# Praise for *USA TODAY* bestselling author
## CAIT LONDON

"You can always count on Ms. London for fiery
passion, heartbreaking emotion and ultimate joy."
—*romantictimes.com* on *Typical Male*

"A new love story from Cait London
guarantees hours of reading pleasure."
—*Romantic Times*

"Cait London is one of the best writers
in contemporary romance today."
—*Affaire de Coeur*

## Praise for CAROLYN ZANE

"Readers enjoy Ms. Z_____ _____ style
and _____

"Caro_____
very funny_____ banter
that will s_____ __le on your face."
—_____antic Times

## Praise for WENDY ROSNAU

"Demonstrating a flair for romantic adventure
and sizzling romance, Wendy Rosnau shines."
—*romantictimes.com* on *The Right Side of the Law*

"Wendy Rosnau's feisty characters and
their non-stop snappy banter provide enjoyable
entertainment as an enticing mystery unfolds."
—*romantictimes.com* on *Beneath the Silk*

## CAIT LONDON

is an avid reader whose books reflect her many interests, including herbs, driving cross-country and photography. A national bestselling and award-winning author of category romance and romantic suspense, Cait has also written historical romances under another pseudonym. Cait says, "One of the best perks about this hard work is the thrilling reader response." She can be reached through her Web site, http://caitlondon.com.

## CAROLYN ZANE

lives with her husband, Matt, and their three children in the rolling countryside near Portland, Oregon's Willamette River. Carolyn finally decided to trade in a decade of city dwelling and producing local television commercials for the quaint country life of a novelist. A change she doesn't regret: the neighbors are friendly, the mail carrier actually stops at the box and the dog, Bob Barker, sticks close to home.

## WENDY ROSNAU

resides in Minnesota with her husband and their six children. She divides her time between her family-owned bookstore and writing romantic suspense. Her first book, *The Long Hot Summer,* was a *Romantic Times* nominee for Best First Series Romance of 2000. Her third book, *The Right Side of the Law,* was a *Romantic Times* Top Pick. She received the Midwest Fiction Writers 2001 Rising Star Award. Visit her Web site at www.wendyrosnau.com.

# CAIT LONDON
## CAROLYN ZANE
## WENDY ROSNAU

## STUCK ON YOU

*Silhouette Books*

Published by Silhouette Books

**America's Publisher of Contemporary Romance**

**SILHOUETTE BOOKS**

STUCK ON YOU
Copyright © 2004 by Harlequin Books S.A.

ISBN 0-373-21814-1

The publisher acknowledges the copyright holders
of the individual works as follows:

TAKING HER TIME
Copyright © 2004 by Lois Kleinsasser

BLINDSIDE DATE
Copyright © 2004 by Carolyn Suzanne Pizzuti

JUST SAY YES
Copyright © 2004 by Wendy Rosnau

Visit Silhouette at www.eHarlequin.com

**Printed in U.S.A.**

# TAKING HER TIME
## Cait London

Valentine's Day is my favorite holiday
and I am so pleased to be invited into
this special Silhouette Books project.

This novella is dedicated to little boys.
May they grow to be considerate and loving men,
sweethearts, lovers, husbands and fathers.

Happy Valentine's Day!

# Chapter 1

*H*er grandmother's house was now Carly's.

All Carly Walker Redford needed to do was to attend the Friday afternoon reading of the will, and the house would be legally hers. During the two weeks she'd arranged away from her demanding advertising position in Denver, Colorado, she planned to complete the ownership paperwork. After an early morning flight from Denver to Kansas City, and a four-hour drive to rural Missouri, she just had time to visit the home she'd always loved.

A long sweet feeling of homecoming filled her in the hot July afternoon. Sadness that her grandmother, Anna Belle Beaumont, had passed away tempered Carly's sense of well-being. It was one o'clock now, but tonight, she would stay in her grandmother's room, and probably cry a bit, about the loving woman who had passed away a month ago. Grams would always be a part of her life, tucked away in Carly's heart. Now, her grandmother's house would become Carly's private retreat from her high-pressure advertising job. She'd take her holidays and extra time to destress, to tend her grandmother's roses and garden and polish the beloved old furniture. Stiles Advertising had agreed that their "hot-shot, prime, killer advertising executive" could work both in Denver and "remote," using her laptop to communicate.

Carly would have her grandmother's home and the challenges she loved.

*Even a person who thrived on challenges tired eventually.*

Carly pulled her rented car into the driveway that curved off the shady quiet street in Toad Hollow, Missouri. She parked beside the little home nestled beneath huge shady oaks and took off her designer sunglasses.

If her future worked out with Gary Kingsley, this might be *their* private retreat. Gary, a man she'd met in Denver, suited what she wanted from life—a rising, sharp executive-type. At thirty-one Carly could feel the warning press of her biological nesting clock, the need to see her own children swinging in Anna Belle's backyard.

Carly slowly scanned the well-kept front yard. July's roses were almost ready to burst into color as they bordered one side of the lot. She made a mental note to thank Mrs. Storm, a next-door neighbor, who had taken over tending Anna Belle's yard.

A curved row of flat stones led down to the street's mailbox that still read A. Beaumont. A light breeze stirred the backyard scents from her grandmother's mint and lavender, where Carly used to swing from the old oak tree.

She badly needed the comfort and quiet and safety of her grandmother's home. The commute she'd planned to the retreat would be easy, since she'd bring her workload with her. In a competitive business, she couldn't afford to lose contact entirely with sales.

With a sigh, Carly picked up her overnight case and laptop and slid from the car. She rounded it to open the trunk and take out two suitcases, placing them on the driveway. The boxes of personal items she had sent to herself would probably be waiting at the local post office. For now, she just wanted to let the house's warmth and memories enfold her, a sweet homecoming. She'd settle into the perfect little house and then start a brief daily working routine, telecommunicating with her office—and Gary Kingsley.

A woman who always planned her life—except for The Incident that almost destroyed it—Carly was a woman who had things to line up.

Hitching up her shoulder bag and laptop straps, Carly took her key chain and walked up to the front steps, just where she'd spent her childhood sitting on her grandmother's lap and watching the night's fireflies dance across the lawn. The house wasn't usually locked, but since Carly had left after the funeral a month ago, she'd thought safety was best. Carly slid a key into the lock and frowned as the old brass knob turned and the door opened from the inside.

Tucker Redford, Carly's ex-husband, stood in the doorway. His dirty T-shirt matched his worn jeans and workboots, sawdust lay in his too-long black hair, and he held a sandwich in his left hand. While Carly was trying to recover, Tucker finished the bite he was chewing and swallowed. His steel-blue eyes narrowed and looked down her body. "Well, well, well. Look who's here."

He slowly took in the practical outfit she'd chosen for the long drive and the move into her grandmother's home—a denim vest and flowing black pants. His gaze rose slowly up to her face and her eyes locked with his.

She'd loved him passionately as a child, as a teenager and as a young wife. Now she wanted to toss him out of her way and out of her life—as if that was possible.

Their paths had crossed several times in the eleven years since they'd divorced, and Tucker's deep, slow voice had never failed to nettle her. Every tone held a taunt she wanted to dive right into and tear apart. In the past, she'd managed dignity somehow, escaping any uncertain situation quickly. But now he was standing in her grandmother's house. He even looked as if he belonged there and that thought ignited Carly's temper. "Exactly what are you doing here?"

Tucker took another bite and chewed slowly. Around it, he said, "Lunchtime."

Then he reached down and slid her key out of the lock, and with a familiar move that a longtime friend and boyfriend and husband could make, he slid the key into the chest pocket of her denim vest.

"Get *out* of my grandmother's house." Carly attempted to push by him, but Tucker at six-feet-two-inches was taller than her. Eight hard inches of tall *EX*-husband. And the rest of him was all muscle, too, even more developed than when they were married.

Tucker's big hand opened on her forehead to gently push her backward on the front porch. His blue eyes darkened within the frame of black lashes and that hard unshaven jaw locked. The long leg he had just extended ended with a big steel-toe work boot that blocked her entry. Tucker always had big feet to match the rest of him and now they were in her business.

It had been a few years since they'd tangled and she'd forgotten how cold those blue eyes could be, as silvery as frost. "Simmer down, Carly," he said. "You're all wound up."

Carly struggled to restrain herself, to cling to some shred of dignity. She was an advertising executive, after all. *But Tucker Redford was standing in her grandmother's house as if he owned it, eating his lunch!*

"It's my house, and you're not welcome in it," she managed.

Tucker braced one hand on the doorframe, and leaned against the other side, effectively blocking her entry. He took another bite and chewed slowly. "So how's Denver?"

She checked her wristwatch and glanced down the street. She didn't want anyone to see that her ex-husband was keeping her from *her property* so easily. "Busy. And so am I. The reading of the will is in two hours, Tucker, and I don't have time to mess with you."

He lifted an eyebrow and that blue gaze slid from

her face around her hair, newly tinted in streaks to lighten the midbrown shades. "Is that so?"

Carly straightened the straps of her overnight tote and the laptop, which had somehow become tangled and threatened to strangle her. "Yes, that's so. Now get out."

"Can't," he said slowly as he watched her.

She struggled not to notice the straps tightening on her throat. To look unaffected, despite her anger and frustration, she propped a hand on her hip. Carly stared at him and asked tightly, "Exactly why not?"

"I live here."

Her grandmother's affection for Tucker had always been there—even when he had stolen a freshly baked apple pie from her window because Carly couldn't wait a minute more to eat it. "Grams passed away a month ago, Tucker, right here in this house. If she wanted you to watch the house until I came for the reading of the will, I suppose that made her feel better, and that's okay. But you'll have to leave now. Get whatever you need and get out."

Tucker reached slowly to ease one strap from her neck to her shoulder. "Lunchtime isn't over. We're waiting for a truckload of lumber. They'll call me before they deliver. Good quality stuff, too. They'll pick me up on their way by the house."

"*My* house, Tucker. I mean, move out, not just go to work."

"Now, Carly, settle down. You know I have to go to work. You know that I took over Dad's construction business. Not a big company, but we manage on small jobs."

"I know all that. I know everything about you. I always have."

At that, Tucker's eyebrow lifted again, mocking her. *On their wedding night, she hadn't been experienced and he had been.*

*They'd been best friends since she was three and he was four, and then they were high school sweethearts. Carly had always thought they would share that first sexual experience—together.*

*Then, before they were married, Tucker had experienced the older, endowed back seat hottie, Ramona Long.*

*On her wedding night, Carly had discovered that Ramona Long had sampled Tucker before his bride!*

He'd always seemed so hot and ready like a simmering volcano before they got married. But of course, back then in their small town, good girls didn't. Or that's what he'd told Carly while fighting her off before their wedding night.

On their wedding night, Tucker had been sweet and tender and patient. *Because he'd already done the deed with Ramona and knew how to prime a woman and—*

None of that mattered now, Carly decided firmly, as she struggled to recover her poise. "I refuse to stand here, on *my* grandmother's front porch, and argue with you, Tucker Redford. I'm going to the reading of the will—"

"Samuel Lawson was Anna Belle's attorney—"

"I know that, Tucker." She was deeply tired from working overtime, carving these two weeks away from stressful advertising campaigns. Now her ex-husband was in *her* house, wasting her time.

"And Sam is at the lunch meeting of Toad Hollow's businessmen. You'll have to wait. They're having elections today to decide who is going to run the barbecue grills on Labor Day."

"Well, my. Aren't you just full of information.... Make sure everything is neat and clean when you leave—before I get back," she said tightly. She wouldn't ask him for a favor of any kind, not even to place her bag and boxes and laptop inside the house until after the reading of the will. She turned and walked down the front steps. Carly threw her bags into the car and opened the trunk. She hefted one suitcase into the trunk and struggled to get the other one to fit beside it. When she slammed the trunk down, Tucker was still standing at her grandmother's door, finishing his sandwich.

Carly rounded the car, slid into the driver's side and jammed on her sunglasses. Through the amber tints, she sent him a silent eviction notice.

He showed his teeth, and the front door swung closed between them.

"Okay, Tucker. Have it your way."

When the lumber truck pulled away out onto the state highway, Tucker strapped on his tool belt and swung up onto the rafters of Tommy Jackson's new barn. On his way upward, Tucker took off his T-shirt and tossed it to another rafter. The bright July sunshine slid through the skeletal framework and Tucker gave himself over to the sweet scent of fresh new Georgia pine lumber.

The barn was small by country standards, but sturdy

and tight. It fit the young rancher's finances. Tucker had designed the barn to allow the Jacksons to build an addition when they could. There wasn't much profit to be had from the little barn, but Tucker liked helping people when he could. Redford Construction, started by Tucker's father, had been in business for years and had no need to spend advertising money; they depended on local goodwill and recommendations. The company motto, No Job Too Small, Or Too Big ran across his truck, which was in Jimmy's Garage for repairs.

Tucker climbed the ladder to a ceiling joist and, standing on it, reached up and hoisted himself up on top of the roof. There, Jace Melba lay on his back, his eyes closed, his expression dreamy—probably because of the empty Fruitylicious Chocolate Pie wrappers in his open lunch bucket. Arlo Newman and Fred Austin hadn't returned from their lunch break down at the MidTown Cafe. Both men were single and eyeing a newly divorced Sally Jo Simon, who had let it be known that she was looking for someone to keep her company.

Tommy Jackson hadn't come out of the farmhouse yet to help, probably helping his wife admire their brand-new baby. Tommy's cows grazed in the green fields, and the fine, warm day should have soothed Tucker.

But it didn't.

He eased down to sit beside Jace. Tucker needed to think and make his gut unknot. Carly always had that effect on him, since they were racing their tricycles down the sidewalk in front of Anna Belle's house.

Eleven damn years since their divorce hadn't changed the way that his heart went flip-flop every time he saw her.

*Hell, after they were married, it took a week to get her to fully make love.*

Carly had a way of destroying any peace he could build around himself—like showing up while he was watching his favorite noon-time game show.

There Carly had stood on the front porch, looking stunned and cute when he'd swung open the door to see who was fiddling with the lock. There she stood, all five foot six of big honey-brown eyes—ones that a man could fall into and his mind would stop—and everything he'd planned and dreamed for since they shared Popsicles on Anna Belle's front porch.

She had done something strange to her hair, putting streaks in it. Her hair had that soft sleek look, just brushing her shoulders. The fitted denim vest reminded him how he used to like to open her buttons slowly, one by one, and the wide-legged black pants clung to her swaying hips as she strode away from the house. The knot in his gut tightened just one hitch, because he surely hadn't ever forgotten how long and curved and soft those legs were, or how they quivered when he came home to them. Add those to the funny little thong sandals with the rhinestones and the red polish on her toenails and the gold band snaking around her upper arm, and he might have been interested—if Carly had been any other woman but his ex-wife.

The sleek muscles in that upper arm said she could probably still throw a baseball pretty well, or hold him tight. Not that he wanted to be held by the woman who had shamed him in front of the whole town by saying, "I need more than marriage to you and a houseful of kids, Tucker. I need to be someone, not just your wife and the legend of Toad Hollow." But she was the only woman he'd ever loved.

That was how he'd always thought of Carly—as his wife, the mother of his children, his soul mate.

But that wasn't enough for Carly; she had to divorce him. Not that he couldn't see it coming with all the arguments they'd had about who played what role in their marriage.

He had been wrong about the woman always washing the dishes and cleaning house. But by the time he figured that out and that a woman just might need more, the argument trail was just too deep and easily ignited.

In the field sprawling below his barn-roof perch, a bull mounted a cow. The sight did little to distract him from thoughts of Carly and the pain that had never healed.

Tucker watched Tommy and his wife step out into the sunshine, a sweet little baby girl in Emma's arms. A forgotten little pain squeezed Tucker's heart. That was how he always thought it would be with Carly, sweet and forever.

"Something bothering you, Tucker?" Jace asked lazily. "You're awfully quiet. I can almost hear you thinking."

"Not a thing on my mind, Jace. Relax a bit before Arlo and Fred turn up."

While Jace yawned and pulled his ballcap lower on his eyes, Tucker settled in to think about Carly. He'd be damned if he'd let the whole town know that the pain was still there, knifing him in his gut. *He hadn't been enough for her; she'd always wanted more. The squabbles in their young marriage had been enough to sour him on any woman. But damned if he'd let anyone know that either.*

Carly had looked drained and thin and shadows spread beneath those honey-brown eyes. She looked like someone needed to cuddle her.

But not him—oh no, he'd had enough of Carly doing everything she could to make his life miserable, haunting his dreams, making him take cold showers at midnight. *She couldn't ever let go of the fact that Ramona Long had him first.*

"Who's that coming down the road like a bat out of hell?" Jace asked, rousing enough to sit up.

Carly's navy-blue car with the rental plates left clouds of dust behind it as she came toward the barn. She didn't slow for the cattle crossing, and the car did a bump routine as the tires passed over the crossing's bars. The car skidded to a stop by the barn. Carly slammed the door and stood looking up at Tucker with her tinted amber sunglasses.

"I am going to kill you, Tucker Redford," she yelled up at him.

"Is that Carly?" Jace asked, clearly stunned.

"That would be her." All one hundred and fifteen pounds of sheer female trouble, and Tucker wasn't having a second go-'round with her.

"I think I'd be scared if she ever said that to me," Jace muttered and his three-hundred pound bulk seemed to shudder beneath his bib overalls. "Everyone knows what she's capable of."

"She's just blowing off steam. Besides, she hasn't done that fearsome stuff since she grew up. She's a big-cheese city executive now." Tucker tried to ignore the warning lift of the hair on his nape—because he knew exactly what Carly could do when in a snit. This time, she looked like it was a whole lot more than a snit. He decided it was safer for everyone if he met her on the ground.

By the time he climbed down from the roof, Tommy and Emma and baby had retreated inside the house. Arlo and Fred had pulled to a stop in the barnyard, but remained sitting in the pickup truck.

On his way to the ground, Tucker picked up a pitcher of water from the bucket and poured it over his head for preventative cooling-down measures. He hadn't had an out-and-out argument with Carly since they'd divorced.

*He didn't want her to know how much she'd hurt him.*

"You bellowed?" he asked politely when he stood in front of her.

Her hands on her hips accentuated a bust that was a whole lot more womanly than when they were married. "I'm *trying* to be calm," she stated unevenly. *"You own my grandmother's house and no one told me."*

"I guess you've been to the reading of the will then." Tucker wondered how many men had touched her like he had and the thought nettled. He tried to push it away—after all, they were divorced and he had no claim.

*He'd always had a claim, ever since they were chil-
dren and sweethearts and—*

But that was done now and Carly wasn't hurting him
anymore—he'd almost died the first time. "Anna Belle
wanted it that way."

"And just how did you ever get your sneaky hands
on my grandmother's house?"

Tucker was hoping for control, but Carly made it
sound like he'd taken advantage of an aging, dear,
sweet woman. "She sold it to me, about five years
ago."

"She lived in it until she went to the retirement
home. Then she came back at the end, and she passed
away last month. Mom and my stepfather, Paul, and I
stayed in it the night of the funeral. It was like Grams
was there with me, like she would always be there for
me when I needed her. Now you've upped and taken
her away from me."

Tucker didn't like that slight nick of guilt; he'd always loved Anna Belle. "That was our arrangement. I
moved in the day after you left. I had to clean out all
the tear and nose-blowing tissues you jammed into the
trash and didn't like it much either. How is your mom?
Are Rebecca and Paul still living in Kansas City?"

Carly didn't answer his question about her mother
and second husband, Paul Fowler. She was staring up
at Tucker with those big, stricken, helpless honey-
brown eyes as if his big, nasty work boot had tromped
all over her dreams. Her next sentence quivered on the
air between them. "Grams left the house and everything in it to you—even her parrot. I love Livingston,

and I always thought she'd give him to me. Why would Grams give him to you?''

Livingston had been a real pain in the butt to care for, but since Anna Belle loved the old bird, Tucker had tried to find its best side—there wasn't one. Just the same, if Anna Belle wanted him to keep care of Livingston, he would. Cleaning the bird's droppings wasn't exactly his favorite job. "Rebecca and Paul already drove down and collected what Anna Belle wanted her to have. The things she left for you are in your old room. You can come by and pick them up—when I'm home, of course. You might even say a word or two to Livingston. He's stopped squawking since Anna Belle passed on.''

That news took Carly backward until she leaned against the car, bracing a hand on it. "Then my mother must have known all this time. She didn't tell me.''

"Maybe she was afraid to tell you. You scared her sometimes. You're not exactly predictable.''

Tucker braced himself against that soft, sinking feeling—the one that Carly could use against him. She had that helpless little girl look that she'd had when her father, Billy Walker, had died. But back then, Tucker and Carly were married and he had a right to pick her up and hold her on his lap for hours, just rocking on Anna Belle's porch. He'd listened to her sob and understood her feelings of guilt and told her that her escapades weren't the reason Billy's heart was too clogged and finally gave out.

As if remembering where she was, Carly glanced at the Jackson's house. "Why did Tommy and Emma go back in the house? Don't they want to see me?''

That soft little wounded kitten sound in her voice reached right into his heart and Tucker firmly tugged it right out again. He crossed his arms and dug his fingers into his flesh, just to remind him that Carly wasn't getting her way this time. "They think we're going to tangle—like we used to. Everyone used to get off the street when we went at it."

"That was over eleven years ago, Tucker. I'm past all that. I can handle you any day," she said, obviously rousing, her brown eyes glinting up at him.

"Honey, your handling days ended with that divorce decree," he said very carefully to remind Carly to keep her distance.

From the furious look that she shielded quickly—the one she used when she was twelve and he was thirteen and eyeing the more developed girls, the one just before she kicked him a good one—he'd scored a hit. Just to remind her that her place wasn't in Toad Hollow and his was, Tucker added, "You make one wrong step with those funny little shoes and you're going to have cow poo squishing between your toes. Don't think you can come into my house anytime you want, either. It's been a while since you've been in the lockup."

Carly's eyes narrowed up at him. She never liked the reminder of the penalties of her great "skunk in the police car" plan when she was sixteen and had just flunked her driver's test. Norma Perry, the police chief, had never forgotten that incident. Each time Carly visited her grandmother, the police car made rounds around the quiet neighborhood as if Norma expected Carly to demolish it.

Of course, Tucker had captured the skunk for Carly

and coached her on how to not excite it before the proper time. To her credit, she'd never told that part.

"I'll just be leaving now, Tucker. But I am going to get to the bottom of how you have *my* house," Carly stated frostily as she slid into her car. She slammed the door, backing all the way past Arlo's pickup, and over the cattle guard and out the curved road leading to the state highway.

Arlo and Fred slid from the pickup and stood staring at Carly's driving maneuvers. Tommy and Emma came out of the house and up on the roof, Jace yelled, "You're in for it now, boy. She's always loved that house and you're smack-dab in the middle of what she wants."

*She'd wanted a divorce, and she'd gotten one. Carly hadn't wanted to stay any longer with Tucker and work things out; she'd wanted wide-open spaces and she'd gotten them.* "This is one time she isn't having her way," Tucker said quietly as he reached for a ballcap and placed it on his head.

He climbed back up the ladder and picked up the nailing gun. For every nail it pounded into the roofing sheeting, that was one less minute Tucker would think about how shattered Carly had looked. She'd gripped the car as if it were the last thing she had to hold onto in life—now that he'd taken her grandmother's house from her.

Tucker pitted himself against the new barn and vowed to burn Carly out of his system....

# Chapter 2

"Now that is just perfect." Carly brushed the tears out of her eyes and when her vision cleared, she focused on the only motel in town—Last Inn Motel—and the big Closed sign on the marquee.

The Last Inn Motel was where The Incident had taken place. Carly had gotten in trouble so deep and wide that when Tucker came to her rescue, it had ended in marriage.

*How was a country girl supposed to know that an aging, career-shot movie star wanted to seduce her—the winner of the Miss Cornbread Muffin Contest? How was she supposed to know that the "party" was intended to be a private one...for two?*

The Incident changed her life and Carly was married to Tucker Redford quicker than Billy Walker, her now deceased father, could pull out his shotgun.

Everyone in Toad Hollow knew about The Incident. However, some of the more unsavory facts had been kept between Tucker and herself.

Carly tried to push back the ugly details, but they still screamed at her…. Carly was eighteen then and had just been crowned Miss Cornbread Muffin. That night her scream at the Last Inn had drawn not only Tucker, but Norma's red flashing lights and siren to the scene of a dead, naked, past-his-prime movie star beneath the sheets. His eerie-corpse smile was offset by a bottle of iced champagne and candles and a sexy negligee in a box with a great big red bow. Another discarded bow beneath the sheets had said that Simon Gifford had tied it on another kind of package.

But Tucker had somehow been nearby when she opened that motel door and screamed. He had run to Carly's side immediately. There wasn't the room full of other contestants fully dressed and celebrating. There was only the dead man on the bed.

It was Tucker's lie that Carly and he were planning a private party of their own in another motel room that pointed the finger of a movie-star's seduction night away from Carly. Tucker had said that he tried to stop Billy Bob Smith's beagle from running through the partially opened motel door—the dog was gone when Norma arrived, of course—but that was when they'd *both* discovered the dead man. And, Tucker had added, he'd just happened to overhear how Simon Gifford, star of one pitiful film ten years ago, loved wearing women's nighties.

It was Tucker's lie—that he was there with the intent

to seduce Carly—that made her father decide that they would be married right away.

The Incident had gotten her wedded and bedded before her time. Before she was someone in her own right.

The motel—the only one in town—was also where Tucker and Carly had spent their wedding night. And for every moment thereafter in their two-year marriage, Carly had resented their "shotgun wedding"—but her father would hear of nothing less than marriage.

It was where on her wedding night that she'd learned that Tucker hadn't waited for her, and Ramona Long had nabbed him first.

Now Carly's father resided in a cemetery outside town and her mother had remarried and Anna Belle's house was Tucker Redford's—to say nothing of Livingston, whom Carly had always adored.

After working fourteen-hour days, she'd planned to unwind by tending those roses and the yard and baking cookies and polishing old beloved furniture…. The pretty picture she'd had of coming home to Anna Belle's house had crumbled, the pieces drifting away on the fragrant summer air.

Cars passed slowly by on the street, and she recognized the few people who waved at her. No one stopped because they knew exactly her history with the Last Inn Motel and how she was trying to deal with it. Of course, they only knew that she and Tucker had discovered Simon Gifford's body accidentally. They probably thought that now she would leave Toad Hollow for good, but she wasn't ready just yet.

*Not with Tucker in possession of her grandmother's house.*

She closed her eyes and leaned back against the car's headrest. She didn't have her grandmother's house. She didn't have her grandmother's parrot, and worst of all she had no place to stay in Toad Hollow. On her way to the reading of the will, she'd picked up her boxes from the post office and she was homeless—not counting her Denver apartment.

"Tucker." He'd stood there in the July sun, tanned and fit and big, with water dripping down his too-long wavy hair and his blue eyes as cold as ice, just like his heart.

The water had dripped down onto his tanned chest and when he'd crossed his arms, muscles jumped beneath those smooth hard pecs, and so did his nipples. Back when they were comparing boy and girl nipples, Tucker could always move his more than she could—

Carly groaned and let another tear slide down her cheek. She just had to know why Anna Belle let Tucker buy her house when Carly had always wanted it.

And there was something in that house that Anna Belle had been keeping for her that Carly wanted more than the house—the diary that told everything she'd ever done or felt or experienced with Tucker. If it ever surfaced, her humiliation would be complete.

As it was, her humiliation was only half-complete.

*She had to get in that house.*

*She had to know why Tucker had the house and Livingston.*

*If he had already found the diary she'd left in Anna Belle's keeping—*

Carly felt an odd warmth creeping up her cheeks. She didn't want to think about Tucker reading her most intimate thoughts, about her lust for him, about how every argument in their marriage had crushed her—she wouldn't let him see how badly she'd hurt.

Carly opened her eyes and stared at the car's upholstered ceiling. She'd never backed off from Tucker and she wasn't going to start now. She could feel herself getting warmed up to get answers and she wasn't leaving until she had that diary in her possession.

She sat up abruptly and fished her cosmetic case out of her bag, repairing the tearstains on her cheeks. The only remedy that she could think to help her red swollen eyes was to pour bottled water onto the tea bags she always carried. With a tea bag over each eye, she settled back to think.

Everyone already knew how much she loved that house—and her grandmother. First she'd visit the cemetery and by the time Tucker finished work, Carly would have a plan in place.

Carly sat up and dropped the tea bags out of the window; in the rearview mirror, she used her best cosmetic concealer to hide the damage of crying. She started the car. She had exactly two weeks to get that diary back—and somehow, push Tucker out of her grandmother's house. Carly would be tending Anna Belle's home and yard, not Tucker.

She glanced at her side mirror, the one with the police car fast approaching. Norma Perry, the police chief, drove by Carly slowly. Then the car made a U-turn and pulled along the driver's side. Norma's silver glasses glinted in the afternoon sun. "Hi, Carly.

Heard you were back in town. The boys at the post office said you'd mailed yourself a lot of boxes and that they had a time fitting them over your suitcases and into the back seat. They said you were expecting more. Are you moving back, or just reliving The Incident?''

Carly saw no reason to hide that she'd come back to the one place everyone knew she loved. "Hi, Norma. No, I'm not moving back entirely, but I worked out a deal with my company that I can work part-time in Denver and part-time here, in Gram's house. I plan to vacation here, too. I guess you've heard a few things today, huh?''

"Heard you couldn't talk after the reading of the will. That was a first. They were thinking about giving you a swig of whiskey to revive you, but then they remembered the time you decided to try alcohol. Samuel Lawson didn't want his new office carpet messed up. Then Arlo called and said you'd made a beeline for Tucker and that whatever passed between you two wasn't sweet. Arlo has never seen a woman put a car into reverse gear and back up like that. You could have hit one of the Jacksons' cows. Cow-icide isn't fun to investigate. I've been hoping for a real homicide for years— Well, never mind that. Forget you heard it.... But after you jumped Tucker, I heard that he had something on his mind for the rest of the day.''

That last bit of information gave Carly hope. Tucker always sulled up when she got to him, otherwise he was even-tempered—but where he was concerned, her emotions swung everywhere. Carly felt it was only fair warning to let Norma know her plans. "I'm going to get my grandmother's house back."

"Tucker is a good, solid thinker. Slower than you, with less flash, but he usually can deliver a bottom line pretty good."

Norma looked straight ahead, as if setting her mind to something. She tapped her fingers on the steering wheel; beneath her uniform hat was a frizzed mass of gray hair. Norma spoke in the clipped style she'd learned on a popular police-crime television show, "When Tucker was teaching you to drive, you ran his truck over a fire hydrant. He's pulled you out of more scrapes than I want to remember. But I don't think he's on your side this time. If you go in that house and he makes a trespassing complaint, I'll have to go by the book—just so you know."

"I like your new perm," Carly said brightly, hoping that Norma wouldn't get that brisk, swaggering, tough police person attitude, as if she were the only crime-killer in the universe. Norma probably hadn't forgotten the skunk episode; she wouldn't hesitate to put Carly in jail for any misadventures that *Tucker* might cause.

Tucker had always been able to sweet-talk Norma. She believed anything he said, including how the beagle opened the door of Simon's motel room, and that Tucker was with Carly when she saw the dead man and screamed. People just believed Tucker, because he was "solid."

"Thanks. Permed it myself. Don't know why everyone has to go to the beauty shop. You can buy a box of the stuff at the drugstore," Norma said before putting the police car in gear and pulling onto the highway.

Carly took one last look at the motel and decided that she wasn't going to cry anymore. She needed to kill time before Tucker got home from work, and she needed to let everyone know how heartbroken she was that he owned her grandmother's house. There were ways to put pressure on Tucker, but first she had to unravel the mystery of why Anna Belle hadn't left it to her. She decided the local MidTown Cafe was just as good a place as any to start.

It was there, over pasta salad, that she discovered Ramona Long had married a minister; she was now the mother of five children and involved with every community event, a real town leader. In fact, Ramona was such a mover and shaker that she was expected to run for mayor in the next election.

Sally Jo, the waitress, took her break and slid into Carly's booth. She counted her tips and sat back to look at Carly. "Tucker has a girlfriend," Sally Jo said carefully. "People like him. And they're not quite certain about you anymore. You've changed. Or that's what they say."

"I grew up here. I have a right to be here—in my grandmother's house."

"Anna Belle missed you. You should have come back more often. It broke her heart when you divorced Tucker. She was never that close to your mother, though she loved her. Your mother always was a bit uppity and your father...well, Billy Walker had a temper. It was just as well you married Tucker when you were caught at the Last Inn Motel."

Carly leveled a stare at Sally Jo. She wanted everyone in Toad Hollow to know that she wasn't giving up
her grandmother's house without a fight. "I love that
house. It holds dear memories for me," Carly said.
"Tucker has no business in it. Whatever he did to get
Anna Belle to sell to him, instead of saving it for me,
probably wasn't—"

"Tucker wouldn't take advantage of Anna Belle,
Carly, and you know it. He kept that place up—"

"Ah. For a reason. To get himself into her good
graces."

With a long sigh, Sally Jo collected her tips, slid
them into her pocket, and stood. "What a crock of you-
know-what. The guy deserves a break, a house and a
wife. You're not getting my sympathy, or anyone
else's."

"He's not sweet, you know, Sally Jo."

Sally Jo laughed knowingly. "Sometimes 'sweet'
isn't what a woman wants."

"I am going to get my grandmother's house back."

"Then you're going to have to go over Tucker to
get it."

"Then I will."

Tucker groaned silently when he saw Carly's rental
car parked in his driveway. He leaped off the back of
Arlo's truck as it slowed, slid on his T-shirt and un-
buckled his tool belt, holding it in his hand. At six
o'clock in the evening, he was tired, sweaty and needing a break from everyone who cautiously watched him
for some reaction to Carly's threat. He stood looking
at the woman leaning against her car, the dying dappled

sunlight burnishing her sun-streaked hair. Her arms crossed as she stared at him.

"Go on home now and tell your parents that nothing is going to happen," he quietly ordered Betty and Ross Wilson's two little boys. The boys had laid their bicycles down on Mrs. Blackstone's lawn directly across the street from his house. They were watching intently, no doubt hoping to see Carly in action, making good on her earlier threat of murder. Tucker knew they were half hoping for real blood and crime-scene tape and being interrogated until they sweated beneath the hot lights and got nervous and spilled their guts. The boys knew Carly Walker Redford's reputation from their parents—that she was capable of stirring up a real mess. Now they were ready to watch Tucker bravely go to his gory death.

"Don't let her kill you, Tucker. I like fishing with you," Tanner said unevenly.

"Me, too," Gavin added as they mounted their bikes and soared down the street to make their report to Betty and Ross who had grown up with Carly and Tucker.

Tucker waved to Mrs. Storm and with a bracing sigh, prepared to deal with his ex-wife. "You'll want the things Anna Belle left for you, I guess. Come on in."

Carly still looked stunned, shadows beneath those light brown eyes, and in her hand was a small bouquet of Anna Belle's budding roses—it looked uncomfortably like the florist's version she had carried when they were married in church. The petals had quivered, reflecting the fear in her face and in her body later that night—until she discovered that Ramona had gotten to him first.

Carly wasn't that sweet girl any longer. In their chance meetings through the years, she'd wrapped her high-nose city ways around her. She'd made it clear that she disdained her ex-husband, who had never wanted anything but to live peacefully and work and grow old in Toad Hollow.

Tucker opened the front door and entered the house, turning to bow and sweep his hand in front of him, beckoning her to enter.

Carly eased around him, just as she always did when they chanced to meet in too-close areas. She stood in the middle of her grandmother's living room, looking slowly around to the things that were Anna Belle's. Carly noted the changes Tucker had made—like the big-screen television set and the big, comfortable leather recliner and sofa, where his pillow and blanket marked his restless night.

"When I came home to visit Anna Belle, I really didn't go anywhere else. I just wanted to stay here and be with her, to enjoy the peace of this house and work in the yard," Carly said softly. "Everyone in town thinks that I'm stuck-up now."

The large parrot who had been silent for a month fastened his beady eyes on Tucker. Then Livingston's iridescent green head turned slowly toward Carly. His rough parrot-language took Tucker a moment translate. "Awk! Awk! Carly. Carly. Carly. My girl, Carly. I love Carly…so does Tucker."

The bird's loud coarse voice startled Tucker, who had tried hours to get the parrot to speak. And now, the first time Livingston said anything, it was a fact that Tucker had buried long ago.

With an excited cry, Carly hurried to the big suspended cage by the window. Before Tucker could stop her, she'd opened the cage and reached for Livingston. She cuddled the parrot against her and Livingston's beady eyes blamed Tucker for keeping Carly away.

"Every time I hold him, he unloads his cargo on my clothes." Tucker turned from the tears shimmering in Carly's eyes. "The last time I let him out, he flew all over—if that's what you can call it—and banged over Anna Belle's cacti in the sewing room. It took forever and a few scars to get the spines out of his feathers—and me. He's got an evil temper and he hasn't been talking."

"He missed me," she said unevenly, easing the bird up onto her shoulder. "Sweet bird," she cooed to the parrot.

"Sweet bird. Sweet bird," Livingston squawked with a parrot accent.

When Tucker had tried to put Livingston on his shoulder, the bird had refused. And he'd left droppings every time, physical evidence of his opinion of Tucker. Now he was nuzzling that dangerous beak in Carly's streaked hair.

Tucker liked her hair better when it wasn't so striped, but more of a natural sun-lightened color. He could feel himself sliding into a weak pool of emotions that he didn't know how to handle—and it would be there in his weak-vulnerable bog that Carly would take advantage of him. "You're not getting him. Friends kept him and took him to visit Anna Belle while she was in the retirement home. But she felt he'd live longer and healthier if he stayed here. She wanted some of the furniture to stay, too…like her bed. I promised I'd do my best to take care of it. Some of it went to your mother. Some of it goes to you, just like she said. Mostly the pictures and smaller stuff. They're in your old room.''

"I…I was grieving so much that I forgot about you, Livingston. I'm sorry. I knew you were being cared for, and I didn't have a place to keep you in Denver. I thought I'd wait until I moved apartments before collecting you."

With Livingston perched on her shoulder, Carly walked slowly to her grandmother's huge spool-leg dining room table, now cluttered with papers and a calculator. She ran her hand across the big antique buffet that once held Anna Belle's favorite pictures—replaced by Tucker's baseball, bowling and bass fishing trophies.

Carly moved through the rooms, her hand touching here and there, where Tucker had removed Anna Belle's knickknacks. She passed into Anna Belle's bedroom, now shed of its doilies and vanity and homey clutter, where the big four-poster was unmade and Tucker's clothes were piled everywhere. "It used to be so beautiful, with her off-white chenille bedspread," Carly said quietly.

"Tucker needs Carly," Livingston squawked.

Tucker tensed and stuck his hands in his pockets. "That's the first time I've heard that bird speak in a long time."

Carly shook her head as if discarding the thought, and moved into the doorway of her old room. Boxes of Anna Belle's things were stacked against the wall and on the floor and on the single four-poster bed and antique dresser. With her back to him, Carly placed her hand on the wooden pinecones of the bed's posters and bowed her head. "There's…just so…much. Her entire lifetime—and mine and Mom's."

Livingston hopped and turned around on her shoulder. His beady eyes condemned Tucker. "Bad boy…bad boy."

Carly slid slowly to the braided rug on the floor and Livingston hopped onto the boxes on the bed. "Bad boy," he said again, eyeing Tucker.

Tucker wished he hadn't seen Carly reach into a box and lift out her old rag doll, bringing it to her chest and wrapping her arms around it. Sitting with her back to the bed, she began to rock.

Before Tucker realized he was moving, he had taken a step toward her. He'd held her when her pets had died and had helped her with their funeral rites. From childhood, they'd spent hours in that big oak in the backyard in perfect understanding, letting go of grief and sadness. At Anna Belle's funeral, Carly had been in her mother's arms, but now there was no one to comfort her—but him.

And he just wasn't that certain about himself now.

Tucker did what he always did years ago, when they were married and his emotions about Carly got tangled between love for a soul mate, frustration that a woman could bring and the ugliness of their marriage breaking apart—he walked out the front door, closing it behind him.

He was halfway down the walkway, headed for the safety of dark places, music, a good beer and steak, when he heard Carly's command: "Tucker Redford, you are not running away from this. You get right back in here and tell me how it was that your name happens to be on the deed of my house."

Well, that was a new one. In their two-year marriage of past arguments, she'd never opened that closed door—unless it was to throw his clothes and his baseball and fishing trophies out onto the front lawn. He stopped and stood still, his mind churning the reasons he should obey an ex-wife. Especially one who thought she had better things to do than to be married to him and raise the kids that now he might never be able to have....

Wait a minute...*wait a minute*. That house was his now, bought and paid, and Carly wasn't his wife....

Maybe it was time to tear her out of his days and nights. Maybe it was cleansing time, so he could move on in life. It definitely was time for a face-off with the one woman who had damn near made him impotent.

But then, how would he know, since his want-to hadn't matched his actual will-do in eleven years.

He turned slowly to the one woman who had given him both heaven and hell.... It was time to finish her off—or at least tell her off and give himself closure.


When Tucker narrowed those blue eyes and looked at her, Carly took a step backward into the safety of her grandmother's house.

She tried to ignore that little quiver of fear as he began to walk slowly toward the house, never taking that piercing blue gaze from her. She'd never been afraid of Tucker, because he'd never hurt her—intentionally. There was that time he slid into home plate and knocked the catcher—that was her—into a roll. He'd gone pale at the sight of the bloody gravel-scratches on her arms and legs. It wasn't until she'd reminded him that she'd hurt herself worse by roller-skating on the street, or climbing up trees or roofs, or falling in a blackberry patch, that his pained and guilty expression had eased.

At a tall, solid two-hundred pounds of muscle, the man walking up the stone walkway looked dangerous and unforgiving. He looked as if nothing could stop him.

Carly swallowed and gave Tucker room to enter the living room. He continued to pin her with those silvery-hot eyes and slowly closed the door behind him. This wasn't the Tucker she'd known all her life, who had taught her how to swim in the river and catch crawdads and frogs. This wasn't the young man who had gently introduced her into sex, playful and the other kind where she thought she had died and melted into a warm, damp, happy, limp noodle curled next to him.

On her shoulder, Livingston squawked, "Kiss... make up."

At the end of their marriage, they were either arguing or making love that when finished, left them lying apart and thinking in the dark—without words between them.

This argument was going to be all heat and fire and fast, hurting words—without the make-up sex later.

"You might want to sit down for this one, Carly," Tucker said. "But first put Livingston back in his cage and cover him. I don't want to listen to you both."

Carly's hands trembled as she managed Livingston into his cage and placed him in darkness. Tucker's voice was deep and cold and he'd just tossed his ball-cap onto the table. In the cool shadows, he looked like someone else. He looked like a hard man with an unrelenting, stubble covered jaw.

It struck her then that she'd never seen Tucker with more than a shadow predicting stubble, because he'd always been careful to shave. He sank into a chair and began unlacing his workboots. He tugged them off, and each one hit the floor with a heavy thump. "You know what? This time, I'm not going anywhere. This is my house now."

He stood abruptly and with a disdaining look down at her as he passed, moved into the kitchen. He washed his hands, reached into the refrigerator freezer, took out a handful of ice cubes and dropped them into a jar, adding lemonade from a pitcher. Clearly, Tucker was taking his time preparing an answer as he heated a skillet, added oil and breaded four pork chops. When they began to sizzle, he took a big bowl from the refrigerator and ladled out a huge pile of pasta salad onto a pie plate.

With her arms folded over her chest, Carly settled against the kitchen doorframe. "How long is it going to take—until you get yourself ready to answer me?"

That hot silvery-blue gaze narrowed at her again. "Unless you want to be evicted on your rear end, I suggest you be quiet—if that's possible. If there's something a man can't stand after a hard day's work, it's a yammering woman."

"Is that why you never remarried? *Because women*

*talk?''* She hadn't meant the gibe to slide through her lips, but it did. She *absolutely* did not care about Tucker's love life.

He showed his teeth, and it wasn't a warm smile, as if he knew just how to get what he wanted from a woman without any rules.

In their short marriage, Tucker had always expected dinner to be on the table when he got home from his father's construction business. He'd learned a few things evidently—or else some woman was filling his refrigerator and just hadn't come over to cook dinner yet.

Carly pushed that idea away. Who cooked Tucker's meals was of no importance to her.

"Take all the time you want," she said when he continued to ignore her, browning and cooking the pork chops perfectly. They were golden and…and hers had always burned.

When Tucker shouldered past her with his two pork chops, Carly caught the eau de working man and the sensation of a big bristling male. This close, he seemed even bigger than she remembered, and she noted a tiny hair whorl escaping the neck of his T-shirt.

That unnerved her. She remembered waiting for the hair on Tucker's chest to sprout with as much interest as she watched her own body develop. Tucker's youthful body had always been sleek and smooth and hairless, but for a small patch.

At the barn today, there was a larger patch of hair that veed down his muscled stomach into his jeans.

While she was dealing with the mouthwatering changes in Tucker's body—and the knowledge that she hadn't had sex in eleven years—he turned on the big-screen television. He sat in a chair holding his pie plate of food and placed the jar of lemonade on a table beside him. Tucker watched the world news as if he'd forgotten she was there.

She'd forgotten how a working man could eat, diving into his food. The few men she had dated didn't eat like it was their last meal.

She could outwait him any day, and she wasn't going anywhere. Carly slipped off her sandals and settled into her grandmother's little rocker, placing her feet over a stack of sporting magazines on the footstool. Stiles Advertising Agency had insured her skills to manage a short visit with an ex-husband. She had taken stress-management classes. She knew how to read body postures, and how to manage difficult people. As the vice president of Stiles Advertising Agency, she dealt with businessmen and male co-workers every day and temperamental graphic artists and copywriters frustrated that their great American novel hadn't sold. Sometimes there were little games before business could be completed, and she could play them to get what she wanted. She could manage Tucker Redford. If he needed to go through his little ceremony, that was fine with her.

Finished with his meal, Tucker stood and padded into the kitchen. She heard the dishes clink into the sink. At any moment, he would come back into the living room where she could unwind the mystery of the house sale and with that in hand, manage to get back her rightful property.

A minute later the shower sounded.

Carly stopped rocking and sat very still, her temper simmering. He was making her wait, and he knew exactly how she hated that.

She walked back through the house—that was rightfully hers—and paused at the bathroom door. She tested the doorknob and found it in the same condition as when they were married and arguing at Anna Belle's house. Carly had locked herself in the bathroom and Tucker had left the house. Her grandmother had then replaced the knob with one that did not lock.

Carly took a deep breath. She could handle Tucker anywhere—and that included a tiny bathroom. Inside she looked at the steam-covered mirror, anywhere but at the shower curtain where Tucker's tall body was moving.

"I'm waiting for an answer, Tucker," she yelled as she closed the lid of the toilet and sat.

After a minute, she got up and flushed the bowl and sat down again. Perhaps a rush of icy water would start him talking.

After a brisk silence, Tucker began to sing. That low, soft, deep voice could always reach inside her and wrap her want-tos into a tiny hard knot that needed unraveling.

Carly hurriedly left the bathroom and went into her old room, determined to find the diary that told too much about her want-tos with Tucker Redford. Her grandmother had promised to keep it safe—somewhere. As Anna Belle's memory faded, she couldn't remember where she had put the diary, and Carly didn't have the heart to press her.

The diary could be anywhere in the boxes. With a

sigh, Carly sat on the floor and tugged a box near her. She hefted out an assortment of worn dolls and toys and albums, then opened another box, prowling through it. Logically, the diary should have been with the old albums, but it wasn't. Nor was it in a box of recipe books. The next box was an empty heart-shaped candy box. Tucker had given it to her and after making her way to the bottom of the box, she had broken out in the biggest zit on her nose—just before she was to be crowned Queen of the Sweetheart Ball.

The box contained all the penny valentines that Tucker had given her since they were children. She'd treasured each one, even when the designs had become more romantic in their teens.

She traced Tucker's first attempt at making a *T,* inside a lopsided pencil heart that had been erased and redrawn more than once. "I like to kiss you," he'd written in the seventh grade, when she was in the sixth. "Let's go steady," he'd written as a high school freshman and the future athletic star of Toad Hollow High School. As a junior, it was "Wear my ring. You've always been my girl and you always will be."

In his senior year, Tucker had chosen a big, pretty valentine and had simply written, "I love you."

And a year after that, it was a huge valentine, which did not erase Tucker's rendezvous with the town hottie and older woman, Ramona.

This happened during the Walker family's two-week, "once in a lifetime" vacation to Florida—because Carly's parents were afraid it would be their last chance for a family vacation. She'd come back to her senior year and the discovery that Tucker had seen Ramona. "I'm sorry," he'd written. "You know what for. Nothing happened. I love you."

*He'd torn the heart out of her. That chip in her trust for him could erupt at any minute—like the night she found Simon Gifford dead at the Last Inn Motel. Tucker's "innocent" date with Ramona was always there. However, back then his hot back seat kissing and petting with Carly had assured her that he didn't have any need for another woman—or so she thought.*

*On their wedding night, she discovered the truth— that Tucker already knew exactly what would happen between them. He'd done The Deed with Ramona.*

The hours of overtime that Carly had worked in order to carve out this two-week niche in Toad Hollow, and the hard day she'd had emotionally slid over her heavily. She could barely wrangle up the energy to put the lid on the box of valentines from Tucker, or to plow through any more unpleasant memories of how they had argued in their marriage.

She was dead tired, but she would wait for Tucker. She would run him down, if she had to, but she would have her answers, Carly decided, as a yawn took her head back to rest on the soft, familiar bed.

She awoke to the old dollhouse poking her in the head, a telephone ringing somewhere and her body aching from a night on the hard floor. She was also sweaty from the weight of the hand-stitched quilt covering her. Carly pushed it away and tried to focus. The telephone kept ringing while she discovered early morning sliding through the lace certains and that her cheek ached from using her rag doll as a pillow. *And*

*she still didn't know why her grandmother had sold the*
*house to Tucker....*

Carly scrambled to her feet, tangled in the heavy
quilt and stubbed her toe on the bed's leg as she tried
to find the telephone. As she hopped by Livingston in
the living room, he squawked cheerfully, ''Hi, Carly.
Feed me.''

''I'll get back with you later.'' She had to answer
the telephone before Tucker—if he was in the house—
because she'd told Gary, her almost-fiancé that she'd
be installed and rested in her grandmother's house this
morning. Gary wouldn't expect her to be with her ex-
husband.

Tucker was probably already at work, she decided,
as she hurried through the living room and kitchen—
but the least a construction company owner and a
small-businessman could do was to have a message
machine.

The sound came from Anna Belle's bedroom and
Tucker was still there. He groaned and rolled over to
reach the telephone on the bedside table....

Carly made a dive for it across Tucker's body, and
half-awake, he caught her with one hand and reached
for the telephone with the other.

''Give me that. Don't say anything,'' she whispered
desperately and struggled against his grasp on her
waist; the rest of her body dangled down the side of
the bed. She braced her hands on the floor and tried to
turn to glower up at him.

And there was something definitely very hard and
big beneath the covers separating her stomach from
Tucker's body and it wasn't his hipbones.

He suddenly released her and Carly was forced to hand-walk until the rest of her body came off the bed. She scrambled to her feet, but not before Tucker drawled in his husky, drowsy, morning tone, "No, this isn't Carly. This is her ex-husband. She's here somewhere...ouch, Carly! Take it easy, will you? That is no place to put a knee into a man."

# Chapter 3

Tucker tossed down the receiver and pushed out of bed, leaving Carly to frantically search through the sheets. When she lifted the receiver, the line was empty, hissing at her, and she could almost feel Gary's anger from Colorado.

*She knew what Gary probably thought, courtesy of Tucker—that she'd spent the night with her ex-husband! In his bed!*

She hurriedly dialed Gary's office number and his home number and then his cell phone number. She left urgent messages, asking him to call her immediately.

Carly automatically translated Livingston's parrot-squawk, coming from the living room: "Five o'clock. Wake up. This is a dark hell. Get me out."

"You owe me for those phone calls you just made," Tucker stated darkly from the doorway. He was wearing boxer shorts and nothing else. Carly remembered that during their married days he'd switched from jockey shorts to wearing boxers in preparation for the babies he wanted. Tucker didn't want his sperm crowded, fearing that they would forget how to be active and swim upstream.

But Carly hadn't been ready for babies. She'd only gotten married because of The Incident. At eighteen, she wasn't certain yet just who she was, except Billy Walker's troublesome daughter and Tucker Redford's steady girlfriend and the town legend, of course.

The telephone rang again, and Carly dived for it, landing across the bed. "Hi, Gary. I'm so glad you called. This isn't as it seems.... Oh, hello, Jimmy. Yes, I know you run the garage now. Okay, I'll tell Tucker that you'll swing by and deliver his truck right away."

"I would have brought it last night, but your car was in the driveway. I figured you two wanted privacy...that old romance-thing, you know. Glad you're back with Tucker, Carly. He was always the only one who could handle you. You're a fast mover. You need a real leveler like him."

"Tucker loves Carly," Livingston added.

"It's not like that, Jimmy. I just came back for my grandmother's house. And I have a boyfriend, and it isn't Tucker. I might even marry Gary."

Jimmy chuckled. "Sure. Tell another one. 'Marry Gary' sounds like some corny song. I doubt that another man could keep up with you."

Carly leveled a bottom-line order at Jimmy: "You just tell everyone who's interested that I did not sleep with Tucker last night."

"Sure," Jimmy said amid a disbelieving chuckle.

When Carly hung up the telephone, Tucker's scent was on the sheets and the pillow that she was hugging. Once Carly realized she was sniffing the pillow and getting that melting feeling only Tucker could arouse in her, she scrambled off the bed and straightened her clothing.

She found Tucker in the kitchen, standing in his shorts, starting to make breakfast.

Carly tried not to think about the reason he had changed from jockey-style to boxers.

While she tried to find words to scathe him for the impression he'd given Gary, Tucker sent her a narrowed look. "I'm not having a conversation with you before I eat. Do you want orange juice?"

The reduce-him-to-rubble words were in her, bubbling and heating. Meanwhile, Tucker took a pitcher from the refrigerator and poured two huge glasses of juice. He let them sit on the counter while he slapped bacon into skillet. With the ease of an expert chef, he cracked an egg on a bowl, opened it with one hand, and dropped it into the bowl. He added more eggs and whisked milk into them.

When they were in another skillet and the toaster was set, he flipped the bacon, shoved it aside and poured in a mountain of frozen potato home fries.

The whole process took her back to when he was disgusted because she couldn't cook home-style dishes like his mother. There they were, high on sexual marathons, and not a clue how to tend to everyday domestic needs.... Now Tucker was cooking....

She still couldn't. And neither could her mother. Rebecca had never been a domestic, or a particularly loving, woman.

While Carly struggled with the transition of awakening on the floor, the telephone call she'd missed, and Tucker cooking, the telephone rang again.

"That would be your friend, Gary Whats-His-Name," Tucker said.

"Gary Kingsley. He's an up-and-coming executive in advertising. We're dating. It's getting serious." She hurried into the bedroom and picked up the telephone.

The excited and happy woman at the other end of the line was Mrs. Storm. "I just want to say how happy I am that you've come back to Tucker, just like Anna Belle always wanted."

"I'm not back with Tucker. We're just sorting my grandmother's things. Some of it I want to go to my mother, and the Last Inn is closed."

"Goodness, dear. There's a new motel at the other end of town—the Taj Mahal. Real spiffy. You zipped into town so fast to visit your grandmother and then you were grieving so, you probably didn't notice. Or you could have stayed with anyone who knows and loves you, you little scamp. Oh, I know how a woman acts when she's set to snare a prize like Tucker. He's had some nice girlfriends—"

For the first time, Carly noted the box lid on Tucker's bedside table. It contained several barrettes and ponytail bands and a brush with several long blond hairs. *He was tending another woman. He'd laughed at Carly's notion of a lover brushing her hair…just the way she'd seen it done in romantic movies.*

She pushed that nettling, hurtful tidbit away and politely ended the conversation with Mrs. Storm. Whatever Tucker did with other women was no longer Carly's business, she told herself.

In the kitchen, Tucker had filled his plate and sat at the table, drinking his orange juice. He ran his finger around the rim of the glass. The resulting squeak raised the hairs on Carly's neck.

"I suppose that was Gary," he said.

"Yes, everything is settled now, no thanks to you," she lied. "You really should get another telephone in here." Tucker did not need to know that he threatened every relationship she'd ever had. Even when he was nowhere near, he came between her and the men she decided she wanted. She planned to seduce Gary, just to get the last remnants of Tucker's lovemaking out of her system—and to nab Gary as a husband, of course. She wondered who was Tucker's naturally blond girlfriend, the one who was sleeping in his bed and whose hair he brushed just like in the romantic movies.

"No need for another telephone. Help yourself."

"Aren't you going to work?"

"Tyrell and I are going fishing. My brother and I usually do on Saturday mornings. I only get up early to feed and take the cover off Livingston. That bird sure does unload a lot. It's a good thing I take the daily newspaper."

Seated across the table from Tucker, Carly devoured her breakfast. Tucker eased back in his chair to study her.

"I bought this house from Anna Belle five years ago," Tucker stated slowly. He glanced at the window as his truck passed slowly down the alley to his backyard. Jimmy was craning his neck to see inside the house. Still trying to peer inside Tucker's house, Jimmy walked past the window on his way back to the street. A car door slammed, signifying that Jimmy was collected by someone else.

"And just why did my grandmother allow you to buy this house? I would have bought it," Carly said.

Tucker breathed deeply and finished his explanation. "Anna Belle needed the money and didn't want anyone to know who didn't have to. People involved with the transaction respected that—I made it a point to talk with them. Samuel Lawson handled everything. It was a better than fair price."

Carly almost choked on the food in her mouth. She forced a swallow and stared at him. "You mean that my grandmother was in need, and she didn't tell Mom or me?"

"Your mother and Anna Belle were never that close. You were just getting set up in your career—or that's how she figured it."

Carly slumped back into her chair, her mind flying. She remembered the new roof, not sagging anymore. Shingles and flooring had been replaced, and new appliances and plumbing had been Anna Belle's pride. Carly frowned as she thought of the hired cleaning lady, and the bottles of pills by the sink, before it had been necessary for her grandmother to enter the retirement home. Those costs alone would have been—

The horrifying reality of her grandmother's age and illness without adequate financial resources stunned Carly. Both Carly and her mother could have helped with bills, yet Anna Belle hadn't turned to them; *she hadn't asked for help.* "I didn't know."

"You look like hell," Tucker said pleasantly, before he stood up and took his dishes to the sink and began washing them. "Now get your stuff and get out."

Carly stood and stared at Tucker, just the way she had when she was twelve and Fluffy, her pet hamster had died. She seemed to hang there, as if someone needed to anchor her, to hold her. Those big honey-brown eyes were soft with pain. Even worse was the slight trembling of her soft lips.

Life was more complicated now with Carly-the-woman than staging the best-ever funeral and burying the hamster's shoebox where he could overlook Toad Hollow.

"I don't know what to do," she said unevenly as she visibly struggled to recover. "I didn't know anything about all this, or I would have helped. I can make a living anywhere, and I could have come back to care for her. She seemed to like the retirement home even though she didn't want to die there. Her friends were there—some of them, and they liked to gossip about the old days and play poker. Mom would have helped with finances, no matter the differences between her and Grams."

Tucker recognized Carly's next expression from their childhood, dating and marriage experiences. She had found her solid emotional footing, dropped the sorrow, and was now getting really worked up. She firmed her convictions and in another heartbeat she launched them at him. "Tucker, you do owe me for saving your life. I'd think you could at least let me say goodbye to Anna Belle as she would have wanted. Funerals and cemeteries just don't cut it. It's a slow ache that takes time to deal with, and I'd planned to work that out right here—in my grandmother's home.''

Tucker poured another glass of orange juice and took his time drinking it as he circled what Carly had just said. He didn't trust her agenda. Even though she looked grief-stricken and uncertain and rumpled, Carly always had a fast mind and wanted her way—but she wasn't getting it this time. The house was his. His drink was finished and so was his patience. He leaned back against the kitchen counter and crossed his arms over his chest. ''And just how did you save my life?''

Those honey-brown eyes had turned to the shade of hot dark chocolate.

When Livingston launched into another squawking session about Carly loving Tucker, she stood abruptly and went into the living room to place Livingston in his ''dark hell.''

She returned and stood, her hands on her waist, glaring at Tucker. ''By marrying you, of course. In doing so, I protected you from my father. Going to that motel that night meant you intended to take my virginity, to seduce me, and my father never liked seducers. If you hadn't said we planned to get married, we never would have been—because you wouldn't have been alive, Tucker Redford.''

Tucker frowned and took a deep breath; he always took deep breaths when he was about to argue his point. ''Now, back up, Carly. Get the facts straight. We'd just had another fight about me seeing Ramona when you were on vacation with your folks. When you screamed, I ran to that motel room, and found you all dressed up in that Miss Cornbread Muffin bathing suit with the banner across your somewhat less than now chest. It's only because you're a lot thinner now than you were, I suppose.... You look bone-tired, Carly, and you're too pale...."

He recovered from thinking about how someone should be holding her and caring for her when she overdid herself—mainly because he didn't like that idea. "I was parked outside that night and I knew what that guy wanted—you. You were set to—"

"I told you and told you, Tucker. Simon Gifford told me it was a party for the contestants. I didn't know what he was planning. And I do not want to relive that nightmare. But I found out on my wedding night that my suspicions about Ramona and you were justified, didn't I?"

"And it took a whole week of everyone thinking we'd consummated, before I could talk you into getting over it."

"That 'But I did it for you, honey' line wasn't believable."

Tucker didn't intend to swear, but Carly knew right where to shove her barbs. At the time, there was no way in hell that he was going to tell his sweet, virginal girlfriend—the one he wanted to have his babies—that Ramona had laid him well and good. His willpower back then broke under the assault of Ramona's capable hands and tongue. That night was his initiation. Tucker had learned then that women had pleasure-muscles that didn't show. "I am not going to apologize for that now."

Carly held up her finger. "The point is, I married you to protect you. You owe me your life, or at least a few days of saying goodbye to my grandmother's house—*which I thought was going to be mine.* She could have told me she was having money problems. Mom and I would have helped—"

"Anna Belle did not want to trouble either one of you, and she knew I wasn't leaving town. You did."

"*I had to,*" she stated unevenly. "I just had to leave, Tucker."

He couldn't deny that fact. He'd always known that Carly was very bright and needed challenges and adventures, one after another. She needed to succeed. Marriage to him wasn't enough for her. She couldn't help her natural instinct to fly away to discover and investigate life.

"I know," he said quietly and walked into his bedroom and slid into a pair of jeans, dressing quickly in his hurry to get away from Carly and the resulting emotions in him.

He went back to the kitchen, took one look at the tears sliding down her cheeks as she looked out at her grandmother's backyard and knew he was about a heartbeat away from giving the house to her. The best thing for him to do was to get out fast, just like he did when they were married. "Do what you have to do, Carly. I'm going fishing with my brother."

"How is Tyrell?" she asked. Her tone said that her mind was really on her grandmother.

"Same as always. Single. He's been engaged a couple of times. Runs a little financial planning office on Main Street.''

She shook her head and a tear dropping from her cheek caught the morning light. It gleamed silvery as it fell to the V of skin exposed by her vest.

Carly—soft and grieving and rumpled in the morning—was dangerous, because Tucker's natural instincts were to comfort her.

But when that tear trailed downward into the soft valley of places he'd better forget, Tucker hurried for his truck and bass boat in the backyard. His hand still felt that soft backside as she struggled on top of him. He'd gone hard at the morning scent of her, the feel of his woman rubbing against him. A tangle of sweet and desperate emotions churned around him. There was an instant when he wanted to tug her beneath him, hold her wrists in the old playful way as she squirmed and laughed before the sweetness came gently upon them.

But she had a boyfriend named Gary, and Tucker always had been too easy where Carly was concerned.

Not this time.

At the lake, with Tyrell sitting at the other end of the boat, Tucker brooded about Carly and the feel of her against him earlier. All the old sweet feelings tangled with bitterness, and frustration that he couldn't take the whole mess and dump it in the lake and forget about everything.

Tyrell was six years younger and not as romantically bruised.

"Sally Jo thinks you need protection from the way Carly was acting at the MidTown Cafe. To help protect you, Sally Jo told Carly that you had a girlfriend,'' Tyrell said softly as he reeled in another bass.

The fish had long ago taken the worms off Tucker's hook, but he hadn't cared about catching them.

"If Carly stays around long, you'd better come up with a girlfriend,'' Tyrell continued. "Carly has gotten to you pretty good in one day. I do not want to have you mooning over at my house and ruining all my good ball games with those long, deep sighs. You're in sad shape, bro. And she wants that house back. You're a solid thinker, but she's all over you when it comes to speed and deal-making.''

"She is not getting to me,'' Tucker said as he felt another fish tug on his hook and dismissed it.

"So how about me dating her?'' Tyrell asked with a grin.

Tucker glared at his younger brother. "She's got a boyfriend named Gary.''

"Probably wants to marry her and live in that house. She's probably in the baby-making mode and needing a donor.''

Tucker brooded on that topic. He'd donated plenty, but Carly hadn't let her eggs play. "She'll be gone by the time I get back. So lay off.''

Tyrell's line sailed out in another cast. "I wouldn't bet on it. She's older and wiser now, and you've still got an ache for her the size of Texas. And you've got that horny look. It hasn't been there in eleven years, since she divorced you and left town. Of course, now and then, when you heard about her visiting Anna Belle, or saw Carly, you got it back.''

"I was over her a long time ago, and I don't want

to hear any more about Carly. She's just passing through.''

''Uh-huh,'' Tyrell said as if he didn't believe Carly would leave easily. ''Remember when we made her clean those fish before we'd let her in our tree house? She got to be real good. I wish she'd clean this big mess of fish for me now.''

Tucker ignored another nibble on his hook. ''Her stuff will be out of the house when I get back.''

''Uh-huh.'' Tyrell's tone was disbelieving.

Tucker dropped his brother at his home two hours later, and dreaded going back to Anna Belle's house—where he'd told Carly the facts of the sale and told her to get out.

He filled the truck with gas, picked up a few groceries, browsed through some home renovation magazines at the drugstore and stopped at the MidTown Cafe for supper. Peter Amos, the local postmaster, came to Tucker's table. ''Carly is having her mail sent to your house. I hope that's okay. She said that you and her had an understanding. Folks are glad about that. Catch any fish today?''

Tucker forced himself to swallow his last bite. The understanding *he* had was that Carly would be gone when he returned. ''They weren't biting.''

On his way out of the cafe, Tucker tuned out the gossip about Carly's car parked overnight in his driveway. He nodded briskly to Jeff Thomas's nosy probing, ''I hear Carly's back in town…that she'll be staying a while…she bought an extra-long phone cord from Mac. Heard she figures that house is really hers.''

''We'll settle that hash,'' Tucker said firmly as he

got into his pickup and almost pulled out in front of Norma's police car.

Her siren drew him back to the side of the street. She was out in a heartbeat, ticket book in hand. "Got to write you a ticket for reckless—"

Tucker shook his head and tried to work up a sweet-talking line and a smile. It was difficult to do when he was on his way to evict his ex-wife squatter. "Your hair looks real nice, Norma."

She patted the big gray fluff around her head. "Thanks. New perm. Okay, forget about the ticket. Saw Carly's car parked in your driveway all last night. I figure you're due a mistake or two. Dealing with her can take a lot of brain-time."

"It sure can," Tucker agreed as he pulled in behind the car that was blocking his drive to the backyard. He parked, grabbed his small sack of groceries in one hand, and strode up to the door with Carly-eviction on his mind.

Inside, Carly was busy at work on Anna Belle's dining room table, punching her laptop's keys. Tucker's business papers were heaped at the other end of the table. A telephone cord ran from her laptop down onto the floor, up over the stacked boxes of her things, and across the living room and into his bedroom.

"Oh, hello, Tucker," Livingston squawked. "I love you, big boy."

Tucker ignored the parrot's make-up talk and surveyed his home. Carly had moved her boxes in from the car and some of them were open. *That meant that her stuff was somewhere in his house!*

Tucker primed himself to tell Carly what he thought

of unwelcome women squatters and how much Norma
would like to evict her. Then he looked at Carly more
closely.

Bundled up on top of her head, her hair had ends
sticking out like a war chieftain's feathers. Some of the
silky strands hadn't been captured and quivered softly
around her face and nape. A pen was propped over one
cute little ear.

He knew that ear very well. He used to blow in it....

Tucker held very still, his heart leaping. Carly was
wearing one of his faded cotton summer shirts, and her
legs and feet were bare. He hoped she was wearing
shorts, because if she wasn't, he'd never be able to sit
on that dining room chair again.

Carly shifted and exposed the requisite cutoff shorts,
and Tucker released the breath he'd been holding.

This woman was a brand-new Carly—a tigress at
work. Bent over her work, her fingers flying over the
keyboard, pausing only to make notes on a yellow pad,
Carly didn't notice Tucker. She unplugged the cord
from her laptop, slid it into the telephone on the table
and punched in a number.

Carly stood, and holding the telephone began to
walk the length of the room. "Look, Tim, the brochure
for Stiles Advertising just has to be updated. It's blah,
blue and black. Not a drop of zest in it. Get a graphic
artist on that, will you? Not a staff person, but send it
out to that last freelancer we had—Iris whats-her-name.
And put her on retainer, if you have to.... Yes, I know
that.... I am not babying some copywriter who doesn't
deliver on time. Give Megan notice that if that copy
isn't sent e-mail to me pronto, she may be looking for

another job…. And Tim, send the photos from the last shoot to me—e-mail—the ones with the jeans. If I can see the model's panty lines, so can everyone else and that is just tacky, tacky, tacky…."

On her way back, she glanced at Tucker who was leaning against the wall, watching her. Carly's expression had a fighter's flashing keep-out-of-my-way look.

He shrugged and swept his free hand in a go-ahead motion. In full stride, and chewing on problems, Carly was fascinating, a tip-top female shark, in the pool and scrapping to get business done her way.

"No, Jessica just had a baby. Don't you dare push her to come back into the office," she continued as she passed in front of him. Her free hand rubbed her temple as if a headache had lodged there.

She glanced at Tucker and momentarily a soft smile crossed her expression. For just a heartbeat, she leaned against him with a little tired sigh.

Stunned, Tucker couldn't think. Then she was off and striding across the floor, intent on business.

While Tucker was dealing with the flow of her long smooth legs and the soft way she'd rested against him for just that instant, Carly continued, "Don't you dare call her in to work on the graphics for the dog show. Get that woman a computer set up at home pronto and everything she needs. Keep her happy. I don't want her going freelance for some other company, and she's already said she plans to work at home. She might as well work for us…. And I want some progress reports from the sales department. I'll handle the digital camera account myself. Express that brochure on the Cayman Islands to me and what you've got on the trade show, and I guess that's all until Monday morning.''

She placed the telephone on the table, closed her eyes and rubbed her forehead. Picking it up again she said, "Listen, Tim. I'm sorry. You're doing a good job. I didn't mean to jump on you. It's just that this stuff has been going on all day—problems that shouldn't arise, especially when I worked overtime to carve out this time for a break. Thanks for being so good about helping me. I'll sign for time and a half on your next check…. Yes, everything is going fine. Same to you…. Bye.''

Carly eased into her chair and shoved her laptop aside to make room for her arms, which she rested on the table. She placed her forehead on them. "It's been hell today," she said quietly. "They've got to make do without me once in a while. I've got the best assistant in the world, but not even Tim can manage what came apart—all in the one day I've been out of the office.''

Did Carly realize that she'd rested against Tucker for that fraction of time?

Looking at her all bent over her work, Tucker wished he would have brushed her hair as she'd read in the romantic novels.

If Carly's work was that demanding, no wonder she needed a getaway. "Do you keep this up all the time?''

"I love it. I'm really good at multitasking and I'm creative as heck. But I'm just handling a lot right now and shouldn't have jumped on my assistant. I feel bad about that.''

Tucker understood how young Carly's energy and

competitive instincts fit well into her adult vocation. "You like the angling and the challenges, the push and the shove, the game. And you're good. That's why they depend on you so."

"I suppose." She reached a hand to her shoulders and rubbed the muscles there, as if they were stiff and aching.

*She'd built herself a whole life away from him. Carly was a different person than the girl he had married....*

*And still, her need to lean upon him when she was tired and frustrated was still there....*

Tucker pushed away from the wall. He preferred dealing with his customers' payments due, than dealing with his emotions right now. He could run, like he did this morning and in their marriage. Or he could stay.

*It was his house. He'd stay, of course. He couldn't run from Carly at every turn.*

Carly's hand slid limply down from her shoulders and the long deep sigh said she was close to dozing.

Tucker shook his head and walked slowly to her. He considered her as she slept, her head on her arms. He forced himself away from her, and into the kitchen, putting away his groceries. One glance back at Carly told him that she hadn't moved.

Drawn to watch his ex-wife without all the flash and barbs, Tucker stood beside her. *She'd smiled that soft old way at him and had rested against him, as if he were home and safety to her....*

He saw his hand reaching for her hair, to ease the pen from over her ear, to smooth back her hair. It seemed only natural to release that twisted bundle of silky hair, to rub her scalp gently with his fingertips.

He'd always been able to touch Carly in a way that soothed her and that pleasured him....

Tangled in his thoughts about the softness of that one moment as she passed him, Tucker began to toy with her silky hair. He lifted the strands to watch the fading sunlight from the window catch the different shades. When Carly sighed deeply, slowly, his fingertips found her scalp, massaging gently.

The first long, soft, erotic purr staked his steel-toe boots to the floor and sent every one of his muscles into hard alert. The next sound simulated a woman beginning her orgasm. Carly angled her head for more, and the very long purring sound caused his throat to dry.

The image of a frisky, just discovered oh-my sex, young Carly flashed across his mind. After they'd made it through that first long week of him coaxing her into lovemaking, Carly was fast and hot, zapping him into a warm boneless mass with a silly grin. He hadn't minded a bit that he'd had to initiate every seduction, but he'd wondered how it would be to have her actually set to seduce him.

Carly had always been a fast learner and a fast runner. These sounds came from a woman who savored a slow, intense sexual climb, waiting there for every particle of pleasure, and the soft fall to earth.... She had probably learned the art of seduction from other men....

Tucker's hands tightened. She'd probably learned a few things—and not from him. He tilted her head, so that she looked up and back at him. "So, did Gary call?"

It took a minute for her drowsy expression to clear and then she frowned, jerking her head away from him. She stood slowly and faced him, her arms crossed in front of her. She took her time in answering. "You knew exactly what you were doing when you answered the telephone this morning. No, he hasn't called. You've probably ruined the only chance I've got to nab him. He's everything you aren't, and everything I want. *He's sensitive.*"

"Big boy," Livingston added.

Tucker leaned down to Carly, making certain she didn't mistake his expression for kindness and understanding. "I told you to get out."

"You told me to do what I had to do. This is it. I had work to do and I'm not ready to turn everything Anna Belle loved over to a squatter."

"Squatter" echoed his previous thoughts about Carly, and began a headache that had moved up from his southerly parts, started by the scramble on the bed this morning and her orgasmic crooning.

Tucker threw up his hands. "I'm getting an aspirin and when I come back, you'd better be hauling stuff out that front door."

"Make me. You are not renegotiating at this point. You told me to do what I had to do, and I am. That's the deal. No post-agreement amendments."

After a minute of deciding just what he could do with Carly, Tucker had no definite course. He didn't trust himself where Carly was concerned. Tucker left the battlefield and marched into his bathroom. He jerked open the medicine cabinet to find it stuffed with feminine facial creams and cleansers, cosmetics, an eyelash curler, pills for "that time of the month," and a tiny pink razor. He closed the cabinet door to find a big circular magnifying mirror that had been stuck to the mirror. The image of his two huge, glaring eyes shot back at him.

He held still and surveyed Carly's invasion of his thinking-space and library. Bottles of women's shampoo and bathing items ran across the window ledge in the shower. "Give Carly an inch and she'll take a mile," he heard himself growl.

Anna Belle's frog planter sat on the back of the toilet stool, replacing his library magazines. *And the seat was down.*

Tucker grabbed the fluffy white net-thing that hung from the showerhead, crushed it in his fist and stalked out to see Carly. She hadn't moved. He was finished with words and unsettled warm-soft emotions sneaking in to confuse him. He tossed the fluffy net-thing at her face, but she caught it. Tucker noted that her catching hand and reflexes were still good, and picked up the telephone receiver. He punched in a number. "Norma? There's a trespasser in my house. Come get her."

# Chapter 4

"I cannot believe you actually called Norma."

Tucker showed his teeth in a cold smile. They gleamed in his late-day approaching stubble. Carly had always distrusted that smile, because it was his "gotcha" smirky look. Sometimes in their dating, it had been matched by the warmth in his eyes. But this time, his eyes were as silver as a cold steel blade. "You've got a few minutes. Norma's car is at Jimmy's getting a new battery. She doesn't think it looks right to make official calls in his wrecker and she's hurrying him. It's Saturday, and Jimmy doesn't like coming in to work on his day off. You'd better start packing your things. Get that junk out of my bathroom."

Carly hurled her bath scrub-net at his face and it bounced to the floor. She'd lost almost an hour sobbing over the shoebox of valentines she'd discovered in her search for the diary. Tucker had kept every valentine from her and no one else. Her handwriting on the back had been crossed out by a big black marker. His adult masculine script had graded every one, from "Not bad for a first attempt at spelling my name" to "Pure Mush Stuff" to "She didn't mean a word of it."

Carly had closed the shoebox carefully. She didn't want Tucker to know that she had seen inside his deep pain. The insight that she had hurt him deeply, that the smell and stain on the valentines was definitely beer and that she'd driven him to drink had upset her for another hour.

She'd lost years because no one seemed to fit her like Tucker—when he was a teen and sweet, her first love. She just knew she could do better on a second or third love, but they never came. *He* was the reason— the man standing in front of her, all six-foot-two of big, stubborn, in-her-face ex-husband.

"I'm not taking your bad mood, Ms. Hot-Shot Redford," Tucker warned too quietly. "If Gary didn't call, that's between you and him. But then, maybe he's seen the light of day—and he's lucky to escape."

"How dare you!"

This was the same old infuriating Tucker, who had changed from the sweetheart-friend into a demanding and sulking husband, one who ran every time they needed an intimate, resolving talk.

Tucker moved to the front door and opened it. "You're getting all worked up, Carly. Maybe Gary didn't call because he knows you've got a wildfire temper. Maybe all he knows is those sounds you make like you're having a long, slow—"

She couldn't bear to let her ex-husband know how she'd never had sex with another man, that somehow, just at the wrong moment, Tucker had managed to ruin everything—and he wouldn't even be close! Tucker was always there, even when he wasn't!

Carly shivered a little and her hand shot out to fist Tucker's shirt. "I was dead-tired and my eyeballs felt like they'd fall out, so I relaxed a bit. My scalp is not an erogenous zone," she lied, because she'd just discovered that it was.

She tugged him close enough to look up and frighten him with a glare. Tucker's blue eyes were starting to get the look that said, "You're so funny when you're worked up."

He reached up and slowly rubbed her scalp. "See how long you can take this and then we'll talk."

*She would not give him one sound of ecstasy. She was a sophisticated career woman, who ran an office staff and negotiated with big business. She'd carved her way in a competitive field, and she was not letting her ex-husband get to her....*

Carly stood very still, keeping her glare full-force and trying not to notice the deepening laugh lines beside Tucker's eyes. The sensuous massage was getting to her and she had to defend herself. "I'll bet your blond girlfriend fakes it. Women like intimacy with sex. You never learned that."

Tucker's teasing expression stilled. His eyes narrowed and a muscle in his jaw tightened beneath the stubble-shadow. He looked raw and tough and big, and Carly knew she was getting to him as he said slowly, huskily, "She likes it fine.... You're trying to hold out.... So do you fake it?"

"Fake it? Fake it?" Livingston squawked.

"Get out," Tucker said quietly and jerked open the door.

He'd always known just how to push the wrong buttons, and now it was about her life without sex. Not even a low-grade on the sex-barometer kind. Not even the mind-blowing kind. With a frustrated, muffled cry, Carly launched herself at him.

Tucker grunted as his arm circled her and his other arm reached out for the doorframe, missing it. Both off balance, they seemed to dance across the porch and down the steps, where Tucker tumbled onto the front lawn, taking her with him.

Carly wasn't done with him yet. He'd primed her and knew it, and he could take the fruits of his punishment. She'd wrestled him to the ground since they were children and later sweethearts, and she could do it now.

In a fast flurry of arms and legs, she intended to wrest him out of her system, once and for all. Since she'd left the dignified businesswoman persona behind, she might as well make the most of it. She'd shame Tucker Redford on her own grandmother's lawn.

They rolled across the lawn, and Tucker definitely weighed more than he had years ago. She hooked her knee around his leg and shoved, and he went beneath her with a soft whoosh of air. She'd always been really good at besting Tucker, at getting him down and sitting on him. This confidence gave her new strength and she held his wrists. They were bigger than she remembered; her hands looked small and soft and ineffectual against the strength of those wrists. "I detest you, Tucker Redford. You've done nothing but ruin my life.''

He rolled on top of her, all of him, his hands completely circling her wrists. He took her hands up to rest beside her head. "Uh-huh. I always let you beat me because I liked you sitting on top of me. Did you ever think about that?''

She struggled against his greater strength and weight, but right there on the grass next to the fragrant budding roses and the happy jumble of purple pansies, Tucker had that quiet, intent look.

His face was too close, and his thumbs were massaging her wrists. She could move—or she couldn't—because her mind and her body were tangling…and waiting, as if the whole world had stopped moving.

"You're a whole lot of trouble, Carly Walker Redford,'' he whispered unevenly as his lips brushed hers and set fire to every flammable, womanly essence in her.

"You're no Prince Charming,'' she managed in a wispy voice as her body began to recognize his and quiver and heat and soften.

With an uneven groan, Tucker opened his lips and fitted them perfectly on hers. His hands released her wrists and his fingers began that slow massage-erotic-thing on her scalp. Tucker seemed to be dragging breath into him, his hands trembling, his face burning near hers.

Or was hers burning?

In the fragrances of home and flowers and lawn and

man, Carly found her arms encircling him, smoothing the hard quivering muscles there, just as her tongue met his. He tasted the same and different and she trusted him, and her lips opened to the nudge of his.

Fire leaped into her blood, a sense of homecoming and new adventure sliding over her, seeping softly into the sweet remembrances of Tucker's big body locking intimately with hers. The beat of his heart raced, a familiar match to her own; she could almost feel that they shared the same pulse, the same heat.

Carly slid her fingers into his hair and smoothed the tense ridge of his broad shoulders. She slid her hands down his sides to lock onto muscular, tight buttocks covered by his jeans. Meanwhile, Tucker's big hand had opened upon her breast, claiming it gently. His other hand framed her face, his thumb slowly stroking her cheek.

She forced her lids open, saw Tucker's grim expression above her—and glimpsed Norma above him.

The cold water pouring down on her caused Carly to gasp and to struggle for breath.

Tucker cursed and wiped her face with a brisk swipe of his hand. He slowly turned to look up at Norma. "She attacked me. I was just holding her down until you arrived," he said darkly as he eased to his feet and stood in front of Carly.

She struggled to sit up and smooth her clothes at the same time, using Tucker's big body as a shield. She struggled to place herself away from the fire and the hunger with Tucker into the reality of the Saturday evening—rolling on her grandmother's front lawn with her ex-husband, the bane of her lifetime.

"Thanks for turning on the water, Norma. The lawn needed it." He reached down and grabbed the back of her borrowed shirt, easily hoisting her to her feet. While she dangled almost on tip-toe, he studied her with a disgusted expression.

"She's all yours," he said firmly, before he shoved her at Norma. Tucker walked to the garden hose faucet, turned off the water and stalked into the house.

"I guess that about says it," Norma stated briskly as she handcuffed Carly. "I gave you fair warning."

*"This is my grandmother's house. You can't do this."*

Norma dramatically adjusted her uniform belt's night stick, leather pistol holster and pepper spray holder. "Watch me. And don't get mud all over the back of my squad car."

"That's not a squad car, Norma. You have to have several cars and more than one policewoman to make a squad. I bet you haven't even used that roll of crime-scene tape you ordered a hundred years ago."

Norma huffed up and glared at Carly. "I can add resisting arrest to the charges. Don't make me. Wipe your feet on the lawn. There's mud between your toes. Since you're already dirty, you might as well clean the fish that Tyrell brought over for my supper. You used to be real good at that."

"I've forgotten how," Carly stated with as much dignity as she could as Norma marched her to the "squad" car and put her in the back seat.

The blast of Norma's siren muffled Carly's protests. The siren brought people to the sidewalks to stare at her—riding in the back seat of the car.

* * *

Tucker took a long, slow shower and, absorbed in his brooding, grabbed Carly's shampoo. He was seated in his recliner, drinking a beer, the television blaring no-channel static noises, before he caught the scent of flowers. He sniffed, scowled as he remembered using Carly's shampoo, and quickly poured beer into his palm. He brushed his hands together and then rubbed his hair hard to remove the scent.

*Nothing would remove the feel of Carly moving beneath him, all full and hot and ripe and hungry.*

*Nothing could remove the need to hear those sounds again.*

*Or maybe the need had grown to hear those orgasmic hungry, sensual sounds, combined with her moving beneath him.*

That Carly had ruined his life, his peace, and his Saturday night was obvious. He was feeling—vulnerable. He had to get Carly out of his system, one way or the other, but just now he had to calm down and think—

When the telephone rang, he supposed it was her single alotted call from jail. Norma wouldn't let Carly ring that many times.

It continued to ring and with a sigh, and he rose to answer it. "Tucker, here."

The silence wasn't typical of Carly. By now, she would have burned his ears and got his temper simmering. A man's deep voice spoke slowly, carefully, "This is Gary Kingsley. I'm calling for Carly Redford. May I speak to her, please?"

"She's not here. She's in jail. If you want her, call

there. I'm not running a message service.'' Tucker gave the number and decided he might as well make Carly's life as miserable as she'd made his. After all, this was *Gary,* the guy she wanted to nab and who was ''sensitive,'' unlike himself. Tucker didn't like the savage jealousy burning and driving him. Unaccustomed to every emotion he didn't want hitting him at the same time, he said, ''She's in jail because she wanted to have sex with me—I'm her ex-husband—and she attacked me on the front lawn *of my house*. The sheriff had to run a hose on her to cool her off. I'd sure be grateful if you could come collect her.''

Tucker hung up and noted that Carly's laptop was still humming. He touched it and it sprung to life, leaping with complex graphs and numbers beside a page layout, advertising for a high-priced car dealership. ''Download complete'' remained on the screen. Another touch brought up a cost-effective list and Carly's notes on marketing to unique groups...she was very good. The yellow notepad beside the laptop contained a neat, thoughtful outline.

He turned off the laptop, watching it do its don't-want-to-die thing. When the need arose, Tucker was still borrowing his brother's office computer, and Carly had hooked up to her office's mainframe in another state.

All he'd wanted years ago was the girl he'd always loved, a stay-at-home wife and a mother for his children, a good safe home for them all. He wanted to protect and love them and—

And Carly had fixed that...she'd gone off and learned how to be a—what? A wrangling, competent, competitive businesswoman with a boyfriend named Gary?

Tucker sat again and rubbed his chest, inhaling the feminine scent beneath the beer's tang. He tried to still the slow hurting ache of love gone wrong—it was then that he noted the drawer askew in the table beside him. He opened it and noted that the papers inside had been rifled.

Still uncovered, Livingston was silent, his beady eyes locked on Tucker. The bird could say more with silence and a beady look than any human Tucker had ever known.

Fifteen minutes later, he was standing behind the town jail, watching Carly clean Norma's supper. The old tenderness was there for the girl he'd known, his first sweetheart. He leaned against the brick wall, nodded to Tanner and Gavin who had followed Norma. The boys had collected five more friends, and they watched the town legend clean fish. "She's good at it, isn't she, Tucker?" Tanner asked.

"Real good. And fast. We used to all go fishing and Carly could clean the whole mess in a half hour flat. We used to time her. She could outswim most of us, too. Her jackknife dive was a thing of beauty. Better go on home now, boys." He glanced at Norma who was standing with one hand on her pistol butt. The pistol probably didn't have any bullets in it. Norma's other hand rested on her pepper spray, ready for a potential prison break.

Reluctantly, the boys rode away, still discussing how the jailbird would escape. Norma studied Tucker as he walked to the jail's back porch. "I guess she's cooled down enough now. What do you want me to do with her?"

Carly was obviously ignoring him, and Tucker's heart tightened at the sight of the tear streaks messing up the mud splatters on her face.

She had rinsed her hands in the bucket of fish water and dried them on the borrowed shirt. She handed the bowl of neatly cleaned and scored fillets to Norma. Then Carly sat with her knees up. Her head rested down on her crossed forearms.

Norma shook her head and spoke quietly. "She's way down, Tucker. Don't pick on her."

"I'll take it from here, Norma, if that's okay."

With a nod, Norma stepped inside the jail and closed the door.

"Go away, Tucker," Carly whispered unevenly.

That's what he usually did when Carly was angry or upset—he left, unable to face her need for intimacy of the talking-relationship kind.

He braced himself for a new experience, because somehow he had to tear her out of his life, his mind and his body. "We may as well talk about this," he said slowly and sat beside her on concrete steps.

Her words were muffled. "The whole town is probably talking about us now."

"That's likely. They have before." He wanted to place his hand on that shiny mussed hair, smoothing it, and rub the tension out of her shoulders and back. Tucker was surprised to see his hand hovering above Carly's head. He lowered it and gripped his jeaned knee firmly, anchoring his need to touch his ex-wife.

"I really did save your life by marrying you," she said.

Tucker nodded; at the time her father hadn't been happy, and Billy Walker had a temper. "Thank you."

She looked at him with suspicion. "Now you're just tormenting me."

"I married you because I was afraid you'd get away from me. You always were a fast mover." His words surprised him; but they rang true in the sweet summer air.

Her eyes widened. "You never said that before."

He took a deep breath and decided to hand her the rest. Because he couldn't bear to look at her tear-streaked face, he looked up at the fading square of blue sky, wedged between the 1890s two-story buildings. "And I didn't think I could catch you. I appreciate that you did try, and I shouldn't have done some things like comparing your cooking to my mother's. What you could do best just ran in a different direction.... I turned off your laptop. You can finish off whatever you have going—that office emergency—and then you'd better leave."

"You were embarrassed because we didn't have sex that first week."

"We made up for that. Things change and so have we." He looked down at Carly. "You smell like fish. Did you find what you were looking for at my house?"

She looked stunned and guilty for a just a heartbeat, before she recovered to come back at him. "*My* house. I don't know what you mean, but I want to make an offer to buy back my grandmother's house."

"You're not getting it, Carly."

"You could make a profit," she insisted. "And you've been drinking. It's Saturday night. Why don't you go to what's-her-name blond-woman and think about selling to me?"

Tucker had just bared his scarred heart to his ex-wife, and she'd stepped right in and started wrangling over property values. He wouldn't let her know that he hadn't managed a relationship after her. Every woman had seemed dull in comparison. *He couldn't think of getting naked and having sex with anyone else. Since they'd rolled on Anna Belle's lawn, that was all he could think about doing with Carly.*

Tucker forced himself to stand and stretch and breathe the alley's hovering scents of summer and fish. He wasn't certain how the intimate-talk business was supposed to go, but he'd just bared his heart, cleaning out a little of the ache, and got a real estate offer in return. His throat was dry and tight, but he managed, "I think I'll just do that. I don't appreciate you messing up my closets and drawers. Whatever you think you want was gone a long time ago."

*Carly could not let Tucker do that to her—just drop something on her that they'd wrangled about in their marriage, that had haunted her since—and walk away.*

Tucker was doing just that—all six-foot-two-inches of broad shoulders, tapering down to narrow hips and long legs in those good-fitting jeans. He'd just given her the intimacy that she'd wanted and ached for in their young, short marriage—and he wasn't giving her a chance to return it. It was just like him to leave the field while he was ahead. "Do not take one more step, Tucker."

He paused, straightened just a bit, then turned the corner into the back street and out of sight.

Carly sank down and let the evening shadows surround her, brooding on Tucker's admission and reflecting on the last bitterness of their marriage. She allowed her tears to drip down her face. Tucker had always been her friend and then her sweetheart, and she'd hurt him. He never lied and he'd just told her how his heart had bled. Valentine-proof lay in a box as worn and tired as she felt.

She amended the "never lied" fact. Tucker's "innocent date" with Ramona hadn't exactly been true.

When she heard the jail's back door scrape open, Carly said unevenly, "I feel like I'm in pieces."

Norma's silence caused Carly to turn and look at the lady police-person, whose expression of sympathy was quickly shielded. "Uh-huh. I have to go home and fry up these fish. I'd rather you didn't sit on the jail's porch all night. Here's a plastic sack. Put the fish heads and guts in the trash can before you leave. Go home."

"I have no home. You'll have to arrest me for vagrancy. Can I stay in the jail all night?"

"No." The door closed and the alley's shadows deepened into night and Carly was alone.

And Tucker was taking his newly developed skill for intimacy-talk to his blond girlfriend. Another woman would be sharing it with him. He was the same and he was different. In the eleven years since they'd divorced and Carly had visited her grandmother, they'd never come close to each other—or said what they had to say for closure. Now Tucker had closed his part and left hers unfinished.

*Just like the need to stake him out and have him.* It vibrated deep and warm inside her—the need to have Tucker. His expression had been tender as he looked down at her, and he was all hot and hungry—but there was something else tangling between them....

Carly sighed deeply and wearily cleared the jail's back steps of fish guts as she reviewed the day's events—her hunt for the diary, the frantic call from her office, rolling with Tucker on her grandmother's lawn and the humiliation of being hauled in by Norma had exhausted her.

So she wasn't in the mood to see Ramona, the minister's wife, the mother of five children and the pillar of the community, dressed in tight jeans and a red satin blouse and matching dancing boots. She wasn't wearing big hair now, but an all-sticking-out-ends cut that framed a pixielike face. "You're a pitiful sight, Carly Redford. I heard you were holed up back here after rolling on the front lawn with Tucker and playing suckface with him."

"Aren't there rules about how a preacher's wife and a mother is supposed to speak? Don't you have to bake a pie for a bazaar or something?"

Ramona's laughter ricocheted off the alley's brick walls. "You've been running away from a talk with me for years. Now, maybe you'll listen. Let me give you a ride back to Anna Belle's. You can clean up and we'll go dancing. If there's one thing I've learned about life, it's that when you think you can't face the world, you'd just better get up and do just that."

After a deep breath, Ramona continued, "Of course, I wanted that fine young stud years ago, but he was hot for you and he resisted. But I nailed him one night when he was down and missing you. I knew when you came back from that weekend honeymoon and glared at me, that he'd finally told you. I knew you'd settle in and dig at that until you made him pay. You weren't in a listening mood then, or later. Then you up and took off and left this whole mess simmering. I've had to live with it."

Ramona walked to Carly and studied her. "Maybe I'd better put a tarp on my car seat before you sit down.... Don't you dare lay any more guilt on me, Carly. I do not want to feel guilty about you and Tucker one day longer. Now pick yourself up and let's go dancing."

"I can't. Tucker just said something that really got me. I don't know how to take it. He didn't give me a chance for a comeback."

"If Tucker said it, he's thought it through and he means it, bottom-line."

"I can't go dancing."

"Sure, you can. You're the town legend. People expect anything from you. It's been real dull here without you. I need you to take the pressure off me. Their expectations are getting pretty high."

Ramona's spiffy little red convertible sportscar wasn't the typical minister's wife's station wagon. She whipped around the city blocks until they squealed to a stop behind Carly's rented car at Anna Belle's house. While Carly showered, Ramona picked out dancing gear and laid it across Tucker's mussed bed. "You should use that bed, with Tucker in it, and loosen up a bit. Your neck got stiffer every time you came home to visit, or I would have told you about having Tucker sooner. Don't think for a minute that it was his fault. I knew what I was doing. He didn't.''

Carly stood still beneath the cosmetics that Ramona applied to repair her crying jag. ''I've got a boyfriend. Tucker has probably cost me the chance to nab him. Gary is sensitive and kind. We're both up-and-coming business executives. We'd make good working partners.''

''I've got a husband. I love him. We argue and make up and balance out life pretty good. I've never looked at another man. Frank understands me, and my need to go dancing on a Saturday night and get my ration of romance without the kids jumping on us in the middle of good sex. They've learned how to pick the bedroom lock…. Frank still lights my fire. I'd say Tucker still lights yours.''

''Tucker is probably at his blond girlfriend's. I am not aching for him. But he started something, and I'd like to finish it. And I want my grandmother's house. I was supposed to inherit it and Tucker bought it right out from under me.''

Ramona pushed the mascara wand into the tube and capped it very slowly. She seemed to be circling an answer for Carly, then she said, ''You're going to have to figure out what is best for you, Carly. Just do it, like you always do. You can't change who you are. You've just got to deal with yourself.''

''You sound like my grandma.''

''Oh, yeah. Well, with my brood I'll probably be a

grandmother soon enough. Face life, Carly. What's the way it is, just is. There's no going back. You just have to deal with what's on the tabletop now, and do the best you can. If your feelings about Tucker are still nagging at you, the best way is to have sex with him and see how you feel after that. You're both wiser now—and I did not believe for one minute that Tucker was planning to seduce you at the Last Inn Motel. I knew that movie star wanted you and I knew the party would be private. I also knew that I had to get to Simon Gifford first if I wanted to go to Hollywood. That's how I was back then.''

Ramona studied Carly in her jeans and long sleeve T-shirt with a red rose on the front. ''You look good. But I can tell you, a man dying of a heart attack during sex did not make my day. You'd think that a movie star would keep himself in better condition.''

While Carly was feeling bruised and tired prior to that knowledge, her agile mind now came to a full stop. ''You wouldn't be fibbing, would you?''

''The undertaker had a time getting that smile off Simon Gifford's face,'' Ramona answered seriously.

Carly rubbed the headache beneath her temple. ''It's been a long day. And I never should have let Tucker get ahead of me. I had my chance, but he pole-axed me with how he felt back then. I was so surprised that I missed my chance and made a bid for this house. I should have evened the score and told him how I felt— back then. Now, he's ahead. I am going to fix that the first chance I get. I don't like being left in anyone's dust.''

''You go, girl.''

At the OK Corral nightclub, the music blared and the dance floor was filled with two-steppers. When Frank left his partner and made for Ramona and Carly, Ramona gently pushed Carly at him. Within five minutes of meeting Frank, Carly could understand why his wife loved him.

Tommy and Emma Jackson invited her to their home, and Arlo and Fred and Jace danced with her.

The band was good, and taking Ramona's advice, Carly smiled at the teasing about being arrested for wrestling Tucker to the ground. She was woman, she was strong and could meet any challenge Tucker threw at her. Then the past would be closed and she could nab Gary. Tucker could marry his blond girlfriend.

She was just fitting all the ugly pieces of the day together—and twirling under Frank's arm—when Tucker and Tyrell appeared at the door. She missed Frank, stumbled, upset a table filled with drinks, and skidded across the spilled beer. Her hand caught on the singer's standing microphone and she gripped it for balance. Once steady on her feet, she met Tucker's cold stare. It cut through the shadows and the crowd to lock with hers. He wasn't backing down and neither was she. Since the microphone was handy and working, Carly used it, because she was never a woman to lose an opportunity to even a score.

She'd lost her dignity today, and probably a potential husband. She'd been tossed in jail, cleaned fish and got her sexual needs all stirred up with nowhere to take them. After all that, Tucker had dropped an intimacy bombshell on her and then just walked off. She would finish the day—and the feelings her ex-husband could tangle in her—her way.

"I've got something to say to you, Tucker Redford. You got away before I could finish today, but I am one hundred percent ready now," blasted across the suddenly silent crowd.

Her words echoed in her brain. She'd been ready on the lawn, hot for Tucker, and they definitely hadn't finished. What she had meant was that he hadn't given her opportunity for closure. Carly felt the heat move up her throat and on her cheeks. "When I was in jail," she added carefully. "And you said those things about how you feel. I want equal opportunity."

Tyrell's grin flashed, but Tucker had folded his arms and was looking up at the ceiling's balloons. From across the room she could see his grim expression.

"Don't just stand there, sing something," she ordered the singer and shoved the microphone at him.

"Same old Carly," someone said quietly after a chuckle.

"The town legend hasn't changed," someone else agreed as Carly made her way around the tables and people to him. The music began and no one moved, staring expectantly at her and then to Tucker, and then back to her.

No one was watching Ramona and Frank's sizzling kiss on the dance floor.

When Carly came to stand in front of Tucker, his eyes narrowed down at her. That vein in his throat began to pulse, a muscle working in his jaw. He looked down her body, and then back up again to her face. "You yelled?" he asked too politely.

"Where's your blond girlfriend?"

"I left her in bed," he said after a moment and gave her that cold wolfish smile. "Exhausted and sleeping. How does it feel to be out of jail?"

That he'd admitted his heart to her and then had gone to another woman for fulfillment shouldn't have taken Carly aback—but it did. "You have a lot of energy, Mr. Redford," she managed.

"What did you want to say to me?" he asked. When she couldn't find the words to even the score, Tucker took a deep breath and slowly placed his hand on her head.

She didn't mean to go soft and wilty, as his fingers gently massaged her scalp, and that sensually hungry look came into his eyes, but she did. Her body quivered just that once and she heard the uneven rush of her words, as if they had been bottled in her for all those years. "I've just got to burn you out of my life, Tucker. I can't go back and I can't go forward. Not until you and I are done. I'm sorry that I hurt you. I didn't know what else to do back then. I knew I wasn't the wife you wanted, and I knew I wasn't settled enough to have your babies. Every day, I fought against what I wanted—to do more, to learn more, to be someone other than Billy Walker's daughter and your wife. But it was always there. I couldn't push it away. Every day it crushed me—what I wanted to be, and what I needed to do. I thought you would be better off without me. You should marry someone and get what you deserve."

She had to stop talking. No one in the universe had probably embarrassed themselves more in one day—or in one whole year. But because she had to, Carly added, *"Do you know how hard it was not to call my best friend when I was starting out all alone in a new place and so scared? Do you know how many times I almost picked up the telephone to call you?"*

It was then that Tucker cursed. With the quick movement of a strong athlete, he bent and hefted Carly over his shoulder. He toted her out of the nightclub as if she were a sack of grain.

# *Chapter 5*

Once seated on the passenger side of Tucker's pickup truck, Carly bristled and tried to find the right words to shake him as she had been shaken. She crossed her arms and settled into the bench seat. It was just like Tucker to be old-fashioned and not have individual seats.

She wasn't leaving the intimacy battlefield to him—not until she'd emptied every last resentment, wrung it out and dropped it on Tucker.

The truck bore his scent—masculine, certain and dark, with subtle layers of frustration that seemed to bristle around her. Papers were stuffed behind the sun visors, a clipboard lay on the floorboard and the seat was set far back to allow for Tucker's long legs. A calculator and papers lay on the seat beside her, a contrast to her ultraspiffy laptop and PDA. Safety glasses hung from his rearview mirror.

Tucker eased those lean legs into the driver's side. He slammed the door, and locked his big hands on the steering wheel. He stared straight ahead, his face grim and hard in the neon light blinking above the OK Corral nightclub.

"Have you had anything to eat?" he asked finally, and not that pleasantly, either.

"One of Ramona's kids left half a peanut butter and grape jelly sandwich in his lunchbox, on the back seat. It was squished flat." The little "I Luv U, Cody" note in the lunchbox had almost made her cry, because it was just like the notes she had sent Tucker in the second grade. As a mature third grader and a boy, he hadn't appreciated the favor.

Tucker switched the truck into life, revved it and shot onto the street. He drove to a fast-food drive-in and parked in a slot near a speaker. At the Red Stompers Drive-In, teenagers were seated in cars, the girls cuddled up to the boys. This was the same place where Tucker and Carly had come as teenagers and as young marrieds. During their marriage, most of Tucker's paycheck had gone to fast food and the cafe. Their grocery bill was high, too, because Carly wasn't able to budget—or to cook.

Now running a million-dollar advertising budget was nothing—but she still had trouble balancing her checkbook.

"I'm embarrassed, you know, Tucker. And you're the cause of my misfortune."

"Sure." The word was flat, giving her nothing, and then he ordered their food.

They sat in silence—until Betty and Ross Wilson brought their boys to Carly's side of the truck. Tanner's and Gavin's eyes were wide, their mouths gaping as they stared at her.

"They've never seen a fugitive from justice before. Or an ex-con," Betty explained with a grin.

"How's it going?" Ross asked, after smothering a chuckle.

"Just peachy." Carly forced a smile. The small town gossip did not observe the protection of secrets and pride. She'd graduated from high school with Betty and Ross and they'd married right away. Between them, they probably rehashed every legend she'd ever made—and Tucker's steadfast ability to rescue her.

"You two getting back together again? Heard you were going at it on the front lawn—"

"No," Carly and Tucker stated in unison.

"Then what are you doing together? The boys said that Tucker came to see you while you were in jail, cleaning fish," Ross, always a reasonable man, asked. When Carly and Tucker were silent, looking straight ahead, Betty discreetly urged her family away into their van.

The food came. Carly and Tucker ate, stuffed the wrappers back into the sacks, and finished their milkshakes—chocolate for him and strawberry for her, same as always. In eleven years, nothing had changed—at least at the drive-in.

Norma pulled in beside them and made her presence known by a loud order into the speaker.

"I thought you were eating fish tonight, Norma," Carly sing-songed across the summer air.

"I'm on patrol. I heard what happened at the OK Corral. Just don't start trouble, Carly Redford. Back when you were roller-skating and delivering orders here, they almost had to shut the place down. You caused more than a few fender benders."

"I rollerblade now," Carly stated darkly. "I'm fast. I bet I could outrace that 'squad' car."

"We'll be going now, Norma," Tucker said. When he had started the motor, he turned to Carly and said quietly, "I do not have a blond girlfriend."

"You have barrettes and blond hair on that brush by your bed," Carly countered.

Tucker squinted thoughtfully out into the night. "Those are from little Samantha Royal. She's six. I fix her hair from time to time. Her father ran out on them a few months ago. I just try to take up the slack now and then, so she'll know that men aren't all the same. I tucked her in tonight. That's where I was. Her dad had called and said he would come see her. He didn't."

Tucker hadn't been with a woman after all. Carly tried not to be jubilant, but she was and couldn't explain that happy, light, giggling feeling. "Fred Royal? The one that you pulled off me when he caught me in that shed?"

He nodded and started the motor. He reversed, gliding the truck out into the night. Norma's headlights followed them to the city limits, then turned back to Toad Hollow.

He drove into the Jacksons' ranch and parked near the new little barn. "Tommy and Emma are honeymooning at the Taj Mahal tonight, celebrating back to marital sex after the baby. Cute little thing, but she's got a good strong grip. I think she'll be pretty good when she starts playing ball. You were. She's at her grandparents.''

"A lot happened all in one day. How are your parents?" After a hard day of discoveries and closures, Carly gave herself an A+ for managing small talk with Tucker.

"Fine. They're in Hawaii, doing the hula. Dad thinks it's good for his arthritis."

Carly forced a swallow down her dry throat. She eased back against the passenger door. This was the first time in years that they'd been alone and had a civil conversation. She was terrified that the unexplainable truce would shatter. And she had missed Tucker.

That fact lodged deep and unremovable within her.

Along with a vibrating and steadily increasing sexual need.

Tucker scowled at her and stepped out into the night, slamming the door behind him. In the moonlight, he looked big and somehow foreign, his hands tucked into his back pockets. His deep voice was quiet and raw in the night. "When you were scared and starting out, you could have called me, Carly. You're right. We were best friends. I would have understood. I was pretty scared when I took over Dad's business."

"I had to do it by myself, Tucker."

"I checked on you, once or twice. Came out to Denver and saw that you didn't need me. You were doing fine. I saw that sleek office building, and your office and your name on that big plaque beside it. I saw you streaking by on the street, dressed in a suit, carrying a briefcase and talking on your cell phone. You looked happy and I knew you were wrangling something by your expression. You looked like someone I didn't know, a sharp businesswoman in action. You didn't need me, Carly.''

''You came to Denver to see me?''

He was silent, gazing out at the cattle. ''I almost called you, too.''

She was terrified of one wrong word, of the past's black arguments. They could tear apart this special fragile moment where the world seemed to stop around them. The stressful day closed in on Carly, crushing her and tears burned her lids.

Maybe it was the physical cleansing that closure brought. Maybe it was the clash between old lifetimes and new. She felt weak and peeled and alone.

She heard a rough sound and looked to see Tucker stand near her, frowning down at her. ''Carly?''

His hand reached for her head and she couldn't let him touch her, lifting her hand to stop him. Her fingers locked on that thick masculine wrist. It was warm and hard and safe, just like Tucker. After a quivering moment in which their eyes locked and her mind went blank, Tucker tugged her against him, her face against his throat. Her arms circled him instantly. She needed his safety, tears burning a trail down her cheek. She rested against Tucker's body, drawing on his strength, the comfort of his arms, his open hand caressing up and down her back.

The hand in her hair had stopped smoothing and his fingers slowly slid into a sensual massage.

She didn't intend to release that sigh, long and low, but it slid into the night air. Beneath her cheek, Tucker's heartbeat had kicked up.

Carly slid her arm around his shoulder and dug her fingers into the muscle tensed there. It quivered beneath her touch, and she held very still, Tucker's skin sending little electric charges to hers. That big span of his hand slid lower on her hip, locking onto the softness there. His breath was uneven and harsh, heat burning around them, in them, though the summer night was cool and fragrant. "You've got that revved woman smell. I'd know yours anywhere, sweet and hot. It hasn't changed."

Carly turned her face slightly and her lips brushed his hard jaw. She didn't move, her lips open on his skin. Tucker was familiar and safe—but he was new, too. And he was dangerous, because most of all, she needed closure from her ex-husband.

"I'd like to burn you out of my life, Tucker Redford."

"Think you could, do you?" he challenged rawly.

Her hand lay over his chest and beneath the cloth, a muscle jumped, a hard nub etching her palm. A huntresslike sense slid over her, almost feline in its awareness, her challenge right under her hand, hot and hard and big and tense. She always loved the game, the hunt, the challenge and the victory.

But she'd never played the game with a man.

In their married, sexual life, Tucker had always done the running, initiating lovemaking—because she wasn't certain if that was a good girl role. While she had debated, Tucker had moved on, gently or wildly taking her to mind-blowing sex. She'd released her riveting need to him, but *she'd* never actually come after *him.* Tucker's need was always right there and revved but never released until she was well on her way to shattering. Now, sexual equality with Tucker was necessary. "I'm thinking I'd like to try."

He spoke impatiently, "Well, think some more. Because I'm not going through that again. Half my heart was torn right out of my chest and when it was still bleeding on the ground, you tromped all over it."

Tucker moved away from her, his eyes silvery slits in the night. "And I'm not changing my mind about selling Anna Belle's—my house—to you, no matter what you try to do to persuade me."

Torn between a simmering desire and Tucker's insinuation that she would use her body to get the house, Carly's mind stopped once more.

She'd always been a fast, agile thinker and her mind had gone blank more times in the two days since she'd been home than it had in her lifetime.

At that rate, Tucker could cost her a future in advertising, where a good mind was a must.

While she felt staked out in the moonlight, vulnerable and unable to move, Tucker got into the pickup cab and slammed the door. A cow mooed as he revved the motor, indicating that he was ready to leave, that he was finished with their brief intimacy. That he was finished with her—forever.

He'd found his closure, while she was still working on hers. In lovemaking, he'd always made certain that they both reached the ultimate finish line at the same time. She'd trusted him to do that. She'd trusted him to understand her need to compete and if not win, call it a draw.

This new Tucker did not care about her feelings.

That fact shook her pride. She'd made a tentative offer and he'd walked away from any negotiation.

Carly did the only thing she could do—she straightened her back and walked to the Jacksons' all-terrain vehicle. Tucker revved his truck, indicating that he was ready to go. So was she. She straddled the four-wheeler and in her hands it lurched to life—unlike Tucker.

She shot off into the night to escape this new Tucker and her shattered emotions.

Tucker heard his curse burn the night. Carly was riding like the proverbial bat out of hell. She'd always acted irrationally when she'd been hurt.

Racing across the pasture toward the road, Carly could be thrown or— He backed the pickup and shot down the road. If she hit that barbed wire fence...he couldn't bear the thought of her bleeding and hurt...or worse.

He almost hit a cow as he raced across the field after her, honking loud enough to send the cattle into a tiny stampede. Carly's vehicle slowed, the headlights swerved and before Tucker knew it, his pickup was into the Jacksons' barbed wire fence. The impact had broken two fence posts. He reversed and found Carly's headlights shooting through the gate.

On the paved road leading back to Toad Hollow, Tucker pulled alongside her and honked. Carly's nose was high in the air, her back stiff.

"You'll get hurt riding that thing. Park it and get

into the truck," he ordered uncertainly. Carly was always one to go the opposite direction of an order, but this time, she could— He did not want to think about the danger.

They continued to drive side by side down the two-lane paved road, approaching Toad Hollow. Carly's hair flew out behind her, and if Tucker hadn't been so worried, he might have thought she was glorious.

Carly always had a really good handle on "glorious."

She turned to him, revved the motor, and then slowed to yell, "I learned to ride one of these at a trade show. We advertised the product. I've raced them. You can see that I am not helpless."

"You've never been helpless, Carly," he said unevenly. When oncoming headlights appeared, he slowed to let her pull in front of him.

The car soared by and Tucker pulled into the lane next to her. She had that stubborn look. "Pull over," he yelled and forced down the temper that never found him—unless he was in the vicinity of his wife.

He blinked, shocked at the new thought. Not ex-wife, but "wife." He'd always considered Carly to be his wife, locked in his heart for good—a maddening, delectable wife, who could tear emotions from him that he hadn't known existed. She always had him on knife-edge, learning about her, about himself, and now about intimacy between them.

She'd wanted him, either for comfort or for sex, or maybe the combination of both. She'd made her statement, and he feared her more than any living creature...rather he feared his feelings for her.

"Pull over," he yelled again and decided that if he got his hands on her...if he got his hands on her, he wasn't certain about himself or what he would do.

Maybe Carly was right. Maybe it was time they burned each other out of their systems.

His hands gripped the steering wheel until they hurt. His sexual need was way ahead of his endangered, vulnerable emotions. This intimacy thing could turn on a man. Carly had always been a fast game, and playing with her could cause real damage—of the broken-heart kind. Payment came in sleepless nights and lonely, aching hours.

"Worry about yourself," she returned over the rev of the all-terrain rig. "Don't worry about me. I've been on my own for a long time."

Another car approached them from the front and Tucker was forced to slow and follow Carly. The car passed and Norma's frizzed hair showed in the interior. She made a U-turn and drove to follow him, her red lights flashing.

Carly shot off the road and into a field. Tucker followed, and winced as he heard Norma's car scrape bottom behind them. They passed Ramona and Frank's family car, parked on a little moonlit knoll. The car appeared empty, until Tucker noticed Frank's white legs and sock-covered feet sticking out of the opened back door. Tucker looked away from the rocking movement of the car. It intensified his own need for Carly.

She re-entered the road and took the route straight down Main Street. Two cars loaded with teenagers pulled in behind Norma, who was by now dragging her exhaust pipe. It rattled loudly as they passed the OK Corral. People finishing the night stood outside staring at the parade. Tucker sank a little lower in the seat, promising he wouldn't—he didn't know what—to Carly.

"Ex" was a big prefix to put in front of "wife." Without reminding himself of the "Ex," he was in definite trouble.

By the time they reached his house, the procession was long and loud. Horns blared, coming from the friendly, whooping crowd behind them. Carly drove the all-terrain rig up into his front yard, parked it by the steps, and ran into the house. Tucker skidded to a stop, one tire up on the sidewalk, and ran after her. While he was testing the locked front door, he heard Norma's car rattle to a stop.

"Carly, open this door," he yelled.

At his side now, Norma huffed, "Problems, Tucker? Need some help? I can shoot off that locked knob. Just stand back and I'll—"

"Nope, not a problem. I can manage," he said, reaching to drag the key out from beneath the doormat. "I'll pay for the tailpipe and damages."

"I'll be glad when you two get it figured out," she said. She sighed and walked toward the people standing and parked on the street, doing her crowd-control waving-off routine.

Tucker entered the darkened house, and walked to Carly's old bedroom. He rapped on the closed door.

"You sure made a spectacle of us out there," he said, because he was obliged to launch a statement of some kind, blaming Carly. He knew it was wrong, because a man was responsible for his actions.

He did not like the sound of muffled sobs. He could handle her crying, Tucker thought darkly, until she was in better shape and he evicted her for good—from his home and his heart.

Carly was his *ex-wife...ex-wife...ex-wife*. He repeated the litany. Otherwise, he'd be in there comforting her. And where would that get him? he brooded. Back into the heartbreak bucket, he decided.

She'd softened to him at the farm, resting against him all sweet and soft, and when she was in her hotshot businesswoman mode this morning, she'd leaned against him in the same trusting way. The old warmth had flowed between them, not of a sexual nature, but the deeper kind that terrified him now.

Tucker took a long, cold shower and practiced putting a big "ex" in front of "wife." There were monumental reasons for that "ex." He shaved, trying to occupy himself and take his mind off Carly in the next bedroom. He pulled on jeans, ate a sandwich he didn't taste and turned on the television to black-and-white static. The sound did not erase Carly's crying, and finally Tucker went to lay on Anna Belle's big four-poster bed. He raked over all the bad things that had happened to him that day—because of his *ex-wife*.

An hour passed and the muffled sobs had turned to hiccups. They tore into his determination to let her come to the conclusion—of whatever.

An unsteady sob quickly took him out of bed and had him walking slowly into Carly's bedroom. She was lying with a sheet over her head.

''Carly?'' He needed to know that she would be all right. *He needed to hold her.*

''Move over,'' he said quietly and nudged her hip a little with his hand. The soft feel of her body clung after he removed his hand.

Either she'd allow him to comfort her—or she wouldn't. She slid a few inches to one side.

''More,'' he said, nudging her again. ''And take that sheet off your face. You'll smother and then Norma will put yellow crime-scene tape all over the place.''

He eased into the single four-poster bed with her, settling gently beside her. He was more afraid of his feelings for her than the collapse of the old bed. Women were more volatile than he realized, and a whole lot stronger and more capable. Carly had ridden that big all-terrain rig like a pro.

He put one arm behind his head and pulled the sheet down from her face. She looked up at the red light that flashed through the window and danced across the ceiling. Her voice was raspy, uneven and low. ''Norma. She's patrolling to keep Toad Hollow safe from me. I suppose I'm up for charges on stealing the Jacksons' four-wheeler.''

''Probably.''

''You're not much comfort, Tucker Redford.''

''I'm lying here, aren't I? I'll call the Jacksons and tell them you'd like to baby-sit to make up for the inconvenience. You should probably put some credit-money in their account at the gas station—they're having a hard time getting started financially.''

''I'll do that. Thanks.'' The red light appeared on

the ceiling again. "Make her go away, Tucker. Please. I can't take any more today. Maybe forever."

With a long sigh, Tucker rose off the bed. When he did, wood cracked and the box springs, mattress and Carly fell to the floor. She pulled up the sheet again, the four-posters rising above her. Beneath the sheet, her voice was muffled. "Great. I just broke my grandmother's visiting bed."

Tucker shook his head and walked to jerk open the front door. "Norma," he called. "Go home."

The police car's red light stopped and the siren whooped just once in disgust as Norma sailed off into the night.

Tucker closed the door, and hopefully the day, away from him. He slid out of his jeans and wearily glanced at Carly's room. Then he turned and headed for the safety of his room.

One step and he was against Carly's soft, T-shirt clad body. His arms circled her and her arms went around his waist. They stood in the shadows, just looking at each other and feeling whatever ran between them—and it was a big, big feeling. It wrapped around them, tightening the ache in his chest, and lower.

"You've put on some weight in the right places," he noted huskily as his hands opened wide on soft, curved territory.

"You're a lot bigger and harder...getting harder." Her hands smoothed his bare back and up over his shoulders.

She gave him something, he decided, and it wasn't only body heat. It was a calming deep inside him, where the uncertainties of life lurked. She gave color to his life, a joy in the unexpected. She'd given him comfort, even when they were fighting. Because he knew they had truth between them, the kind that had grown from childhood until their marriage—and then something had gone very wrong.

He eased the silky hair back from Carly's cheek and studied her. "You're looking at me like you used to look at some big project you'd tackled, all fierce and determined to succeed."

Carly's arms were around his shoulders, her fingers in his hair, massaging his scalp. "Do you like that?"

He couldn't move. Then he did. To see her intent expression better, Tucker ran his hands beneath her bottom and lifted her to his eye level. Her breasts were just inches beneath his chin and he decided that Carly was a whole lot of good-feeling, sweet smelling, warm-blooded woman. "What are you doing?"

Her legs circled his waist. The movement of her fingers in his scalp was slow and erotic. "Watching you. You've got that dark, bristling look, like you do when you're uncertain. You're feeling fragile, aren't you?"

"A part of me is," he admitted, because the other parts that were pressed against Carly's soft heat felt strong enough to do any job.

"Do you want to talk about it?" Her face was close, her lips just a fraction of an inch away.

"Only to say that I offended you earlier, and I shouldn't have done that. I know you wouldn't make love with me just to get your grandmother's house. You'll scrap with me, and try to bargain, but you wouldn't do that. If you wanted me, it was because you wanted me. You're an out-there-honest kind of woman.''

"You were uncertain then, too.'' Her fists gripped his hair and tugged lightly. "Have you ever had a woman in my grandma's bed, Tucker Redford? Because if you have, that would just be purely evil of you.''

"No, I never have.'' He'd never had a woman since Carly, because it hadn't seemed right.

Carly was quiet, her fingers tracing his face slowly, her gaze intently following them. "I'm thinking that if we're going to burn each other out of our systems, then maybe we'd better get started.''

"Maybe,'' Tucker agreed after weighing his will and won'ts. Still holding her, he began striding for his bedroom.

In the kitchen, Carly's hand locked onto the doorframe, stopping him. "Wait.''

Tucker held still, his prize in his arms, his want-to revved up and at the ready. "What?''

"Let me down. This isn't what I want.''

He closed his eyes, braced himself against taking her anyway, and lowered Carly to the floor. "It's not what I want either,'' he said to keep his pride. "I was just doing it for you.''

She grinned up at him. "Liar.''

Her hands reached to smooth his bare chest, to linger in the hair triangle there, and to spread over his nipples. Slowly, she eased closer, and took one nipple in her hot mouth, suckling it gently, and finishing by flicking it with her tongue. When she finished with the other nipple, Tucker's hands had circled her waist and he was shaking. "I hope you don't try to back out at this point with your other men. Because that could get rough."

"But not with you," she said firmly. "You would never force a woman. Tucker, when we were married, you were always the leader. That left me behind—but enjoying it just the same. It left me feeling like I didn't do my share. And that's an awful burden for a woman to bear for almost thirteen years…. And Tucker, I've never wanted to share my body with another man. I've tried, but I just couldn't…. I wanted to tell you that before you found out later. And because I'm a little scared right now."

"So am I." He'd have to be very careful with her, holding back his primitive desire to claim her fully, quickly. "I appreciate that information."

Every molecule in Tucker locked onto the fact that Carly hadn't taken another man to her body. While he was still dealing with that, Carly stepped back and lifted her borrowed T-shirt away, leaving her body curved in the shadows. "You're shaking, Tucker, and I'm going to take that as an indication that I'm not the only one who is quite uncertain now. This time, I'd like to have equal opportunity, if you don't mind…please."

"I don't mind," he managed rawly as Carly came closer to slide her hands inside the elastic of his boxer shorts. She eased them away. From the trembling of her hands and her hesitation when the fabric caught on his body, Tucker knew that she wasn't certain of herself or what was happening between them. He closed his eyes and gripped the doorframe with his hands, because if he didn't, he'd be placing them over those full, sweet, darkly tipped breasts. The wooden doorframe creaked beneath his hands and he wished his deep, aching groan hadn't escaped his keeping.

"My, my," she whispered in a tone of awe, which did truly please him. "Would you mind if I took a shower?"

"I like your fragrance the way it is—all woman. But suit yourself." That would cost him, he decided uncertainly, especially if Carly decided to change her mind. To indicate his thoughts on the subject, he found her hips and locked his fingers onto the softness there. "You smell real good, Carly," he stated unevenly.

"So do you, Tucker."

He started to walk her backward into his bedroom, but Carly put a firm hand on his chest and inched around until she was pushing him backward. He accepted the maneuver, because more than anything, he wanted Carly to choose how she came to him.

They stood beside the bed, the back of Tucker's knees against it, looking at each other. "You can change your mind," he offered, praying that she wouldn't.

"So can you." Her tone said she was gauging him, deciding where to start—or when to stop. Her hands smoothed his face, sliding over his eyebrows, his lashes, his cheekbones and trembling on his lips.

He kissed her fingertips and gently suckled the one that came prowling over his lips.

More than he wanted air, Tucker needed Carly to show him that she desired and cared for him still; he'd know the truth in the way she took him. She'd always given him one-hundred percent, but there was something new and mysterious about her now...and even more fascinating.

"I've been reading a lot about women taking the sexual lead in magazines," she whispered. "They're very educational."

"Uh-huh."

"You won't get scared?" Her fingertips walked downward slowly, her eyes locked to his.

"Ah..." He wanted to talk, say something sweet and tender, but that was difficult. Her hand had gloved him briefly before moving to smooth his chest.

"I...do...think I want that shower, if you don't mind. I'd like to compose myself...before. I'd like to understand the whys better as we go along. Why we are the way we are with each other. I'm afraid I could get too carried away and forget why I need to understand. If you don't mind," she repeated carefully.

"You need to do that right now, do you?" Despite his hunger, he knew that Carly always evaluated a project carefully, before taking it on. And just now, he truly wanted to be taken on, in the physical sense—and maybe in the tender way, too.

All he had to do was to let her take the lead and do her part, like she wanted—if he could. Maybe he had always pushed too hard and just maybe Carly, being the competitor that she was, needed angling room to know how she felt. Right now, it was hard—everything was hard—Tucker corrected, to think of anything but holding and cuddling her later.

"Go ahead," he managed, though his body might burn a hole into the bed's mattress while he waited for her.

## Chapter 6

Carly stepped into the shower. She changed the shower stream from pulse to spray. She didn't need any exterior vibrations when her interior was already pounding like jungle drums.

Tucker's face had that honed, primed look; his high cheekbones looked as warm and hard as the rest of him.

A shampoo would take too much time. Carly went straight for the shower gel. In a way, she felt like a bride. But in another sense, she felt like an experienced woman who hadn't used all of her emotions, who hadn't tested herself fully against a man she trusted.

Tucker was an all-man testing site. If she did burn him out of her system, then it was a "go" for her grip on life. She would then understand why thoughts of Tucker always leaped to life when she was with another man.

She inhaled the steamy herbal fragrances and cooled the shower's temperature. It wouldn't do to come at Tucker too fast and eager. She wanted to seduce. To revel in her power as a woman. By the time the night was finished, she hoped she'd understand the hum of her senses when Tucker looked at her with those stormy blue-silver eyes.

With a sigh, she decided to enjoy the seduction of Tucker, ex-husband.

As she applied body cream, Carly studied herself in the steamy mirror, a woman now, certain in her course—and powerful and feminine at the same time— an equal participant set on equal opportunity, taking just as much as giving. She remembered how his notes on the valentines from her had reflected his pain. She picked up a tube of lipstick and decided that she would give him a great big valentine to remember their night together. Or if Tucker didn't notice, she would have physical proof that she had scored—well, other than the sated fuzzy tingling that she was certain would be an aftermath of Tucker's lovemaking. Then they could flow separately into the rest of their lives, leaving behind the darkness of the past.

She carefully drew a big heart between her breasts, overflowing a bit onto the twin softness. She blotted the lipstick carefully; it marked her advent into an equal partner in pursuit. It also surpassed any of the valentines they'd given each other in the past. Sexual games hadn't been their agenda, but maybe their eagerness to have each other ruled out everything else.

Carly decided that she needed to remove her toenail polish and apply new, just to mark her new start in life as a woman taking an opportunity when it presented itself. She smiled as she sat, waiting for the polish to dry...because Tucker did look like six-feet-two-inches of perfect opportunity, all revved and ready to go.

The brisk knock on the bathroom door was followed by Tucker's "Carly? You'd better get out here."

A woman in control of a situation, understanding herself better than she ever had, Carly smiled softly. Tucker desired her, that was evident, but she did truly need to seduce him. She'd always been capable and now she was ready—at the second rap, she answered, "Do not hurry me, Tucker."

"Get your butt out here," he stated darkly, unlike the loverlike tones she had hoped to hear, the little sweet talk that Tucker had never given her, and that she wanted to wring from him tonight—those intimacies every woman needed.

"In a minute," she singsonged. She studied herself in the mirror and smiled at the red heart Tucker might never see. It would mark her trophy-win of the night. A mark that Carly, the huntress, had scored.

She'd find her diary, and finish it with a memo that said, "I got every bit of what I wanted."

The door jerked open and Tucker's big hand thrust the red sweater and jeans she had worn into the bathroom. "We've got company."

"Tell Norma to go home."

The door shut and Carly dressed quickly. She decided she would tell Norma herself.

In the brightly lit living room, Norma was hitching up her uniform belt in her officer-on-duty role. Bits of face cream and pink curlers in her gray frizz spoiled the look.

Gary Kingsley, looking road-weary with weekender bag in one hand and a laptop briefcase in the other stood next to her. Dressed in a cotton shirt and wrinkled khakis, his up-town eyeglasses, and his cutting-edge attitude, Gary looked harried and tired and threatening. Tucker, his muscled, tanned arms crossed over his bare chest, wore only his jeans and a scowl. His slitted, steely stare ripped down Carly's sweater—where her braless nipples peaked against the light cloth.

"Did you lose something, Carly?" Norma asked. "This man says he knows you. Mrs. Storm called about an unknown car and prowler. Took me just two minutes to get dressed and out the door. Another minute here. The perp offered no resistance when I collared and frisked him."

The telephone rang and Tucker jerked it from its cradle. "Yes, Mrs. Storm, everything is fine. Carly will call you tomorrow."

"I drove all the way from Denver in one day to check on you. Who is this?" Gary said, while he appeared to be sizing up Tucker. Tucker was doing the same to Gary.

"This is my ex-husband. He lives here. Temporarily. Tucker, this is Gary Kingsley."

Gary dropped his bag and the men moved closer to shake hands. A shade taller than Tucker, Gary looked delicate beside Tucker's workman-muscled body. The men gripped hands—tightly—and Gary's forced smile indicated pain. They resembled two battling stags, locking horns over the female in heat nearby—which had been basically true, Carly admitted uncomfortably.

She did a double take at Tucker's wolfish smile as they stepped apart. Gary stealthily rubbed his hand against his side.

"You must be tired," Tucker said pleasantly. "Carly, why don't you get the bedding for your friend? He can sleep on the couch. You two must have a lot to talk about. I want to check on the new barn in the morning and I have things to do. So you can have all day to show Gary around town, Carly. I'll make extra coffee in the morning for you."

Just as the mighty slugger of Mudville had struck out, so had Carly.

Tucker knew exactly what he was doing, making her face the reality of a potential lover and an aroused ex-husband. If he'd been rude, she could have had reason to— "Go home, Norma," she ordered and turned to smile at Gary. If Tucker could play games, so could she. "So glad you could come, Gary."

"I was worried about you, Carly. Your messages sounded so desperate."

"Yes, well, we can discuss all that in the morning. Let me get your bedding...." She paused to look at Tucker, who was unfolding the sleeper couch.

"I'll put out fresh toweling," he said cheerfully. "I'll just get that bedding. And how about a beer for you, Gary? Just a little something to wind down on? There are earphones by the sound set, they should reach to the couch and you can relax—or you can stay up and talk with Carly. Don't worry about cooking tomorrow night, Carly. I'll pick up a few things on the way home and we'll have barbecue.''

After dumping the bedding on the opened sleeper couch, Tucker left for his bedroom. Despite his pleasant host manner, his bare muscular back had a definite bristling male look. The door closed with an ominous too-quiet click.

Gary glared at Carly. "What's going on?"

"We've been friends a long time, Gary. It's a lot to understand, I know. But this is *my* grandmother's house, and I'm going to get it back. Tucker was in residence when I came back on Friday, and we're just discussing how to settle things." If a woman ever felt foolish, it was Carly, standing and talking to her potential husband with a big red heart meant for her "ex" painted on her chest.

"Where do you sleep?" Gary demanded as he leaned to one side to peer into her bedroom.

"There, where I always stayed overnight. Tucker has his own room."

"Cozy." The single word was a derisive sneer and too much at the end of a long, long day, which had turned into a three-o'clock morning.

"Don't you have something to say for yourself? I came all this way, because I was worried, and find you shacked up with your ex-husband? I thought we could have a little time away from Denver and work, and now I find you...*like this*."

He reached into his pocket and pulled out a cell phone, clicking it rapidly with his thumb. While he answered his messages, Carly made Gary's bed.

She wondered if a cell phone could distract Tucker

from greeting her and kissing her and holding her....
She doubted that anything could distract Tucker from
making love with her—unless it was another man
sleeping on his couch—her boyfriend and potential
husband...who had come to vacation with her.

The lipstick on her chest was the no-fade kind; she'd
be wearing that impulsive valentine for a long time.

Gary looked so uncertain and tired as he finished his
calls that she couldn't help coming to kiss his cheek.
She hugged him. "You'll feel better after some sleep."

"I just wanted to know that you were safe," he
stated unevenly. "I've always cared about you. There
was always a part of you that I couldn't get close to,
and maybe it's here. With him."

Gary looked wounded now as he held her hand.
"Have you had sex with him? The kind that means
something between two people?"

He wasn't menacing at all, just a friend who had
come a long way to make certain she was safe. She
owed Gary the truth and gave it to him as gently as
she could. "Not yet. But I'm hoping. He's probably
going to be a little difficult right now. But he's been
my best friend since I can remember. He stuck up for
me when I wanted to play on the boys' baseball team.
He made a really nice high school sweetheart—but
things got a little uneasy when we got married. There
was a big incident that could have looked really bad
for me, so he stepped up to bat like he always did when
I was in trouble. He married me. I married him to protect Tucker from my father—who was a righteous kind
of guy."

She paused and hearing her own words, understood

herself better. She explained her feelings slowly. "All of it wasn't clear until a few hours ago. I wasn't ready years ago, and we made mistakes. It's time to sort them out now. He's always been in my heart, I guess. We know we don't want to go back—I guess, speaking for myself. But I'm not too certain what I want now, either. Except Tucker. He's solid. I'm a fast game. I speed him up some and he holds me to the ground. It's sort of a yin and yang between us."

Gary looked at her blankly, then he sank to the couch. He held his head in his hands. "It's been a long day."

"Tomorrow, I'll show you where I grew up. I'm the town legend," she said to lighten his dark mood.

"I believe it," Gary stated firmly.

In her bedroom, lying on the mattress and looking up at the four-posters above her, Carly heard Gary begin to snore gently. The sound developed into a full nasal symphony. There was no way, without passing by Gary that she could reach Tucker's room. If she could, she'd ask about his gracious-host motives.

Carly turned and twisted in the sheets. When she awoke she floated between reality and the dream of Tucker making love to her. She hoped the sounds echoing in her head weren't the remnants of her own orgasmic purrs. She lay quietly, coming awake. She listened to Livingston squawk in the living room and the sound of men's voices rumbling quietly through the house.

Tucker jerked open the door before she came fully awake. "Gary and I are going fishing. You're not invited."

She flopped over on her stomach, preparing to meet another exhausting day facing the past, an ex-husband and Gary, who probably should have been perfect for her—but who was just a friend now. "I am not cleaning your fish."

Carly decided to hide throughout the day. Livingston, happy to have her near, squawked and talked regularly. His weight on her shoulder was a comfort she needed, his beak prowling through her hair was tender and soothing. Determined to put the men out of her mind, Carly worked on her laptop and made business calls—not answering any incoming ones from Norma or Mrs. Storm. The revelation that she had shared with Gary tangled around her. Exhausted, she slid into Tucker's bed for a nap.

The men came swaggering home, bragging about the size of the ones that got away and carrying a six-pack of beer. The new friends ignored her throughout the dinner they cooked together, clearly enjoying each other. Then they did dishes together and settled into television while debating baseball stars' batting averages.

In her bid to escape, Carly came out to lie on the front lawn and to look up at the stars. After a while Tucker and Gary came out, and they lay on either side of her, each taking her hand. "I'm leaving in the morning," Gary said. "But I'd like to come back to visit occasionally. If that's okay."

"Okay with me," Tucker said cheerfully. "How about you, Carly?"

"Fine." She didn't try to disguise her peeved tone. "Tucker, do you know where my diary is?"

"Sure. But you're not getting it. Anna Belle said I should keep it, that it held the heart of you, and I'm not letting that go until I'm ready."

She flipped over on him in a minute and straddled him, pinning him to the lawn. Carly ignored Gary's roaring laughter. "Give it to me."

The hot look he sent her said he truly would, and she scrambled off Tucker and hurried for the safety of the house.

After a long hard night of tossing and turning, she did not care about how she looked, or who she saw, or what they thought as she trudged for the coffeepot. She poured a cup and sat down to mull the dark bog of her life.

Gary, fully dressed and chipper, bent to kiss her cheek. "Call you later, Carly. Thanks for the nice time."

She gave him an airy wave that said she did not care about anything and for him to go away. Drained and exhausted, she listened to Tucker and Gary—new best friends—trade jovial goodbyes. Livingston added his "Awwk. Come back. Come back."

Then Tucker was standing beside her kitchen chair. "That bad, is it?"

She wanted to wallow in the pits—without her ex-husband. When the calendar year turned over, she just might pick herself up for another go at life. "Shouldn't you go to work?"

"Have to deal with life today, honey. There comes a time when it's just more important than work," he said as he bent and picked her up and carried her to his bed, easing her beneath the sheets. He slid in behind her and curled around her, giving her the safety that she'd needed for years. She rested against him, the soothing stroke of his hand on her hair causing her to doze.

When Carly awoke, Tucker lay sprawled on his back, sleeping deeply in the morning shadows. He looked young and new and sweet, and vulnerable. He was perfect for the taking. Carly eased off her T-shirt and her briefs, then eased to lie beside him again, comparing his length to hers. In their marriage, she'd been uncertain of lovemaking rules, but now she'd read how-to magazine articles.

And she knew what she wanted—Tucker. "I'd like a real go at you," she whispered when his eyelashes fluttered.

"Come ahead," he whispered back rawly. "The ball is in your court."

"There's a lot of you."

"Start anywhere. I can take it. But first, why don't you lie on top of me and let me tell you a few things. Then maybe you could tell me a few."

At his invitation, Carly eased over him, found the hardness that said he wanted her and captured it between her thighs. Tucker's hands were easing back her hair, his expression serious and tender.

Before he could speak, the words came flowing from her lips, "I love you, Tucker. I always have."

He sighed deeply and closed his eyes as his hands opened and trembled as they skimmed her body. "Tell me I'm not dreaming."

"Gary told you what I said, didn't he? That's why you changed your mind about going to work."

Tucker turned her so quickly that he took away her breath. She lay beneath him, and fire burned their skin, his eyes flashing and hot, his skin tight across his cheekbones. "He told me. We talked. I thought I'd try some new romancing techniques on you, because I was too fired-up to do that years ago. You need sweet talk and erotic play, and—"

"You're not going to do that now, are you?" She hoped he wouldn't.

"You're a fast game, Carly Redford. You can't always have your way. That's what was wrong before— you'd just look at me and I'd start burning. I'd come at you before I knew what I was doing."

"You made the advances. I need to do some of that."

"Now?" he asked tightly, rawly.

"There's not enough time." She moved and turned him easily, moving over him again. His hands flowed to her breasts, along her sides and up to her face, drawing her down for a long, slow tender kiss. "Hi, Carly."

"Hey, Tucker," she whispered against his lips and then suckled the bottom one just a bit, tasting this new person. He lay still as she experimented with the fit of their bodies, the way his skin smelled as she nuzzled him, the rough texture against her smooth one. She caressed the hair on his chest, the width of his shoulders and met the heavy-lidded stare of those hot eyes. She bent to nuzzle his throat, to trail lower, to find his nipples, flicking them with her tongue.

Tucker's big body quivered beneath her touch, but yet he held still, waiting for her to complete her journey. "How long is this going to take?" he asked breathlessly.

"I'm trying to control the pace—make it last. My wants are running faster than I'd planned." She was starting to heat and clench and burn.

Tucker groaned unevenly, his body rigid and quivering. He looked so ripe for the taking that she had to. She took his mouth, tasting his stark hunger, meeting it, as she opened her body to ease down on him slowly, so slowly. When she arched back, riveted, concentrating on the incredible pleasure, Tucker cradled her breasts. He plied them with heat and suction and the torrid uneven sweep of his breath.

The sudden burst of pleasure staked her high and hot and Tucker eased her down gently, until she was limp upon him, her face resting against his throat, feeling the racing pulse here. "Oh, darn," she whispered. "I was going to make you tell me where my diary was."

"You could try again." Tucker eased her to her back and began moving slowly within her, plying her with little, tender kisses. His fingers moved in her scalp, the erotic motion soothing. His teeth caught her earlobe, his breath uneven and warm in the whorls of her ear. Carly began to stretch and heat and undulate beneath him, locking her legs around his, taking him deeper.

She forgot what good girls don't do and went for the primitive gusto, her fingertips digging into his back, placing her lips and teeth on his shoulder, urging him on with tiny nibbles. There were no words this time, only hot open kisses, bodies moving as one, rising into the pleasure that when it burst, seemed to last forever.

They lay in the morning shadows amid the rumpled

sheets, hands soothing each other, hearts slowing their paces, lingering in the sweet aftermath. Tucker cuddled her closer, and she fitted her body close to his, rubbing his shin with her insole, her arm tight around him.

"Whatever you have to do, Carly, you go do it," Tucker said quietly, firmly. "I'll always be here for you."

She smoothed his broad chest, his heartbeat strong and sure beneath her palm. "I think I've done it. But don't think I'm finished with you. There are things I need to do to you—for you."

She could feel Tucker's smile against her temple. "Likewise," he murmured and turned to kiss her.

His finger traced the valentine on her chest, valid now that she had scored with Tucker. "Now what is the purpose of that big red heart on your chest?"

Carly took her time in answering. "I found your valentines and saw the pain in them. I thought I'd give you a very special one, one you'd remember more fondly."

Tucker started to chuckle, and despite the heavy sated feeling of her body, Carly started to wrestle with him. Too easily pinned beneath her, Tucker lay still and suddenly quiet. His hands rose to smooth back her hair, his expression tender. "I've never even wanted another woman. There's been no one but you—ever. You take your time, honey, and decide just what you want."

Carly eased down close to him, filled with peace as Tucker held her close. "We'll argue."

"And make up. Take your time, Carly. Do what's right for you this time."

* * *

On Valentine's Day, Tucker left work early. He carried his lunch bucket into the house, excited because every day with Carly was amazing.

Inside Anna Belle's house, which they shared now, Carly was striding back and forth in the living room, talking on the cell phone. Livingston was adding regular comments and squawking.

Carly was in a big deal, pushing her ideas on a hefty account. Tucker stood still, enjoying the sight—Carly, like a tigress, wrangling in the business world and loving it. He could tell she was winning by the smirk on her lips, that little flush on her cheeks.

Carly came to stand on tiptoe and kiss him, then leaned to snuggle against him. Her free hand smoothed his face and that soft, sweet look she slid him said he was loved well and good. Then she moved away, back into her business mode and Tucker took his shower.

In the steamy mirror, he considered his reflection, angling his face to see what Carly saw in him. He was pretty good-looking, he decided, full of happiness that she had brought into his life. He was comfortable as a "big stud, macho man, hot-blooded lover." But the best label Carly had ever pasted on him—because he'd learned that in advertising, "buzz" words were a big deal—was "my guy."

Tucker wasn't pushing for anything this time around, not even marriage. When Carly was ready, she'd develop a full-scale business project development plan. Equal opportunity between them had become her goal, and sometimes she just came after him full-steam. Other times, she was into seductive moves.

And to top that off, they were fishing buddies—no more men's-only days for him—unless Carly was busy reinstituting herself as the town legend. He rather enjoyed cooking for her business friends when they came to visit.

In full huntress mode, she'd be coming for him, wanting her diary. It was more of a game now, played between them, and he'd be ready, his body gearing up—because one of the benefits of having a business-woman who celebrated her coups—was the fast, hot, sweet lovemaking. When the doorknob rattled, he smiled and put his shaving gear away. He slapped on the aftershave Carly loved; he wanted to be just as delectable as he could when she made her move. He wouldn't be too easy, because she liked the challenge, but he was at the ready. A man yielding to a woman had definite pluses.

"We got that account," she reveled, a woman riding high on business triumph and power, and determined to get everything else she wanted, too. "Tucker, I am going to *make* you give up that diary. Where is it?"

Tucker braced himself as Carly hurled herself against him. He swooned a bit as her tiny kisses around his jaw almost sunk his plans to let her seduce him. He reached to the shelf high over her head and lowered a small box for her. "Anna Belle wanted you to have it when you were happy and knew what you wanted. You look happy now. I never read your diary. It was only a part of you that I wanted to keep."

Carly held the box without opening it. She frowned and eased back from him and studied his chest. "I just wanted it because I didn't want you to know how I

fantasized about loving you and you loving me....
You've shaved your chest, Tucker. There's a big red
heart—"

When her brilliant smile shot up at him, Tucker got
a little light-headed and managed unevenly, "It's a valentine. And it's all for you."

\* \* \* \* \*

# BLINDSIDE DATE
## Carolyn Zane

For my new infant son,
Silas Matthew, one cuddly, bundle of fun.
Thank you, Jesus, for blessing us with sweet Sy
and turning our four into five.

# Chapter 1

*Monkey see, monkey do*
*You cheated on me*
*Now I'm cheatin' on you.*
*How does it feel, ya two-faced primate*
*To watch me swing from date to date?*
*Uh-huh, oo—oo—oo, uh-huh, oo—oo—oo*
*Uh-huh, oo—oo—oo, uh-HUH!*

At the top of their lungs, sixteen-year-old best friends, Amber Springer and Brianna Davis rapped to the beat that vibrated from the stereo speakers in Brianna's family room. Knees bent and wobbling to and fro and fingertips to armpits, they danced with the unrestrained vigor of youth.

It was spring break. No homework and, since both

sets of parents were gone on errands or at work this Saturday morning, they had the home theater all to themselves. Was anything better than a morning spent caterwauling with Top10TV—*America's Favorite Music Channel*—guzzling a gallon of diet soda and polishing off a box of toaster tarts?

They didn't *think* so.

When *The Gorilla Blues* video by *Marsha's Inner Child* was over, the girls flopped, exhausted, to the sofa and sucked noisily at their straws between a lightning round of teenaged chatter. A commercial break came on and stopped their conversation in its tracks and had them staring alternately at the TV, and each other, in giddy wonder.

"Hi guys! The Bodacious Candie Walsh here with the latest insanity from Top10TV—"

Brianna leaned forward, knees to elbows. "I love her hair. I wish mine would do that."

"I wish I could fill out her bra."

"Start saving."

*"Uh-huh, oo—oo—oo!"*

The girls snickered and turned their attention back to Candie.

"People, Top10TV is bringing you a brand new Reality TV show for lovers! Yes, it's your turn to play professional 'Cupid.' Participate in the three-hour Valentine's Day pilot episode of *Blind Side Date* by helping us ambush two people who have never met...with a blind date! Yo, it's gonna be the baddest reality show of 'em all. We're shooting all this summer and fall, and airing the pilot on Valentine's Day next winter. Uncensored, unvarnished and unbelievably exciting, the whole ugly mess is coming right to your living room, so *get psycho!*

"We are looking for two lucky winners to participate in our first episode and we need your help. If you know of two people who are never going to get off their duffs and find Mr. or Ms. Right, then this is your chance to give them that kick in the booty they so richly deserve. Your incentive?" Candie pointed at the girls. "The selected 'Cupids' will win backstage passes to *Marsha's Inner Child!*"

Brianna caught Amber's eye and their jaws dropped. *"Ah-ma-gad!"*

*"And,* if your couple completes the date and agrees to go out a second time for the 'Love in the Steam Room' round, you could win a cameo appearance on Top10TV's smash hit, *BEAT!"*

The girls shrieked and leaped to their feet. "I *love* that show!"

*"Aaand,"* Candie lifted her pencil-thin brow and, pursing her lips in a sexy moue, breathed into the camera lens, "if they are ready for the honeymoon by the end of next year, the Grand Prize is—" she paused for dramatic effect, "One hundred *thousand* dollars!"

The girls fell back on the couch and gaped at each other. "Those are only the coolest prizes *ever!"*

"Please enter your submission in an essay form of no more than five hundred words, and send it to us here at Top10TV to the address at the bottom of the screen. Winners will be notified by a surprise visit from the *Blind Side Date* crew on the morning of June 14th. Filming will begin that day, starting with a complete makeover for the lucky lovers."

Across the bottom of the screen, the crawl read, *Selected Lovers must be 18 years of age or older....* Blind Side Date *will not be held responsible for awarding prizes if lovers fail to complete their respective dates.... Void where prohibited by law...some restrictions may apply....*

Amber and Brianna clutched each other's hands and fairly vibrated with excitement.

"Let's enter!"

"Okay!"

"Who do we know who's over eighteen that we can enter? Someone who won't kill us," Brianna said.

"How 'bout your big brother? He's really cute and he won't care if we make him go on a date. He goes on blind dates like..." Amber waved her hands, "every day."

"Garret?" Brianna considered him for a moment. "Okay. Who should the woman be?"

"For sure," Amber snorted, "*not* my sister."

"Why not?"

"Because she's socially challenged. And even though she's already twenty-five, she has, like, this holier-than-thou virgin thing going. I don't think she'd go for a stunt like this...."

"Yeah, but she's probably the only woman we know that Garret hasn't already met, and dated."

"That's true."

"And opposites attract, right?"

"Nobody is attracted to Jayde."

"Good point. But Top10TV doesn't know that. If she wanted, she could be really cute and we can make her sound superhot when we fill out our essay."

* * *

Jayde Springer arched back in her hard wooden chair and stretched, deeply inhaling the musty smell of books and institutional cleaning supplies. She pushed her reading glasses high on her head to better rub her bleary eyes, and then finger-combed her unruly pony-tail back into some semblance of order. Mmm. Again, she stretched. A full morning spent at the Portland University library was murder on her back, but necessary if she was ever going to get a jump on the Doctoral program she planned to begin next fall.

Silence governed this hallowed environment of academia, the first Saturday morning of spring break. Perfect for the deep thought she'd need to compose notes, gather resourses and photocopy bibliographies. Plus, there was that article she wanted to do on her involvement with Habitat for Humanity for the Lifestyle section of the *Sunday Oregonian*. She hoped to have it published early this summer, to drum up crewmembers for a new project in North Portland.

So much to do, so little time.

She sighed and, tugging off her reading glasses, chewed the thick, plastic stem as she glanced over her shoulder to the clock. Nearly noon. Her belly rumbled. With a yawn, she decided to run over to her parents' house and raid their fully stocked refrigerator. While she was at it, she'd fix some lunch for her younger sister, Amber. Lord knew, while their parents were working and running errands, the kid had probably eaten nothing but toaster tarts in front of the boob tube that morning.

Though she lived on campus in a dorm room by

herself now, Jayde still enjoyed going home and mothering her younger sister and the kid's goofy friends. She began to gather her study materials. Maybe she'd take the Max train and swing down to a small farmer's market in the area and get some fresh produce before she went home. The weather was certainly perfect for a little jaunt.

Her gaze floated from the hands of the clock and out the windows.

Just outside in the garbage area, a grizzled man everyone on campus knew as "Soda Pop" foraged the Dumpster for bottles and cans to turn in for deposit. Jayde watched with interest as he dug up a stubbed out cigarette and after straightening it, lit it and took a long drag. Once he'd smoked it to the filter, he stumbled out of the Dumpster, gathered his spoils and shuffled away.

Jayde wondered where he would spend the night tonight. It was early spring, and still pretty chilly after dark. She swallowed and refused to indulge the pity she felt welling. He'd be okay. Jaw firm, she reminded herself, it was people like him she'd someday be helping on her quest for social reform. Jayde was a doer. Not a talker. By fall, Pop would have a place to call home.

Until then, she would remember to put several sandwiches in her backpack from now on. If Pop was around, she'd give him one.


"—and I'm out there, hangin' from the steel girder by my harness, helping one of my guys do some tricky spot welding and a spark lands on my boot."

Exceptionally good-looking, charismatic, smart, funny and an all-around wonder boy, people always gravitated to Garret Davis. As he stood in the common garden at his condominium complex, he was surrounded by a bevy of beauties and buddies, sharing in the usual neighborhood Saturday afternoon beer and brag hour.

"So," Garret continued, "I figure, no problem. It'll burn out like usual. But I didn't know that my sock was sticking up between my boot and pant leg—"

The girls—all neighbors and all nubile beauties— gasped appropriately and sidled in closer.

"—Yep, it slipped into my sock, burned like a son of a—" he glanced in deference at the ladies and said, "—gun. Which I could have handled, I guess, but damned if the stupid thing didn't begin to smolder, then catch fire."

"Ooo!" The girls clasped his biceps in alarm.

The male neighbors all nodded as if to say, "Yeah, I know what you mean, that happens to me down at the office, every day."

"What'd you do?"

Garret gave his leg a vigorous shake. "Talk about hotfootin' it. I'm sure I broke repelling records getting off the top of that building."

Everyone laughed. The girls wanted to kiss his boo-boo better. The guys wanted to slap him on the back. Someone else suggested heating up some pizza for lunch. The brand-new condo complex pool and its connecting hot tub had just opened that weekend, and they could eat at the umbrella-covered tables.

That sounded great to Garret. Beat having to forage about in his empty fridge for something edible. He was bushed from all the overtime he'd been putting in to build his construction business. Plus, he glanced at the Lucero twins, already stripping down to their bathing suits, the company was excellent.

For Garret, his free time was worthless if it didn't involve the company of a beautiful woman. Preferably several beautiful women. No woman had ever deflected his charms and the funny thing was, the women never appeared to mind sharing Garret. Everyone just seemed to know that he was light-years from settling down.

He tipped back his beer and listened to one of his neighbors tell a rather lackluster tale about a client. Over his shoulder, he could feel the Lucero twins eyeing him and he grinned.

Life was good. At only thirty, he owned his own commercial construction business, and they'd just won a bid on the latest high-rise to be built in downtown Portland later this summer. He was the king of his domain and didn't have to answer to anyone except his maker. And even that was pretty much relegated to the times his socks caught fire. Yeah. Like Frank Sinatra before him, Garret was doing things his way.

Candie Walsh waited for the director to call "cut" before she allowed her phony smile to fade and moved from her stool in the studio over to the water cooler. On the brink of forty, she hated the whole bimbo persona she'd created, feeling that if she hadn't been so well endowed by Mother Nature she'd be on the national evening news by now. But alas, no one ever figured her for having an IQ much higher than her bra size, so here she was.

The Bodacious Candie Walsh.

Responsible for the success of yet another in a string of reality rip-off shows. And the clock on her career was ticking. She dug a couple aspirin out of her pocket, yanked a Dixie cup from the dispenser, filled it and turned to find Fred Dalton and Arnie Bridges—who along with her, were two of the senior producers at Top10TV—standing behind her. She tossed back the pills but knew they'd do nothing for this particular brand of pain.

Fred's toupee was listing a bit, and Arnie had that nervous tic that he developed whenever ratings took a dip.

"You gotta make this *Blind Side Date* thing work, Candie." Fred fingered the thin ropes of gold looped at his neck. "The brass says this is it. If this one fails, heads are gonna roll."

"Would you stop worrying, Freddie? Everything is going to be fine. Trust me. It's all about who we pick to be the," Candie drew air quotes and husked, "lovers."

*Blind Side Date* had been her idea at last quarter's reality pitch session to the honchos upstairs. She had no idea if this turkey would fly, but she hoped a little spurious reassurance would keep her inevitable pink slip at bay. She had one kid in braces, the other one was off to UCLA next year and her husband had just been laid off from his dot-com gig.

"Why?" Arnie's nostrils flared spastically.

"Because sex sells, honey. Everyone knows that. We'll scrutinize the essays, looking for the perfect combination of sensuality and animal magnetism. With the right clothes, hair and makeup, they won't be able to keep their hands off each other. And that stuff equals ratings. And big ratings equals big promotions.''

Arnie and Fred exchanged sly, relieved glances.

Turning her back, Candie rolled her eyes and dug another aspirin from her pocket.

Arms aching from being unable to resist big, beautiful vegetables, Jayde shifted her bag of organic produce to a more comfortable position and climbed out of the Max train at the stop nearest her parents' home. For lunch, she'd make a Greek salad and a pot of vegetable bean soup. Amber would eat that, but only if garlic bread and Starbucks coffee were involved.

As she stepped off the curb and crossed the street, she entered a quaint neighborhood of aging brick buildings turned condo, several blocks into the West Hills, and not too far from her parents' home. From the windows of the building she approached at the corner, came the smells of pizza baking and the sounds of televisions blaring sports and music à la Top10TV. The old, brick, U-shaped Ambassador condominium complex sported a beautiful atrium, visible to the street. Behind a wrought iron fence, lay a newly installed pool and hot tub and the surrounding area had been landscaped attractively.

Only the nouveau riche could afford to live there Jayde knew and she wrinkled her nose with something akin to disdain. Lavish lifestyles weren't her cup of tea. She preferred the modest existence of a meager graduate student, working hard to make ends meet. In Jayde's humble opinion, a person's expendable income should be directed to loftier goals than a useless hole in the ground, filled with chlorinated water.

The joyful sounds of pool games and flirtatious shouts traveled from the pool area, and unable to contain her curiosity, Jayde paused in her tracks and watched the horseplay. Looked like a pool party. She hadn't attended one in years. She swallowed back the tiniest bit of yearning to be part of such carefree camaraderie.

The water sparkled in the sunlight. Everyone was smiling and laughing. A really handsome man executed a perfect dive off the board and into the middle of the pool. Time was when she could dive like that. She shifted her load and pressed closer to the fence.

No.

*Don't go there,* she cautioned herself, and took a step back.

Just as turned to go, a Frisbee came whizzing out of the pool yard, over the fence and landed under some bushes at her feet. She paused and debated. She doubted she could reach it even if her arms were empty.

She'd pretend she hadn't noticed it and move on.

"Hey! You just gonna leave it there? Have a heart, huh?" A smiling man with double dimples and chocolaty brown eyes waded to the shallow end of the pool, revealing his rippling abdominals and sinewy upper torso.

"Pardon me?" Apparently he couldn't see that she was loaded like a pack mule.

Though she was annoyed, she couldn't help but notice that he oozed a certain boyish charm as he clapped his hands. Clearly, he was used to getting his way. Holding his arms out, he gestured at Jayde to fling the Frisbee back into the pool. Again, the urge to play niggled. The water looked so very cool and inviting. As did he.

She groaned.

Okay. How was she gonna do this? She jockeyed her packages and slowly bent at the knees. She scrabbled about amongst the thorny bushes, booted feet spread, her filmy broom-handle skirt stretched to the limit, packages slipping and sagging and coins pinging out of her purse and rolling around on the ground. She reached for the plastic disc, but it simply bounced off her fingertips, out of the flower bed and proceeded to scrape along the sidewalk. Ugh. Why had she even bothered to stop?

"Garret, leave the bag lady alone, and come with us," a voluptuous bikini-clad woman called.

Someone shushed her.

Everyone giggled.

"Garr-rhett! C'mon," another woman cajoled. "We're going to get in the hot tub now."

Frozen with shock, Jayde gasped at the sidewalk. *Bag lady?* Did she really look that…that…she swallowed around a lump of hurt in her throat, frumpy? Granted, her cardigan was a tad Annie Hall and her boots weren't the latest in fashion, but c'mon, she was a poor student. Working her way through school. Trendy apparel wasn't a luxury she could afford.

"Coming." Garret waved at them, but didn't move in their direction. Seeming to gather that she was in no position to help, he hefted himself out of the pool and wet footprints followed him to the gates where she stood bent over his neon disc.

As he gripped the iron, water dripped from his hair and sluiced off his lightly fuzzed chest. Through the bars, he looked her up and down, then grinned. "Never mind. I'll get it. I can see you're cartin' a load."

"Ya think?" She clutched her packages a little more tightly and grunted as she returned upright. Sometimes she felt a hundred years old.

"You want to leave some of your...things," his eyes dipped to her bags, "here? You can come back for them. I can get dressed and help you carry them to, you know, wherever."

Face flaming, Jayde realized that he, too, had mistaken her for a street person. And, for some idiotic reason, it stung. Her gaze skittered to the sexy, scantily clad group frolicking in the pool and then back to the dripping man. "No." She masked her humiliation with a curt voice. "I'm fine. Get back to your...friends."

She could feel him watching as she strode away.

Brianna tapped away on her mother's laptop, hunting and pecking as Amber dictated the essay they were preparing for Top10TV.

"—powerful hunk of throbbing manhood? *Garret?* My *brother*, Garret?" Brianna paused and giggled. "Don't you think that sounds kinda over the top?"

"No. Trust me. They'll eat this stuff up. Everyone knows sex sells. We gotta make these guys sound like they're going to burn up the screen or we won't stand a chance."

"Okay...uh, how do you spell 'loins'?"

"We'll run everything through spell check when we're done, don't worry. Let's get started on your sister."

"We're gonna have to make up a whole bunch of stuff."

"Not really. We just have to practice the art of embellishment. First of all, we have to stop thinking of her as the frigid student, and start thinking of her as the love-starved co-ed."

Tongue protruding, Amber slowly tapped out the words "love-starved." "Okay, but if she's so hot, why is she love-starved?"

"Because she's so hot that ordinary men are afraid to approach her. They cower in her mere presence."

"You got that right. Except for the 'hot' part." Again, Amber hunched over the keyboard. "Wouldn't it be excellent if we won? Just think, you and me backstage with *Marsha's Inner Child*. Everyone will be so totally green."

"Yeah, but I think getting to be in an episode of *BEAT!* would be even better. If we win, we *have* to get them to make it to round two."

"What if we actually made it to round three?"

Brianna stared unseeing at the wall and slowly shook her head. "Never gonna happen."

"I know. But if lightning struck and we won, what would you do with the money?"

"My mom and dad would make me stick it in the bank for college. What would you do?"

"I'd get a whole new wardrobe and then I'd give some to my sister."

"Jayde? Why?"

"Because even though she's a total geek, she would make sure that someone hungry or hurting was better off in the long run. And that's really cool." Amber shrugged. "She's pretty cool. That way, anyway."

# Chapter 2

*Two Months Later...*

> *Monkey see*
> *Monkey do*
> *You took my heart*
> *And ripped it in two.*
> *I used to think that you were 'the man'*
> *But now I know you're an orangutan*
> *Uh-huh, oo—oo—oo, uh-huh, oo—oo—oo!*
> *Uh-huh, oo—oo—oo, Uh-HUH!*

"**B**rianna!" Amber jumped up and down on the family-room couch. All night long, Top10TV had been promoting this very moment. The morning of June 14th had finally arrived, and they were about to go "live" to the home of the winners of the *Blind Side Date* contest in Anytown, Anystate, USA. "Hurry! When this song ends and these commercials are over, they're going to announce the winners!"

"Relax already. It ain't us." From the family room kitchenette, Brianna ripped open a bag of cereal and poured it into a pair of bowls, then grabbed two bottles of diet pop from the tiny refrigerator and headed into the home theatre.

"They said the winners lived on the West Coast."

"So? Probably a bazillion other kids entered really slammin' people who weren't their loser brother and sister. They probably wrote about super-exciting, extreme people and here we enter geek girl and playboy. Besides, I'm not lucky that way. The biggest thing I ever won was free tickets to 'Barney on Ice.' I gave 'em to my cousin Sybil's kids."

Suddenly deflated, Amber flopped down on the couch and sighed. "Yeah, I know. Me neither. If there was a raffle with only two tickets, the other ticket would win."

Brianna yawned and slumped down beside her friend and handed her a bowl. She closed her eyes and murmured, "We should just go back to bed. I haven't been up this early on a Saturday since we flew to Hawaii last summer."

After another two excruciating minutes, the commercial break was over and they cut "live" to the Bodacious Candie Walsh, who was riding in a television van and gushing into a microphone about the *Blind Side Date* contest and how the moment had come to reveal the results. Brianna sat up.

"Bizarre. Looks like Portland."

"As we are approaching the winner's house, we can now divulge that we have a pair of winners and they live in...*Portland, Oregon.*"

Brianna and Amber froze as the screen flashed with beauty shots of Mt. Hood at sunrise, the distant snow-capped hills and the gleaming city skyline as they traveled down the road.

"What? No *way!*" The girls exchanged slack-jawed glances.

"Don't get your hopes up," Brianna whispered and clutched Amber's hand.

"Okay."

Candie continued to burble. "This is my first trip to the Pacific Northwest. So far, Oregon is a quaint little state. Looks like a perfect place for lovers, huh? This morning, we're winding through a funky little downtown area and heading over into some 'burbs in the hills where our lucky winners live—"

Again, Brianna and Amber exchanged dumbstruck glances and begin to vibrate. "*We* live in the 'burbs in the hills!"

"—on the west side—"

Cereal bowls forgotten, they jumped to their feet. *"We live on the west side!"*

Candie checked her notes. "It's right up here—"

"Look!" Amber cried. "There's our school! Ohmygosh! And there's my church!"

"And there's Hippie's Granola Factory, and Puddles Ice Cream, and the 7-Eleven and look there's TJ. Hi, TJ! Ah-ma-gad. *Ah-ma-gad! AAH-MAA-GAAD!* They're turning down *Pierce Street!*"

"—down Pierce Street toward the address, given to us by our lucky winners." Candie held a slender finger to her pouty lips and shivered à la Marilyn Monroe. "Now, on this show, the element of surprise is everything—"

Screaming and running in circles, Brianna grabbed Amber, who was suddenly glassy-eyed and suffering from shock. "*We won!* They are coming to my *house!* They are going to be here in two *minutes!* How's my lip-*gloss?* How's my *hair?* We are going to be on *NATIONAL TV!* Why did I wear this stupid outfit?"

"I'm going to faint."

"No! You can't! You have to help me clean up the breakfast dishes and stuff." With wild arms Brianna gesticulated at the chaos on the coffee table. "Why'd we make such a mess?"

"We don't have time to do the breakfast dishes."

"We have to. Get started! Pile them under the couch cushions! My mom will have a cow if the nation sees our family room in a mess." Brianna began to shove bags of chips and cereal under the cushions.

"But what if we didn't really win?"

*Dingdong.*

They stopped stuffing dishes and gaped at the TV. The *Blind Side Date* van, followed by two limousines, had parked at the curb in front of Brianna's house. Having already disembarked, Candie was standing on their porch.

"We won," Brianna breathed.

"Answer the door," Amber whispered.

The girls flew to the door and then stopped cold.

Brianna waved a hand before her face, tugged her top down and adopted a smooth look of sophistication.

On the other side of the door, Candie was doing the same thing.

The iridescent glow of morning twilight on fog told Jayde that any minute now the last vestiges of night would give way as the sun scaled the Cascade mountains to the east. Melodic birdsong was increasing in volume, as were the sounds of the morning commute on Portland's city streets. The air was cool and fresh with just a hint of last night's rain. The light fog rolled and swirled, giving the campus an otherworldly feel.

Jayde loved this time of day. So peaceful. So refreshing.

This Saturday morning, she was standing in a Dumpster, just outside the campus library, tucking cans and bottles amongst the refuse before she went inside for a morning of study. So that Pop wouldn't think she was trying to give him charity, she did her best to make these gifts look "natural." Pop might be a shiftless vagrant, but he had his pride.

Bending low, she arranged a bit of crumpled newspaper over a carton of her sister's empty soda bottles. Unfortunately, as she did so, her foot sank into a soft, slippery pile of waste—courtesy of a nearby cafeteria—and she suddenly found herself mired up to her hips in the plate scrapings of yesterday's dinner menu. She stared at her gooey hands.

Gravy. Mashed potatoes. Meatloaf. Limp lettuce soaked in Ranch dressing.

Ish.

Her sigh was heavy. So much for heading straight to the library.

After flailing a bit in the muck, she finally made her way to the far wall of the Dumpster where the refuse became a tad more "solid" for easy escape. It had become clear that she'd need more help cleaning up than the few antibacterial towelettes she kept in her pack. The stench was overwhelming. At least she was the only one up at this hour to witness her ignominy.

Then again, maybe not.

Startled, she realized that heavy, irregular footsteps headed her way through the shroud of morning mist were too close now for her to duck and hide. Her heart began to pound. Perhaps she could simply ignore the passerby. Act as if there was nothing unusual about wading through a Dumpster at this hour. Hopefully, it wasn't campus security. Or an ax-murderer.

The footsteps stopped. A hand clutched the side of the Dumpster and from the shadows a voice with a bit of a slur inquired, "Now why would somebody throw away a perfectly good woman?"

Heart pounding in her throat, Jayde hoped her businesslike demeanor would mask her fear. "Amusing. Now. If you will kindly step aside, I will attempt to disembark."

"Hey." As this man's face came into focus, Jayde could see herself being scrutinized through bloodshot eyes. "Didn't I meet you outside my place a while back?"

Jayde snorted. She had salad in her hair and gravy on her neck and this loser was giving her a pickup line. "No. I'm quite sure we don't run in the same circles...." She studied the man's swaying face and slowly realized that he was the owner of the Frisbee. "Oh..."

"Yeah! It was you. I'm Garret. From the pool?" He belched and the fumes of alcohol could have embalmed her, had she been standing any closer. "Listen, you tried to do me a favor, it's my turn to help you out." He fumbled in his pockets and withdrew several crumpled dollar bills. "I have this left over from tipping the stripper. Since she went home with our bartender, I didn't have time to give her the rest." Sheepishly, he held out the money. "It's not much but maybe you can get yourself something to eat."

Jayde was irrationally affronted. Normally, she would applaud his willingness to help, but his prejudiced assumptions stung and her blood began to boil.

*What was with the blasted bag lady thing?*

Normally, she didn't give a flying fig what some frat-rat type thought of her, but she still burned when she thought of those bobbing bimbos laughing at her from the pool. At her. A master's student. An eventual Ph.D. The unmitigated gall of some people.

Glancing down, she had to admit that since she was standing in a Dumpster and covered with Dumpster gook, his supposition would be a natural one. But still, she thought she'd looked presentable that day. That broom handle skirt was *supposed* to look wrinkled.

"Whoa." He wobbled a bit and clutched the edge of the Dumpster again. The dollar bills fell into the mire. "I'm a little wrecked this morning because I overdid the celebrating at a bachelor party last night. Since I'm best man, I had to host. Then I had to loan my car to the designated driver because he got towed and somebody had to make sure all those bozos got home.''

As he reiterated about the stripper, the drunken brawl, the fact that the groom was in the bathroom throwing up half the night, Jayde stood there and stared at him, aghast.

''Sounds like an evening of moral bankruptcy. You should be real proud of yourself.''

''Yeah. It was a great party.'' His grin was lopsided.

''You realize that if you don't clean up your act, you're going to end up a derelict. Like me.''

''Dibs on the other Dumpster.'' He indicated the recycle bin. ''We'll be neighbors.'' He hooted at his joke then seemed to feel compelled to explain that his inebriation wasn't a habit. Though his attempts to affect sobriety were failing at the moment, he seemed genuine enough as he blathered on about the fact that he was a good boy, really. Practically a choirboy on most days. The ones during the week, at any rate. Last night had just been one of those…obligations.

When he told her that he didn't know why he was confiding all the sins of the night before, but she was just so easy to talk to, Jayde rolled her eyes. At this point, no doubt he'd find the lamppost good conversation.

''So,'' he blinked up at her, ''how'd you get to be a bag lady?''

''I prefer the company of garbage to hanging around trash such as yourself.''

''Okay. Ouch. You're judging me.'' Expression

wounded, he pointed at her. "Plus, I'm sensing a bit of hostility. Toward me in particular, or all men?"

"Toward all moral degenerates who think a fat bank account gives them respectability."

"Hey now. Somebody's fat bank account provided this Dumpster over your head."

Jayde exhaled her exasperation. "Don't you have something better to do than stand here and argue with a bag lady?"

"You'd think, huh? Yeah, I'd probably better head home for some shut-eye. Luckily, I took the day off work."

"Yeah. Me, too."

Garret's grin was filled with a woozy admiration. "You're funny."

"And you're drunk. Go home." She pursed her lips. *And back to your bimbos.*

Brianna yanked open the door and feigned polite surprise at seeing Candie standing on her stoop.

"Brianna Davis?"

With a tilt of her head and the smile she'd practiced for two months—just in case—Brianna nodded. "Yes?"

"Your essay has been selected as the lucky winner of the *Blind Side Date* contest. You and Amber Springer have won backstage passes to *Marsha's Inner Child!*"

Unable to keep up the facade of sophistication, Brianna shrieked and ran into the house to leap into Amber's arms. As they spun and shouted with glee,

Candie and her people rushed inside after them to capture the excitement for live television.

Finally coming to their senses, the girls composed themselves and led Candie to the family room where they offered her a seat on the couch. From beneath the cushions came a crunching, tinkling and vaguely rude noise as the hostess sat on a hidden pile of dishes, plastic soda bottles and exploding chip bags.

The consummate professional, Candie rearranged her slight frown and smiled at the camera. "We're *live* on Top10TV to announce the winners of our Valentine's Day Contest! Behind the camera is Tony, our cameraman, Fred and Arnie, our producers and I'm—"

The girls screamed. *"The Bodacious Candie Walsh!"*

Candie grinned. "Right. And these two lucky girls *won* and will be playing 'Cupid' for our pilot episode of *Blind Side Date* coming to Top10TV next Valentine's day. Introduce yourself, girls."

Tony zoomed in on the girls.

"I'm Brianna, and she's Amber and this is our family room here. I can't believe we won! *We won!*" Brianna grabbed Amber and they shook each other half-senseless.

Tony swung the camera back to Candie.

"So far, these girls have won front row seats and backstage passes to *Marsha's Inner Child,* who will be playing at the fabulous Rose Garden in Portland, Oregon this summer. And, after we wrap up our vigorous shooting schedule today, we'll know if your 'lovers' agree to another date and you win the cameo appearances in our hit behind-the-music-scenes program, *BEAT!*''

Tears of joy streamed down Brianna and Amber's faces.

Candie continued. ''And next year at this time, if your 'lovers' are engaged or married, you'll each win the grand prize of $100,000 dollars! Should be a piece of cake.'' Head back, lashes at half-mast, Candie zeroed in on the camera lens. ''If our 'lovers' are even a fraction as hot as their essay promises, then cock your fire extinguishers!''

Amber bit her lower lip and stole a look at Brianna.

''Right now, we are going to go ambush our 'lovers' and begin shooting the most intrusive, pushy, risky, lurid, shocking and undeniably sensuous show of all time. So, be sure to join us this coming Valentine's Day for the premier episode of *Blind Side Date!* You won't want to miss a sexy second.''

''Aaaand…cut.'' Tony glanced at Candie from around his viewfinder. ''We're clear. I'm gonna grab some cutaways for the show and promos. Then we'll start taping the show.''

''Yeah, okay. So,'' Candie turned to face the kids, ''where are Jayde Springer and Garrett Davis hiding?''

The front door burst open and Jayde stumbled in, reeking of day-old buffet. Mucking a bit of gravy out of her eyes, she blinked at her sister, then at the Bodacious Candie Walsh.

''What's going on?''

# Chapter 3

"You're trying to tell me that I have won a date with this…this…" Jayde stared in disbelief at the party animal sprawled out on the bed before her, "drunken derelict? Is this some kind of practical joke? Am I on *Candid Camera*?"

"Oh, I know he smells a little ripe," Candie strode across the pigsty of a bedroom, tossed the drapes aside and threw open the window. Brows high, she shot a rueful smile at Jayde. "But then I wouldn't go calling the kettle black."

"I fell, okay?"

"Sure. Whatever. I got a show to do. Maybe you could—" her tone exasperated, the Top10TV hostess gestured to Jayde's hair, "—run a comb through your dinner, there?" Candie turned her attention to the man in the bed. "Garret, honey. Wakey, wakey, eggs and bakey."

Garret grunted, but did not move.

"Excuse me? I demand some answers!" As Jayde stood behind Candie, and watched the woman slap the lucky "lover's" cheeks, she had to wonder why fate kept throwing her in the path of this self-destructive man. And why wouldn't anybody talk to her? At the very least, she deserved an explanation.

"Somebody get me a glass of water," Candie ordered. "And put on a pot of strong coffee. If this guy is going to make it through the date, we have to have caffeine. Lots of caffeine. And a few aspirin." She dug into her pocket and popped a couple into her own mouth. "Get me a bottle." At Fred's raised brow, she clarified. "Of aspirin." Still, she ignored Jayde.

Bristling, Jayde glanced at her watch and saw precious hours at the library slipping away. All right. Enough was enough. "If someone does not tell me what's going on right now, I'm going to call the cops and cry kidnapping."

Tony swung the camera to Jayde. Fred and Arnie huddled in the corner and wrung their hands. Clearly, this was not turning out the way anyone had expected.

Fine by Jayde.

Humiliating people on national TV was a terrible idea and didn't deserve to succeed. Fuming, she began to search the hopelessly cluttered room for the cordless phone that was missing from the nightstand's base unit. Time to summon 9-1-1. So far she'd been hustled— against her will—out of her parents' home and into a complete stranger's limousine, rushed through the neighborhood to the Ambassador Condominiums and into the bedroom of a degenerate and then told she was being forced to accompany him on a *date?*

Certainly this was against the law.

She glanced at the lump that snoozed on the bed. Okay sure, normally, she was an advocate for people with problems, but this guy ought to know better than to throw his life away on cheap booze and cheaper women.

Suddenly worried, Jayde glanced around. "What have you done with my sister?"

"Here I am!" Out of breath and radiating with joy, Amber, and her friend Brianna, burst through the door. "Wow! I have never ridden in a limo before. I bet everyone thought we were rock stars, or something."

Ignoring the camera that swung back and forth between the two of them, Jayde squinted at her sister. "Would you mind telling me just what the hell is going on?"

"I entered you in a contest for a new show on Top10TV called *Blind Side Date*. And you won!"

"I...*won?*" Jayde stabbed at her chest with a forefinger. "*I* won?"

"Yes! They needed people to participate who were having trouble finding a soul mate and settling down, and I thought of you."

"Me? *Me?*" Tongue clicking in exasperation, Jayde sighed. "Why me? I mean, what on earth gave you the idea that I'd want to be blindsided with a date? Especially with him?" She jerked a thumb at the groaning Garret.

"Because he's Brianna's big brother. And normally

he's really cute. Seemed like a good idea at the time?"
Amber's shrug was a tad sheepish as she glanced at
the bed. "Anyway, we won a fabulous prize! Backstage passes to *Marsha's Inner Child!*"

Jayde dragged a hand over her sticky face. "Amber,
you know I don't have time for this kind of fool—"

"Jayde, please. Please don't wreck this for us. We
are so excited. We never get to do anything like this.
This is a dream of a lifetime and all you have to do is
to go out on one lousy date. And it'll be fun. I promise."

"With him?"

"Yes! He's totally nice and trustworthy."

Jayde shot a skeptical brow at Garret whose jaw
hung slack in deep slumber.

"Honest. All the girls love him. You will, too."

Garret mumbled something profane in his sleep and
rolled over, his arms flopping off the bed.

Jayde would forever wonder how she ended up in a
limousine, squeezed between the Bodacious Candie
Walsh and Brianna's hungover older brother. Directly
opposite, producers Fred, Arnie and the camera-
wielding Tony shared a well-padded bench seat. The
girls followed, in their own limo.

Garret's firm torso rested heavily against her side,
and she squirmed a bit, wishing she had a tad more
personal space. She carried a vivid recollection of his
beautiful bod as he'd climbed out of the pool, water
running over his smooth tan and dripping to the
ground. Yes, even his feet were beautiful.

It was intimidating. The laughter of his girlfriends

echoed in her mind and caused her cheeks to flame. Since she'd been given no time to clean up after the Dumpster incident, she felt every inch the bag lady at the moment.

Jayde glanced at Garret who—feeling her gaze— lolled his head toward her and winked. She rolled her eyes out the window. How could this be happening to her? Trite television such as *Blind Side Date* went against everything she stood for and believed in. And here she was, participating. All because she could never simply say no to her younger sister.

Jayde had always feared that since their father had been in the military and they'd moved a lot, Amber had sometimes fallen through the social cracks at school. Being an independent person herself, moving hadn't mattered so much to Jayde. But it had been hard on the bashful Amber.

In fact, Brianna was her sister's first real bosom buddy. Because of this friendship, Amber had blossomed this past year. Come out of her shell and finally begun to fit in. Now was not the time to put the kibosh on her enthusiasm.

But this?

Garret belched and let his head flop back against the seat. "Man. I'm so ruined."

"Okay you two lucky lovers," Candie chirped. Tony swung from a tight shot of the grimacing Garret to a two shot of Candie and Jayde. "You are being treated to a morning at Edgar Sonoui's Spa and Salon for a…" her eyes flicked with doubt over the disheveled pair and she cleared her throat, "…makeover. From there, you will be limo'd over to BeBe-Deena Monroe's

Fashion Boutique to select the clothes you'll need to get through the day.''

Garret dragged a hand over his beard-shadowed jaw. ''Now?'' He groaned. ''I'm gonna kill those kids.''

''Get in line.'' Jayde's jaw ached from the clench.

''But right now, we need to get some 'first impressions' from you for our 'Cupid's Arrow' segment.''

''What?'' Garret opened one eye and squinted at Candie.

'''Cupid's Arrow' is what we will call a series of little Q&A vignettes where we will interview you both and cut your answers together in a snappy montage so that the viewing audience—'' she indicated Tony's camera ''—will be able to gage how 'hot' you two are for each other.''

''Hot?'' Jayde gaped at Garret. ''For him?''

Candie sighed. ''Work with me here, okay? Now. Jayde. What was your 'first impression' of Garret?''

''You mean the drunken slob you had to drag out of his bed this morning?''

''Hey? Excuse me? The drunken slob is sitting right here.''

Jayde ignored his indignant expression. ''I don't know where you came up with the ludicrous idea that we are even from the same planet, but my first impression,'' Jayde thought back to the humiliating Frisbee incident, ''well, it's not prime-time material, and that's saying a mouthful these days. My second impression,'' she referred to the Dumpster, ''is not for viewers with weak stomachs and my third impression is that you'd better have a damn good lawyer working for your company.''

"Great." Candie's smile was tortured. "Garret, what about you?"

"What?"

"Your 'first impression' of your date." Candie gestured to Jayde.

"I thought I was dating you."

"No," Candie burbled some phony laughter. "You are dating Jayde, here. Come on now, 'first impression,' please."

"Well," Garret dragged his eyes from Candie and settled them on Jayde. "I'd have to go with disappointment. She smells bad. Like meatloaf. Is it like date a vagrant week on Top10TV, or what?"

Ignoring their barbs, Candie said, "I know you'll both clean up very nicely. Now, off to the spa where we'll get you ready for phase one of your date."

Jayde stared at Candie. "You mean there's more than one phase?"

When they arrived at Edgar Sonoui's Spa and Salon, Garret held his hands over his face as he disembarked from the limo. The sun was blinding and his head was throbbing. Never had he regretted a party more than he did Vinny's bachelor shindig last night. But he was best man. He'd had no choice.

But this was it, baby. Time to turn over the proverbial new leaf. At thirty, he was getting too old for this crap. Besides, watching his buddies get plastered and chase women was not as funny as it had been a mere decade ago. These days, an evening at home with the local news was preferable to the debacle that went on last night. Even he was disgusted.

Garret groaned.

What was happening to him? Talk about turning into a dud. He was beginning to resemble his old man. Respectability loomed drearily ahead, along with a mortgage and a marriage license. When had he gotten so old?

As he stumbled after the homeless woman and into the spa, he wondered what kind of charity mess his twerpy sister had gotten him into this time. He watched a sputtering Jayde being settled in front of the shampoo bowl and gave his pounding head a teensy shake. Even Brianna had to know that this idea crossed the line of good taste. This poor woman needed a shelter and a good meal. Not a day of pampering at some fancy-schmancy spa.

Candie was issuing instructions to her crew and at the same time the staff at the spa had gone to work on Jayde. As he sipped at a glass of orange juice that had been thrust into his hand, Garret moved in for a closer inspection. This Jayde character wasn't really all that bad-looking. Now that the muck was being rinsed from her head—and her eyes, and mouth, were closed—he could see she had the makings of a reasonably normal appearance. His gaze dipped. And her figure wasn't half-bad either, if he was correctly reading what was going on under those baggy sweats.

Too bad she was such a hellcat.

She'd never fit in to normal society with that mouth on her.

A hand on his arm tugged Garret from his reverie.

"Mr. Davis? Time for your shampoo."

\* \* \*

The longer the girls talked about how they'd "embellished" the assets of the "lovers," the more Candie's stomach began to roil. She'd taken the girls into the spa's elegant waiting room to tape the "From Cupid's Mouth" segment. And now, the unfortunate truth was winnowing to the surface.

"So, let me see if I have this straight." Candie searched her purse for a bottle of antacid. "You two embellished the facts in your essay in order to win backstage passes to the concert."

"Mmm-hmm." Amber nodded, unaware that she was incriminating herself and Brianna. "To be honest, Jayde is a complete prude. She like, hates anything that remotely involves, like, breaking a commandment or wasting time."

Brianna nodded. "Yeah. Study, study, study. That's her mantra. So, when you asked if we knew anyone who would never, ever, ever in a zillion, billion, gajillion years, ever get off her duff and find a date the, like, totally *natural* person we thought of was Jayde."

"She's a total virgin."

"Yeah. And she doesn't even like to hug a guy or anything."

"Right. She's like always saying stuff like 'my body is mine. If I don't respect it, no one will. I don't need some creep slobbering all over me to reaffirm my womanhood' and all stuff like that." Amber shrugged. "I don't even think she's made out with anyone yet."

Brianna heaved a worldly sigh. "Probably never even Frenched anyone."

"Nope."

Candie could fairly hear the toilet flushing on her career. "And how old is your sister?"

"Super old. She's already twenty-five, if you can believe that."

"And she's still in school?"

"Graduate school. She insisted on working her way through and not taking any money from our mom and dad. And she wants to be a doctor, so it takes time...."

"Ahh," Candie murmured and wondered how early the unemployment offices opened on Monday morning. "Okay then. Why don't you two tell me about Garret."

"He is a total pagan."

"Yeah," Brianna agreed. "And he doesn't go to church either. Unless my mom nags him to go on a special occasion, or if one of his buddies gets married."

Candie scratched her head. "So, he likes to party?"

"It's his middle name. So, like when you said that part about who do you know who would never ever settle down—"

Bosom heaving, the Top10TV hostess sighed. "In a bazillion years, yada, yada, yada. And you thought these two would be super hot for each other...why?"

The girls looked at each other and shrugged. "Opposites attract."

"Five, four, three, two—" Tony pointed at Candie. Standing between the soaking wet—and none too happy—winning couple, she assumed a bright smile and began to talk to the camera.

"Now that we have captured our 'before shots' and finished up at the shampoo bowl, our lovers—"

"I wish you'd stop calling us that," Jayde snapped. The word was ridiculous and embarrassing. It connoted an intimacy that she'd never share with the likes of— she glanced at Garret's freshly shampooed locks—him.

"Maybe you'd like to be called Oliver Twist." Garret's expression was deadpan.

"Only if we can call you Hugh Heffner."

Candie ignored their biting repartee. "—are both being treated to a total head-to-toe makeover."

"Excuse me? I thought I mentioned that I have a tight schedule? Could we just cut to the chase?"

"Yeah." For once Garret seemed to agree and Jayde was grateful, however cocky he sounded. "I don't really see that I need a makeover." His gaze dropped to her stained sweats. "Miss My-Undies-Are-In-An-Oliver-Twist, here, could use a bath, though."

Jayde gasped. "I beg your pardon—"

"Oh, no need to beg—"

"—you…you…*arrogant* jerk—"

"—be grateful for the chance to better yourself—"

"—grateful? *Grateful?* To *better* myself? *Myself?*—"

"—instead of throwing away a perfectly good opportunity—"

"—to what? To date *you?* Don't make me laugh—"

Deciding that this would no doubt go on for a while, Candie summoned Edgar to come and gather his clients.

The entire time Garret was being snipped, clipped and shaved, he could hear Jayde, hidden from his view just over the partition, fighting her good fortune hammer and tong. What was with this kooky broad? Here she was, being handed a day of pampering, and all she could squawk about was getting out of there and back to—he'd could only hazard a guess here—the street. Although he did have to agree that this was a colossal waste of money.

Voices carried to him from only a few feet away, Garret couldn't help but eavesdrop. "Here, Miss. Go, strip and put this on. I'll be back to rub you down with essential oils of love in a minute."

"No way." Jayde was vehement.

A lighter snicked and Garret watched some smoke curl above the partition. "Perhaps I'll just light a bit of sage to clear the air of evil spirits?"

Jayde snorted. "That won't change my mind."

"How about if I just lay on the crystals to improve your chakra?"

"Forget it! I'm quite certain I do not have, or need, a chakra."

The man sighed. "How about a pedicure?"

"Fine. But I keep my pants on."

"I can see what kind of date this is going to be," Garret muttered.

"I heard that," Jayde snapped.

After a good two hours of pampering, it was time for the makeover reveal. Hair had been cut, dyed, shampooed and coiffed. Garret had been clean shaved and Jayde wore the makeup she'd irritably referred to as "war paint." Up to this point, neither of the lovers had been allowed to see each other.

Garret knew he didn't look much different than

usual, but he had to admit that he was curious about the Dumpster diver. He couldn't imagine what she'd look like.

Candie was out front in the spa's lobby area, yabbering at the camera, introducing this segment. Luckily for him, the caffeine and aspirin had finally kicked in, and he was feeling a little more like his old self. Although, he could use some serious z's.

Or not.

He was jolted to full wakefulness as Candie summoned him around the corner and he got his first gander at Jayde. His jaw came unhinged and he stood there, glassy-eyed, and stared. Even in the spa's white terry cloth robe, she was…well, she was stunning. Hot. Sizzling.

Shapely, well-muscled legs were protruding from beneath the robe's hem. Looked as if she'd finally agreed to a shower at least. A glimpse of her full bust peeped from between the folds of the collar she clutched in her delicate, manicured hand. Slowly, Garret's gaze traveled north and settled on her face.

She was an angel. Her long, straight blond ponytail had been cut and highlighted into a trendy do that suited—and softened—her features. Her plump lips were rosy and kissable and her blue eyes sparkled beneath a heavy fringe of newly darkened lashes. Her cheeks were high and lightly bronzed and she was easily ready for the cover of a magazine.

Sultry.

Pouty.

Sexy.

All these words flitted in and out of Garret's brain.

He knew he must look like a real dope, standing there, drinking in every detail, but he couldn't seem to help himself. Gears whirred as Tony zoomed in on his face. He could hear the pounding of his heart. The delighted laughter of the TV crew and the spa's employees. He could see the answering interest flickering in Jayde's eyes.

What was this woman's story?

Such an enigma.

Garret had never felt so curious or so many mixed emotions. One minute, he wanted to turn her over his knee, and the next...

He tried to swallow.

"Okay, good." Candie clapped her hands twice and nodded at Tony. "Let's set up for another 'Cupid's Arrow' segment. 'The Second Impression.'"

# Chapter 4

Jayde felt naked.

Even though she was wearing a huge, fluffy bathrobe and at least a pound of makeup, she felt buck naked. And not just because she would appear on national television in front of millions of people. Nor because the cast and crew of *Blind Side Date*—not to mention the entire entourage at Edgar Sonoui's Spa and Salon— were staring at her and applauding their handiwork as she followed Candie to tape the next segment.

No. Jayde felt naked because of the expression on Garret's face. He looked as if he'd seen some kind of ghost. Had she changed that much? In his eyes, it seemed as if the change was shocking.

From bag lady to ingenue.

She couldn't help but meet his eyes and grin. He'd leaped to a preconceived idea where she was concerned. That's how most folks were. Never bothered to look past the cover of the person and into the pages of the soul. Suddenly, her mood was buoyed. This *was* kind of fun.

As she stood there, the center of attention, Jayde shifted her focus and caught her reflection in the mirror. Wow. She really did look different. Sophisticated. Every inch the Ph.D. she someday hoped to become. She gave her head a tiny shake and her hair floated around her head like a well-behaved cloud. Her skin was luminous, her lips dewy and her eyes wide set and sparkling with the color of summer sky.

These people really knew their stuff.

Excitement filled her lungs and she slowly exhaled. Really, she ought to pay more attention to her appearance. And she would. If only she wasn't so busy trying to save the world.

Although, she doubted she'd be struck dead if she took a few minutes each day to spruce up a bit. At the very least, get the occasional haircut—she glanced at her beautiful nails—and a bottle of polish. She lifted her eyes to the ceiling and looked into the heavens and gave the good Lord a nod of thanks. It was nice to be reminded about the lovelier things in this life now and again.

Her gaze floated over to Garret.

He was still staring.

*My, my, my.* He did clean up nicely. She knew he would. She couldn't help but wonder which of his bimbos he'd call tonight, and have come over and inspect the merchandise.

The teeniest feeling of rogue jealousy tickled her

brain and she pondered the strange feeling for a moment. Jealousy? Why? Certainly not because she worried about his opinion of her. No. She mulled for a moment.

Probably because this was *her* day. *She* was in the spotlight. She sighed. Though she hadn't asked for it, here she was. And by golly, she was enjoying herself. Would wonders never cease?

"Okay, people." Candie gestured to a pair of stools, situated in a pool of television lights. "Have a seat. It's time for another segment of 'Cupid's Arrow.'"

## "CUPID'S ARROW"

Candie: "Garret, tell us about your version of a 'dream date.'"

Garret: "Well, Candie, I like sports, the more extreme, the better. My dream date would be to meet a woman who would take chances. Jump out of a plane, surf, moto-cross, snowboard, bungee jump, you know, whatever gets the adrenaline pumping. She would have to love arena football and the fights and hockey and the fights at hockey. The kind of sports where people get creamed. Then, I don't know, pizza, a few beers and some time spent getting to know each other in the hot tub, if you know what I mean."

Mouth open, Jayde could only stare. Amazing. And for a moment back there, she'd found him to be the tiniest bit attractive.

Candie: "Jayde, what about you?"

Jayde: "*My* version of a perfect date would be to

attend a book or poetry reading down at Powell's bookstore. Then, a save-the-whale beach trip or some time spent on highway beautification would be worthwhile...."

Garret leaned forward to squint at Jayde and laugh.

Garret: "I'd rather set my boots on fire and hang from a hundred-foot girder."

Jayde: "Be my guest."

Candie: "Well, Jayde, we're not going to do any of that today."

Candie turned and smiled into the camera. "From here, we're off to BeBe-Deena Monroe's Fashion Boutique to select the clothes our lucky lovers will need to get through the day."

Again, Jayde winced at the use of the term "lover." How could they throw such a beautiful, sacred word around so casually? Clearly, the word had lost its true meaning. How sad. The sanctity of sharing one's body with another—she inadvertently glanced at Garret's tightly corded chest as it rose and fell with each breath—escaped them.

When Jayde first allowed a man to possess her, it was going to be pure magic. Heavenly. Holy. A moment she'd never forget as long as she lived. For, in that moment, she would become one with her lover. One spirit. One flesh.

She tore her eyes away from her perusal of Garret's bulging biceps and tried to swallow. As if she'd ever fall for a hedonist like him.

"You have got to be kidding! I wouldn't be caught dead in public in this getup. I look like a slut."

In a nearby waiting area, Garret could hear the poor BeBe-Deena wrangling with Jayde over what to wear on this dream date.

"But girl, the collar accentuates your cleavage."

"What collar? Get me something more than two handkerchiefs and a string and we'll talk. I'm not wearing this. Period. That's my final answer."

BeBe's beleaguered sigh could be heard round the world. Garret couldn't help but grin. Jayde had moxy. He hated moxy. But on her, it was amusing at least. Already sporting a pair of wraparound sunglasses, leather pants and a silk shirt, Garret lounged in a club chair and waited for BeBe to come out here and deck him out in outfit number two. BeBe had gasped and fussed over his tush and how the leather hugged it to perfection. Garret didn't know about that. He only knew it was going to be hot today. And heat and a leather-sculpted butt didn't make for comfort. He was hoping for a nice pair of chinos and a polo shirt. Something simple. He didn't give a damn if it was "something that spoke to the hours he'd put in at the gym." Whatever. He wasn't into fashion.

Seemed he had that much in common with the squalling Jayde.

On the way over here, he got to ride in the limo with his sister and her little friend, Amber. They'd given him an earful.

Seemed Jayde wasn't homeless after all. Intriguing. He should have seen that from the beginning. But he'd heard the bag lady title hung on her out at the pool, and it had stuck in his brain. Stumbling upon her in a Dumpster had only cemented the impression. So. She was a graduate student. Wanted to be a doctor. Yeah. He could see that. She was brainy all right.

And loud.

"No, no, no! I am not a stripper! I am not a call girl! I am a *student*. Think political science. Think conservative. Does the term 'button-down' mean anything to you people?"

"But girlfriend. This is a *makeover*. We are looking for change. You have to meet us at least halfway."

Behind him, in his peripheral vision, Garret spotted Fred and Arnie, heads together, a cloud of worry fairly radiating from their rigid bodies. His eyes disguised behind his spendy shades, he tuned out Jayde's grunts of frustration and tuned in theirs.

"I don't think this is going so well."

"What was your first clue, Arnie? The harridan in the dressing room, or the hangover in the club chair." They eyed Garret with malice.

Garret untangled himself from his slouch and sat up straight. His hangover was gone. And Jayde wasn't a harridan. She was simply exhibiting good taste. The muscles in his jaws worked as the men raked his character over the coals. Then Jayde's. Then Candie's. And all, it seemed, because he and Jayde weren't likely to hit the sack before the end of the date.

Now, Garret was no prude, but that was rushing things a tad, even for him and his crowd. And on national TV, no less? Talk about performance anxiety. He hadn't had time to contemplate the logistics of kissing a hellion like her, let alone bedding her with a camera watching.

He lowered his sunglasses and glowered at the men. From what he could tell, all they cared about was sex. And money.

Swallowing, a nasty realization struck as he watched Fred adjust his toupee. Would that be him in a few years? Good grief. He sure as hell hoped not.

With the help of the thoughtful driver's hand, Jayde emerged from the back of the limousine and tried to ignore the fact that Tony was capturing her every awkward move for posterity. At least she knew she looked good. The expression on Garret's face had again given her self-confidence a lascivious little boost when she'd come around the corner for the ''The Third Impression'' segment.

A grin flirted with her lips.

He really was an open book. Didn't hold his cards close to his chest, the way some men did. And though she may not have shown it, she had to admit, he looked wonderful in his snug jeans and form-fitting designer shirt. He carried his leather jacket slung casually over his shoulder, held only by a finger, and she could see her reflection in the shiny lenses of his sunglasses.

She teetered a bit, unused to such spiky heels. Together with the pedal pushers and the sleeveless suntop, she felt delicate. Feminine. Certainly not up for a romp in the Dumpster. So, she'd have to relegate this outfit to the back of her closet, practicalitywise. But she'd keep it.

''Here we are,'' Candie chirped to the viewing audience, via Tony's lens, ''at the Multnomah Kennel

Club for phase three of our whirlwind dream date! Right now our lovers—''

Jayde winced.

''—will spend a day at the racetrack gambling on the dogs. From there, we have them scheduled to take a scenic boat ride on the beautiful Willamette River. For happy hour and a gourmet dinner overlooking the city, it's *Sebastian's Lounge and Grill* in the Galleria Tower, and then dessert and drinks at a local jazz club. It'll be grueling, but what better way to get acquainted?''

Grueling? Jayde was already exhausted and they hadn't even placed a bet. She glanced at Garret. No telling what he thought from behind his two hundred dollar sunglasses.

With extreme care, Jayde teetered after Garret and toward the enclosed stadium, to make her gambling debut. She gave her head a sorry shake. The moral foundations upon which she based her very existence were morphing into something that would make even Al Capone roll over in his grave.

''They don't seem to be connecting.''

With loathing, Candie watched Arnie's nostrils flare. ''Your whining isn't helping matters,'' she snapped. ''The way you and Fred stand around fidgeting and calculating ratings, it's enough to render even Romeo impotent. Will you just relax? They'll get into each other. The evening we have planned is sure to generate the heat. I promise.''

Fred snorted. Arnie twitched.

Candie crossed her fingers.

\* \* \*

As the show progressed, it became increasingly clear to Garret that he and Jayde had nothing common, aside from the fact that they were both human, and the jury was out on Jayde, as far as he was concerned. It seemed that the more he turned on the charm, the more he turned the antisocial Jayde off. And to make matters worse, the more his frustration became palpable, the harder Candie worked the angle to make it seem like they could barely keep their knickers from bursting into flame.

It just wasn't there.

As much as Garret hated to admit failure at wooing a woman, especially on national TV, there wasn't so much as a spark between them.

Oh, she was real cute in her new hairdo and outfit, but that was the extent of her dubious charm. All she had to do was open that mouth of hers to frustrate the holy crap out of him. Nevertheless, Garret would not be the one to cry "uncle." Nosiree. He'd never flown the white flag on a date. He wasn't about to start now.

"So." Garret smacked his racing form on his thigh. "You're not going to place a bet?"

"No."

"May I ask why?" Not that he wanted to hear her pontificate, but their conversation had been dead in the water since they'd been seated. He felt for Candie. The poor woman looked as if she were suffering from a two-hour-long panic attack.

"Yes." Jayde nodded. "You may. Did you realize that after your dog 'retires' from a losing streak, he's euthanized. Killed. Kaput."

Garret snorted. "That's not true. They get adopted into nice families and live happy ever after. I've seen the commercials on TV."

Jayde nodded. "A few do. But as a former card-carrying member of the Greyhound Rescue Squad—"

Face scrunched in disbelief, Garret stared at her. Of course she was into rescuing greyhounds. And a card-carrying member at that. What better way to sour his love of gambling?

"—I can tell you that 'happy ever after' isn't always a reality. In fact—"

Blessedly, over the loudspeaker, the announcer's voice alerted the betting crowd to the beginning of the race.

"*RRRrrrrrrrr-Rusty's ready!*" The trumpet sounded, the gates flew open and the electronic rabbit began to race on its track, just out of the reach of the lead dog.

The crowd roared.

The announcer called the play-by-play. "Number five, Kiss Me Kate, is in the lead, closely followed by number one, Cat Man Do. Closing in, number six, Born Free." Legs pumping, heads straining after the prized rabbit, the dogs rounded the first and then the second corner. Falling behind the mayhem, was a little straggler known as Angel Baby.

"Come on," Jayde muttered. "Come *on!*"

Surprised by her sudden burst of enthusiasm, Garret stole a covert glance in her direction. Knuckles white, she gripped her program and strained toward the track. Television monitors overhead brought the race in closer, but Jayde couldn't seem to take her eyes off the dog bringing up the rear out on the track.

"And, in last place, Angel Baby," came the announcer's ominous declaration.

"Come on, Angel Baby," Jayde urged. The chords at her neck stood out and the veins in her forehead bulged.

*Ah.* Garret's gaze traveled from Jayde's face to the race and then to the struggling Angel Baby.

The underdog.

Of course. Amazed, he watched her jump to her feet and begin to shout.

Tony climbed over the bleachers for a better shot.

"Losing ground to Cat Man Do, Kiss Me Kate slips to second. Jimmy's Good Boy closes inside and takes a tumble...uh-oh, we have a dog down. Two...no... three. Cat Man Do in the lead, Kiss Me Kate falling to third behind Rogue Wind and Angel Baby moves into fourth in the stretch. As we come to the corner, it's Cat Man Do and Rogue Wind. Long shot, Angel Baby closes the gap. Cat Man Do. Rogue Wind. Angel Baby. Cat Man Do. Angel Baby pulls to second."

Jayde began to jump up and down. "Go, Angel Baby! Goooo!!"

Her enthusiasm was so contagious, Garret forgot that this woman drove him half out of his skull with irritation and jumped to his feet. *"Go, Angel Baby!"* he roared.

Arms waving, eyes buggy, face a brilliant shade of crimson, Jayde tottered on her heels and screamed till she was hoarse. The crowd's cries fairly rattled the rafters.

"—aaand into the home stretch, it's Cat Man Do.

Angel Baby pulling up to neck and neck. Long shot Angel Baby hell-bent for leather. Cat Man Do surges. Falls back…and it's a photo finish…."

Time suspended. Jayde froze. To Garret it seemed that Jayde glanced up at him in slow motion. Their gazes locked. In that super-suspended time of the *Matrix,* they willed Angel Baby to win.

And he did.

By a nose.

The crowd went wild.

Jayde went berserk. Reaching out, she grasped Garret's shirt and shook him till he was sure his teeth rattled. But he didn't care. This was the most fun he'd had in like…forever.

"He *woooooonnnnn!*" she cried and jumped and jostled and high-fived him. She gave Tony two big thumbs-up and the tears of joy welled in her eyes and streamed down her cheeks. "I *knew* he could."

As she turned and grinned up into Garret's face, it was then he saw the stuff of which Jayde Springer was made. And it was a beautiful, multifaceted thing. Far more complex than he could ever decipher in a day. Or a month.

Or, perhaps, even a lifetime.

Yep. She was one interesting broad. He'd give her that.

Garret took a huge bite out of his hot dog and shook his head as he chewed. Amazing. Simply amazing. He swallowed and stared at Jayde, who was picking at her fruit salad.

"So. Tell me again."

"Hey. It's not like I have three eyes or anything."

"Yeah, but a 'virgin'? At your age?"

"What's that supposed to mean?"

"You're not exactly a teenager, and these days, even a teenager has done—"

"Oh, I cannot believe you *said* that! Teenagers have no business getting their bodies involved in relationships that their brains and hearts are not ready for. Do you have any idea about the statistics for unwed mothers and venereal disease in this country? Kids are having kids, not to mention dying, precisely because of the kind of ridiculous expectations that people like you are perpetuating."

"Say that again."

"What?"

"Perpetuating. You're very sexy when you say that."

"There is really no hope for you, is there?"

"Are you really a virgin?"

"Could you say that just a tad louder? I don't think the dogs heard you."

"Sorry. It's just that I find your…condition, fascinating."

"Why?"

"I don't know. It turns me on."

"Well, you can just turn yourself right off. You're not touching me."

Behind them, in a mobile control unit, in the stands, Fred and Arnie—wearing headsets and watching the proceedings between their "lovers" on a monitor—fidgeted and twitched.

"They're never going to end up in the 'Steam Room' at this rate," Fred complained.

Arnie twitched.

But Candie leaned in toward the monitor and listened closely. Something was happening here. And it was sexy. In an old-fashioned, puritanical kind of way they might just be on to something. Ignoring the rumblings and grumbling of the Muppet-like Statler and Waldorf behind her, Candie pressed her headset more tightly against her ears.

"So. No fooling around for you." Garret crumpled his napkin and tossed it to the floor. Another race had come and gone, but they'd decided to order some food and study their racing forms before they placed an actual bet. "Not even a good-night kiss?"

"No."

"Oh, come on. Don't tell me you've never even been kissed."

Jayde colored.

"You *haven't!* You haven't been properly kissed!"

"Would you just shut up? You're embarrassing me."

"Why should you be embarrassed? I'd think you'd be proud of your unsullied state."

"I am."

"Why?"

"Why should I want to kiss you?"

"I've never had any complaints."

"Oh, that's about as sexy as licking a water fountain. Who knows what I'd catch from a sexual addict like you."

Garret issued some strangled laughter. "I am not a

sex addict, c'mon, try not to romanticize me so much, huh?''

"Is it romantic when you lose track of the sheer numbers?"

"Criminy! What numbers? What has my dingy sister been telling you?"

"I know your type."

Garret guffawed. "You do not. And, because you'll discover I'm really a nice guy at heart, I bet I can get you to kiss me before the end of the evening."

"Pretty sure of your potent allure, there, huh buddy?"

"Yup." He chuckled. "So, what'll it be? The common cold, or a colorful case of the stomach flu?"

"Nothing thanks."

"No good-night kiss?"

"No. Not unless you plan on saying 'I do' first."

Candie leaned forward and stared agog at the monitor. "Holy cow. She's gotta be kidding."

Garret leaned forward and stared agog at Jayde. "Are you kidding? You are not going to let anyone kiss you until you're...*married?*"

"Yep."

*"Yes!"* Jumping to her feet, Candie pulled her fists back under her breasts and did a little jig.

Fred and Arnie exchanged puzzled glances. "What?"

"Gentlemen, I'm beginning to think we just may have a hit on our hands."

# Chapter 5

Garret simply couldn't wrap his brain around Jayde's lifestyle choices and she could feel it in his unrelenting gaze as they traveled by limo down I-84 and to the Willamette River for phase four of their dream date.

"Would you just *stop* it?"

"I can't help it. I never met an old virgin before."

"I'm also a vegan."

"No way." His jaw dropped. "What's that?"

Jayde laughed at his comical expression. Clearly he was envisioning something shocking, and for a moment, she was tempted to put him on, but decided against it. They were on television, after all.

Funny how easy it was to forget that, and let one's hair down. Tony had a way of becoming nearly invisible with his camera, and Candie had kept Fred and Arnie confined in the van. The girls were happy following behind in their own limo and jamming to the sounds of Top10TV on the throbbing stereo system.

So, they were alone.

Just the two of them.

And, of course, Tony.

And a couple million viewers.

"A vegan does not eat any animal products."

Garret rolled his eyes. "What a crashing bore of a diet."

"Now, Garret. Tell me how you really feel."

"You mean to tell me that you've never kissed a man and you don't eat steak? What exactly do you do for fun?"

"I…I'm not 'in' to fun." Jayde shrugged. "I don't feel that 'fun' is my mission in life."

"Man. You make eating a simple steak sound like a sin."

"Hey, if the shoe fits." She wriggled around in her seat to better see his handsome face. "What's yours?"

"My what?"

"Mission in life."

She could tell she'd taken him aback. A guy like Garret didn't usually spend a lot of time working out a mission statement. She made no attempt to let him off the hook as he groped for an answer.

Finally, he shrugged. "I don't know. I have a very strong work ethic. I work hard, so I figure it's fair to play hard. I try to be a good son and brother. That's about it."

"Is that all you want out of life?"

Garret looked out the window as the city of Portland rose on the horizon. The river sparkled before a small berg of skyscrapers, several of which he'd told her he built. A series of bridges connected the two halves of the city. Today the sun was brilliant and the foliage was lush in the City of Roses.

Jayde had never failed, in all her years of living here, to appreciate the beauty.

Garret shifted his gaze back to Jayde, but didn't really seem to focus. "I don't know." He lifted and dropped a shoulder. "Never gave it much thought."

"And you're...how old?"

He grinned. "Thirty-one, in December."

She clucked her tongue. "So old to be so aimless."

"This from the world's oldest virgin."

"My sexual status really seems to bother you."

"Yeah. But not in a bad way."

"Then how?"

"It makes me want to conquer something."

"Never gonna happen."

"Don't be so sure."

Jayde stood on the edge of the bobbing dock and watched the Willamette Speed Boat jockey into position for loading. Oh, this was not good. She didn't have any Dramamine, and if the wake that swelled behind the boat was any indication, she'd need it. Without looking, she knew Garret was watching. Along with the rest of the world. Great. Nothing like puking for pure family entertainment.

"You're not lookin' so hot."

"Gee, don't go telling that to BeBe and Edgar. You'll hurt their feelings."

"I mean you're a little green around the gills."

"I tend to get seasick."

"No way. A tough cookie like you?"

"Yep. I don't do boats, or heights, or anything that even remotely resembles one of your fantasy 'extreme sports' dates."

"Bummer. And here I envisioned us climbing Everest together."

The captain of the boat signaled that it was time to load up and get started. Curious passengers and out-of-state tourists stared at the TV crew, clearly wondering what was going on. Some of the kids recognized the Bodacious Candie Walsh and bummed an autograph. Brianna and Amber acted the part of junior divas and enjoyed the attention of several teenaged boys. Everyone was excited about being on Top10TV. Even those who'd never heard of the channel.

After the civilians were loaded, the 'lovers' were seated in a prominent place of honor right behind the captain, then Candie and Tony, and, in the very back of the boat and looking leery, were Fred and Arnie.

"Everybody in?" The captain gunned the engine for effect. "Good. Hang on tight to the one you love. We don't want to lose anybody."

Jayde's shoulders shuddered and Garret put his arm around her and gave a reassuring squeeze. "Hang in there. It will all be over soon."

"Tell my parents I loved them. And tell Amber I'm going to haunt her."

Garret's laughter was lost to the four winds as the captain put the throttle to the metal. The boat lifted up out of the water and seemed to skim the water's glassy surface. Overhead, gulls wheeled and a few fluffy clouds floated. The passengers squealed at this first burst of speed, loving the wind in their hair and the cool spray on their cheeks. Jayde buried her head in Garret's armpit and inhaled the spicy scent of his deodorant. Hopefully, this would keep her from upchucking and embarrassing herself for time and eternity.

"Okay, everyone. Holding on?" the captain queried his passengers after several minutes of flying over the top of the water.

A few bold sailors shouted, "Yes!"

"I can't hear you!"

"*Yes!*" came the roared response.

"Good! Here goes!"

Jayde moaned.

Suddenly the boat bucked and shimmied and then spun in several horrible circles that soaked everyone on the starboard side.

Including Jayde.

Half-frozen, she burrowed more firmly beneath Garret's arm, and he pulled his new leather jacket around them both for protection. Ensconced this way, Jayde could feel him radiating comfort. And warmth. And strength.

When he wasn't questioning her commitment to her virginity, or touting his liberal lifestyle, he could be quite charming. In an animal way. A magnetic, virile way that did something tingly to the pit of her stomach.

She tried to ignore these rogue feelings and chalk them up to what they were. Proximity. After all, she was only human. Snuggling this close to a hunky guy like Garret was bound to make her thoughts stray in directions she usually tried to reserve for the day of her honeymoon. But, oh, it was hard.

Garret was a sexy man. Jayde saw the looks that he'd gotten at the kennel club. And here. On the boat. Even that granny in the back seat that passed out chocolate chip cookies to the kids had raised an interested brow when she'd spotted Garret.

Under the pretext of nausea, Jayde allowed her cheek to rest on the swell of his chest. She snaked an arm around his middle and inhaled the leather. Listened to the steady beat of his heart. Felt the safety of his arms. And enjoyed the trip down the river.

Once again, the captain warned everyone to hang on. And once again, the boat spun in crazy circles that had everyone screaming with laughter. Garret had a deep, velvety laughter. She could listen to that all day.

When his laughter continued, Jayde ventured from beneath the confines of his jacket for a quizzical peek at his face. Everyone, it seemed was laughing. And here she had yet to vomit. What on earth was so amusing?

"What?" she whispered up at Garret.

Bringing his lips to her ear he urged her to turn around and take a peek at Fred, whose shiny pate was suddenly reflecting the afternoon sun. Sometime during the last one-eighty, his toupee had taken flight, and now a herd of gulls was scrapping over the piece as it floated down the river.

Jayde forgot all about her rumbly stomach and laughed with Garret. They clutched each other and snorted and hooted until the tears flowed and they had to gasp for breath. Jayde could not remember having this much fun in…well…forever.

### "CUPID'S ARROW"

Candie: "I'm no psychic, but it seems to me that the sparks between Jayde and Garret are beginning to flare to life."

Brianna: "I *know!* And no one is like, more shocked than us! We thought they'd fizzle for sure."

A stricken Amber gave her friend a covert kick in the shins.

Brianna: "Ouch. What? We *did*. My brother is a total slut and your sister is a prude. Who'd have thought they'd like each other, let alone 'flare to life.' Oh, this is so exciting. Candie, do you think we have a chance at winning a part on BEAT!?"

Candie: "Of course, I can't make any promises, but it's looking really good."

Brianna and Amber shrieked and gripping each other's sleeves, jostled each other back and forth on their stool perches.

Brianna: "Did you see how Jayde was all over him on the boat?"

Amber: "I don't know. I think she was just trying to stay dry. You guys don't know my sister. I don't think she'll go for it in the 'Will They Smooch?' round."

Brianna: "Don't be such a thrill-kill, Amber. I think she'll do it. Nobody ever resists my brother. Seriously. He could get a woman to kiss him with one lip tied behind his back. I don't think it's even a challenge for him anymore."

Amber: "I don't know…"

Brianna: "Just trust me."

Candie turned her attention to Tony and his camera. "Right now, our 'lovers' are dining at the exclusive *Sebastian's Lounge and Grill* at the top of the Galleria Tower. Perhaps Garret is finally convincing Jayde that she can't live another minute without his kiss. Let's listen in on their private conversation, shall we?"

"So," Garret leaned back in his chair and took a sip of his after-dinner coffee. Dining with Jayde had actually been amusing. The conversation had never lacked for a topic and they'd discussed everything from her lofty goals to save the world and his lofty goals to build it. "Tell me why you have decided not to kiss a man until your wedding."

"We're back to that again?" Jayde shifted her gaze to the stunning view out the window. The sun was low now, just tickling the tips of the West Hills. Feeling mellow and sated after a fantastic meal, and some pretty stimulating conversation with Garret, she allowed herself an amused smile at his pestering. He really did have a one-track mind.

Tony and Candie were seated at a table nearby, recording their every move, but already Jayde was inured to it. Fred and Arnie were in the lounge, drowning their fears in a bottle of Jack Daniel's over this sexless mess of a show. They'd made it clear that they thought Candie was crazy if she thought there was anything re-

motely titillating about some frigid freak of a woman
spurning a playboy's ardent advances.

And, until someone started stripping, well, to them,
the whole thing equaled not only a ratings fiasco, but
also the ax falling on their careers as Top10TV producers. Candie had joked to Tony that thankfully Fred
had stepped up to the plate and done his part for the
"Will They Strip?" segment, when his hair had gone
sailing overboard.

"Jaye?" Garret angled his head and searched her
face. "Anybody home?"

She smiled. "Mmm. I was just giving your question
some thought and I really don't think you can handle
the answer."

Garret issued a little snort of disbelief. "Try me."

"Okay. Call me a prude—"

"Prude."

"—but I think that making love is a sacred act. It
should be shared by people who have made a permanent commitment to each other because it involves an
intimacy that links you forever to that person. It carries
a responsibility not to be taken lightly. A lot of people
today scoff at that. But look around. The people who
use another person's body for a quick thrill, usually
have issues."

"I don't have issues."

"Then why does my virginity make you so uncom-
fortable?"

"It's not just that. You won't even kiss me." He
sounded almost petulant. Boyish and somehow vulnerable.

"Why bother?"

"Because you might find you enjoy the experience."

"And then what? We kiss some more, and end up in bed and you never call me again. Sorry, but I have more respect for myself. Not to mention the nine Commandments—"

"Ten."

"Ah, so you *have* heard!" Jayde grinned. "Anyway, I have more respect for my body, and my heart, than to set myself up that way. I want to wait. Find a man who loves me, warts and all."

"I love your warts."

Jayde laughed at the ceiling and shook her head. "You just want to get in my pants."

"That, too."

"Forget it."

As Candie listened in on the headset, a look of admiration crossed her features. This kid was special. A real old-fashioned heroine. You just didn't find people with gumption like that anymore. And it was too damn bad. Fred and Arnie might disagree, but Candie felt the American public was longing for more people like Jayde Springer and her ideals.

In its way, Top10TV had gone a long way toward making sex cool for kids. She thought of her own children with niggling worries. Perhaps Top10TV could begin to turn the corner and make it hip, once again, to be square.

## "CUPID'S ARROW"

Candie: "Jayde, what was your favorite part of the day so far?"

Jayde: "Watching Angel Baby come in first."

Candie: "Right. You won some cash at the race-track. What are you going to do with it?"

Jayde: "Pay off some school loans and buy some new clothes for this guy I know."

Candie: "A 'special' guy?"

Jayde: "No."

Candie: "Care to elaborate?"

Jayde: "No."

Candie: "Fair enough. Garret, so far, what has been your favorite part of this dream date."

Garret: "Kissing Jayde."

Candie: "You haven't kissed Jayde."

Garret: "I know. But I will."

# Chapter 6

"I gotta get out of here." Jayde tugged on Garret's sleeve and lifted her voice to be heard above the revelry. "The noise and the smoke are giving me a headache."

Scatting had never been on Jayde's playlist and tonight's artist *do-be-doo'd* and *sha-be-daw'd* up and down the scales with the frenzy of a French ambulance siren accompanied by a drummer who worked out his psychosis on his instrument. The air—if one could call it that—was a choking blue haze, stagnant with the heat of wall-to-wall bodies, sweating to the beat.

Why this cramped hole-in-the-wall was so popular was beyond Jayde. She gestured to the door and Garret nodded.

She felt his sure hand at the small of her back as he guided her through the Saturday night throng at the

Red Sky at Night jazz bar. Out on the sidewalk, a long line wound around the block as people waited their turn to enter the popular establishment. The live music filtered beyond the doors and several couples danced in the street when the traffic light was in their favor.

A burly bouncer kept a stealthy eye on the comings and goings of the ebullient patrons as, seamlessly, Tony followed the "lovers," never losing them in his viewfinder. In the van, parked at the sidewalk behind the limousines, Candie monitored their every move when she wasn't taping "Man on the Street" promos for the pilot episode of *Blind Side Date*. As they had been at the docks that afternoon, people were delighted to meet the Bodacious Candie Walsh, collect her signature and wish their mothers a boisterous hello on national TV.

And, oblivious to the action that swirled around them, Brianna and Amber dozed in their limo, guarded with care by their chauffeur and new best friend.

It was nearly midnight. Cool, mountain fresh air gave Jayde and Garret a renewed energy and the light of a city at night bathed them in soft shadows as they strolled.

"It's past my bedtime," Jayde murmured. "I should really be getting home. I still have a ton of reading, if you can believe that."

"I don't. I think it's just an excuse to avoid the inevitable."

"And that is?"

"The 'Will They Smooch?' and 'Steam Room' segments still loom."

"Shyah. Right." Jayde shivered, hating how close

he was to the truth. Staying out any later would be a mistake. Already her defenses had taken a pummeling. "Is that all you can think of?"

Garret shrugged. "Now, yeah."

She stopped walking for a moment. Tony rushed around in front of them for a better angle. "Why, for heaven's sake when you can—and *have done* I might add—kiss any woman you want? Why me?"

"Because I've never met a woman who said no."

"If it makes you feel better, I don't kiss anyone."

"You have to admit, that's unusual in this day and age."

"So? I have to play tonsil hockey with you to prove I'm a woman?"

"No, Jayde." His eyes raked her body. "It's abundantly clear that you're a woman."

Jayde was glad the light was too dim to capture the heat staining her cheeks. A delicious shiver skittered up her spine. She waited for a curious couple to pass before she spoke. "I had a great time today. I didn't think I would, but I did. So, let's not spoil the beginnings of a lovely friendship, okay? Besides, after tonight, this will all just be a funny, distant memory."

"No. I don't think so." Garret grasped her hand and tugged her into the doorway of a Niketown store. There, he cornered her against a wall with one hand and with the other, rubbed at the tight muscles at the back of his neck. "Jayde."

Her name was gritty on his lips. Raw. Needy. She'd have to have been dead not to feel an urgent response roiling. Setting her on fire.

"I don't know what you've done to me." Slowly,

his gaze traveled over her face. For a long moment, he studied her mouth. Then, her eyes. "I'll admit I've dated a few women in my time. But, I have *not* been the bed-hopping Don Juan you seem to think I am—"

"Garret, you don't need to whitewash the truth—"

"I'm not!" He dragged a hand through his hair. "If I spent as much time wooing women into my bed as you believe, I'd never have been able to work seven days a week to build my business. Just ask the guys I work with. I'm pretty much there, 24/7."

Jayde opened her mouth to speak, but Garret silenced her with a fingertip to her lips.

"I'm not claiming to be some kind of a saint. I've had my share of relationships. But they came easy. And they went easy. I don't want that anymore." He rubbed his thumb over her lower lip. "I want you."

Jayde went liquid inside. Oh, why was he making this so hard? She wanted to scream at the injustice. Life could seem so unfair. Why was everything good in life so horribly unhealthy?

"I...I..." She searched for the words to protect everything she believed to be right and true. "Garret," she whispered, her words tinged with torture, "it's not about what we *want*. I want lots of things, but that doesn't mean they're good for me...."

"Dammit, Jayde. Don't you ever just give in and enjoy life?"

"Dammit, Garret. Don't you ever, ever, just once in your life, deny yourself?" Her eyes flashed, warring with his. *Oh, Heaven help me.* It was a prayer. "Don't you see? By giving in to your every whim, you've become..."

"Jaded?" His smile was self-deprecating. Rueful.

"Yes. And, sometimes," Jayde pulled her lower lip between her teeth and gnawed for a moment while she gathered her wild thoughts. "Sometimes…certain things…" She grew distracted as his nose touched hers and his eyes went out of focus. "Certain things…" She licked her lips, "…are worth the wait."

Oh, how she wanted to press her mouth to his. To taste everything she'd denied herself all these many years. Her body went suddenly hot. Her legs, molten. It was becoming impossible to think straight.

"I really hate it when you're right." Garret groaned, his breath fanning her lips.

"So do I."

"I don't want to wait."

"To be honest, neither do I."

He drew her into his embrace and, of their own volition, her arms rose and wound around his neck. Jayde had never been this close to a man and, she knew now, it was for a good reason. The temptation was overwhelming. Her curves fit his planes as if they were born to mold to each other and it didn't take a boatload of experience with men to know that he felt the same.

Much to her surprise, Garret's breathing seemed as labored as her own. Beneath her breast, her heart was beating out of control and a wonderful dizziness made her head light and her limbs heavy.

She had only to tilt her head a fraction of an inch to find his mouth with hers and lose herself in his kiss. Just standing here, breathing his breath was incredible. The sensations of heat and strength were marvelous. Wonder filled. Everything she ever dreamed they would be. Instinctively, she knew his kiss would be, too.

With one tiny exception.

This man was not her husband.

And, as much as she wanted to throw caution to the wind and revel in his possession, she couldn't. Not now. Not ever.

And certainly not on national TV.

As Garret lipped her neck, gooseflesh roared down first her right side, and then her left as he changed the angle of his head. Yes. The man had moves.

Moves best left to her imagination. With a terrible regret that he'd never begin to fathom he'd created in her, Jayde pulled her arms from around his nape and gently pushed at his chest with the palms of her hands. "Stop."

"No. Please. Don't go." His voice was low in her ear. Pleading.

"I have to. You know it."

His sigh was long and heavy. "Yeah."

"Garret?"

"Mmm?" He ran a palm over his face and took a step back. Then another. He turned and began walking away.

"Wait…" Jayde paused and it hit her.

Suddenly she knew that she had to take a frightening risk and that if she didn't she would regret it for the rest of her life. But she simply had to know the answer. Terrified, she blurted out the awkward words.

"What would you do if I asked you to be the first?"

He stopped in his tracks, his head dropping back on his shoulders as he slowly turned. "To what?"

"Kiss me."

*"Now?"*

She took a step forward. "Yes. Now."

"I'd run like hell."

Eyes closed, Jayde sighed in relief. Somewhere, under that muscular chest, beat the heart of a good man.

Now, to make him see it.

Candie leaped from the van as Garrett and Jayde headed back for the Red Sky at Night, and their personal belongings. She pounded on the limo door to rouse Brianna and Amber for this last segment. The two girls staggered sleepily to the sidewalk, yawning and blinking beneath the bright television lights.

"Hey, guys!" Candie waved at Jayde and Garret. "Time for another segment of 'Cupid's Arrow'! This segment is called 'Will They Smooch?'" She thrust out her microphone as Garret stalked by.

"No." Without pausing, he disappeared into the Red Sky.

"Never?" Candie lifted a brow. "Jayde, question please?"

"Yes?" Jayde paused and sighed wearily. Would this damned date never end? How on earth would they ever be able to compress every thing that happened into a three-hour premiere? They'd been at this forever.

"You have finally reached the end of your dream date—"

"Thank God," she said on a heartfelt breath.

"But, before we take you and your sister home, everyone is waiting anxiously to see if Amber and

Brianna will win cameo appearances on Top10TV's hit show, *BEAT!*"

Jayde looked at the hopeful expressions on the girl's cherubic faces. "What do I have to do?"

"You only have to go out on a second date with Garret. All expenses paid—"

"No."

And with that, Jayde disappeared into the Red Sky to find her jacket.

### "CUPID'S ARROW"

Candie: "Wow, girls. I didn't see that coming. I'm so sorry. I thought for sure you'd have a chance at a spot on *BEAT!* However, you will both be our guests backstage at the *Marsha's Inner Child* concert and we're also sending you home with some lovely parting gifts—"

Brianna: "But wait! They *have* to go out on a second date! Don't you see? They're *perfect* for each other. You think so, too, Bodacious Candie. I know you do. Please. Just give us one more chance. I want to go talk to my brother. Amber, you talk to Jayde. I really think they would go if we could just make them understand what's at stake for us."

Candie: "I don't know about that…but okay. We can certainly let you talk to them. Bring them back here and we'll see if they change their minds."

Amber: "And if they do, will we get to be on *BEAT!*?"

Candie: "Honey, if you can talk them into going out again, you can star on the stupid show."

Brianna and Amber squealed, leaped off their stools and rushed to the bouncer at the door of the Red Sky at Night and asked him to please get the stars of the Top10TV show out here on the double. Looking for his fifteen minutes of fame—and the admiration of the girls—the thick-necked man was only too happy to comply.

Back out on the sidewalk and under the television lights once again, Jayde could feel the pressure. Everyone was anxiously awaiting her response. It was suddenly all riding on her, it seemed. The ratings, the prizes, the very future of the show. Her sister and Brianna were watching with hopeful, doe eyes, the thrill of victory within their grasp. Fred and Arnie were watching with hopeful, bloodshot eyes, while visions of ratings danced in their heads. Even Candie and Tony, the consummate professionals, were holding their breath.

Only Garret was silent. He'd agreed to go on a second date, but he was as expressionless as Plymouth Rock.

"Jayde?" Candie urged. "Time for your decision. Will you go out with Garret for a second date?"

Closing her eyes, Jayde inhaled a huge breath. "That depends."

Everyone strained forward. "On what?"

"On Garret."

"How so?" Intrigued, Candie squinted at Jayde.

His gaze enigmatic, Garret crossed his arms over his

chest. Though his posture was unnerving, Jayde held her ground. She took a step forward, looked into his eyes and, marshalling all of her courage, laid out her condition.

"If Garret agrees to withdraw from the dating scene and instead put his…energies into projects that will benefit the community for an entire month, I will go out with him again. Same time, next month."

Garret remained frozen. Immobile.

"Let me see if I'm on the same page, here." Candie's gazed bounced back and forth between them. "You want Garret to stop dating."

"Yes."

"Anyone."

"Right."

"No casual dinners with 'friends.'"

"Correct."

"No talking on the phone?"

"No."

"No parties."

"Uh-uh."

"No physical contact with the opposite sex."

"None."

"Instead, he is to pick a 'community-type service' such as…"

Jayde shrugged. "A soup kitchen. Reading to prisoners. Visiting the elderly. I'm not picky."

"And in turn you will agree to a second date?"

"Yes."

"How do you know that he will be a good boy?"

Jayde turned from Candie, her gaze colliding with

Garret's. "Because I know that beneath that playboy exterior lurks a man of honor."

All eyes swung to Garret. "Is that true?" Candie asked.

Garret shrugged. "We'll see, won't we? But before I agree, I want to know if Jayde will agree to a kiss. At the end of the date."

Jayde didn't hesitate. "No. You know the rules."

"Yeah. I *know* the rules."

There was something in his expression. Something that had Jayde looking deeper. Straining forward. And, as realization dawned, her heart threatened to fail.

"And," she whispered, "you still want to kiss me?"

"Yes."

"What?" Candie's head whipped back and forth between them. "What's going on?" She turned to Tony and then the girls. "Did I miss something here?" The girls shrugged and the camera bobbled.

"He..." Jayde swallowed and blinked, unable to finish.

"I want to marry Jayde."

## Chapter 7

After Candie and the girls had finally stopped screaming and jumping up and down, it still took Jayde a good minute to recover her sensibilities and become skeptical once again. He had to be kidding. She took a step closer to him, and sniffed the air. No. Didn't smell like he'd had a drink when they'd returned to the bar. Still, what would possess him to make such a ridiculous statement? Angling her head, she scrutinized his face.

Wait a minute.

He was serious.

Slowly, Garret grinned. As if he'd read her mind, he cupped her face in his palms and lightly exhaled. "I haven't been drinking."

Jayde's eyes slid closed. Minty. *Mmm.* "Doesn't matter. I'm not going to marry you on our second date."

His hands trailed from her cheeks to her elbows. "Okay, I can see how that might be rushing things, so to prove my intentions are honorable, we'll take it in stages starting right now with stage one. I stop dating anyone else."

Jayde's laugher was incredulous. "You? C'mon."

"Yes. Me. I'm going to prove to you—" he scratched his chin and stared off down the street for a second, "—and maybe me, that I'm capable of denying myself."

Jayde felt the tiny chink in the armor she'd built around her heart begin to crack and grow. Try as she might, it was impossible to steel herself against the earnest expression on his face. He really meant what he was saying.

At least for now.

He returned his focus to her. "Stage two starts this week with me doing some volunteer work of some kind in the community. On one condition—"

She sighed. "There's always a catch."

"Hear me out." He looped his thumbs on his belt loops and rocked back on his heels. "During the month that I prove to you that I'm worthy of caring about our community, you have to try something new, every day."

Tony moved in for a close-up. Candie and the girls strained to catch every word over the typical night noise of the city. The jazz from the bar was still going strong. Cars honked, people gathered to watch the show being shot on the sidewalk and murmured amongst themselves over the nature of the show, and the Bodacious Candie Walsh. Off in the distance, a siren wailed.

Who, everyone wondered, was this couple, standing so close, and having such an intense exchange? Everyone, with the notable exception of producers Fred and Arnie—who'd given up on the show and gone inside to seek a little action—slowly inched in around the pool of television light.

"Something…new?" Jayde lifted a skeptical brow. "Like what?"

Garret shrugged. "Whatever you want to do. The only caveat is that it cannot benefit anyone. Or any group. Or any animal. Or any group of animals."

"But…"

Garret steamrolled right over her protestations. "Why don't you go swimming? Just for fun, though. No lifesaving classes. Or take a pointless bike ride. Try kickboxing lessons. Go to a Blazers game at the Rose Garden or a Winterhawks hockey match. Learn a hobby or two, something like photography, or knitting or shopping. Anything but saving the world."

"But…that's…"

Garret shook his head and shushed her sputtered protests with a palm over her lips. "Hey. If I have to expand my horizons, I don't think it's asking too much for you to return the favor. What better way to prove to each other that we're serious?"

Jayde had to admit he had a point. "Okay. And then what?"

"Then, at the end of the month, we'll meet again for the big date and you agree to marry me."

Her heart began to pound and her blood roared in

her ears. "But that's crazy! I can't marry someone I've only known a month!"

"Ohh, for crying in the night...of course not." Garret buried his face in his hands and groaned long and loud. "Right. You're right. Okay. So. We'll get engaged. I give you a ring, you can set the date."

Candie interrupted. "You won't mind if we shoot all of this stuff for our show?"

"I don't care. Jayde?"

"Why? Why are you doing this?" Jayde still couldn't believe any of this was happening. This morning, she'd been minding her own business, climbing around in a Dumpster and doing her thing, and now...now this man...this impossible, insane, wonderful, completely weird man was asking her to break out of her shell and maybe even think about spending her life with him. No. Never. It was too rash. Too out of character. Far too soon.

Marriage was a holy sacrament. It took time. Consideration. Planning.

On the other hand, she knew people who had planned for years and ended up divorced. And then there was the matter of her own parents. They met at a New Year's Eve party, were engaged on Valentine's Day and married in June. Married, and they'd only known each other six months. Crazy. But they were still married after thirty years. And still in love.

She could feel Candie and the girls staring at her. Willing her to give Garret a chance.

Garret rotated his head from side to side to ease the tension. "I know it does sound crazy. And, it probably is. But I also know that I'm ready. And you're the one.''

"*The* one. You can be so certain?''

"You are a rare beauty, Jayde Springer. Both inside and out. I would be a fool to let you get away.''

Large tears welled in her eyes. If only he really believed what he was saying.

"So. You'll agree to my plan?''

Jayde turned to stare haplessly at Candie and the girls.

"Say yes, Jayde!''

Tears spilling, Jayde laughed at the expressions of hope on their faces.

"All right. Yes.''

A second date seemed harmless enough. And chances were, when Garret began to feel the strain of her demands, he'd bail out and none of this—winning one hundred thousand dollars for their sisters—insanity would ever even be an issue.

Candie headed into the Red Sky and finally found Fred and Arnie bellied up to the bar, attempting to make time with several rather seedy looking goodtime girls. Straining to be heard over the din, she wedged herself between the men and shouted that she wanted to discuss some changes in the concept for *Blind Side Date*.

"Now?'' Arnie looked at her over the rim of his shot glass. His shirt was unbuttoned down to his navel, revealing his sagging pecs and penchant for gold medallions.

"No. Not now, stupid,'' Candie muttered.

"Pardon?" Arnie leaned forward.

"No. Not now." Candie lifted her voice. "In the morning. When you are...fresh."

Arnie grinned. "For you, I can be fresh now." He pinched her backside and she slapped his hand. He laughed.

"What changes?" Fred peered at her through his drooping, crimson-rimmed eyes. There was the tiniest slur in his speech that indicated he wouldn't remember much of their conversation in the morning.

It irritated Candie to no end to have to run her ideas past these bozos, let alone ask for their vote to go ahead with a project. They were clueless when it came to what interested today's teens. "Don't worry. It's all good."

"It's all good. It's all good," Arnie mimicked. "What the hell does that mean, Fred?"

"It means that it's good," Candie snapped. "You guys just go back to what you were doing. I'm going outside to wrap this episode. Then I'm going to my hotel room to call my family. May I suggest you do the same?"

"May I suggest you join Arnie and me and our new friends," he winked at the haggard, world weary barflies to his right, "at our hotel room and we discuss your good thing?"

"Her good things," Arnie corrected, staring pointedly at her bustline and they all laughed raucously.

Jaw clenched, Candie ignored them. "I'll meet you two tomorrow, before we head to the airport, for a quick meeting to outline the idea I have for a new direction for this show. Be in the lobby at nine."

"Ten," Fred corrected.

"Eleven," Arnie said.

"Nine." Lips pursed, Candie refused to indulge them in their immature debauchery. Pushing off the bar, she nodded her good-night.

Maybe, she mused as she barreled through the crowd and back out to the set on the sidewalk, just maybe Jayde was beginning to rub off on her. She smiled.

Good.

When it came to Fred and Arnie, she was long overdue for a little backbone.

This was certainly the strangest day of Jayde's life.

Amber was slumped against her side, a satisfied smile gracing her lips. Her eyelids were heavy with exhaustion, but she battled sleep with jabber, rambling on about her winnings and Garret's proposal as they made their way home in the back of a limo.

"Now, *that's*," she yawned widely, "what I call a successful date. When the guy asks you to marry him…you *know* he had a good time and will probably go out with you again. I am so gonna be on *BEAT!*"

Jayde stroked her sister's hair, only half-listening to her sleepy teenaged prattle. She knew she should set her sister straight with a healthy dose of reality. Tomorrow the clear light of day would bring them all to their senses. They'd all share a good laugh about how they'd all gotten so caught up in the moment. And then—Jayde sighed—they'd all get on with their lives. At the moment, however, she'd let her sister enjoy her girlish fantasies about love and romance and happy ever after.

"I bet you never thought you'd get a marriage proposal today, when you got up this morning," Amber murmured.

"Never."

"I bet he's a good kisser."

"Mmm." Jayde shrugged. She'd probably never know. The thought make her strangely melancholy.

"You really gonna marry him to find out?"

"Yes. No. I mean, that's the only way I'd kiss him."

"Wow. That's so weird."

"Thanks," Jayde said dryly.

Amber lolled back and grinned up at her. "No. I mean it in a nice way. What you're doing takes guts. You probably won't believe this, but you're a good influence on me."

"Really? Me? On you? How so?"

"Well, don't tell Mom and Dad, but T.J. wanted to kiss good-night after the prom, but I said I wasn't ready."

Jayde was touched. "Because of me?"

"Yeah. And also, he had a wad of Copenhagen in his lip."

"That's attractive."

"Yeah. It was so gross." Amber made a face. "Jayde?"

"Hmm."

"No pressure, but if you marry Garret, we'll make a ton of money."

Smile bemused, Jayde said, "No pressure."

"You could do a lot for charity and stuff, with that money."

Jayde kissed her sister on the head. "I'm not getting married for money."

"Right. You'll marry for love. You love him, you know. You just don't know it, like, yet."

"Mmm-hmm."

First thing in the morning, she'd set Amber straight.

The next morning, Candie was on the verge of leaving when Fred and Arnie finally stumbled out of the elevator and into the hotel lobby.

"C'mon," she ordered, barely disguising her disgust for their tardiness, "the coffee is this way." She hustled them into the busy coffee shop and asked for a booth. When the coffee had arrived and they both looked sufficiently conscious, she laid her cards out on the table.

"I don't want to hold this show till February sweeps. I think what we've stumbled onto is too good to keep on the shelf that long. I want *Blind Side Date* to debut with the fall lineup." More excited about a project than she'd ever been in her entire career, Candie barged ahead before either of them could protest.

"I'm telling you, this show is going to be a mega hit. The bride has never been kissed! And she is holding her ground until the wedding. And better still, the hunk of the century is going to save himself for her. Can you believe it? We're gonna place up there with *The Bachelor* and *Survivor*."

Fred and Arnie were speechless.

Staring at her. Without comment.

Unnerving as it was, Candie took the old proverb

"no news is good news" to heart, and valiantly carried on.

"So, next month I want to come back to Portland and follow Jayde and Garret through another date. They've already agreed. After that, I think they may become engaged, and if we're lucky, married. We'll get ad contracts for Jayde and Garret. We'll film the birth of their children. They'll be the 'it' family—like *The Osbournes* only innocent. We'll do a whole ad campaign built around their dates, and then we can air the possible wedding on Valentine's Day, instead of the pilot. Their kiss will be the season finale."

"A stupid kiss? A season finale? What kind of crap is that? Who wants to sit around all season and wait for some old maid from Backwater, Oregon to get her first kiss?" Arnie's cup clattered to his saucer. He winced.

Fred gaped at her. "You want to base an entire season on that self-righteous prig? Have you lost your marbles?" His phony chuckle was meant to be condescending. "Candie, if this flops, it will be just another in a string of flops for Top10TV. I don't think we can afford it."

Candie began a slow boil. Throughout her career, she'd never been taken seriously. Ever. The muscles in her jaw jerked as she ground her back molars together. Even in middle age, she was still treated as the airhead with the boobs. She was sick to death of it. Mad as hell.

And she wasn't going to take it anymore.

Still, she was a professional. She forced herself to

smile. "And if you're wrong? If this is the mega hit I'm predicting? What then?"

"I don't think the playboy can take the 'no woman' dry spell."

She clenched her fists. "I think he can."

Fred reached back, as if to retrieve his wallet. "Care to make it interesting?"

"No. And I want you two to leave them alone."

"I think we should cut our losses. Sex sells. You said so yourself, Candie."

"I was wrong, okay? Other things sell, too. Especially today."

"No. You weren't wrong, Candie. Let's find a couple who will give the audience what they're dying for."

Elbows to table, Candie gave her brow a vicious rub. "So, you two immature Peter Pan types would prefer to watch some bimbo, like your drinking buddies from last night perhaps, lose her virginity for the thousandth time? Talk about boring. Where's the human interest story in that?"

Fred chuckled. "I'll tell you a little 'human interest' story from last night, honey—"

Candie interrupted, her voice low with repressed rage. "And I'll tell you one. We are going with my plan, you two overaged, oversexed sleazebags."

Faces agog with shock, Fred and Arnie stared.

"And if you say one word," she held up a shaking finger and hissed, "one *damned* word against my plan, I swear on all that's holy I'll sue the pants off both of you for sexual harassment. Got that?"

Fred gulped.

Arnie's nostrils grew round.

"Good. Now, I am going to the airport and flying home to my husband. I suggest you both do the same for your poor wives. Got *that?*" Her fist caused the dishes on the table to dance.

The producers paled and exchanged glances before they both nodded.

"Good."


Garret rolled over and looked at his bedside clock—6:00 a.m. He wondered if Jayde was up yet. Was it too early to call? It was Sunday. She'd said something about getting up for church, but he doubted church started this early. Then again, how would he know? He hadn't attended a service since he was a kid.

The digital readout changed—6:01 a.m.

He'd hardly slept a wink, but for some reason he was wide awake. Fairly vibrating with an eagerness to begin his day. To turn over that new leaf.

He'd call Jayde a little later. He could hardly wait to talk to her. To reassure her that he was serious about their agreement.

Throwing off his blankets, he leaped out of bed and into the shower. When he was finished dressing, he jumped out to his porch and retrieved the paper as it landed on his stoop. He'd read it over breakfast.

After leisurely browsing the sports section over his coffee, Garret flipped through the remaining pages until his eyes landed on the lifestyle section. There was a continuing story on Habitat for Humanity that caught his eye. Interesting. He sipped as he read. Seemed they needed people to work on a project in North Portland.

They'd listed some contact numbers with message machines. Garret reached behind his head to the counter and picked up the phone. Since he was between building projects at work, he had plenty of time on his hands. He'd volunteer.

Then, he'd spend some time cleaning house. He'd throw out his cadre of little black books and various scraps with the jotted phone numbers of women he barely knew. Didn't need them anymore. Because, even if Jayde told him to take a flying leap after their second date, Garret was done with his old lifestyle. *Fini.* Kaput.

He'd make that clear to all of his cronies at Vinny's wedding, next week. And, if they didn't like it, well, maybe it was time to find some new cronies.

He glanced at the clock—6:50 a.m.

Still too early to call Jayde. Man. He missed her bad. Already. He gripped the phone. He'd leave his number at the Habitat for Humanity office, and then what? Sunday morning yawned endlessly. Pent-up energy had him drumming his fingers on the table. Normally, he'd sleep till noon, then go find someone to hang with.

Not today.

No siree, Bob.

Today was the first day of the rest of his life and all that. He pushed away from the table and stood up. Just to seal the deal with the Big Guy Upstairs, he'd take his sorry butt to church.

Two weeks later, Jayde limped into her dorm room and flopped down on her bed. That was the last time she'd make fun of those stuck-up bimbos who took kickboxing classes for grins and giggles. That stuff wasn't for wimps. She was so sore, even her hair hurt.

The phone rang.

She groaned. Oh, how was she going to find her phone when she could barely move? "I'm coming!" Moaning, she rolled off the bed and crawled toward the incessant sound. "Hello?"

"Hi."

"Hi!" she sat up, instantly perky.

"How are you?" Garret's voice washed over her, electrifying as a summer thunderstorm.

"Fine," she lied. "How about you?"

"I miss you."

Smiling, Jayde crawled back to her bed. "Mmm. Me, too."

They'd talked on the phone every day since the Sunday morning after their date, several times a day and long into the night. He knew everything about her now, her hopes, her dreams, her aspirations to make the world a better place. She'd even confided her dreams to get Soda Pop off the street someday. And he hadn't laughed.

She knew everything about Garret now, too. When he'd had his tonsils out, his first home run, his grade point in junior high, his most embarrassing moment, all the names of his first cousins, and even such personal details as his family's health history, his taxable income and his unrequited crush on his first grade teacher.

But still, he wouldn't talk about the changes he was making in his lifestyle. He'd only admonish her to "trust him."

*Trust* him.

Trust...*him.*

So, though her usually skeptical nature urged her to beware, her heart had no reservations where Garret Davis was concerned. With every conversation, they grew more intimate. Closer. Tighter. And though they'd only spoken on the phone these past weeks, Jayde had never felt so close to another living soul in her life. It was scary. And exhilarating.

"It's only two weeks until I see you again," Garret murmured, "but why does that seem like forever?"

"I don't know. I used to wish for more hours in the day, but now every minute seems to drag by."

"Yeah. I know what you mean." Garret's sigh crackled heavily across the line. "So, what did you do today?"

Jayde rolled onto her back and propped her feet on the wall, ankles crossed. "After school I dropped in to a kickboxing class."

"Umm. I love a woman who can kick butt."

"Kickbox. And yes, I'm learning to defend myself, so don't try anything funny on our second date."

"Nothing?" His voice was loaded with innuendo. "Not even a little hug?"

"No!" Giggling, Jayde shivered at the memory of dallying in Garret's arms. Garret's sigh whooshed heavily across the line. At his groan she said, "Okay. A little one."

"Oh, good. How about a little peck on the cheek?"

"Maybe. A little one."

"And one for your nose. Can't forget that."

"No, can't forget that." Jayde's eyes slid closed.

"How about your ear?"

"Mmm."

"Your neck?"

She sighed.

"—and then—"

"Garret," she whispered.

"Yes?"

"I'm learning to kickbox."

"Right. So. What else did you do today?"

"Why do I have to tell you all about how I'm expanding my horizons with square dancing classes and cooking lessons and shopping for a new wardrobe at the mall with our sisters, and you don't say a word about all the good deeds you're supposedly doing?"

"I told you. It's a surprise."

Jayde snorted. "It had better be some surprise, cuz I'm killing myself for you."

"It is. Trust me."

"I do." And God help her, she did.


"Finally."

"I know. It's all I can do to make it through each day to hear your voice." Garret lay stretched out on his couch, the phone tucked between his ear and chest, the volume on ESPN turned down low. During *Sports Center* at that. He never missed *Sports Center,* but to talk to Jayde he'd skip his dear old granny's funeral. Not that he had a granny, but if he did...

"How was the wedding?"

"Great. Vinny was a blubbering idiot. We all thought Kayla would be a mess, but she was a rock. It was really a beautiful wedding. Made me think about our wedding."

Jayde laughed. "You still want to marry me."

"To get that kiss, uh, yeah."

"What if I'm a horrible kisser?"

"Then I'll just have to spend some time teaching you technique. But I have a feeling you'll catch on quick. Real quick."

"I hope so."

"Aha! You hope so, huh? So, you're going to kiss me."

"Shut up."

"Vinny kissed Kayla twice. Which of course made me think of—"

"Our wedding."

"Right. I think we should go one better than Vinny and kiss three times."

"Ooo. Sounds fun. Maybe we should consummate the marriage, right then and there," she teased.

"I can tell I've been a bad influence on you. So, I'll have to veto that idea. Besides, that would be too showy. I don't want Vinny to look bad, I just want to show him up."

They laughed and murmured another night away.

"I dreamed about you last night."

"Really?" Jayde was amazed. "Me, too! I mean, I dreamed about you! What did you dream?" Per usual, she was cuddled up with her phone, whispering another evening away with Garret.

"I'll show you on our wedding night."

"Oh." She blushed.

"You're blushing."

"Am not."

"Are, too. You're cute when you blush."

"How do you know?"

"I remember."

"So, you've been thinking about me?" Jayde closed her textbooks and shoved them and the wrappers from her sandwich back on her desk and settled in for some dinner conversation with Garret. "What have you been thinking?" She adjusted her headset so that she could eat and talk to him at the same time.

"I've been thinking that I love you."

Jayde sat stock still, her heart suddenly hammering, her sandwich falling from her hand and to her desktop with a thud. "I...I..." She tried to swallow. "You just said you love me."

"Yeah. That's cuz I do."

She blinked at the wall. "You do?"

"Yup. And this is where you're supposed to say you love me, too."

Mouth hanging slack, Jayde considered the gamut of emotions she'd been wrestling lately and could only come to one conclusion. Bursting into laughter she blurted, "I love you, too!"

And she did. God help her. She did.

Jayde fumbled in the dark for the shrilly ringing phone. Thank heavens she'd left it under her pillow. Finally, she had it right side up and at her ear. "Lo?"

"Good morning."

"Mmm. Good morning. What time is it?"

"It's 4:00 a.m."

"Four? Four?" Jayde blinked at the clock on her nightstand. Sure enough. It was four. "What's wrong? Why are you calling me at four?"

"Because today is the day."

"What day? Oh. Mmm. Right." A slow smile started deep in her belly and spread to her cheeks. "Our second date."

"Yep. Candie called me last night with last-minute instructions."

"Yeah. Me, too."

"Six tonight. That little Polynesian place on Northwest 23rd."

"Right." Jayde yawned. "What are you wearing?"

"Nothing."

"What? No! Not now, you goose! Tonight."

"Oh! Tonight. I don't know. Edgar is sending something over for me to wear."

"Same." Jayde rubbed her eyes. "So are you really naked?"

"Buck."

"Oh, my gosh. And I'm talking to you." She laughed.

"You are so cute." He chuckled. "I can't wait to see you."

"Ditto. You gonna pop the question?"

"Hell yeah. You gonna say yes?"

"Maybe."

"Then you'll kiss me?"

"Hell no." She hooted with laughter. "Yes. Maybe. Someday."

"Soon?"

"Maybe."

"Just maybe?"

"I have to keep you interested."

"Jayde." The frustration in Garret's voice crackled across the line. "I'm more than interested."

"I know. The same way I knew Angel Baby would win. Gut feeling."

"You are such a bleeding heart conservative weirdo. Marry me?"

"We'll see, won't we?"

## Chapter 8

Candie sat in a chair in the darling Polynesian restaurant they'd selected for Garret and Jayde's long anticipated reunion. She and Tony were discussing last-minute camera angles under the little tiki hut set the crew had constructed for the 'Cupid's Arrow' segments, while Fred and Arnie stood nearby, sporting headsets and pretending to call the shots in front of the gathering crowd.

Candie rubbed her temples and emitted a low, rumbling groan. What a couple of egocentric fools. They strutted around, issuing time-wasting instructions for the benefit of the beautiful, young waitress who was currently taking an order for their second round of cocktails.

"Hey, sweetheart," Fred said, "you got a sister for

my friend here? We could really party after work tonight.''

Disgusted, Candie signaled Tony to stop setting up for a second and turn on his headset. These two dim bulbs seemed to have forgotten that she and Tony could hear their every word when their headset mics were switched on.

''Want me to unplug 'em?'' Tony mouthed.

''No! Listen.''

As the waitress collected their empties, Fred muttered to Arnie, ''She's built like a brick outhouse.''

''Great assets.'' Arnie har-de-har'd at his inane humor, then lifted his voice so that the waitress could hear as she worked. ''Ohhh, yeahhh,'' he brayed, ''this is our show. *Blind Side Date.*''

''We're the producers.'' Fred threw his drooping shoulders back and sucked in his gut. ''We could get you on our show.''

''Yeah, baby.'' Arnie's left nostril twitched. ''We could make you famous.''

''Hey! Idea! New show! Pick the Producer! We could wine and dine you, and you could pick between us!''

Exchanging narrow glances with Tony, Candie ground her teeth as she covered her microphone with her hand. ''Remind me that I am a professional. That it would look bad on my record to beat up my business associates.''

''I'll help you pound 'em, if you want.''

Candie smiled. ''Thanks, Tony. You're a pal.''

The waitress made good her escape with a tray full of empty glasses.

"Yeah, well, maybe later," Fred called after her retreating form. He turned to Arnie. "I sure hope the boss gets on board with us. I hung my butt out there in the wind, telling him this stupid thing was our idea. Bodacious had better be right."

Candie watched as he smoothed his toupee with a shaking hand that would probably take another drink to kill.

No one—with the lone exception of the waitress—noticed a nervous Jayde arrive and hover just behind Fred and Arnie. Smiling in welcome, the waitress took her order for a diet drink and moved away, leaving her alone.

As wobbly as she was, Jayde decided she'd stay back here in the shadows until Garret arrived. She glanced around. Okay, where was he? *Ohh, hurry,* she mentally pleaded. She couldn't believe how excited and happy she was to finally get to see him after a month apart. It was all she could think of all day long. Talking with him on the phone had been wonderful, but it simply wasn't the same as seeing his beautiful, sexy eyes.

Moments later, the waitress returned with the drink and made change for Jayde's bill.

"Keep it," Jayde whispered, took her soda and waved the girl away as she moved farther into the shadows. As she took a deep sip, Jayde attempted to collect her thoughts. The ice cubes in her drink jangled along with her nerves. Why was she behaving this way? A mere month ago she would never have let herself fall into such a dither.

Luckily, so entrenched in conversation were Fred and Arnie, they didn't even notice her clinging to the totem pole-style pillar behind them. Good. Until she could get her vibrating pulse under control, she'd bide her time back here, out of the way.

The waitress returned with Fred and Arnie's round and then cleaned their table of napkins and lemon rinds. Their conversation grew suddenly loud, seemingly aimed at impressing the waitress. Jayde rolled her eyes. Though she was loath to eavesdrop on these dorks, she couldn't seem to tune them out.

"This was a pretty good idea of ours. 'The Playboy proposes to the Prude.' The more I drink, the more I like it," Fred said.

Jayde's lips froze to her straw. *What?*

Arnie yucked it up. "Yeah. I gotta tell ya, back when we came up with that idea, I had my doubts that 'The Playboy' would 'play' along. I mean, he don't seem like the type to forgo a woman's 'company' for a whole month. And certainly not for a glacier like her, if you get my drift."

"I doubt that he was actually celibate all month, but who cares? As long as he completes the second date and proposes marriage, he gets the money. Did you tell Bodacious that we upped the stakes for him, just to make his incentive a tad more interesting?"

"No. I don't tell her anything," Arnie said. "And, I'd call a cool mil more than just a tad interesting."

By now, Fred and Arnie were feeling no pain. Fred tossed back the last of his current drink and attempted to set his empty on the nearby table. He missed. "Million bucks. That's a lot of money."

Arnie's laughter raked the chalkboard. "But if this thing is a hit, it will be worth every penny."

Jayde clutched her glass until the ice had turned her fingers numb. Light-headed, she leaned against the wall and listened to her heart try to jackhammer its way from her chest. What were these men saying? *That they'd bought Garret off? That the marriage proposal had been their idea? That...* Her eyes fell closed to forestall a wave of dizziness...*he'd been dating other women?* She had to leave. She'd managed not to vomit on the boat, and she wasn't going to embarrass herself now.

Not any more than she already had, anyway.

Blinded by tears and shaken to the core, Jayde's glass tappity-clicked against the window as she tried to set it on the sill.

"I'll get that for you," the waitress said as she swished by. "Anything else?"

"No. Uh...I...no, thank you." Jayde turned to go, then paused. "No, wait. Please tell Candie Walsh that I had to leave. Something...unexpected came up and I...I...I...can't...well, that's all. Thank you."

"Sure." A slight frown marring her brow, the waitress shrugged.

Jayde rushed passed the grass-skirted hostess, through the lobby and to an open elevator. Jumping inside, she stabbed the button for the parking lot and once the doors had closed and she was well and truly alone, allowed herself to cry.

Everything she believed to be true since meeting Garret was simply based on lies. Lies told for the purpose of making money. And making a fool out of her. Well, Jayde Springer was nobody's fool.

She swiped at her tears with the edges of her palms.

So. This had all just been a big setup to get her to fall for Garret, and to win prizes for the kids and get ratings for the Top10TV network, and to make Garret rich.

Well, they could all forget it. Jayde wasn't playing anymore.

After Candie'd had a bellyful of listening to Fred and Arnie yammer about how smart they were, and speculating about the ratings share, she finally snapped on the microphone to her headset and whispered sweetly, "Fred, Arnie."

Arnie jumped and squinted over into the television lights where Candie stood behind Tony.

"Could you boys save your self-congratulations for later? We're about to get started here."

Fred and Arnie started and exchanged glances that said, Uh-oh. She'd overheard their conversation.

"Has anyone seen Jayde Springer?" Squinting past the TV lights Candie searched the room. Garret had arrived moments ago, but she had yet to see Jayde.

The waitress approached and tapped her on the shoulder.

"There was a tall, blond woman standing right behind those two clowns for a while. She told me to tell you that she had to leave, and that she was sorry, but something came up and she had to go. She looked really strange. Kind of pale. Like she'd seen a ghost."

"She had to...*go?*" Mouth sagging, Candie stared for a moment until it dawned on her. *Uh-oh.* Jayde had overheard Fred and Arnie bragging about how the show—and the proposal, not to mention the money—had all been *their* idea. Good grief. From the poor kid's perspective this was huge. Horrible. Humiliating.

Candie didn't blame Jayde for splitting. Given the same set of circumstances, she would have taken off, too. Unfortunately, when Jayde took off, she took the show with her. Snatching her headset from her head and flinging it behind her, Candie rushed over to Garret. To explain. To apologize. To send him after the star of her show.

His heart in his throat, Garret drove like a madman through town to the one place he figured he just might find Jayde. Calls to her parents and her classmates hadn't turned her up at any of the obvious retreats so that left an obscure alternative upon which he was placing his hope.

As she scribbled her cell number on a cocktail napkin, Candie had agreed to stall the crew for as long as possible while he searched. And groveled. And begged her to listen to the truth. In the meantime, Candie had assured him she'd be in a meeting with Fred and Arnie.

After parking illegally in a campus lot near the library, Garret jumped out of his car and hit the ground running. Shadows were long and dark in the light of the setting sun, but even so, he could see well enough to spot Jayde sitting on the ground, her back to him as she leaned against the Dumpster. Beside her lay a bag of cans she'd collected for Soda Pop.

Slowing to a walk, Garret ran a palm behind his neck and gave his head a tiny shake. How like Jayde to revert to the distraction of good deeds, even in anger. He stopped and wondered at the best way to approach this mess. There was no way she'd ever simply believe that he had well meaning intentions. Not now. Not after all of the incriminating evidence she'd heard against him. He had to make her understand the truth.

But how?

He flexed his fists and with his thumb, popped the knuckles of his fingers. Jayde was a person who believed that actions spoke louder than words. So, that being the case, Garret had to come to the conclusion that his only course of action was…action.

Surprise was on his side as he padded up behind her, gripped her by the arms and then hauled her to her feet and up against his chest. Feet flailing, fists swinging, she emitted guttural grunts of terror and inflicted some seriously painful damage as he swung her away from the Dumpster.

"Jayde! Stop it! It's me, Garret."

She froze.

But only for a second. The sound of his voice seemed only to infuriate her into a redoubled effort to render him unconscious.

"Jayde! Would you please stop...ouch, *hitting* me? Criminy, woman, that *hurts!* Listen to me. I need to explain."

"Oh, no you don't," Jayde grunted, "I *heard* everything I need to know and more."

*"Sshhhsssssssssss."* Her elbow found his breadbasket and left him sucking wind. "Stop," he rasped and struggled to maintain his hold on her by lunging for her waist. "Just hear me out! I need you to come somewhere with me. I have something to show you."

"No! Never. You're a big, fat liar! And a womanizer and a—" face crimson and spitting like a cobra, she twisted around in the circle of his arms and faced him, "—gold digger! All you care about is—"

Garret sighed in the face of her rampage.

"Okay—" he muttered as she dove into a litany of his inadequacies, "—you can tell me all about it on the way there because this is a waste of perfectly good daylight." Bending low he positioned his shoulder into her waist and stood. Ignoring her outrage Garret carried her—bob-bob-bobbing along like a shrieking sack of spuds—to his car.

As he wound through the unfamiliar neighborhood, Jayde sat with her mouth tightly shut, refusing to respond to Garret as he explained his side of the story. Lies. All lies. A silver-tongued orator. That's what he was. Smooth. Practiced. No doubt he'd given this speech to all of his bimbos at one time or another. Well, it wouldn't work on her, dammit. Nostrils pinched, lips pursed, fillings a-grinding, she stared out

the passenger window of Garret's car. She was immune
to liars and their packs of lies.

"—because I respect you. Are you listening to me?
In fact, I've never met anyone I respect more than you,
Jayde."

Oh, yeah. Respect. Sock it to me, sock it to me, she
urged the old tune to drown him out in her head, sock
it to me, sock it to me…

"—and beautiful to boot. How could a regular guy
like me get so lucky?"

Jayde exhaled a sharp snort through her nose.

"But even though I'm physically attracted to you
like I've never been to any other woman I've ever
met—"

Sure. Mmm-hmm. Right.

"—my feelings for you have nothing to do with the
way you look." He glanced at her. "Which, yes, surprised me, too. But, Jayde, it's everything about you
that attracts the hell out of me. Your ability to stick to
your guns. To do what's right in the face of adversity.
To hold true to your belief in what is good and right
and true, no matter what anybody else thinks. Hardly
anyone does that anymore, Jayde."

Breathing shallow, Jayde found herself listening in
spite of her vows to tune him out.

"I admire the hell out of you. Everyone does. You
are an inspiration. And, in spite of what you may think
you know, you have had a profound effect on my life."

Garret rounded the corner from where they'd been
wending their way through an established neighborhood, and onto a street of half-built houses. Jayde

frowned. What was this? He pulled into the driveway of the last house on the street, and cut the engine. It was a smallish ranch-style, simple, yet attractive in its design.

A push of a button sent his seat belt zinging over his chest and into its holder. "C'mon. I have something I want to show you. And, if you don't like what you see, I'll accept defeat. I'll understand. I'll tell Brianna and Amber that it was all my fault. I'll tell Candie and everyone, but first, just come with me."

"Why?"

"Because I thought you might like to see what I've really been doing with my days since I've seen you last."

Jayde blinked in confusion as Garret got out of the car and came around to help her. As he led her up the front porch stairs, he fumbled with his key ring and finally opened the door.

"What is this?"

"This house is a project we've been building for Habitat for Humanity."

Immediately, Jayde forgot her fury and tears of disbelief burned at the back of her eyes. "It is?"

"Mmm-hmm. I read about this organization in a fascinating article for the *Sunday Oregonian,* 'bout a month ago."

"I wrote that article!"

"No kidding?" Garret's grin was knowing. "I called 'em up and told 'em I was between jobs, had a few spare weeks and knew a thing or two about building."

He swept the room with his arm. "The rest, as they say, is history."

"You...have...been *working* for...*Habitat for Humanity?*" Jayde could barely digest what Garret was saying to her. "But what about the million dollars? What about all the women? What about the deals you made with Fred and Arnie? When did you have time to do all this?"

A loud groan of exasperation seemed to literally explode from Garret's lungs. "*What* women, Jayde? Criminy damn, woman, I built a house in the past four weeks with a crew of senior citizens and college kids!" He waved his arms. "When the *hell* would I have time to date? And then spend hours talking on the phone with you? And eat? And sleep? And go to church?"

"Church?"

"Yeah. What's so strange about that?"

"Nothing, it's just that—"

"And *what* deals with Fred and Arnie? If you're talking money, it's true that they tossed around the idea of throwing some money at me, yeah, and I pledged whatever they actually fork over to Habitat for Humanity. If you don't believe me, ask Soda Pop. He's one of the guys I recruited for my crew. Turns out, he knows a thing or two about wiring. He's applied for one of these places with some members of his family and if things turn out the way we all hope, you and I are standing in their new living room."

Jayde could only gape in wonder. "So, you really have kept your promise."

"Yes. And not just for you. Dump me now if you

must, but the past month has been the most satisfying of my life. I'll continue to build houses for these guys in my time off. And I'll spend even more time, pining away for you. It will take me a long time—years—to get over you, Jayde Springer. And maybe I never will. Maybe I'll have to spend the rest of my life, proving myself to you, to change the way you see me. But it would be worth it. Because Jayde, I've said it before and I'll say it again, a man would have to be a fool to let you go.''

Gooseflesh ran amuck and Jayde's heart began to flutter. Her cheeks went hot and her hands icy. Waves of dizzy wonder seemed to fill first her chest, then her head. She was floating. Soaring. Falling.

Falling in love.

Again.

With this new, improved, wonderful, crazy, special, fabulous man. And it was then she knew that she, too, would be crazy to let him go. She loved Garret Davis. More than ever.

He stood there, spilling his guts and growing emotional to the point that tears welled in his eyes. "I love you, dammit, Jayde. And I really want to ask you to be my wife. Here. Now. In private. Not on TV in the middle of some cheesy three-ring reality circus. Say yes.''

Jayde met his gaze from across the room, tears of joy spilling down her cheeks. "Yes." She laughed. "I will.''

Garret dragged the ends of his sleeves over his

cheeks and eyes, but did not move from the spot where he was rooted. He sniffed. "Good."

Jayde took several tentative steps in his direction. "Good."

"Good. Fine. You. Me. Get married. Now, stay over there where you are until I cool down. Because if you so much as move a muscle in the next few minutes, I'll grab you and kiss you senseless. After that, I can't be held accountable for what happens."

"Can I tell you that you're wonderful?"

"No."

"Can I tell you that I love you?"

"Jayde, you're skating on thin ice."

# *Epilogue*

*Valentine's Day*

In the months that passed since Garret proposed to Jayde, they'd become household names. *Blind Side Date* had become the smash hit that Candie Walsh had predicted and more. The ratings continued to soar through the roof as the public followed these two through their courtship and waited breathlessly for them to finally share a kiss.

But true to form, Jayde insisted on waiting, and Garret backed her in her decision.

So, the day of the wedding had arrived and millions of people everywhere tuned in to Top10TV for the big event to be held at the Old Ivy Cathedral in downtown Portland. The crowd was already standing room only and spilling out to the sidewalk. Inside, the stunning sanctuary was bathed in candlelight and adorned with fragrant red and white roses. A stringed quartet played softly as the hands on the clock approached 6:00 p.m.

Camera crews and their equipment were everywhere and at the ready. Advertisers had pitched in to provide goods and services for the wedding and cater the reception to be held in the ballroom at the Benson Hotel. Jayde had been fitted for a one-of-a-kind designer wedding dress, handmade by one of Hollywood's most favored rising stars of haute couture. Her bridesmaids, Amber, Brianna and her matron of honor, Candie Walsh, were dressed in gowns of rose-red in honor of Valentine's Day, and Garret, Vinny and Soda Pop's tuxes had deep crimson cummerbunds and a red rosebud in their lapels.

Everyone was ready for the ceremony. Even Angel Baby—who Garret had adopted and given to Jayde for an engagement present—had been trained to deliver the rings on cue.

Everyone was ready, with one exception.

Jayde.

She was standing alone in the private powder room, just off the pastor's office and staring in the mirror and shaking like an aspen leaf in the midst of an avalanche. This was it. She was getting married, which was admittedly a big step, but once the vows were taken, she would share her first kiss with Garret.

Oh, this was not good.

Panicking, she smoothed her beautiful gown with trembling hands. She had no idea what she was doing. Aside from the loving pecks she'd shared with her family, she'd never kissed a man before. And here she was, about to learn how in front of record-breaking audiences around the world. The pressure was incredible.

Garret.

She needed Garret.

Maybe, if they hurried, she could send for him. He could meet her here, in the bathroom, and show her the ropes real quick. She could get some idea of what to expect. For pity's sake, she knew nothing. What a doof. Which way should her nose go? What if she smashed her nose into his? What if it bled? Should she keep her lips pursed? Loose? Tight? Open? Shut? What would he do? What would he expect her to do back?

Jayde turned on the cold water and plunged her wrists beneath the flow. There was a light tap at the door and then Candie's voice filtered through.

"Jayde, honey, are you all right in there?"

"Yes. I…uh…Candie? I need Garret."

"Now?"

"Yes. Right now."

"But, honey, it's already after six o'clock. The wedding planner has signaled for Garret and his guys to take their places. You father is waiting in the vestibule and the girls and Angel Baby are good to go."

"Ohhh, no!" Jayde ripped the door open and stared at Candie with wild eyes.

"Honey," Candie peered into her face, "what on earth is wrong?"

"I don't know…I don't know…I don't…"

"What, Jayde, what? What is it that you don't know? Work with me here, honey. Here," Candie grabbed a manila envelope off the pastor's desk, dumped out the contents, blew into it and handed it to Jayde. "Breathe into this until you feel better. Good girl. Now. Slowly. What is it you don't know?"

"I don't know how to kiss," Jayde wailed.

"Is that all?" Candie sighed and laughed with relief. "Oh, honey, now that's as easy as falling off a log backward. You just get yourself up there. Your man will take care of the rest."

"—and so, by the powers vested in me by the state of Oregon and as an ordained minister in the service of our Lord Jesus Christ, I do now pronounce that you are husband and wife."

Flashbulbs popped.

The silent crowd inhaled a collective breath of anticipation.

Camera lenses zoomed in, and the crowd leaned ever so slightly forward.

"Garret, you may now—"

There were several loud whoops from the eager audience. Then, a swell of laughter combined with a wave of ooh's and ahh's. When it became silent again, the minister continued.

"—at long last, kiss your wife."

Time froze for Jayde as Garret stepped forward and gingerly lifted back her veil. The sweet expression on his face drove burning tears to the backs of her eyes and throat. Oh, he was such a beautiful, tender man.

Just over his shoulder, she could see that Vinny and Soda Pop were both fighting their emotions. This time, when the crowd whooped, Jayde barely heard it. All she could see was Garret.

Gingerly, he disentangled his hands from the netting and cupped her cheeks in his palms.

"I love you," he whispered.

"I love you, too."

The room fell silent.

Only the occasional sniffing of family and friends could be heard.

Very, very slowly, Garret tipped her face up and angled it to the side. His eyes grew dark and his lids fell to half-mast. His nose rested lightly against hers for just a moment and then he whispered against her lips with words, featherlight. "Don't be afraid."

"No. Never."

For how could she be afraid when he held her like this? As if the world had begun rotating backward, time slowed, then...stopped. It all happened so naturally. Garret's mouth found hers and possessed it in a way that had Jayde feeling as if she'd finally come home. His nose brushed hers as he fit their lips together and coaxed her to open up to him. The kiss immediately became deep. Sexy. Hot.

Her arms rose and circled his neck. She filled her fingers with the hair at his nape and reveled in the spectacular sensations coursing through her noodlelike limbs.

Guttural sounds emanated from each throat as they hungrily learned the secrets of each other's kiss. Their hearts pounded and their breathing was irregular. It was heavenly. Every bit the thrill Jayde had imagined it would be. And more. For she was one with Garret Davis now. They were a family. One mind. One spirit. One flesh.

Somewhere, in the recesses of her muzzy mind, Jayde could hear people screaming. Streamers falling from the ceiling and the sound of corks popping. The recessional music began to play, but Garret paid it no heed as his kissed his wife. Once. And then again.

Then, once more.

Releasing her just a bit, he tipped her head back and grinned. "Worth the wait?"

"Ohhhhh, yeah."

"Damn, woman. Me, too." He shook his head in wonder. "Wanna skip the first hour of the reception?"

"Mmm-hmm."

They shared a secret smile. And much to the delight of viewers around the world, Garret kissed his wife again.

And then, once more, just for good measure.

\* \* \* \* \*

# JUST SAY YES

## Wendy Rosnau

To the fans of my Southern books.
Ya'll know who you are.

# *Chapter 1*

The sign read, Beer with Breakfast. Home of the Buzzard Burger.

Stephanie Arnou read the sign twice while her silver Mustang idled in the dirt-packed parking lot of the Muddy Bar & Grill. She reached for the letter in the empty seat beside her and tried once again to decipher her cousin's directions. It was no wonder she'd made a wrong turn somewhere. Arley's instructions were as poor as his handwriting.

She reversed the Mustang and backtracked to Crawford, again noticing how small the Louisiana town was, and the general age of its population. When she'd stopped for gas at the Henny-Penny on the outskirts, there had been a moment when she'd considered this might be a retirement community. Then she'd gone inside to pay, and was relieved to see two young women in their twenties working a lunch counter in the back. Twins with big brown eyes, identical glasses and the same crooked smiles in reverse.

She parked in front of Crawford's police station— an aging building in need of a fresh coat of paint and a carpenter's estimate on a new porch railing. One quick look at the town's lean but clean main street and she knew she would be spending her free time in New Orleans sixty miles away. After all, she had been born and raised in a big city and was used to buying milk at 2:00 a.m. if she felt like it, and shopping for shoes on Sundays.

She exited the car, grabbing Arley's letter at the last minute. As she entered the police station she saw that the interior mirrored the outside. The walls were gray, and it wasn't the color they had been painted twenty years ago. She noticed the chipped linoleum, another shade of gray; and the metal desk stacked high with papers. The skinny file cabinet in the corner had a similar paper stack.

There was a door behind the desk, a noisy hum coming from inside. Stephanie circled the desk to read the name plate on the door. On closer inspection, she saw that the plate had been stripped from the wood frame and replaced by a single piece of white paper that read Sheriff William Walker.

She knocked on the door.

"I'm here. 'Bout done with supper, too."

She arched a delicate blond eyebrow at the unprofessional greeting, then opened the door and stepped inside the sheriff's office. She found him behind his desk relaxing in a cheap swivel chair, his jean-clad legs stretched across the desk like a paperweight holding down another stack of papers.

The man had dark brown hair, brown eyes and looked to be in his early thirties. He had bulky shoulders that went along with a wrestler's chest and sturdy legs.

"Sheriff Walker—" Stephanie raised the letter to find the paragraph that was most important in her cousin's letter— "I'm looking for the M…ondy Restaurant." She looked back to the sheriff, eyed his run-over black tennis shoes, then the gray cat perched on the corner of the desk enjoying the remains of the sheriff's high-fat evening meal—a burger, onions and cottage fries. Heavy on the grease.

In spite of her long and exhausting two-day trip, Stephanie smiled. From the looks of the leftovers, Crawford could use some of her heart-smart recipes.

She'd been the manager and top chef at Cafe Lean in Minneapolis for three years. Last year she'd received the lean and tasty award—an honorary gold star and an engraved plaque for being the most cognizant chef in the Twin Cities—an award her employer had insisted on displaying in the restaurant lobby under glass. Which is where it had been until three days ago.

"Did you say Mondy?"

"That's how I read it." Stephanie offered the sheriff her cousin's letter.

He pulled his feet off his desk to reach for the letter, sending a dozen papers off the pile to the floor. Ignoring them, he scanned the letter.

Stephanie noticed his cheeks slowly turn an ashy puke color. "What is it? Am I lost? Do I have the wrong Crawford, Louisiana?'' She pointed to the letter. ''As you can see, my cousin writes like an eight-year-old, and spells like he didn't make it out of the fourth grade. He never put a return address on the envelope, either, so I'm not sure if he lives in town.''

''You say this letter was sent to you? That you're my...Arley's cousin?''

''Yes.''

''Then you'd be Melvin's...''

''Daughter. Stephanie Arnou. My friends call me Stevie. Did you know my uncle Clarence?''

''Clarence? Oh, you mean Buzzard. Sure thing. Everybody in Crawford knowd Buz.''

''And Arley? Do you know if he lives around here?''

''Brown house south of town about a mile.''

Stevie laid her hand on her chest and sighed. ''Thank God I'm in the right town. I was beginning to wonder if Arley had spelled that wrong, too. I won't go into what an awful time I've had this past month, or how much I'm looking forward to a fresh start. Believe me, February can't come close to being the nightmare January was. You just don't want to know.'' She glanced at the narrow floor fan doing the shimmy in the corner. ''Is this heat normal? I expected low seventies this time of year. It must be eighty outside. Not that I'm complaining. I left the Twin Cities in a snow storm and single-digit temps.''

''Gets warm some days. Nowhere near what we're used to come July and August, though. Back to this here letter. It's addressed to Stephan.''

''Stephan, Stephanie...'' Stevie shrugged. ''Considering all the other misspelled words in there, I'm not surprised he left out a few letters in my name.''

The sheriff mumbled something, then dropped the paper on his desk. "He's gonna skin me."

"What? Are you talking about Arley?"

"No. Justus. And he's good with a knife, too. Nobody can skin croakers faster that I know of."

Stevie had no idea what the sheriff was talking about. "Who's Justus?"

"Your business partner, Stephan…ie. He's over at the Mud… Mondy."

The man's complexion had gone from puke to paste. It was that hamburger he'd eaten. It had started to congeal. And no wonder. Whoever had fried that grease bomb should have known it would explode the minute it hit bottom.

She glanced at the sheriff's soft belly. His cholesterol was probably off the charts and through the roof.

"I'm anxious to see the Mondy, but if you could direct me to my uncle's house, that would be even better. I'd like to unpack and take a shower. I've been driving all day."

The unpacking wouldn't take long, Stevie mused. An electrical fire had swept through her apartment building a week ago. She'd lost nearly everything she owned. Her cousin's letter two days earlier had been a gift from God—though at the time she hadn't realized that inheriting her uncle's home and half of his business would come to be such a blessing.

Everything happens for a reason. Stevie had heard that expression, though she'd never understood it. She had been twenty-one when her parents died, and she had often contemplated what possible reason God could have had for allowing a tragic accident to take them from her. An only child, there had been no siblings or close family to lean on. She'd been left alone with her memories, and the Arnou instinct for survival.

"In the letter, Arley says Uncle Clarence has lakeshore property. For the record, I know how valuable lake frontage can be, but that's not why I'm here. It's not the land, but the house that interests me. I've always wanted a place of my own. A real house with a full-size refrigerator and stove, and a bathroom with a tub, and a shower."

The sheriff came to his feet mumbling something Stevie couldn't make out. He stepped away from the desk and gave her a thorough up and down, followed by a low whistle that could have been taken as a compliment if it hadn't been for the loud belch that climbed his esophagus a second later.

It was rude of him to stare. The belch, worse, without begging pardon. Stevie would have mentioned both, but she was a midwesterner who knew protocol, as well as a few rules that had saved her butt more than once in the big city. One of those rules was never present attitude when asking a stranger for a favor. Or bring attention to his shortcomings. Truthfully, the belch was tacky. But she'd forgive him this once because he really did look like he was suffering from indigestion.

"You gotta pickup I s'pose?"

"I have a car. It's right outside."

"You wanta get back in yer car and go on out to the fork. When you—"

"The fork?"

"The stop sign a block back. Take a right and head out of town 'bout a half mile. Then take a left. The Mudd... Mondy is another half mile, and then some, down Turtle Road. Caint miss it. It's the only waterin' hole... I mean, building out there with a string a cars out front."

"Business is good, then?"

"Real good. Busiest grill...ah, restaurant in town."

"That sounds wonderful."

"Don't it though. Buzzard's floater— Ah...Uncle Clarence's place is on the same road. Can't miss that, neither, on account they both are on the same swam...lake."

"My house and restaurant share the lake? That's fabulous."

"Ain't it though."

"You bet."

"No, I don't gamble much. Play a little bingo, though."

Stevie frowned, wondering how they had gotten on that subject.

He walked past her and swung the door open. "You take off and I'll give Justus a call and warn... I'll call him and tell him you're on your way."

The minute Stephanie left the police station, Arley grabbed the phone and dialed the Muddy. When he heard the busy buzzer, he swore, then slammed the receiver down. Fayda Mae must still be scrapping with Hawg. Those two had started that feud two days ago, and it didn't look like Hawg was making much headway at getting back in his wife's good graces.

Fayda Mae had a cannonball temper, and held a grudge longer than a skunk's stink. Thirty years on the same dog leash, Hawg should have known that. Should have known, too, that when he gave Henrietta that fool wink over at the Henny-Penny, the whole town was gonna pay the price.

Arley glanced down at the letter on Justus's desk. His cousin Stevie had said he wrote like an eight-year-old and spelled like he hadn't made it out of the fourth grade. But that wasn't so. He'd made it all the way through high school. Damn hard thing to do, it was, but he'd gotten his diploma right alongside William Justus Walker and Elroy Fachon.

He'd wanted to quit plenty of times, but Justus wouldn't let him. No, siree, the orphan from Bogalusa never believed in quitting at anything. The townsfolk had all known Justus was special the day Mamma Dula brought him home. He was smart as a whip, and friendly as a puppy.

Arley picked up the letter and examined it for errors. How Stevie had gotten Mondy out of Muddy, he didn't know. He squinted at each of the letters and decided he'd spelled Muddy just fine. Maybe not her name, but then that was old Buzzard's fault. The chicken scratch on his uncle's will had been about as clear as Turtle Bayou after sunset when the mosquitoes came out to feed.

*My friends call me Stevie.*

They should have nicknamed her Steamin' Hot. Arley had no idea they grew 'em that curvy in Minnesota. Must be all that cold weather up there. A natural fat burner.

"A blonde with lips," Arley muttered. "No, not just lips. A pair of heart-shaped yumbuggers that would taste sweeter than Fayda Mae's seven-minute frosting."

Arley's cheeks turned red. Shame on him for thinking that way. Stevie was his cousin.

He tried to call the Muddy again, then gave up. He wasn't going out there. No, siree. Not until Justus got a good look at his *partner,* and she got a good look at the Muddy and Buzzard's floater.

Stevie sounded like she had her heart set on indoor plumbing. A picture of Buz's *House of Plenty,* as it had been named, formed in Arley's mind. The outhouse sat back in the woods between a stand of Mayhaw trees. It was a pretty spot. Real quiet. A thinking man's place.

Maybe he ought to go out there and take down that *Playboy* calendar him and Justus had given Buz last Christmas. Maybe he ought to take home the old ones stacked between the two-seater, too. He was partial to last year's August issue anyways. Jinx had mentioned the '93 November issue was his favorite. Maybe he'd pass a few out to some of the boys.

Arley winced thinking about how often this week he'd screwed up. Only none of them had been as bad as this.

What would Justus have to say about his partner being a steamin' hot female with seven-minute lips? Probably nothing. Justus never talked a lot when he got mad. He'd just skin his best friend without saying a word. Then dig up old Buzzard and skin him, too.

# Chapter 2

The jukebox hadn't taken a rest all day, and neither had Justus. He would never admit he missed Buzzard Arnou—certainly not his onion breath—but he did miss the old bird's talent in the kitchen.

Since they had buried Buz a week ago, the Muddy had been operating on a cylinder and a half—Justus and Fayda Mae. He'd closed the Bar & Grill for the funeral in honor of his partner's sudden exit. It had been the first time in its history that the Muddy had closed its doors in the middle of the day.

At age fifty-eight, Buzzard hadn't been old enough to croak, but as Mamma Dula had recited graveside, Buz had been invited to cook for the King, and the fastest way to get there had been by car.

Justus had been relieved when Mamma had skipped over the details. It had taken him and Arley half a day to get Buzzard's Mercury out of Turtle Bayou—he'd really sent her to the bottom when he'd sailed over Cottonwood Bridge.

Fayda Mae let out a yell from the kitchen, and Justus knew what that meant—another Buzzard burger had just gone up in smoke. Her two-day feud with Hawg was getting expensive. Not to mention the fallout effect it was having on his customers—she'd burned up more orders in the past two days than Buz had burned up in the Muddy's thirty-year history. But that wasn't the worst of it. She was serving the burnt offerings—daring the customers, and him, to complain.

No one had. Everyone in Crawford would agree Fayda Mae had a short fuse and a long memory. He was still on the outs with her since he'd suggested she might be putting too much shrimp in the gumbo and not enough crispy in Nate Gruber's bacon.

"Burger's comin' right up, Jinx." Justus stepped behind the bar and slid LaMarr Jenkin's a cold brewski.

"You tink dat nephew of Buzzard's is gonna come claim his half of the Muddy?"

Justus sure as hell hoped so. Fayda Mae was a waitress, not a cook. He could put up orders, but if he was in the kitchen, no one would be behind the bar. And to make matters worse, a month ago he'd been appointed sheriff of Crawford. Today he'd had to have Arley Arnou hang around the station house just in case something happened in Crawford that required his attention.

"You ain't gonna close down the Muddy are ya, Just? Hawg's been spreadin' that rumor."

"No, I'm not closing."

Jinx let go of a heartfelt sigh along with a loud belch. "That's a relief. I'd starve if'n that happened. You know I can't cook. That's why no matter what that burger looks like when it comes out dat kitchen door, I'm gonta eat it. The Muddy's been feedin' me three squares a day for thirty years, 'cept on Thursdays."

Everyone in town knew that on Thursdays Jinx drove over to Belle Chasse to visit Onella Simons. They all knew why, too.

"So how you gonna split yourself between here and your other doins as sheriff, Just? Best thing is for dat nephew of Buzzard's ta get off his honky and come down here and lend a hand. Where did Arley say he sent that letter?"

"Minnesota," came a gravel-crusted voice from a high-sided booth on the right side of the dining room.

"Is that above Nebraski, or Coloradi?" LaMarr asked.

"Iowa," Nate Gruber offered, still keeping himself hidden inside the booth.

Justus headed into the kitchen to check on Jinx's burger, and to remind Fayda Mae—as gently as possible—that Jinx liked his burger open-face, with a mess of cheese grits over the top. Grits on a Buzzard burger, and bacon grease, still warm from Nate's double decker BLT, drizzled over the top.

The order didn't look quite like it should when Fayda Mae handed him the plate. The burger was under the grits somewhere, Justus had faith, but it was anyone's guess what kind of shape it was in. The black specks mixed in with the grits were a mystery, but Jinx didn't mention them when Justus slapped the plate down in front of Crawford's seventy-six-year-old barber, so neither did he.

When the screen door squeaked, Justus didn't need to look up to know that Mamma Dula was on her way in. It was five-thirty, and the two things you could count on in Crawford were the turtle population and Mamma's routine.

He reached for the glass of iced tea he'd just made for her a minute ago, then cut across the dining room to meet up with the woman who had raised him.

The tea glass was on *her* table next to the window before she got comfortable in *her* chair. For his efforts, Mamma smiled, then turned her soul-searching eyes on him to take inventory. Her look told Justus she was still debating the issue she had been debating since he'd moved back to Crawford a year ago—whether or not he was going to stick, as the townsfolk called it.

The general consensus was, if you were lucky enough to leave Crawford, you were usually smart enough not to come back.

"Evenin', you handsome blue-jean devil, you," Mamma drawled. "The sight of you sure makes a woman wish she was twenty years younger and forty pounds lighter. How you've kept single all these years is beyond me."

Justus gave Mamma his famous wink, the one he used on Saturday nights to get the Folly twins up on the bar to entertain the crowd for free. "You know you're the only woman who has my heart, Mamma," he teased.

"You tell it good, just like you should." Dula sang the words, then took a sip of her iced tea. When the glass was back on the table, Mamma said, "I heard Sue Ann left you."

Jinx's granddaughter hadn't exactly left him. They weren't married. Not even living together. Sue Ann had come to Crawford on a visit last summer and had ended up staying through Christmas.

"She never intended to stick," Justus reminded. "She's back in New Orleans were she belongs."

Mamma snorted. "Does that mean this is gonna be one of those long-distance affairs, or do you plan on packing your bags one of these days for good?"

Mamma must have heard the rumor, Justus decided. "Sue Ann did ask me to move in with her." He reached for a chair, turned it around and straddled it. "But you and me made a deal, remember? I plan on keeping my end of it. I've come home, just like I said I would. Guess you could say you, and the good folks of Crawford, are stuck with me."

Mamma had rescued Justus from the orphanage in Bogalusa when he was nine. She'd raised him and sent him to college after high school on one condition—that he return to Crawford an educated man worth something by the age of thirty.

Justus had studied hard, gotten his law degree and returned a little over a year ago at age twenty-nine.

"I was hoping that Sue Ann would like it here. A prize stud needs a flashy filly," Mamma said. "That's what my daddy used to say. We don't have too many fillies in town under the age of forty. Jinx said you was laughing and having a good time with those Folly twins the other night. Maybe you ought to see if one of them can fill the bill."

"Now that Buz is gone I've got my hands tied being sheriff and keeping this place open," Justus offered. "The twins are entertaining, but you know it ain't no fun playin' with your hands tied if you're too tired to fight the ropes."

His comment, followed by a wide grin, had Mamma shaking her head. "When you was a squirt, I shoulda used barkeepers on that smart mouth of yours ta keep yer thoughts clean. But I didn't. Spoiled you stink rotten, I did."

Justus chuckled.

"It's probably just as well you leave them twins alone. Everybody knows those girls ain't gonna marry unless they can marry the same man. I don't think those two have ever done one thing without the other. Now don't you say it, 'cause I can see in those devil-blue eyes of yours what you're thinkin'."

Justus tipped his head back and hooted.

Dula made a half-hearted swipe at his head, then changed the subject. "I hear Buzzard's nephew might be coming ta Crawford."

"Buzzard didn't put Justus in his will." Jinx spun on his bar stool, a piece of Buzzard burger—resembling a charcoal briquette—pierced on the end of his knife. "Buz gave all he owned to some kin he never met before. That nephew."

"He what?" Mamma's eyes bugged.

"Some doo-dah big city duffer." This time Nate's hand shot out of the booth, the middle finger on his bony hand extended to let everyone know how he felt about Buzzard's betrayal.

"Buz promised me that he'd…"

"Promised you what, Mamma?" Justus asked.

"Nothing."

"What did he promise?" Justus reached out and took Mamma's plump hand in his.

Dula made a face, like she was trying to decide what to spill and what to keep to herself. Finally, she said, "He promised he would see to it that you stayed in Crawford. What I thought he meant by that was he was going ta sign over his half of the Muddy to you before he…"

"Before he what? Died? How would he have known when that would be?"

Mamma pulled her hand free and tugged on the edges of her orange and pink turban. "I musta heard him wrong. Some days I swear I'm losin' my ears."

Justus studied Mamma's face as she reached for her tea while trying to avoid his eyes. She was hiding something. But what? He said, "I'm here because I want to be. I told you when I came back, I was here to stay. The Muddy isn't what's holding me here," he clarified. "And I agree with Jinx. I can't run this place and be a good sheriff, too. I was thinking that I'd offer to sell my half of the Muddy to Buz's kin when he gets here. What do you think?"

Before Mamma could comment, Nate Gruber's middle finger left the booth once more. No words followed. He'd clearly given his opinion on Justus's sell out.

Dula plunked her tea glass down on the table, this time having no trouble looking Justus square in the eye. "You can't walk away from the Muddy. Crawford needs this place."

"They'll still have it."

"This city duffer is a stranger. We don't know nothing about his character. Putting the Muddy in a stranger's hands is reckless. You've never been reckless your entire life, Justus. No, that's a bad idea."

"I second that," Jinx muttered, working his false-teeth hard to get his burger off the end of his knife.

"That makes it three to one, Just," Nate yelled from the booth. He knew protocol. He was president of the bingo club that met on Tuesdays on the Muddy's back porch—that is, unless it was windy.

Mamma grinned, then patted Justus's arm. "Now that that's settled, am I gonta get my usual Tuesday night special, or is Fayda Mae on strike? I hear she and Hawg are still shouting their words."

Justus stood, spun the chair around and slid it back. "Fried cheese grits and blackened catfish." He leaned forward and kissed Mamma's smooth brown cheek. "Coming up."

"You know I don't like my catfish blackened," Dula reminded, spearing a handful of Justus's white T-shirt tucked into his low-riding jeans. "Beer-battered, lightly golden. Double tarter."

Nate Gruber let go of a loud snort from inside his booth. "That's a tall order for today, Dula. Shoulda gone down to the Coffee Cup if'n you wanted something you could recognize 'cause everythin's blackened on the Muddy's menu today. Even my crispy bacon."

It was after six, and the number of vehicles in the Muddy's lot had doubled within an hour. Stevie parked her Mustang in the third row. There was nothing else she could do but go inside and ask for directions.

She couldn't believe she'd missed the turn again, but that was the only explanation she had for ending up back at the Muddy Bar & Grill.

While she sat in the car, going over the sheriff's directions in her mind another time, five more pickups pulled into the lot. By the looks of it, the entire town had plans to eat cheap and dirty tonight. Hoping that wasn't the case every night, she climbed out of the car and picked her way between the pickups to reach the screened-in porch, where a number of customers were seated around picnic tables enjoying the warm evening air. Or maybe they were trying to get away from the loud music. Stevie could feel the pounding beat of Zydeco coming up through the weathered steps beneath her feet as she made her way to the front door.

Inside the Muddy, the vibrating music was bouncing off the walls. The ventilation system must be broken, she decided. The windows were open and still the smoke was hanging in layers. Either something in the kitchen was on fire, or the bug zapper arcing in the corner frying mosquitos was doing double time.

No, it wouldn't be hard to steal this crowd away from the owner of this dump once she settled into the Mondy. A little soft music and a wine list, and this crowd would be making reservations a week in advance.

For all the noise and good time being had by all, Stevie managed to turn heads. She smiled pleasantly at one and all—potential customers for the Mondy—then started toward the bar, aware she was a little over-dressed in her electric-green shift and white sandals.

"Hey, sweethin', you can sit on my lap!" a grinning

fool in a muscle shirt and jeans called out from a table in the middle of the room. He was wearing his hat backward and straddling a chair as he played cards with three other men who had similar tastes in hat fashion and, no doubt, shopped at the same thrift store.

Another man, this one older—a silver fox three times her age peered around a high booth and answered the fool with, "She's mine, Elroy. I sawd her first. And you know the rules. Age before beauty as long as she's willin'. Name's Nate, Missy, and there's plenty of room in my booth."

Stevie slipped onto a stool at the end of the bar. She kept her eyes averted from the other men seated next to her on the line—all over the age of fifty.

"Call it, and it's yours."

Stevie looked up, confronted by a pair of scoundrel-blue eyes. *Call it, and it's yours?*

Don't expect something for nothing, that was one of the golden rules she'd grown up with in the big city. "I'll have a cosmopolitan, heavy on the cranberry juice, please."

The bartender winked, then offered Stevie a beamer of a smile that parted his lips wide enough to guarantee that he had all his teeth. There must be a dentist in town. That was positive, Stevie thought.

Like the good ol' boy at the card table, Stevie noticed the bartender also had a broad set of shoulders, nice biceps, and when he turned to retrieve a glass off the shelf behind him, a great ass. The all-in-one package immediately brought back a solid memory of her ex-boyfriend, Tony. He was a body builder. A brawny beefcake who had decided to go professional after winning the midwestern Big & Beautiful title. Six weeks ago Tony had moved to California without a lengthy goodbye or an invitation to go with him. They had dated for over a year.

The bartender turned up the wattage on the beamer, and with it came Connie's warning just before Stevie had left Minnesota. "Remember, girlfriend, the way to tell if a man in the south is an oversexed animal is his beamer. I roomed in college with a girl who was born in Mississippi. She said that if you smile back at a beamer, he takes it to mean she's agreeable." "Agreeable to what?" Stevie had asked Connie. "Agreeable to whatever. Oh, and she said the hunky, good-looking beamers are the worst. They're the ones who prey on whoever, willing to do whatever, whenever."

Stevie locked her jaw in the midst of a return smile and looked down the line of men seated at the bar, noticing that they had all shifted their butts like dominoes and were now drinking their beers—all the same kind—left-handed, while they stared a hole through her.

To the bartender, she said, "I'll take a beer, if you don't know how to make a cosmo."

The bartender pulled a bottle of vodka from under the counter and, still flashing his glow-in-the-dark smile, said, "One Bullfrog coming up."

"They're not the same." Stevie's mouth was moving into a polite smile to soften her contradiction, when she freeze-framed it. *Whoever. Whenever.* "No way."

"Pardon?"

She hadn't realized she'd spoken out loud. "I said, I don't think a Bullfrog has cranberry juice in it."

"You sure, honey?"

"Pretty sure."

"Is that pretty sure leaning left or right?"

"I'm sure," Stevie answered, refusing to back down.

"And will you have a twist of lemon with a cherry, or without?"

"No cherry."

A cosmo wasn't served with a cherry. The bartender's unwavering grin told Stevie he knew that. He knew that and a lot more.

He wore jeans and a T-shirt, like his customers, and talked with a thick syrupy drawl. But there was something different about him. Like he'd been educated somewhere else. In the midst of her musing it registered that the room had grown quiet. Stevie glanced around the smokey bar, spied the jukebox, and decided that someone must have turned it down.

Okay, so a few more people were going to hear her ask Mr. Beamer for directions. At least she wouldn't have to shout over the top of the music when she asked where the Mondy was hiding? And if he didn't know what she was talking about...if no one did?

Then Stevie would assume that after she'd turned off I-10 she'd driven through a vortex and into the *Twilight Zone*.

# Chapter 3

It was while Justus was pouring the cosmo into a glass that he realized the smoke coming from the kitchen was thicker than usual and that Fayda Mae was burning more than just another Buzzard burger.

He heard her scream, only that was nothing unusual either—she'd been back-flashing to Hawg winking at Henrietta Penny every hour on the hour for two days. But when he saw a streak of green join him behind the bar, then dart into the kitchen, Justus followed. Not as fast, of course—folks born and bred in the south didn't rush anything.

Not that he wasn't fast on his feet. Three weeks ago he'd been dozing on Mamma's front porch in her rocker with his feet propped up on the newel post just after sundown when Willy Carr had snuck by and swiped Mamma's favorite broom. Barefoot, four beers loose, he'd caught the little snot before he'd made it to the post office.

The little lady's cosmo in hand, Justus watched the cute blonde with the spitfire eyes grab the fire extinguisher off the wall and race to the stove, where a small puppy of a grease fire was making an awful stink. She took a stance, gripped the tank like a pro, then told Fayda Mae to stand back.

Her aim was true, and in a jiffy she had smothered the puppy. Applause went up behind him lickity-split, and Justus turned to see that the Tuesday night barstool, shoot-the-bull crowd had followed him and was jockeying for the best spot to watch the show in the kitchen. When he turned back, the curvy blonde had pivoted on her sandaled feet, her look-at-me green fitted dress covered with white powder retardant.

Maybe curvy wasn't the right word, Justus decided, getting a full, front-and-center view. She was fine-boned, narrow-waisted and small-featured—well, not all her features were small. She had a pair of those Angelina Jolie lips, big violet snapdragon eyes and a sizable pair of knockers that had knocked his eyes half out of his head the minute she had come through the front door.

She was either wearing one of those padded pushup affairs or she'd opted for surgery and a set of rubber playmates. Justus would never hold either against her. He liked the natural look best, but if a man was just going to look and daydream without getting his fingers in on the action, this sweetheart was every man's fantasy gal all the way.

Small-bodied women—compact perfection, Justus

called it—turned him on without a doubt. A man was a fool if he couldn't admit to plain facts that were staring him in the face. Truth being, the short-haired blonde was one of those beautiful fillies Mamma was always talking about—and this one, no doubt about it, would be the one he'd cut away from the herd first.

He sauntered toward her and traded her the fire extinguisher for the drink she'd ordered minutes ago.

"Here you go, honey. One cosmo, with a twist of lemon, plenty of cranberry juice, hold the cherry. It's on the house for saving Fayda Mae and rescuing the Muddy. You wouldn't be interested in rescuing anything else I own, would you? Say something south of my heart?"

She ignored his teasing way and his easy smile. The cosmo on its way to being half-gone, she asked, "What I would like is directions if you don't mind. Decent directions to the Mondy? I'm Clarence Arnou's niece. I was over at the police station, but the sheriff's directions were as bad as the ones in the letter I received from my cousin, Arley, a week ago."

Justus thought he had heard wrong. She'd used the words Clarence and niece in the same sentence. Buz had a nephew named Stephan. That's what Arley had told him, anyway. And he knew every restaurant in town. There were two others besides the Muddy: the Coffee Cup downtown next to the post office, and the lunch counter at the Henny-Penny gas station on the outskirts near the I-10 turnoff.

A chorus of mumbling started up behind him, and Justus turned back, gave all the ears a look, then closed the door in their faces. What he didn't need now was a confab going on while he tried to sort out who was who.

When he turned back, he said, "You spoke to the sheriff?"

"Yes. William Walker."

She hadn't talked to William Walker. He knew that to be a fact. He knew that because *he* was William Walker, and unless he'd had an out-of-body experience, he hadn't seen her before she'd stepped into the Muddy and turned his head—and every other man's head, to boot.

Arley was at the station sitting in for him like he'd been doing ever since Buzzard had cashed in and he'd been forced to spend more time at the grill.

"You said you're Buz's niece?"

"Yes. I'm Stephanie Arnou, from Minnesota. Stevie, if you like."

There was no doubt he liked her no matter what name she went by. He liked, and then some. The bouncers up front. Her pouty lips. Her sexy northern accent. Even her cute short hair, which was a switch for him.

Justus was deciding how best to explain the situation to Buz's niece, when the phone rang and Fayda Mae picked it up. A second later she was striding toward him, her mood a bit tempered, saying, "It's him. He says it's urgent."

"He used the word urgent?"

"Uh-huh. Strange word for Arley, don'tch think? You suppose he knows what it means?"

Justus shifted his attention back to Buz's niece, and as he spoke into the receiver, he decided a more in-depth inventory of Stevie Arnou wouldn't hurt. Perfection to this degree was rare. There had to be something he wasn't seeing. A flaw of some kind that he'd disregarded in the confusion. A crooked tooth, or a double-wammy wart. A furry mole tucked under her chin. Or maybe she was knock-kneed. Justus angled his head and sent his eyes south. No, her knees looked perfect just like everything else.

He kept looking. Something would eventually crop up. It better, or the stiffy in his jeans was going to hemorrhage soon.

"Hello, Arley. You got something urgent on your mind?"

"You have anythin' ta drink tonight, Just?"

"No."

"Not even a beer? Maybe two ta slow down your reflexes?"

"Not a drop, Arley."

"Been busy, then?"

"*Oui.* Busy. What's on your mind, Arley? Or do I already know why you were hoping I was half-snauckered?"

"Ain't she's perty, Just?"

Justus was still looking for that flaw that hadn't cropped up yet. She was one flashy filly, all right. Only flashy fillies didn't stick in Crawford.

"Guess you being quiet means she's in earshot, ya?"

"She is."

"Did you get a whiff of her, yet? Gaalee… And what about those lips? I ain't never seen yumbuggers like them ones. Anywho, I think the mistake in this,

Just, was made on Buzzard's end. You know he wrote his own will, and it was damn hard ta 'cipher.''

"I'd have to take your word on that, Arley. I never saw it on account you said you'd handle it, remember?"

"I did say that. Yes, I did. You had your hands full with the funeral doin's, and I wanted ta help, too. After all, Buzzard was my uncle, too. Not just Stevie's. But his chicken scratch is about as poor as..."

"Yours?"

"Now don't go saying something mean you're gonna hafta apologize for later, Just. It was a honest mistake."

"I don't think she's going to agree, Arley. She says she stopped by the station and talked to Sheriff Walker." Justus turned his back on Stevie. "She's looking for a place called the Mondy, but then I figure you already know that."

"She read my letter wrong. And I can explain about her thinking I was you when she walked into your office. I was having my supper at your desk when she showed up."

Justus turned back the minute he heard water running. Stevie was at the sink trying to wash the retardant off the front of her dress. He said to Arley, "You sent her here so I would have to break the news to her."

"You're better at soothing feathers than me, Just. You're the one with the law degree. Ah...there's one more thing. I think she's expecting a little nicer house than Buzzard's floater. She mentioned a full-size somethin' or other on lakeshore property. I reckon I coulda called the cabin *property*, but I knows I never used the word lakeshore in the same sentence. How long do you think it would take us ta fix up the floater?''

"She's not going to be here long enough to worry about it, Arley."

"S'pose not. She mentioned something about a bathroom. That would take running water, right?''

"That it would, Arley."

"Thought so. I don't s'pose the rain barrel would—''

"No, it wouldn't. You should have told her you were her cousin, Arley."

Justus eyed Stevie's trendy white sandals, then her silver ankle bracelet sporting a mini red heart. His gaze followed the length of her slender legs, enjoying every inch. He shifted his stance, trying to get air moving between his legs to keep the noose from tightening into a choke hold. In the middle of Arley's weak explanation, she turned and the water from her efforts of washing the retardant away had plastered her dress to her million-dollar assets.

Justus, still looking for flaws and having no luck, felt the noose tighten, and he hung up on Arley.

"Did I hear my cousin's name?"

Justus set the phone on the counter. "That was Arley on the phone."

"I'm anxious to meet him. We've never met. I've never even seen pictures of my father's family."

"You know anythin' about the restaurant business?"

"As a matter a fact, I do. I've been a chef for three years in Minneapolis."

"Nice place?"

"Five star."

"Why did I already know that?"

"Excuse me?"

"Nothin'."

Justus wanted to blame Arley for the sour situation, but he knew it was his fault, not his friend's. He should have attended to Buzzard's will himself. After all, he was a lawyer. More to the point, Arley's track record in the mistake department had a history. He was no longer on the Baptist Church board of directors after mixing up his numbers on their supply slip. Arley had purchased enough toilet paper to outfit the entire town for the next ten years.

He said, "I'll get you another cosmo, then we'll take this conversation outside. You hungry? Want somethin' to eat?"

She glanced around the kitchen, wrinkled up her cute nose when she spied the six dead Buzzards laid out on the grill. Shaking her head, she answered, "Just the cosmopolitan, thanks. No cherry."

Justus made the cosmo stiffer than a steel pecker and poured it into a sixteen-ounce water glass. Before he corked the vodka, he took a healthy swig from the bottle, then returned to the kitchen with Stevie's drink, minus the cherry.

He told Fayda Mae to get Nate behind the bar. The seventy-year-old logger had never been behind a bar in his life, but if you could believe his tall tales, he'd spent plenty of hours on a stool in front of one in his wilder days.

Justus ushered Stevie out the back door and headed for the biggest oak tree in the backyard. Encouraging her to use it as a back rest—she was going to need the support—he said, "So, you're from Minnesota."

"You bet. Minneapolis, all my life."

While she took a sip of the cosmo, Justus pivoted on one boot heel and motioned to the Muddy, then to the dirt road that led to her lakeshore property. "This is it, Stevie. This is the Mondy."

"What?" She wrinkled up her nose again. "You're joking, right?"

"Afraid not." Justus started over, pointing once more to the two-story building with weathered clapboard siding. The Muddy had needed a paint job for over ten years. "This is what you own half of. The Muddy is the…Mondy. Arley's not too good with putting words or numbers down on paper."

She stared at the Muddy. "But…but this can't be it. In the letter it sounded so nice. This…this place is a dump."

"Dump?" Justus took offense. "The Muddy's no dump."

"Trust me," she sniffed, "it's a dump where I come from."

"Trust me. Here, it's called a lucrative investment. Money in the bank."

"I can't believe it…hell has followed January. The devil's followed me through four states and into February."

She looked at him with a pathetic ray of hope. Like maybe he was going to slap his knee and tell her he was pulling her leg after all. He wouldn't mind getting his hands on her legs, but for other reasons entirely.

"Didn't you say earlier that the Muddy was yours?"

"Half mine. The other half is yours."

She shook her head. The small ray of hope in her eyes died, and they suddenly turned glassy. "Then you're Justus. The sheriff told me my partner's name was Justus."

"*Oui.* I'm your partner."

She gripped her stomach. Laughed. The sound was as offensive as her use of the word dump. Justus jammed his hands into his back pockets and lost his smile. He never lost his smile, not even when he got mad.

She took a sip of the cosmo. "This can't be happening." She laughed, again, then took another sip. "It's the third of February."

"Which means?"

She looked at him like he was an idiot. "February is fix-a-heart month."

"Heart month?"

"That's what my dad used to call it. Valentine's Day. It's my favorite holiday."

"Every holiday is a favorite here at the Muddy," Justus offered, remembering how busy it was last year. Buzzard had made the burgers extra big and in the shape of hearts. They had hung out of the buns like they had grown wings.

Her gaze shifted to the Muddy. She looked like she was going to cry, but instead she raised the glass and up-ended it.

Holly hell! "No…" Justus lunged forward to stop Stevie from emptying her drink like a good ol' boy would a beer on a scorching hot day, but he was too late. The Bullfrog was a goner, and Stevie Arnou would be, too, in a matter of minutes—the vodka was eighty proof, the cranberry juice mostly red food coloring.

If he intended to get all the facts out, he'd better get to it before she passed out. "There's more," he said. "Before you need to lie down, let me finish."

"I'm not going to need to lie down. Cosmos are my drink. I assure you I can handle cranberry juice with a stiff shot of vodka in it."

She had the ingredients right, but she was way off on the ratio.

"You don't have to accept Buzzard's gift, you know. You can always sell your half to me and go back to Minnesota," Justus suggested.

"I can't go back." She closed her eyes. "At least I've got the house."

Justus realized too late he should have agreed with her.

She blinked open her eyes, read his thoughts, and asked, "What's wrong with the house?"

Nothing, by Justus's standards. But he was sure Stevie wouldn't see it that way. Arley mentioned she was expecting indoor plumbing.

"I think you should sit down."

"Oh, God…not the house, too. Lying bastards!"

She pulled back her arm and lobbed the empty glass at Justus's head. He ducked and the missile sailed over his shoulder. "What the hell was that for? I wasn't the one who wrote you that letter, or spelled Muddy wrong."

"I'm going to kill my cousin!"

"Now, hold on. Arley made a mistake, but it wasn't intentional."

She moaned and pressed her hand into her stomach. "I feel sick. Ohhhh…" She glared at him, leaned against the oak. "What did you put in my drink?"

Justus lunged for Stevie and caught her before she slid down the tree. Gripping her arms to keep her on her feet, he said, "Easy, honey. Lean on me. *Oui,* that's a good girl."

She looked up at him. "What did I drink, you slippery weasel? My stomach is on fire, and my head… Ohh… I need to lie down."

"There's a bed in the cabin," Justus said.

"My cabin?"

"*Oui.* It's yours."

"A real bed?"

"A real bed."

She sagged against him. "I can't feel my feet." Justus ran his hand along her slender waist, then over her shapely backside and lifted her into his arms. "You're going to be fine—" he assured "—after the vodka comes up."

She laid her head on his shoulder and closed her eyes. Still looking for flaws, Justus checked under her chin for the furry mole. Nothing.

He started walking down the road toward Turtle Bayou. A million stars were peeking through the tall oaks that framed the road, their branches heavy with Spanish moss. Around the bend stood the magnolia tree, and next to it the sign Buz had made welcoming one and all to Turtle Bayou.

He reached the landing and stopped. Stevie's arms

were wrapped tightly around his neck, and he glanced down at her doing one last flaw check.

Under the crescent moon, he was so mesmerized by her perfection, it didn't register she was trying to get him to put her down until she cried out, ''I'm going to be sick. Put me down. Hurry! Put me down. It's coming up!''

# Chapter 4

She stood on the deck of her uncle's cabin in the morning sunlight. To say her uncle had lived a simple life was an understatement. The one-room cabin sat on wooden poles thirty feet from shore, accessed by a wooden dock that had been built almost on top of the water.

The cabin was beyond primitive. There was no running water. No kitchen. No bathroom. There was, however, a rain barrel on a corner of the wraparound deck.

The entire scenario was something out of *Swiss Family Robinson*, Stevie decided. The only thing that didn't fit—thank God—was that the bed wasn't tied between two trees. There was an actual *real* bed in the cabin—double-wide, complete with a soft mattress and a yellow quilted bedspread. Stevie didn't know if she should laugh or cry. Her hangover warned her, however, that both acts required effort and movement, and that in either case, she would be chancing another stomach eruption.

Yes, the vodka had come up. She vaguely remembered Justus Walker holding her around the waist to keep her from going to her knees as she retched.

Stevie moved her hands slowly to her temples and rotated her fingers, hoping to ease the pounding in her head. Squinting across the marshy bayou, she focused on the sign at the end of the dock.

> WELCOME yawl ta TURTLE BAYOU
> HOME of The BIgGEST SnappeR thIs Side of
> NAWLiNS.
> We Got oUR Own JAWS. SAY HEllO ta HUSH
> PUppY.

The early morning breeze swept past Stevie's bare legs just as she finished reading the sign and she nearly jumped out of her skin. Moaning from the sudden movement, she scanned the water looking for Jaws. When nothing showed up, she sent her gaze back to the shore and located her Mustang parked beneath a carport a short ways from the dock. She didn't remember moving it, but then she didn't remember much.

She was wearing a T-shirt and panties. That was it. She didn't remember removing her dress last night. But then she didn't remember going back to her car for her luggage, either. And if she had, she wouldn't have found anything that resembled an oversized white T-shirt in her suitcase.

Stevie glanced down at the T-shirt. It looked familiar. She lowered her head. Sniffed. It smelled familiar, too. Like smoke and a hint of cologne. Men's cologne.

Just then it all came rushing back. The Bullfrog and the bad news about the Mondy. Her partner had gotten her falling-down drunk. And then... Stevie looked down at the T-shirt once more. And then what?

She closed her eyes and moaned. What had she done? No, a better question to ask was, what had he done?

She shook her head. Regretted it. No, she didn't want to know what he'd done. It was clear as day what had happened.

"Stephanie?"

Stevie blinked open her eyes to see a woman standing on the end of the dock. She was African-American, in her mid-fifties, maybe, and wore a loose shift in shades of red and orange. Her hair had been twisted into a knot on the top of her head along with a strip of red cloth.

Framed by the Spanish moss hanging from the oak trees along shore, the woman carried a paper sack in one hand and a red heart-shaped helium balloon in the other.

"Jinx said you saved the Muddy," she called out as she started forward. "He said, 'Buzzard's niece saved the Muddy, Dula.' So I'm here ta thank you, *cher*, and welcome you ta Crawford." When she reached Stevie, she added, "Jinx told me you didn't look nothing like Buz, but land sakes, he didn't mention you was a filly. Oh, my..."

Stevie felt self-conscious in the T-shirt and bare feet.

"You'll have to excuse my appearance. I'm not feeling well this morning."

"Of course you're not. That's another reason I stopped by. My name's Dula Walker and I come ta bring you a gift. Here, this is from me." She handed Stevie the paper sack. "And this—" she tied the balloon to the railing "—is from Justus. Why he insisted on a Valentine heart, I'm not sure. But he was specific about it. I found it over at the Henny-Penny. Henrietta is always good at keeping the holidays straight."

The woman let go of the string and the balloon floated upward until it caught and held, high above the cabin on the morning breeze.

Once Dula was facing her, Stevie said, "My cousin lied to me. He misrepresented the restaurant and..." She glanced back at the cabin door. "This cabin is no house. And it's not on a lake, it's in the middle of a swamp."

"This morning I looked over Buz's will and the spelling of your name was written shabby. It was clear how Arley could have made that mistake. Especially Arley." Dula motioned to the paper bag. "That's my special tummy tonic. I call it Mother's Milk. I came up with it years ago for my dearly departed. Ojoe enjoyed his whiskey, sometimes a little too much. I put together the tonic so he wouldn't have no excuse to lay in bed all day long. Course I never told him that. That first morning he took my tonic, he said, 'That concoction, Dula, is as soothing as mother's milk.' So I named my tonic Mother's Milk."

While the helium balloon danced overhead, Stevie opened the bag and pulled out a pickle jar. The tonic was the color of the scum floating to the left of the dock and as thick as mud. Just looking at it made Stevie nauseous all over again.

"I guarantee it'll turn toad scum into cream."

Stevie looked at the jar once more, then Dula. "Excuse me?"

"That means it'll cure what's ailing you, *cher.*" Dula leaned close. "He told me what he done. He came knocking on my door before sunrise lookin' guilty as sin."

*He told me what he done.*

The doomsday in that statement sent color into Stevie's cheeks. "Do you mean Justus told you about last night?"

"*Oui,* child. There are no secrets in Crawford. But don't you think for a minute I didn't give my son a piece of my mind. I taught him better than that."

*My son...* Stevie let the words settle around the situation and decided that Justus must be adopted.

"And what did he say...happened exactly?" Stevie considered her question a moment, then quickly shook her head. Was she nuts? She didn't want this strange woman detailing something that had ended up with her wearing a stranger's T-shirt and having no memory as to how she'd come to be wearing it. "No, don't answer that. I don't want to discuss this, or the weasel responsible."

Dula chuckled. "I don't think it was right, my Justus doing what he done. But he's no weasel, child. He's the pride and joy of Crawford. The best thing that ever happened to me, and this ink-spot in the road. He could be the best thing that happens to you, too, *cher*. That's, if'n you can stick.''

"Stick? What does that mean?"

Dula didn't answer. She simply patted Stevie's hand where it still gripped the railing, then turned away. As she sauntered toward shore, she hollered back, "You need anything, *cher,* more Mother's Milk, or a good ear, my house is the pink one on the corner of Main and Tickle. Only pink house in town. As I always say, I'd be tickled pink if'n you come by for a visit. Oh, almost forget. Justus brought me your dress. I washed it and hung it on the line. Be ready by noon."

The Mother's Milk had gone down hard, but the good news was, it had stayed down. Dressed in a pair of jeans and a lavender tank, Stevie parked her Mustang in front of the police station. She still had a headache, but she was thinking more clearly.

It was two in the afternoon, and she had just come from the Muddy. She'd gone looking for Justus Walker and found Fayda Mae Daniels instead—the woman she'd helped out in the kitchen last night. Fay had been friendly and sympathetic, too. She'd told Stevie she could find Justus at the police station. She'd even ransacked a drawer to locate a bottle of headache pills when she noticed Stevie massaging her temples.

When she entered the front lobby at the station, she heard voices coming from the back room, confirming that no doubt Justus was speaking to the sheriff. He was probably anticipating trouble and trying to cover his ass...the snake.

She had been practicing what she was going to say

to him. Had considered filing a formal complaint with the sheriff, too, over *what he'd done*. But she hadn't planned on doing both at the same time.

She knocked on the door and the male voices inside quieted. A moment later the door swung open and Stevie found herself staring into a pair of familiar crystal-clear blue eyes.

"Mornin', Stevie, honey."

He had the nerve to keep his smile in place, but this time Stevie had no problem keeping her expression as cold as an arctic ice cube.

"How do you feel this mornin'?"

Stevie removed her RayBans and pushed her way past him, quickly locating the sheriff in the guest chair on the opposite side of the desk.

"Stevie, honey, I asked how—"

She spun around. "I feel like pressing charges. Do you think I have a legitimate reason?" She turned back. "What do you think, Sheriff? Do you think if a woman passes out, then wakes up the next morning wearing a stranger's shirt and not much else, she has a justifiable case?"

The sheriff looked first to Justus, then back to Stevie. Then back to Justus again. "You said nothin' happened, Just. You said—"

"He's a liar." Stevie stepped close to the desk and thumped her finger on the metal surface. "Aren't you going to take down my statement?"

"Yeah, Arley. Take down her statement."

"Shucks, Just, you know I caint do that." He shifted his torso forward, his hands resting on his knees. "B'sides, I was fixin' ta take Nate fishin' right about now. Listen, Stevie, if Justus said he didn't do nothing, then I bleeve him. He's my best friend and he's the squarest deal in town.''

Stevie scowled, looked from one to the other. "Did he call you Arley? I thought you told me yesterday your name was William Walker.''

"I didn't say that, Stevie. *You* said that.'' He pushed to his feet, rocking back on the heels of his black tennis shoes. "I feel bad about not telling you who I was yesterday, Stevie. Real bad.'' He glanced at his left hand, rubbed it on his jean-clad thigh, then stuck it out. "I'm your cousin, Arley.''

Stevie backed up, feeling sick all over again. She took a quick inventory of the man she'd been led to believe was the sheriff, noted the classic Arnou over-sized nose, with deep-set brown eyes to match. These were two strong traits she hadn't been blessed with. She had taken after her mother's Swedish heritage. "Oh, God...''

"Yesterday you didn't let me explain, Stevie.''

"That's not true.'' Stevie felt another wave of nausea. How had everything gotten so mixed up? "You're Arley? *You're* the cousin I want to kill?''

"Yes, siree, Stevie. I mean...no, not kill. We're cousins, after all.'' That said, a goofy grin peeling his lips back from his teeth and he stepped forward, lifted Stevie off her feet, and pulled her into his arms. After giving her a bear hug, he set her down. "My daddy was Harlen. He was your daddy's big brother.''

"If you're not the sheriff, then where is he? I'd like to speak to him, Arley. I'd like to—''

"You don't hafta look far, Stevie. You wanta talk

to the sheriff, he's right over there." Arley pointed over Stevie's shoulder.

She slowly turned, her stomach balling into a knot. No, she thought, not the slippery weasel. But by the look on his grinning fool face she knew he was Sheriff Walker. Then suddenly it made sense. It was William Walker. Sheriff Walker.

"Arley—" Justus unfolded his arms and shoved his brawny body away from the jamb "—why don't you go roust Nate out of that rocker on his front porch and take out the boat?"

"Sure thing, Just. I'll catch you a perty catfish, Stevie. See ya later, Cuz."

When the door closed behind Arley, Stevie finally managed to get her tongue unglued from the roof of her mouth. "You're the sheriff of Crawford? You're William Walker?"

"William Justus Walker. Townsfolk call me Justus. Sometimes they shorten it up. I'm the sheriff, and the only lawyer in town. Own some rental property."

"And you own the Muddy?"

"Half of it. Buz needed to make some improvements a year ago. I offered him the money, but he insisted on making me a partner in his business. He said that's the only way he'd take it."

"It sounds to me like you practically own the entire town." Stevie's stomach was slowly turning into an acid ball.

"More like it owns me."

Stevie wasn't going to ask him to explain that. His eyes were drifting away from her face, moving over her, giving her a slow, thorough shakedown, reminding her of her state of undress that morning. "What happened last night?"

"You had a little too much to drink."

"I know that. And?"

"You were having trouble standing up. I carried you to Buz's floater and put you to bed."

"You got me drunk on purpose."

"No. I was only trying to help."

"Help yourself, you mean."

"No, last night it was all about helping you get over this first hurdle."

"Remind me to refuse your help next time. Your help made me throw up."

"It did that, all right. Soaked my boots."

"That wasn't my fault."

"No, ma'am. I take full responsibility for the Bullfrog goin' down and comin' up."

His drawl was low and deep. And annoyingly soothing.

"What happened *after* the Bullfrog came up?"

"I was a lawyer in Houston for a few years. I have to tell you, honey, that admitting you can't remember what happened last night shoots a hole in pressing charges against me. It's called conjecture, and it's not admissible evidence in a court of law. They deal in facts."

Stevie's nose shot up. "I woke up without my dress on. That's a fact."

"I would have to plead no contest to that. But then I would have to explain why I found it necessary to remove it. I'd have to say you threw up on it after getting snauckered. I'd have to tell the judge, and those big ears on the jury, I was concerned with getting the stink off you. Then I'd have to ask the judge, and those ears, if they knew a better way.''

Stevie dug in her canvas bag and hurled his T-shirt at him. "I suppose you have an explanation for why *you* found it necessary to undress, too."

"Your bags were still in the car. The car was back at the Muddy. I took off my T-shirt and put it on you, after I pulled your dress off. Plain and simple, it was an artifice."

"What?"

"A trick. It's obvious you tricked me, honey. You were naked underneath, except for them candy-pink panties. You looked real good in that dress. Out there and perky. Figured it was due to one of those special bras. I would never have stripped you if I had known you were into trifling with a man's mind and playing tricks."

What was obvious to Stevie was that Justus Walker was a smooth-talking southern lawyer with a silver tongue. He had completely turned the whole incident around and was blaming her for the entire ordeal.

The writing on the wall was that there would be no filing charges. Not even an apology. Stevie started past him, intent on leaving. But before she could open the door and escape, he stretched his hand out flat against the door, then followed her around, trapping her between the door and his body.

He lowered his head, his left cheek making contact with her right. "I did look. Maybe longer than I should have, but I didn't touch. Not that I didn't want to. You're the real thing. I knew that the minute the dress came off. But I didn't touch…nothin'. I looked, honey. That's all.''

Stevie spun around, her eyes blazing. ''You, Justus Walker, are an immoral, silver-tongued—''

''I got morals, honey. I just said I never touched you. And I won't. Not until you say so.''

He was smiling as if he was expecting an invitation any minute. ''Stand aside and let me leave, snake,'' Stevie insisted.

Her words weren't meant as a challenge, but she could see that he had taken them that way. His smile spread—if that was possible. He was a grinning fool, she decided.

He closed the few inches between them. Toe-to-toe, she could feel his breath on her face.

''I could lock you up for bad-mouthing an officer of the law like you just done.''

''You wouldn't dare.''

He angled his head, his smile touching his eyes and adding another level of handsomeness to his tanned rugged face. ''You're right, I wouldn't lock up my business partner. I need her. Things have been crazy around here since Buz died.'' He studied her face without laying a hand on her. ''Mamma bring by her Mother's Milk?''

Stevie fought the relaxing effects of his never-get-riled, slow-and-easy drawl. It was soothing her feathers even though she was angry. Even though she wanted to stay angry.

She closed her eyes and told herself she was still recovering from the Bullfrog. That was the only explanation she had for wanting Justus Walker to lean closer. To lean in and use that mouth of his for something other than grinning.

She couldn't help wondering if he kissed as slow and easy as he spoke.

"Stevie, honey, where did you go? I asked if Mamma came by?"

Stevie blinked, then refocused her thoughts. "Yes, she came by."

"And did you drink the tonic?"

"Yes." Stevie remembered the heart-shaped balloon that was still tied on the railing. "If that balloon is supposed to be some kind of peace offering, you can forget it. I just traded my favorite job in the world, and my best friend, in on a greasy spoon, no plumbing and a lying snake for a partner."

"I'm no liar, honey. You woke up in a bed this morning, *oui?*"

Stevie made a face. "One truth. I have a bed wrapped in fishnet."

"*Baire,* honey. It's called a *baire.* Mosquito nettin' has a finer weave to it than fishnet. This here is mosquito country. Turtle Bayou's got a healthy crop. Don't sleep without it, hear?"

"Turtle Bayou also has the largest turtle this side of Nawlins," Stevie drawled poorly. "I was considering an outdoor bath this morning until I read the sign."

"You don't want to bathe in Turtle Bayou. The snappers aren't the worst of it. There are water moccasins, and gators out there, too. So far, I ain't found one flaw on you. I'd like to keep it that way." He reached out and brushed her cheek with the back of his hand. "You can use my shower."

"Thanks, but no thanks."

"Come on now, honey. Don't go gettin' uppity. The door locks from the inside. You can have the place to yourself anytime you want."

"And your place is where?"

"Top floor of the Muddy."

"You live above a bar?"

"And grill," he finished. "It's small, but I'm hardly ever there, so it don't matter much. What matters most is—" his scoundrel-blue eyes lit up "—I've got running water. Hot running water. Sounds nice, don't it?"

Stevie was dying for a shower, and he knew it. "And this is an offer out of the goodness of your heart?" she asked, knowing the man's heart was as black as sin.

He straightened and laid his hand over his brawny chest. "She noticed I have one. Smart lady."

"Smart enough to question everything," Stevie countered.

"Spoken like a woman who's been hurt a time or two."

Yes, she had, but Stevie had no intentions of discussing Tony with Justus Walker. Or the other three before him.

"Okay, I'll accept your offer, and in return, what do you want? I'm sure there's something."

"Well now...let me see." He rubbed his clean-shaven jaw, thinking. "Okay, for starters, two things."

Stevie snorted. "No, and no."

He chuckled. "Whoever hurt you, he was a fool, you know."

"I agree. Men are fools."

His chuckle turned into laughter. Easy laughter.

Stevie had never met anyone so comfortable with himself.

He sobered, but his smile remained. "I like a woman who has a sense of humor and can make me laugh."

Stevie scowled at him. "You said two things."

"Yes, ma'am, I sure did. I want you to believe me when I tell you I never touched you last night. Believe I'm a moral man and no liar. That you can trust me."

Well that wasn't going to happen, Stevie thought. "Number two?"

"The Muddy has been a staple in Crawford for thirty years. The folks here are afraid I'm goin' to close it down. I don't want to do that. I need my partner. I need her experience and her willingness to share it. I need her to be a stand-up gal and lend a hand. I need you, Stevie, honey… I need you to stick."

## Chapter 5

If she was going to be a stand-up gal things were going to have to change. Stevie had come to that conclusion the day after Justus had made his speech to her at the police station. The next morning she'd toured the Muddy, and, seeing what there was to work with, she had started making a list.

Three days later she was still adding to that list. She didn't know the first thing about making roux, or what exactly went into gumbo or jambalaya, but from what she could tell by watching Fay, it really didn't matter. The people who frequented the Muddy were a forgiving crowd.

Fay was in her mid-thirties, was married to the local banker, Hawg Daniels, and had stepped into Buz's shoes in the kitchen after his funeral. She admitted she knew the basics of cooking, but that she was actually the Muddy's one and only waitress, and had been for ten years.

With no hesitation after she'd explained the situation, she'd removed her apron, handed it to Stevie and picked up her order pad—promptly handing the kitchen over to Stevie.

So it began, Stevie spending long hours in the Muddy's kitchen learning the menu by trial and error. And in between times, Fay had enlightened her on the primary characters who lived in Crawford. Today, she was discussing Justus Walker.

"So that's how Justus came to Crawford," Fay said. Dula had adopted him. "The town loved him as a boy, and they love him still. Especially since he lived up to his promise and came home after he got educated at that fancy college in Texas. Some of the folks in town didn't think he'd come back. But I did. Justus Walker is the most reliable and honorable man I know."

"He told me he was a lawyer."

"He worked for a big law firm in Houston for four years. Jinx says that's not how he made his money, though. He says, Justus played at investments and struck it rich. That's how Buz got the money to fix this place up. There never used to be a deck looking out over the bayou. They done all new plumbing, too. Put in them two microwaves, and got all new tables and chairs for the dining room. You should have seen it a year ago. This place was a dump."

Stevie listened to Fay, as she had Arley yesterday. The general consensus in town was that Justus Walker was a saint. And if that was true, then she should have every reason to believe him when he said he never touched her three nights ago.

*I did look. Maybe longer than I should have. But I didn't touch.*

Every time she thought about his smooth liquid drawl next to her ear, her heart started to race, and she felt warm all over.

"He's all man, that one," Fay continued. "Dontcha think?"

Stevie blinked. "What?"

"Justus. He your type?"

"Type? Ah…no. He's too…" He was too what? Stevie scrambled for the right word. "Too happy."

"Happy? You don't like a happy man?"

"I think it's the smile," Stevie clarified. "I don't think I would like being around someone that happy all the time. It would be too depressing."

Fay was looking at her like she was crazy, then suddenly smiled. She lowered her voice even though they were alone in the kitchen, and said, "I shouldn't tell you this, but folks are making bets on whether you're going to stick it out here, or head back to Minnesota. Most think you're too uppity for the likes of Crawford."

Stevie had heard the rumors. "Is that why the tables in the dining room have been full every day since I arrived, or is the Muddy normally this busy?"

"We're always busy, but you're packing 'em in a little tighter than usual. That's a fact. You're the most exciting thing to happen to Crawford since they redid the county road and added shoulders to it. So have you made up your mind yet? You goin' to stay, or is it too early to tell?''

Fay was looking at her with hopeful eyes, but Stevie couldn't promise something she wasn't sure of. She said, "I'll have to see. I've been thinking about adding some of my favorite Minnesota dishes to the menu. Do you think I stand a chance of selling the idea to Justus?''

"She claims she can take the grease out of the Buzzard burger. You ain't gonna let her, are you, Just?''

That rumor had been circulating a full two days now. Arley's worried face was just one of many who had come to see him on the same score.

Justus listened to Arley's continued whining, while he worked at getting the pile of papers on his desk filed away. On a day when he didn't need one more problem stacked up on his busy plate—he'd already been out at five that morning to pull Elroy out of the ditch, and over to the Folly twins' house to fix their washing machine—he wasn't in the mood to hear more about how dry the Buzzard burgers would be without any grease.

When the phone rang, Justus looked at it not sure he wanted to pick it up. He didn't have to. Arley reached for it, and said, "Crawford Po-leece. Service with a smile. Oh, hi there, Nate. Say what? Uh-huh... Uh-huh... Hmm... Uh-huh... Just a minute, I'll ask him.''

"This here's Nate on the phone. He's over at the Muddy. He wants to know which side he should sit on?''

Confused by the question, Justus shoved himself up from the chair behind his desk. "What does he mean, which side? He always sits on the right, second booth from the door.''

"You hear that? You always sit on the right. You having a senior moment, Nate? Uh-huh… Uh-huh… Hmm… I'll tell him.'' Arley scratched his head with the butt end of the phone. ''He says the booths are in the middle now, and on the back wall where the picture of Hush Puppy used ta be.''

Justus closed his eyes and counted to ten. Blinking them open, he said, ''Tell him I'll be right over.''

"He's on his way, Nate. Have a beer at the bar, and— You're sittin' at the bar now. Uh-huh… Uh-huh… Hmm… Been sittin' there for a while. Well, have another bottle. He's comin'.''

When Arley hung up, Justus said, ''Stay here.''

"I was goin' fishin'.''

"Later.''

"But—''

"Later.''

Justus parked his black 4x4 Ranger in the lot. Nodding to the crowd out on the porch, he stepped inside the Muddy, and finally understood why Nate had been confused. The booths had been moved into a line down the middle, with tables on either side.

How she had managed to move the solid oak booths was beyond him, but she had, and with it she'd successfully drawn an imaginary line down the middle of the grill.

"I don't like this new arrangement at all, Just,'' Nate grumbled as Justus rounded the bar on his way to the kitchen. "I like Stevie's cookin', but she needs to stay in the kitchen."

"She in the kitchen now?" Justus asked Fayda Mae as she waltzed past him with an order.

"She is. But ifn' you've come to yell at her, you'll have to go through me first. She's a sweetheart, Just, and she makes pancakes lighter than a cotton ball. Don't you mess nothing up, you hear?"

When he stepped inside the kitchen, Justus, again, noticed how clean everything was. Unless she was planning on scrubbing the paint off the walls, he didn't know what more she could clean. Even the pots and pans were shiny. He didn't ever remember them being shiny. He glanced at the grill, then took a second look. Holly hell, she'd scrubbed every speck of grease off the grill; she'd unseasoned the seasoned grill. Buzzard must be rolling in his grave.

He found Stevie on a ladder five feet in the air in the narrow storage room. She had a clipboard in one hand and a pencil between her teeth. She was wearing a yellow sundress with skinny straps that sent his eyes straight to those beautiful breasts he'd been dreaming about since the unveiling.

He took a deep breath, wished he didn't have such a damn good memory, then cleared his throat.

She looked down.

His gaze went from her chest to her face. "We need to discuss what's going on out front."

She gave him a placid smile. "Later. I'm working on my grocery list in between orders. I need to know what to have shipped in for my new menu."

"New menu? The Muddy's menu has been the same since Buz opened the door thirty years ago."

"Exactly. I respect the staples, as you call them. Actually, I'm not changing much on your side of the menu. I'm assembling my own."

"Your own what?"

She looked at him as if he was a dunce. "Menu. You don't expect me to serve grease without an option do you? I'm a heart-smart expert, not a lard lover. I received an award for responsible cooking last year. I care about my customers' health. I can't, in all good conscience, deliberately clog arteries, and put extra pounds on Arley that he doesn't need. You're right, the people of Crawford depend on the Muddy. That means it's our responsibility to offer them a choice."

Justus grinned. He could not, no matter how hard he tried, get angry with her. Besides, this wasn't going to amount to anything so there was no reason to get lathered. As nicely as he could, he said, "I'm sorry, Stevie, honey, but Arley's an adult and if he wants to eat Buzzard burgers all day long, that's up to him. And about these alternatives. Serving the good folks of Crawford a diet of lettuce and tofu is gonna get a few laughs, nothing more, but if you need to find that out for yourself, you go on. So, how was your shower this mornin'?"

"The same as it was yesterday and the day before. Inconvenient."

"If you want to leave your soap and shampoo, I'll clean out a drawer in the bathroom."

"That won't be necessary. I don't intend to share your shower indefinitely."

"We haven't shared my shower yet, honey, but I'm willin' whenever you give the go-ahead. Now, about the booths..."

"A two-sided menu, or separates altogether, Justus. That's your choice. What will it be?"

"You mean you're thinkin' of splittin' the Muddy in half if I don't agree?" He chuckled at the thought.

"I'm trying to meet you halfway. Can't you do the same?" She backed down the ladder and brushed past him. "Have you really looked at the Muddy's menu?"

"Of course I've looked at it. I grew up with it."

"It was put together by a man," she said.

"No argument there."

She turned to face him. "I checked with Marge at the Coffee Cup, and Henrietta Penny over at the gas station, and they both think some fresh salads would be a nice addition. Broiled fish for a change instead of fried. And some low-calorie desserts."

"You ever think that maybe the reason they're in your corner on this is because it'll drive business their way?"

"Are you saying they're vengeful women?"

Justus shook his head. "No, but we do get triple the business they get." More, lately, he mused. He had been doing double time behind the bar since the word had gone out that Buzzard's nephew was really a niece—a blond baby-doll with hooters. After that had circled for half a day every man in the parish—young and old—had made the Muddy a regular stop off at least once a day to take a look at Crawford's new filly. Once they'd found out Stevie could cook—cook better than Buzzard—the place had been humming.

He wasn't the only one who was seeing her as flawless. The scuttle at the bar had been steady. She'd been nicknamed Miss Purr…fect. But they didn't know the half of it.

"And raspberries. I'd like to offer fresh fruit for breakfast. Melons, pineapple and fresh raspberries."

Justus blinked. "Raspberries?"

"Do you prefer strawberries? I have a low-calorie strawberry pie. Dula has expressed interest in losing twenty pounds, but she loves the Muddy's bread pudding and pecan pie. I told her I would support her by coming up with a few alternatives."

"Anything else?"

"You bet. I've got a ton of ideas to make the menu healthier. Oh…and we'll need to hire two waitresses. Fay has agreed to give up her past position and become my assistant in the kitchen. That way we can all get a day off now and then. I think it wouldn't hurt if you trained in a bartender, too. Arley has expressed interest."

Justus winced. "I don't think Arley's a good choice. Measurements are too much like numbers and letters."

She angled her head, one pretty eyebrow lifting. "Okay, so I suppose I could learn the bar. That way you can spend more time at the police station."

The idea of her serving the men at the bar with those sexy lips smiling at each and every one of them would drive him crazy in a week. "I'll think on it."

"We'll need a salad girl, too."

"What's a salad girl?"

"She cleans the vegetables and makes the salads. What are you staring at?"

"You sure look pretty in yellow."

"Thank you."

"I've been had, haven't I?"

"What?"

"Changin' the booths around, that was to get my attention. Get me hightailin' it over here?" Justus's smile widened. "If you wanted to see me that bad, honey, all you had to do was whistle and I'da come runnin'."

"If you don't like the booth arrangement out front then you'll have to agree with changing the menu."

"That's blackmail, honey. Plain and simple."

"That's such an ugly word."

She may have thought it was ugly, but the mischief in her eyes told Justus that she wasn't beyond a little ugly if it got her what she wanted. Determination, then. *Oui,* he liked that in a woman. Especially in bed.

"All I'm asking for, Justus, is equal representation. To let me perk up the menu a little."

The word perk sent his eyes to her breasts. Remembering how unbelievably perfect he thought they were, he slowly came toward her, his fingers itching to touch her. He kept moving until he had her backed against a stack of boxes. She raised her chin, set her jaw.

She was an intelligent woman, with looks. Some men found that a scary combination, but not him. He liked smart, and he liked pretty. Combine the two with curvaluscious breasts, and he was willing to sell his soul for fish bait for one night in Stevie Arnou's bed.

"How about I come by the floater after I close up and we'll talk this out?"

"You mean try to change my mind. No thanks. I

have to be here bright and early tomorrow morning again, and I'm going to bed before midnight so I can get here on time. Last night I noticed the lights were still on until way after one. I can't stay up that late and be any good in the morning.''

"I'll kick the stragglers out by eleven. How's that? Be over five minutes later."

He broke his promise and brushed a damp strand of hair away from her temple. "Maybe we ought to get one of those air-coolin' units back here in the kitchen.''

"You would agree to that?''

"Sure. Whatever you need.''

He had money to do pretty much whatever she wanted to do to the Muddy. He'd offered the air-conditioning idea to Buz, but the old bird was too stubborn to change too much.

"You're not wearin' a bra again today, are you?''

She had been on the verge of giving him a smile, but he'd gone and stuck his foot in his mouth and ruined it. She gave him a shove instead and left the storage room in a huff.

Justus trailed after her. "Now, hold on. That came out wrong.''

Her hands were on her hips when she spun around and glared at him.

"Don't give me that pissed off look, honey. My eyes are twenty-twenty, all right?''

"Meaning?''

"Considerin' what I know about the artifice and all… Well, I—''

It wasn't normal for him to sputter, but she'd had

him tongue-tied and restless for days. She turned away, and he started trailing her again.

"Fay," she called out. "We won. Tell Elroy he and his brothers can move the booths back the old way. Tell him I'll meet him at eight o'clock at the bar so he can collect on our deal."

Justus lost his smile. "Deal? What kind of deal did you make with Elroy Fachon?"

# Chapter 6

At a few minutes to eight Stevie left the cabin to meet her date. She had wanted to pay Elroy Fachon for moving the booths...twice, but he had refused to take money. When she'd offered dinner, she hadn't meant dinner with her, but Elroy had jumped to the wrong conclusion and, before she knew it, he was calling it a date.

To refuse Elroy would have been rude. She had smiled and they had arranged to meet at the bar at eight sharp.

Dressed in a cropped black tank, a skinny leopard print skirt, and black strapped sandals, Stevie walked the short quarter mile to the Muddy. Instead of meeting her at the bar, however, as she rounded the building, Elroy was in the parking lot leaning on the hood of his brown pickup.

He was the owner of the local junkyard on the north side of town. Stevie hadn't been there, but Fay had filled her in, saying the Fachon brothers bought, sold, swapped and borrowed. If the hardware store didn't have it, Elroy Fachon likely did…somewhere.

Average in height, average in weight, with short brown hair and deep-set brown eyes, Elroy was the same age as Justus—thirty and single. Fay said Elroy didn't date much because everyone in town knew after four beers he got as obnoxious as a woodpecker—he just wouldn't shut up.

Determined to hold Elroy to three beers, Stevie smiled and waved at him. He waved back, then shoved himself away from his '73 Ford. Quicker on his feet than she would have guessed, he sprinted toward her.

Grinning, he said, "Guess we timed that perfect." He eyed her outfit. "Dayum, you're gonna start a riot in there dressed like that, woman. But don't worry—" he flexed his muscles "—I'll tell 'em they can look but don't touch."

Stevie slipped her arm around Elroy's and tugged him toward the door. There was only one man she wanted to notice her tonight, and that was the man juggling the kitchen orders and the bar at the same time.

She had come to Crawford with her pride bruised. Tony walking out on her had been more of a shock than an emotional setback. Still, she wasn't interested in backsliding into thinking a relationship is what she needed. At this time in her life, what she needed most was a house with running water and a bathroom of her own.

But in the dark of night her needs shifted. Recently, as she fell asleep, Justus's face would appear. She would fall asleep thinking about his infectious smile, and, in the morning—like a pet toothache—she would wake up with him still there, grinning at her with that look in his eye.

They entered the Muddy, greeted by an expectant crowd. It was as if the entire town had turned out to witness Elroy's *date*.

Stevie's eyes went straight to the bar where Justus was serving a line of old-timers. As he slid beers in both directions, he glanced up. It was almost as if he had sensed she was looking at him. She noticed his smile slid a little, before he wiped his hands on a white towel tucked in the waistband of his jeans, then went into the kitchen.

They managed to find an empty table smack in the middle of the dining room. Suspicious, Stevie sat, noting that they were now the center of attention.

It felt odd being a customer in her own restaurant, especially when the person who came to take their order was Justus. Stevie frowned and asked, "Where's Fay?"

"She went home sick."

"Sick? So you're running the Muddy all by yourself tonight? The kitchen, and the bar? Why didn't you send someone to get me?"

His smile was back. "You deserve a night off, honey. You've been at it all day. I can handle it."

"But we're packed."

Someone called from the bar, followed by Nate from his favorite booth asking where his BLT was.

"Be right there, Nate." Justus slapped a menu down in front of Stevie, then Elroy. "I'll be back to take your order, you two." He winked at Stevie, then hurried off to get Nate his BLT.

For the next several minutes, Stevie watched Justus working the room, the kitchen and the bar. He was handling it, but he was doing it on the run.

"This is ridiculous," she muttered.

"Say what, Stevie?" Elroy had his head stuck in the menu. He laid it down and pointed to the all-you-can-eat fish platter with a choice of three side dishes. "That's what I'm gonna have," he stated.

"A good choice," Stevie said, standing, "I'll get right on it."

"What?"

"I'm sorry, Elroy, but we're going to have to do this another time. As you can see, the Muddy's shorthanded tonight." She reached for his menu. "If I don't help Justus, you're not going to be eating for an hour."

"An hour. I usually eat before seven. I'm an hour late already. An hour? You sure?"

He looked hungry and disappointed. Stevie touched his arm and smiled. Elroy melted like a butter patty in the sun. "Okay, Stevie. You go on and put up the order. I'll just sit here and, if'n you get time, you can come sit and watch me eat. How's that sound?"

"That's real generous of you, Elroy," Justus said appearing suddenly to plunk a beer down in front of her date. Then without further ado, he started herding Stevie toward the kitchen.

The Muddy didn't slow down all night. Elroy ate alone while the crowd watched him ask for seconds, thirds and fourths. About nine-thirty, he joined his brothers for a few hands of poker. By ten, he was on his seventh beer, his laughter drowning out the jukebox. By eleven, he was howling and pounding his fist on the table, and shortly after that, Justus advised his brothers to escort Elroy home.

By eleven-thirty, Justus entered the kitchen saying, "I shooed everyone out. I'll walk you home."

They left by way of the back door. Side-by-side, walking slow, and in silence, Stevie kept her eyes straight ahead. The night was warm and the moon was out. When they rounded the bend in the road, the red heart balloon came into sight high above the cabin.

"I see the balloon's holding its own," Justus drawled.

"Yes, it is. Why did you send it?"

"You don't remember?"

"No."

"The night we were out by the tree you said February was one of your favorite months on account of Valentine's Day. The holiday seemed important to you, so I sent the balloon hoping it would cheer you up."

He grinned down at her, and Stevie couldn't help but smile back.

He ushered her onto the dock, his hand on her back.

"Careful now. I don't want to have to fish you out of the bayou."

"The sandals were a mistake," Stevie confessed. "But they make the outfit."

"*Oui,* that they do. Just not too practical for standin' at a grill all night. Guess I'll have to take you to Nawlins one of these days so you can dress up."

Stevie reached the deck, put a hand on the railing and slipped out of the sandals. Then, opening the cabin door, she tossed them inside. "I haven't spent any time in New Orleans. That would be fun."

"Then it's a date." He leaned a hip on the railing next to her and propped his elbows behind him on the top rail.

"Sorry about you havin' to pull a double shift. You're right. We need more people working for us. Buz lived for the Muddy. He didn't mind being there day and night. But it's different now."

He angled his head, and looked at the moon. "Beautiful evenin'. No mosquitoes to speak of. Perfect night."

What was beautiful was Justus Walker's smile, Stevie realized. She had lied to Fay. It was fun being around someone happy all the time. It wasn't depressing, it was therapeutic.

She asked, "Don't your lips get tired of smiling all day long?"

His eyes found hers. "You got somethin' against smilin'?"

"I've just never known a person who can keep one up that long."

The words weren't meant to be sexual, but when Justus's smile turned into a nasty grin, she knew what he was thinking. Her cheeks flushed. "You have a dirty mind, Justus Walker."

He shoved away from the railing and turned to face her. "It must be your outfit. It's leadin' me astray."

"You don't like it?"

"It's not a matter of liking it or not, it's just a major factor in what I'm thinkin' and how I'm feelin'."

Stevie felt her knees go weak as his hips hemmed her in and she was forced to lean hard against the railing. "Justus…"

He took his sweet time putting both hands on the top railing on either side of her. "You know I'm crazy about you."

"No… I didn't know."

"Sure you do. I've been wantin' to kiss you for days. You gonna let me?"

"I…"

"I told you I wouldn't move on you without your say so. But if I've been missin' your subtle go-ahead, I'm all ears."

He couldn't move much closer. She was tight against the railing, his thighs brushing hers. He was dressed in hip-hugging jeans and another fitted white T-shirt.

"Invite me, honey. Go on."

Stevie released a heavy sigh. "Justus, we're business partners. I don't think mixing—"

"Don't tell me what you think. Tell me how you feel, honey. Let's start there."

"Feel? You mean right now?"

"*Oui.* Right now."

"I…I'm feeling warm."

"Warm is good. What else?"

"Short of breath."

"*Oui,* me too. And my heart—" He reached for her hand and laid it on his chest over his heart. "It's trying to keep up with my head. Feel that?"

She felt it…him, and it was heavenly. "What's going on in your head, Justus?"

"You, honey." His eyes studied her face while Stevie sucked on her lower lip. "Say it. Say, 'Yes, Just, I want you to kiss me.' Say it, honey, just like that. Say it and we'll get started."

Stevie had never had a man sweep her off her feet before, but Justus Walker's southern drawl and lazy smile had been keeping her off balance since she had arrived in Crawford.

"This is different," she sighed.

"Different? How?"

"I've never been asked to ask for a kiss."

He didn't answer, just waited.

Stevie wanted him to kiss her. She really did. She'd wanted it for days. "Yes, Just. Kiss me."

"That'll do. That'll do fine, honey." He reached down and took hold of her wrists. "Now then, I think you should hang on to something sturdy."

"Something sturdy?"

"Somethin' you can lean on if you feel the need. Something dependable." He placed her hands on his chest, then slowly slid them up his chest and around his neck, all the while watching her reaction. The act dragged Stevie forward and flattened her breasts against his chest.

"That's it, honey," he crooned. "That feels nice."

Stevie tilted her head back. "I like your drawl."

He blew out a slow breath. "I like the way you talk, too, honey. Even though it's got a few people in town confused."

"Confused?"

"That expression, you bet, has got Jinx stumped. He's been wondering for three days what kind of bet you're talking about and how much it's gonna cost him."

Stevie laughed.

"You sure got a sweet laugh, honey."

"Whatever."

"See, there's another one of those meaningful expressions. What exactly does whatever mean in Minnesota?"

Stevie shrugged. "It means whatever *yawl* want it to mean."

This time it was his turn to laugh. When the laughter played out, he asked, "Am I sturdy enough for you?"

"Like an oak."

"That kind of flattery is goin' to get you everything you want, honey."

"And you think you know what I want?"

"My ears are open. I'm told I'm a good listener."

He leaned forward.

She angled her head.

It was time, she thought—time to stop wondering what it would be like to be kissed by Justus Walker. Time to stop thinking, as he said, and address her feelings directly.

Stevie parted her lips.

Justus lowered his head.

It was going to be perfect, she could feel it. Wonderful.

She closed her eyes ready for contact, but the moment was halted by a familiar voice calling her name.

"Steeevieee… Steeviee, it's me, Arley. I come ta

warn you it smells like rain. If'n you ain't closed the winders, you best get to it. Steeviee, you awake?''

Justus was a second away from claiming Stevie's sweet lips when Arley's voice reminded him that it was Saturday. He raised his head at the same time a loud splash sounded from somewhere in the middle of the bayou.

He released Stevie, took a step back. "Hell, I think he fell in."

"And that's not good, is it? You said Hush Puppy wasn't the worst of it."

Justus reached for the flashlight on the side of the cabin dangling from the end of a long rope, then walked around the corner of the cabin. "Arley!"

"That you, Just? What you doin' out here at Stevie's place?"

"Arley, did you fall in?"

"Yes'um I did." He laughed. "Lost my balance. Don't worry. Didn't roll the boat. The croakers are safe."

"Croakers?" Stevie had followed Justus. "What is he talking about?"

"Bullfrogs. It's Saturday."

As if that explained everything, Justus turned on the flashlight and scanned the water until he found Arley's head bobbing beside his boat twenty feet from the dock. Ruby Duke, Arley's hound dog, was still sitting in the bottom of the boat, her butt planted between two plump gunnysacks. She was looking over the side at her owner with a bored look on her face.

"What is he doing out there after midnight?" Stevie asked.

"He's been out froggin'."

"Froggin'? He sounds like he's been out drinking."

"He's been drinking, too. Arley always drinks when he goes froggin'. But he's not stink-drunk or he wouldn't be bobbing. Arley can't swim. Crazy-drunk he'd of sunk by now."

"Oh, God!"

"Don't get riled," Justus drawled. "In this case, drunk is good. It means his gunnies are full of croakers."

Stevie was looking at him as if he was a half-wit.

"Your cousin is the best frogger in Crawford, honey. Only problem is, he's also squeamish when it comes to handling them. Especially the fat ones. Hoppin' Froggies is the Sunday night special at the Muddy. Saturday nights Arley takes a bottle of whiskey and Ruby Duke out with him to get the job done. If he comes back snauckered he's had a good night."

"Who is Ruby Duke?"

"Arley's hound dog."

"That's a strange name for a dog."

"There's a story behind that. A year ago, Arley picked out a puppy. He wanted a male, and he thought that's what he'd picked out at Jinx's place. Swears to it to this day. The way Jinx tells it, though, Arley was like a kid in a candy store looking at those puppies. Picking up every one of them at least twice like he couldn't decide which one he wanted. And Gloria had sixteen."

"Sixteen puppies?"

"That's a fact. Arley named the pup Duke. Guess it was about a month later he noticed the pup was a female. Only problem was, by then she was coming real good to Duke, so Arley decided to give her two names."

"Say, Just... You wanta get the fetch pole. You wanta hurry. I reckon I heard Hush Puppy come off that log he likes ta sleep on."

"Oh, God!"

"Take it easy, honey." Justus retrieved the long pole that hung on the side of the cabin, then walked to a section of railing that opened like a gate. He unhooked the gate and swung it open. Sticking the pole out, he said, "Come on, Arley, get swimming. Move your ass." To the hound, he said, "Ruby Duke, get off yours and bring the boat in."

As Arley began to swim for the pole, Ruby Duke stood and found the rope in the bottom of the boat. Taking it between her teeth, she leaped into the water and started swimming for the dock.

"She's doing it," Stevie said excitedly. "She's bringing the boat to the dock, just like you told her to."

"Women like it when I talk forceful to them." Just winked, then wiggled his eyebrows at Stevie. "How about you goin' on over there to meet her, honey, and loop that rope around a post for me?"

"Only if you can guarantee those frogs are still in the gunnysacks. I don't like frogs any better than Arley."

"I'm sorry to hear that, honey. Tomorrow night

we're gonna be knee-deep in customers orderin' Hoppin' Froggies. I'm gonna need two fryers goin'."

While Stevie headed to the dock to tie up the boat, Justus waited for Arley to reach the pole.

"Is Ruby friendly to strangers?" She called back.

"She's gonna like you fine, honey," Justus assured, then seeing Arley was almost within reach, he stretched the pole out to his friend, and he pulled him in hard and fast.

When Arley was at last standing dripping wet beside Justus, he leaned close and said, "I knowd what you was doin', Just. You were kissin' her, weren't you?"

Not yet, Justus mused. But he had been damn close.

"You was," Arley continued. "Elroy's been wantin' a taste, too. Them frosting lips is sugar sin, he says. But he says he'll gladly suffer a toothache if'n he gets a chance to suck on 'em."

Justus felt the green-eyed monster start growling inside his gut. It had been a long while since he'd felt it, but it was there. A solid growl. No mistake. That's why he'd sent Fayda Mae home tonight...*sick.*

"Elroy says that heart balloon out here on her porch ain't gonna stop him from going after Stevie for himself. He says she's hotter than Buzzard's pepper cabbage, and it's open season on her. He's even been havin' dreams 'bout her. He says it's an omen. Specially since Stevie asked him to flex his muscle for her at the Muddy moving them booths."

Justus's nostrils flared even though he hung on to his smile. "You can tell Elroy that if he don't stop dreamin' about Stevie and omens, he's gonna be in for a nightmare he ain't gonna wake up from." '

The words were out before Justus could take them back. It wasn't often that he let loose with a threat. The worst of it was that he'd exposed his feelings to Arley, and by morning his words would be all over town. He only hoped that Arley was drunker than he looked, and that he wouldn't remember half of what Justus had said, or what order he'd heard it in.

"No, Ruby! Get down. Ohhh... You're getting me all wet."

Both Justus and Arley turned to see Ruby Duke on her hind legs, her paws wrapped around Stevie's trim waist. "See, honey," Justus called out. "That hound likes you just fine."

"Everybody likes Stevie," Arley muttered, suddenly turning a sober face toward Justus. "'Member when you said she wouldn't last a day? It's been four full days now and I'm wondering if'n that means she's gonna stick? I'm thinkin'...no, she's too smart and pretty for us. But then, it sure would be nice if'n she would. You given it some thought, Just?"

He'd given it a lot of thought. And, like Arley, some days he thought, no, she wasn't going to stay—he wouldn't be that lucky. Then he'd see her in the kitchen making her little improvements, or hanging her panties out on that line behind the cabin, and he'd think she was here to stay.

She sure wore skimpy panties, and in the damndest colors, too.

## Chapter 7

Arley sized up Justus and decided he was holding up progress. If they were going to get Stevie to stay in Crawford, Justus was the only man who could make it happen.

"Best be gettin' them croakers tied down and head for home. You gonna whack 'em for me, ain't ya, Just? You know I hate that part."

"You hate any part of froggin', Arley. But you're a good sport about it. There isn't a man in Crawford who's got a better nose for sniffin' out croakers than you."

Arley puffed up. "Yep. I do have the knack. But whackin' and skinnin'…" His puff deflated, and he made a face. "My stomach caint keep nothin' down for two days afterward. A man can starve if'n he don't eat for two days."

"Tie the sacks down and leave 'em in the boat. I'll whack 'em and see they get into the fryers tomorrow night."

Arley left Justus holding the fetch pole and sauntered toward the dock where Stevie was still fighting off Ruby Duke's affectionate nature. He sometimes wished he was a dog so he could take liberties like that. He hadn't ever climbed all over a woman, and lately he was starting to wonder if it was ever gonna happen.

He hadn't told Justus all that Elroy had said about Stevie. But he was in agreement with Elroy on a couple of points. One of those points was none of them was getting any younger. Him, Elroy or Justus. Bachelors they were. Thirty-year-old virgin bachelors. Well, all except Just. Arley suspected he hadn't been a virgin since high school.

Elroy had announced at the barbershop that afternoon when he was getting a little trim for his date with Stevie, that he would be willing to change his ways, and then some, if he could turn Stevie's head even a snail's inch. And he must have meant it, because there were changes being made over at the junkyard. There was grass showing in the front yard, and Jinx had said Elroy's lawnmower was over at the fix-it shop. There was some talk about him putting in an indoor outhouse with all the trimmings, too.

Wringing wet, Arley stopped two feet from Stevie. "Come on, Ruby Duke, get on down and stop slobbering on your cousin. Thanks for catchin' my boat, Stevie. Justus said I should leave it here. I'll pick it up late mornin', if'n that's all right."

"Whatever, Arley."

"What does that mean, exactly, Stevie? You say that an awful lot."

"Whatever means sure, Arley. Whatever you want is fine."

Arley grinned. "That's pretty slick. Okay, I'll come by for my boat whatever."

"You mean whenever."

"Huh?"

"Never mind. I'll see you tomorrow."

Arley got down on his knees and tied up the gunnysacks. On his feet once again, he started past Stevie.

"Are you all right, Arley?"

He stopped and turned back. "Wet. A little hungry. Fine mostly. You?"

"I'm fine, too." She reached out and ran her fingers through his wet hair to push it off his face. "You didn't drink so much that you won't be able to find your way home, did you?"

"Ruby Duke knows the way. She's got a nose on her that won't quit. We'll be home lickity-split."

"All right, then." Stevie leaned forward and kissed Arley's cheek. "I'll see you tomorrow."

Stevie watched Arley until he'd joined Ruby Duke on shore and the two disappeared around the bend toward town, then she returned to the deck where she'd last seen Justus. But when she found him nowhere in sight, she rounded the deck and started through the open door into the cabin.

The sight of Justus stripping off his T-shirt had her stopping dead in her tracks. The cabin had few lights, and the ones it did have were oil lamps—two small wall sconces and one larger table lamp that sat next to the bed. The table lamp was lit.

Stevie studied Justus in the amber lighting. He was broad-shouldered, long-legged, with a butt that put her in a pinching mood every time she saw it.

For days she'd struggled to keep her mind on the restaurant and off that butt, but the memory of their first night here in the cabin had made a lasting impression on her subconscious. Or the lack of memory.

Yes, Justus Walker, without a doubt, was the most handsome, smooth-talking man she'd ever met. And happy. She hadn't seen him in a bad mood yet.

He turned, his all-day-long smile in place. "Shame on you for staring."

"If you don't like being stared at, keep your clothes on and your body out of my house," Stevie countered, admiring his six-pack.

"That kiss on Arley's cheek, honey, made his night. You gonna make my night, too?"

"And how would I go about doing that?"

His grin spread. "I think you know what would make my night. Those gorgeous arms of yours hanging around my neck would be good for starters."

Stevie had never met a man so honest about his thoughts. "I was thinking that maybe out there—" she pointed to the deck behind her "—what was about to happen before Arley showed up was maybe not such a good idea."

"The word *maybe* is an ambiguous word. Used twice in a sentence it strengthens debate. In a court of law it's a discreditable word if you're a witness for the defense. Then, too, if I'm the prosecutor and I hear the word maybe, I feel down right hopeful. Maybe means, *maybe* the witness can remember, and maybe she can't.'' He paused, then said, ''See where I'm going with this, honey? Maybe we should kiss, and maybe we should kiss and then some.''

''And then some?''

''*Oui*, then some.''

His lazy speech and slow-never-get-riled demeanor was misleading. It fooled you into thinking he was a slow thinker, too. But the truth was, Justus Walker was a sharp-as-nails lawyer.

Still, she wasn't sure stepping over the line was a good idea. They were partners and that was probably the safest relationship to be in with Justus Walker, even though she couldn't think of a better way to end the evening than in his arms, kissing his lips.

She said, ''Mixing business with pleasure can be—''

''A whole heap a fun with the right partner.'' He finished for her.

When he started toward her, Stevie held her breath.

''You sure do make me feel good, honey.''

He didn't stop coming until they were toe-to-toe. His free hand stretched out to rest along the jamb a little ways above Stevie's head. His T-shirt was in his other hand, and he tossed it through the open door. It landed near the string that anchored the balloon to the railing.

''It's gonna rain, like Arley said. You ever make love in the rain?''

The question sent a rush of heat between Stevie's legs and she shivered in response. ''Justus…''

''Hmm…'' He leaned forward and sniffed along her jaw, moving in the direction of her ear. From there, his lips grazed her temple, his nose drawing a path for his lips to follow.

Stevie sighed, reached out and slid her hands up his warm, bare chest.

"That's it, honey."

"Just…"

He slid his arm around her waist and encouraged her to touch him further. "We're goin' to kiss now," he drawled. "We're goin' to get it done."

Stevie raised her chin, angled her head and slid her arms around his neck. "Yes, Justus," she whispered, "we're going to get it done."

He ran his hands over her backside, then outlined her hips. "I'm gonna put my hands on you, honey. Put 'em everywhere before the night's over. You alright with that?"

"Yes, but…"

"Yes, but what, honey?"

"If you spend the night, I don't want the people in town to know about it. Do you understand?"

"Only a scumball kisses and tells."

That said, Justus covered her mouth and kissed Stevie with all the passion and expertise she knew he would. The kiss was slow and deep. Unhurried, just like the man. Straightforward. All or nothing.

Stevie was glad she had wrapped her arms around his neck. She felt a rush of heat go through her, felt her knees grow weak. Sometime in between the third and the tenth kiss, Justus lifted Stevie off her feet and carried her outside. It had started to rain, a slow, sweet-smelling sultry rain that felt warm on Stevie's skin.

He backed her against the cabin, tucked her under

the eave and kissed her again. Seconds later, his hands began to explore her body. He slid his fingers beneath her black top and cupped her bare breasts. "No bra."

He let go of a heavy sigh, an honest reaction to the amount of pleasure she offered him. He flattened out his hands and when his palms rolled across her nipples, Stevie moaned and closed her eyes.

"I want to see," he whispered against her mouth on the end of another kiss.

"Shouldn't we go inside?"

"No, not yet."

When he shoved up her top and revealed her breasts to his eyes and the warm night air, Stevie locked her knees.

He was going to look at her now, look his fill. Stevie closed her eyes anticipating his mouth on her breasts. But when it came she nearly collapsed. His lips were hot, but gentle as he stroked and licked, teased and sucked.

"Ohhh…"

Stevie sagged against the wall, thankful for its support. She raised her hands and threaded her fingers through his black hair to keep him close. "That's amazing."

"I agree. You're amazing. *Bon Dieu, ma douce.*"

Stevie sighed. "I don't speak French."

He looked up, his smile strong. "How 'bout I teach you this summer?"

"Does it take a long time to learn?"

"*Oui.* A long time. I'm a slow teacher. But I'm thorough." He kissed her breasts, sucked on her nipples.

"A stickler for details, my college professor used to say. Unzip your skirt."

Stevie reached behind her and slid the zipper down at the same time she arched her hips forward.

"That's it, honey." Justus took over and he tugged her skirt past her hips. She felt suddenly nervous, but then his fingers were stroking her belly and making her forget about everything else but him.

"Oranges…"

"What?"

"Your panties. They're the color of an orange. I like the taste of oranges, honey."

He had crouched in front of her, his words followed by a series of kisses starting at her belly button and moving downward. Another shiver sent Stevie writhing on the wall as Justus's skilled lips began to work their magic. Slowly, his fingers slid their way into her panties and eased them down her hips to expose her to him.

"Just…"

"Shhh…"

"We'll need a condom?"

He stood slowly, his hand cupping her triangle of hair. "I wager more than one, honey." His fingers followed the seam of her, parted her slightly. "At least three before morning. Maybe four. Breathe, honey."

She did what he said. Concentrated on keeping air in her lungs while his fingers touched her.

"You ever do any marathon running?"

"No."

"How's your wind?"

"My wind?"

"Your endurance, honey."

"I can hold my own."

"And then some, I'll bet." He kissed her again, moved his hands away from her heat. "You want to touch me?" he whispered close to her mouth.

Stevie angled her head back to look into his eyes. "Do you always say what's on your mind?"

"It's the fastest way to communicate that I know of."

Stevie considered that, then offered him a mischievous smile. "Oh, I don't know, sometimes actions speak louder than words. Let me see if I can get across what I'm thinking without talking." That said, she moved away from the wall, stepping out of her panties and skirt at the same time. Wiggling her tank top back into place, naked below the waist, she pushed Justus against the wall. "We'll call this silent communication. Let me show you how it works."

Stevie started to kiss her way down his hairy chest, then bent her knees and kept going. Her fingers found the snap on his jeans, then the zipper.

She was going to touch him, all right. Touch him with more than her hands. Justus watched as Stevie peeled his jeans off his ass and down his thighs, taking his shorts down at the same time.

Hard and hurting something awful, he never took his eyes off her as her hands slid down his belly and into the hair around his swollen shaft. On his way to dying of pleasure, he spread his legs and arched his hips. She slipped her hand around him, squeezed.

He kept reminding himself to breathe. Telling himself that this was just the beginning. Hell, he hoped it was just the beginning.

He kept watching, kept his mouth shut, hoping hers would open soon. Then like a psychic nurse moonlighting for the good of mankind, she said, "Say, yes, Justus. Say, yes, and I'm there. One word is all it'll take."

At the moment, Justus couldn't think of anything he wanted more than her mouth on him.

"*Oui*, honey," he drawled. "You're there. I'm yours."

# Chapter 8

Justus sat with his back against the headboard, his eyes fixed on Stevie asleep beside him, while the rain continued to fall, tapping out a tune on the roof.

He had been right about the condoms. They had used three. And for never running a marathon, Stevie definitely had amazing stamina.

He slid his legs off the bed, pushed the *baire* aside, and climbed out of bed. He had noticed earlier that she had been cleaning the cabin. She had boxed up Buz's clothes, and some of his personal things. In doing so, was she making a statement? Was she planning on staying?

He walked to the dresser and eased open the top drawer. Inside he found underwear and a few bras, some T-shirts. He smiled seeing the bras. She hadn't worn one yet as far as he could tell.

She'd brought only two suitcases. He'd wondered about that from day one. Yesterday Fayda Mae told him Stevie's apartment in Minneapolis had burned just days after she'd received Arley's letter. The fire had been extensive, she'd lost most everything she owned.

He spied a small red book on the dresser and turned it over. *203 Ways to Drive a Man Wild in Bed.* Well, now, Justus mused, it looked like his little playmate had been brushing up on silent communication.

"Just…"

He turned around and found Stevie sitting up. The sight of her naked behind the *baire* sent his body on another growth spurt. Her eyes were heavy-lidded, her bare breasts beautiful. In the amber lamplight her full lips and her pixie-short hair reminded him of an exotic doll—her perfection breathtaking.

"What do you have in your hand?"

Justus carried the book back to the bed. "Is this why you're such an expert in communicatin' without words?" he drawled.

"An expert? I never said I was an expert."

"Trust me, honey, you're an expert."

She stretched like a lazy feline, thrusting her pretty breasts high so he could see that her sweet nipples were puckered tight. He drew the *baire* aside, his body reacting to her uninhibited nature. He flashed her the cover of the book, then stretched out beside her.

"Where did you get that?"

She reached for the book, and he easily rolled her onto her back, flattening her to the mattress with his weight and a long hairy leg across her thighs. "Don't get riled. It was out in plain sight on the dresser."

"I don't think so."

"*Oui,* it was…sorta." He grinned. "So what should I make of this book, honey?"

"Let me up."

"You want to trade places, do you?"

"Don't get me mad," she warned.

He chuckled, kept himself tight against her as he flipped open the book. "So this is where you learned all those fascinatin' tricks." He flipped to chapter four. "Here it is, 'Oral Treats.'"

"I didn't buy that book," she protested. "Connie gave me it as a gift. A little joke between friends."

"Was the bookmark stuck on chapter four a gift, too?"

She narrowed her eyes. "Give me the book."

Justus scanned the first page of chapter four. "Learn the three C's," he read out loud.

"Oh, God… Don't you dare read it."

"There's even a checklist. Crave it. Concentrate. Continuous movement." Justus looked down at Stevie. "I think that describes your technique perfectly, honey."

She squeezed her eyes shut, causing her cute nose to wrinkle up. Justus bent down and kissed the end of it. "I like your nose. Almost as much as your mouth and…talented tongue."

She blinked open her eyes. "You're embarrassing me."

Justus snapped the book closed and laid it down on the bed beside them. "*Mais non,* honey. You have nothin' to be embarrassed about. Not with me."

"I've never owned a book like that before. January

was a tough month, and Connie was just trying to cheer me up. She and I have been through a lot together. We both lost our parents at the same time a few years ago, and we met at a grief meeting.''

"Then I owe Connie a thank-you." Justus lowered his head and kissed her sexy mouth, then nipped her lower lip to urge her to join in on the kiss. "That's it," he encouraged, when she responded.

Just as they were coming up for air, she bit him.

"Ouch."

"I want you to know I've never done anything like that before. What I did outside. Honest. I don't usually…"

"Shhh… I liked everythin' you did." Justus couldn't put into words what it had been like for him—Stevie Arnou on her knees loving him with her mouth. Loving every inch of him.

"That book title is pretty accurate. You did drive me wild," he admitted, lowering his head to kiss her again. "And now it's my turn."

"Your turn?"

"It's early. Too early to get up." He slid down her body and took a perky nipple into his mouth and cherished it. "Your heart's pounding, honey. You excited?"

"You make me hot," she sighed. "I want…"

"What do you want, honey? You want me everywhere?"

"Yes…everywhere."

"Say, 'Yes. Just, drive me wild.' He moved to her other nipple and sucked on it. "Say it, and I'm there."

"Yes. Just, drive me wild," she mimicked. "I'm yours."

"You bet you are, honey. All mine, and then some."

She closed her eyes when he parted her legs and began kissing a path to the blond curls between her legs. She arched for him, and he liked it, liked watching her beneath his touch.

This was nothing you could plan for, Justus decided. In a man's wildest dreams, he couldn't have ever dreamed this. He'd been stripped naked—literally and figuratively—by an angel with pixie hair and seven-minute frosting lips. Stripped and pleasure-tortured into surrendering not only his body, but something more. He'd gone willingly knowing the price would be high. Knowing the odds of a happy ending were slim.

But for now, Stevie Arnou was his. She'd just given him the go-ahead to know every inch of her, and he was determined to read every page of her just like that book. Read her cover-to-cover, and take his time doing it.

Rushing was a fool's game. Justus was glad he'd never learned how to play that game. Stevie would be, too, before the night was over, he intended to make sure of that.


Stevie's body writhed between the sheets as Justus kissed her again—an illicit nasty kiss that left her breathless and aching.

His hands and mouth were everywhere, and she loved the way he was never in a hurry. Loved the gentle words that went along with his touch. Loved his smile. Loved the way he talked.

Loved...him.

Stevie sat straight up in bed. Her eyes wide open, she glanced around the room looking for the man who had been occupying her dream, but Justus was gone. She turned her head to the window, confused by how light it was outside. When she glanced at the small clock on the table she gasped.

How could it be eleven-thirty? How could she have slept the entire morning away? She was supposed to cook for the breakfast crowd at the Muddy. The breakfast crowd that had now turned into the lunch crowd.

She'd set her alarm for five-thirty. Justus must have turned it off before he left at dawn.

It didn't matter now. She was late. Late!

Stevie swept the *baire* aside and leaped out of bed. In a matter of minutes, she'd tugged on a pair of jeans and pulled a white tank top on. She raced through the door and was halfway to the dock when she heard voices. She glanced around, saw the boats. She had never seen so many fishing boats.

For a moment she thought there must be some kind of fishing contest going on, that is until she noticed no one was fishing. They were all looking toward the cabin. No, they were looking up in the sky above the cabin.

Slowly she turned around to see what they were looking at and nearly keeled over. There were balloons everywhere, big red heart-shaped balloons floating high above the cabin.

They had been tied to the railing, and they went around the perimeter. They were identical to the balloon that Justus had sent to her days ago.

Justus…

He had said he wouldn't kiss and tell. He had said it so matter-of-factly that she'd believed him.

"Lying…scumball," Stevie growled, then looked back at the many boats. The *men* were no longer looking at the balloons. No, of course not. Their eyes were now on her.

"Mornin' Stevie. Beautiful day, ain't it?"

Stevie could feel hot color rise up in her cheeks as she glanced at the two men occupying a boat less than fifteen feet from her dock. It was Arley, with Nate. Arley lifted his hat off and waved excitedly.

Stevie returned his good morning with a wave much less enthusiastic, then hurried to shore, ignoring the catcalls and whistles that had started up from several of the other men who had come to witness her humiliation.

"Scumball," Stevie growled again as she raced up the path to the Muddy's back door. Swinging the door wide, she entered, not expecting to find the person responsible for her anger behind the grill flipping Buzzards. When she laid eyes on him, the hurt and betrayal overwhelmed her and she fought tears. Shaking them off, she spat, "Only a scumball would kiss and tell. Well, Mr. Scum, I hope you choke on the ball."

Justus looked up, his smile widening at the sound of Stevie's voice. That is, until her words registered. He wasn't sure what was wrong, but something sure was. Stevie's spitfire eyes were blazing.

He sent the burgers, one at a time, into the open buns

on the three plates he'd lined up, then said, "Fayda Mae, take over."

He made a move toward Stevie, but she scurried backward as if she couldn't stand to be touched by him. That was crazy. He'd touched her everywhere there was to be touched last night and she'd purred like a kitten the entire time.

"Don't you touch me, you…you…lying pond scum."

"What's going on?" he asked calmly.

"As if you don't know."

"I don't," Justus assured her. "And I won't until you tell me, honey."

"Don't you 'honey' me." Stevie waved her hand in the direction of the back door. "How could you do it, Just? Why would you deliberately humiliate me like that? Advertise like that?"

"Advertise what? Come on, honey. Make it simple and spell it out. I've been here in the kitchen all mornin', so you're goin' to—"

"I said don't call me that! Never again. In fact, don't call me at all. And as far as this stupid partnership goes, there will be no joint menu. No joint…anything!"

"Stevie—" Justus trailed her to the back door. "Come on now, honey. Don't chew my head off and leave me bleedin' without knowin' why. Stevie!"

By the time Justus decided to go after her, Stevie was running flat out down the road toward the cabin, making Justus winded just thinking about how fast he was going to have to move in order to overtake her. But there was no need to consider that. As he started off the back stoop, he heard her car start up. Seconds later the silver Mustang was churning up a cloud of dust as Stevie shot past the Muddy, shifting into fourth before she hit the parking lot.

He turned around and stepped back into the kitchen, his eyes finding Fayda Mae where she stood balancing three plates loaded down with Buzzard burgers and fried okra.

"What do you make of that?" he said, not really expecting an answer.

But he got one anyway. Fayda Mae blasted him with both barrels. "Justus Walker, if you've hurt my friend Stevie, you best fix it, and fix it fast, or this whole town is gonna whack you into next week. She's ours and we all want her to stay. We ain't gonna give her up 'cause you done her wrong. So, fix it. Whatever you screwed up, unscrew it, or I quit."

"He bought out Henrettia's entire balloon stock!"

"I heard. Now, you just take it easy." An hour later Mamma Dula steered Justus away from Arley and into the rocker on the front porch of her house. "Sit down."

"Have you seen the cabin?" Justus asked.

"Arley's motives were pure." She gave Justus a little shove and his butt landed in the rocker.

"There are heart balloons tied to everything."

"He had your best interest at heart."

"You knowd I wouldn't do nothin' to hurt you, Just. Not Stevie, neither," Arley drawled. "Elroy's been talking about puttin' in indoor plumbin'. I thought the best way ta squelch that right quick was ta let him know Stevie was already taken."

Never before had Justus wanted to strangle Arley

more than he did right now. His scowl red-hot, he branded Arley where he stood leaning against the railing with his hands shoved into his pockets. Arley lowered his head.

"Justus, you stop it right now," Dula scolded. "He didn't mean any harm. Besides he's feeling bad enough."

He ought to, Justus thought. Most days he could overlook Arley's blunders. But this time he'd outdone himself; the cabin looked like a bandbox on the Fourth of July. No wonder Stevie was hopping mad.

"I went ta pick up my boat," Arley began. "Went just before sunup. I noticed the door was open on the cabin and I got worried about Stevie. I went ta check on her and that's when I saw."

Justus's scowl deepened. "Saw what, Arley?"

"You and Stevie curled up like two possums."

"That's all you saw? Us sleepin'?" Justus stared down his friend, feeling both protective and possessive of Stevie.

"I didn't see nothing I shouldna, if'n that's what you're askin', Just. I decorated the cabin with the balloons after you left so's Elroy would know cutting his grass was gonna get him nothin' more than a better view of the road."

"It's true, Justus. Elroy's got his lawnmower runnin' for the first time in ten years," Mamma confirmed.

Justus rubbed his jaw, his anger cooling slightly. "Either of you see Stevie since she tore up the parkin' lot and run Jinx off the road?"

Mamma shook her head. "No. I've been asking around, but no one's seen her."

Arley looked at his feet.

"Arley, out with it," Justus insisted. "You've seen her haven't you?"

"I saw her at the Henny-Penny. She was gassin' up the silver bullet."

Justus stood. "Did you talk to her?"

"Uh-huh. We had words."

Arley kept looking at his tennis shoes, which Justus took to mean there was bad news coming his way. "And?"

"She said she was goin' into Nawlins. I asked her if'n she wanted some company, but she said no. I asked her if'n somethin' was wrong 'cause she looked like she'd been cryin'. She said real sad like, 'Somethin' awful's happened, Arley. That's why I have to go back to Minnesota.' Then she kissed me and hugged me real tight. That part was nice. I was still thinkin' about how good she smelled when I heard the bullet start up. I blinked twice, and she was gone."

571~0293

# Chapter 9

Stevie's plane landed at the Minneapolis airport at 7:00 p.m. in a snowstorm. She'd worried her lip the entire flight, going over in her mind what the nurse had told her on the phone. Connie had been in a serious accident.

She flagged a cab and told the driver to take her to Abbott Northwestern Hospital pronto. Asking at the desk where she would find Connie Nelson's room, she took a deep breath outside the door, then opened it. To her surprise she found Connie sitting up in the hospital bed talking with the nurse.

When Connie saw her, she stopped talking and started crying. "Oh, Stevie, you flew back!"

"Now honey, don't cry. Of course I flew back." Stevie came toward the hospital bed noticing Connie's left arm was in a cast. She hugged her friend carefully, her worried gaze finding the nurse.

"Don't worry. She's going to be fine," the nurse assured. "She has a broken wrist and sprained shoulder. The other gal was treated for minor injuries and released."

Stevie stepped back and looked Connie over like a mother hen.

"They say I can go home tomorrow," Connie said. "But I don't know what I'm going to do for money. A secretary with a broken wrist. Dilby is going to fire me. I just know it. I'm the one who made that order mistake last month, remember? The one that caused the overdraft from the bank. It wasn't really my fault, but after I hit his car in the parking lot a few days earlier, he wasn't willing to listen to any excuse I had."

"Don't worry, Connie," Stevie patted her friend's hand. "What are you staring at?"

"You look different."

"How can I look different? I've only been gone six days."

"I know, but you do. You look really good. Does that mean you're happy with the move? Are you going to stay in Louisiana?"

The question was a hard one to answer. Stevie definitely wanted to stay in Crawford, that is if she could live down her humiliation after the balloon fiasco. It would have been so easy to tell Connie everything if Justus had been the man he had led her to believe he was.

But now... How could she tell Connie she was in love with a scumball?

"Dilby's going to fire me," Connie started again.

"No, he won't," Stevie crooned. "Think positive."

"You don't know about the coffee."

"What about the coffee?"

"I soaked Dilby's desk two days ago."

"Accidents happen," Stevie consoled.

"His crotch got it good. By the look on his face I cooked the whole meal."

"The coffee was straight out of the pot?" Stevie questioned, already knowing what the answer would be. Connie reminded her a little of Arley. She had good intentions, but often those intentions turned on her and took a healthy bite out of her own behind.

Connie nodded. "The girls in the phone pool said they heard him as clear as they do the fire drill that goes off once a month. This is it for me. I just know he's going to fire me this time. He's been looking for a reason, and when he sees my arm in a cast he's going to break out in a song and dance."

Connie was probably right. Her friend rarely stayed longer than a year at any one job. Stevie brushed Connie's long red hair away from her face to examine the small bruise on her forehead. "Tell me how this happened. The nurse who called me said something about being thrown on impact. If that's true, you're lucky to be alive. Was your car totaled?"

Connie lowered her head and chewed on her lip a minute. Finally she said, "No, the car's fine."

"It's fine? Meaning you can still drive it, right?"

"There's nothing wrong with the car. The collision happened at the supermarket."

"That's what probably saved you. You weren't going all that fast."

"Oh, I was going pretty fast. I was running late for my yoga class." Connie went back to munching on her lip.

Stevie could see there was more to the story. "Okay, so you were speeding. What else?"

Connie stopped munching. "I was speeding inside the supermarket with my shopping cart and somehow it just flipped over."

"Your cart flipped?" Stevie's eyes widened.

"Don't give me that look, Stephanie Suzanne Arnou. I never saw that woman in the motorized shopper, okay? Actually I think she was the one who sideswiped me, but it happened so fast I'm not sure who hit who first. I did go flying. A witness said I was airborne when I took out the peanut butter pyramid. Jiffy, I think. The good news is the woman has decided not to sue."

Justus had never had trouble holding onto his smile, but the past four days it had been hard. Still, he made a conscious effort as he slid a beer across the bar to Jinx.

"So what do ya say, Just? You takin' off after her?"

"You got a wager on this, too? Is that what you're telling me?"

"No. I didn't bet on you, boy. I bet on Stevie. I bet she was the one for you, and that sooner or later you would stop lickin' your smartin' pride and go fetch her home. I'd like it to happen sooner than later, 'cause there's a time factor involved. I lose fifty if'n things don't change in two days. Nate says you ain't gonna go after her. I say he's wrong. What do you say?''

"I say your burger should be about ready." Justus headed for the kitchen.

"Fayda Mae said she'd come back if'n you asked her. Now that she knows it wasn't your fault Stevie hightailed it.''

Fayda Mae had already come back. Justus had gone to see her early that morning. She had been amicable. Especially once he told her he intended to fix the situation.

He returned to the bar with Jinx's open-face Buzzard burger. "There you go. Hot and greasy.''

Jinx reached for his fork. "Back to Stevie. I'm in agreement with Arley.''

"And what would you two be in agreement on?''

Jinx lowered his voice. "Arley says Stevie's done the dirty with you, and she's triple H'd you. We all know the dangers of that, Just. When your heart, head and hammer get involved with a woman it's a done deal.''

As much as Justus would have liked to have argued with Jinx, his words rang true. Stevie had turned his head and snagged his heart the first night they had met. The other night at the cabin his hammer had gotten in on the action, and he'd been bagged quicker than a dizzy croaker.

*Oui.* Stevie had triple H'd him using the three C's.

Justus locked the door on the Muddy at midnight, then ambled outside. A few minutes later he found himself standing on the deck of Stevie's cabin in the middle of Turtle Bayou thinking about how soft and cuddly she had been in his arms.

He heard a noise and turned to see Mamma on the dock sauntering toward him. He said, "Kinda late, ain't it?"

"Sky's clear, a mess a stars out tonight. Figured I'd go for a stroll and enjoy 'em. You don't look so good."

"I'm fine."

"I'll be the judge of that. I'm your mamma, remember?"

Justus grinned. "How could I forget, you remind me of it every day."

"That's 'cause I'm proud of it. Proud of you. If'n a mama caint speak her mind and tell her son important stuff, then what good is she?"

"So what important stuff did you come to tell me? You can see the stars from your front porch as well as out here," Justus pointed out.

Mamma leaned against the railing. "I come ta say a bunch. First off, Stevie belongs here. She's a one-of-a-kind. The prettiest filly I ever saw. We caint lose her."

Justus leaned his backside against the railing next to her. "Okay. What else?" He motioned to the paper in her hand. "What's that?"

"It's a letter from Buz. I found it tonight in my cookie jar under the chocolate delights."

"He wrote you a letter?"

"It's a little hard ta read, but I finally made sense of it. It explains what he done and why."

Curious, Justus held out his hand. "Can I read it?"

"You can. You should. It'll clear up some important stuff. Loose ends." She put the letter in his hand, then started into the cabin. "Best read it inside. Buz's chicken scratch is poor. Worse when you're straining your eyeballs."

She lit the lanterns, while Justus pushed the *baire* aside and sat down on the bed. After scanning the letter, then reading it again, he looked up and said, "He was dying and he knew it. A tumor in his head."

"I remember him taking a trip into Nawlins. Remember him being vague about where he'd gone and why."

"He was having headaches a lot," Justus said. "I caught him taking painkillers more than once."

"Had some dizzy spells, too," Mamma added.

"So he knew a year ago he was dying, and set me up to become his partner to take over the Muddy."

"That's how I see it. I had confessed my concerns about you sticking in town when you first came back home. I said I wished you had a better reason to stay than just your promise to me. I guess he decided to find you one. From that letter, I take it that Buz had plans to leave Stevie the other half of the Muddy once he was gone. You think he knew she was a cook in Minneapolis?"

"Probably."

"I don't think he meant to con us into thinking Stevie was his nephew. He just wrote the name down wrong and Arley took it from there, screwing it up like usual."

Justus stood, handed the letter back to Dula. "I agree."

She took the letter then hung her head. "You don't think Buz drove off that bridge deliberate, do you?"

Justus wrapped his arms around Dula and hugged her. "Buz didn't kill himself, Mamma. He'd been feeling poorly for a long time. Worse lately. I caught him taking those painkillers daily that last week. I figure one of those dizzy spells happened that afternoon on the bridge."

Mamma looked up, smiled sadly, then patted Justus's arm. "You're a good boy. My boy. Thank you for setting me straight on that." She stepped back. "Now then. Are you gonna go after our Stevie, or wait till she gets good and homesick and comes back on her own?"

"Homesick for Crawford?"

"Silly boy," Mamma stuffed the letter back in her pocket. "Homesick for that smile of yours. It's a killer, don't you know? It was all I could see that day you was brought to me in that orphanage office. You was a sorry sight. Skinny as a broom handle. I 'spect you hadn't had a good meal in years. You was pale as flour, too. But in spite of all that, you was smiling. Smiling like you was the luckiest little duffer alive. You stole my heart that day. Stole this whole town's heart that afternoon I brought you ta church with me. From what I been seein' this past week, you've stolen our Stevie's heart, too. She ain't been able to take her eyes off you since she got here."

Arley saw the lights on in the cabin as he rounded the narrow channel that led into the bay. Stevie had cleared out with no word, so there was no reason for those lanterns to be burning, unless someone was robbing her after dark, or poking around snooping.

That was it. Somebody was snooping. The folks in Crawford were generally honest. Nosey, and ready to gossip a second after the spit hit the street, but they weren't thieves.

He paddled toward the dock, then tied up the boat, motioning to Ruby Duke to stay put. In a crouch, he snuck up on the cabin, then flattened himself out as much as he could against the wall. Inching to the window, he spun his hat backward, then peeked inside.

He made out one person, not clearly, but from the back the redhead looked either like a woman or a long-haired drifter. The minute the drifter idea entered Arley's head, he realized he'd been wrong about the situation. What he was witnessing was a robbery.

The idea that someone had the gall to steal something from his sweet cousin, Stevie, soured Arley's disposition. He wished he had time to go get Justus, but by then the thieving varmint might be long gone.

Arley made a quick decision, counted to one, then made a mad dash for the door and swung it open. He gave one banshee yell as he entered the cabin and charged the intruder.

The yell startled the thief, and the long-haired drifter spun around. Arley saw it was a woman seconds before he plowed her over, following her down, his weight and momentum flattening her into the floorboards with a loud thud.

It happened so fast, his speed and accuracy dazed him. When his head cleared, he got his hands under him and shoved himself up. He shook his head, blinked twice, then focused his eyes on the prettiest female he'd ever seen.

The freckle-faced Bambi finally found her voice, and surprised him with, "You must be Arley."

"Uh? Yes, 'um. That's me."

"I'm Connie. Stevie's friend from Minnesota."

"Ah… Stevie ain't home."

"Not at the moment, no. She took a walk. She said there was something she had to do, and that I should make myself comfortable. I don't think this is what she had in mind, though."

Arley heaved himself off Connie, then reached down to help her up. Once she was on her feet, he took a quick tally—green eyes, flaming hair, twice-blessed hooters, and a broken wing. "Sorry I laid you out. Thought a thief was stealin' from Stevie. You mentioned she had something ta do. You sayin' she's here? She's come home?"

"She's home. So tell me about this partner of hers. Is Justus Walker good enough for my best friend, Arley? Or should we shoot him between the eyes and bury his body in the swamp?"

# Chapter 10

Stevie paused outside the Muddy's back door and inhaled the sweet, sultry scent of tropical heat and lush foliage. It was amazing how fast she had grown to love her new home.

She opened the door, knowing it wouldn't be locked. Justus had told her that most people in Crawford didn't bother to lock their doors.

The minute she stepped into the kitchen she was overwhelmed by a mix of emotions. She didn't want to call it homesickness, but that's what it was. She'd been homesick for days. Homesick for her new friends, Uncle Buz's cabin and the Muddy. Most of all, Justus.

Stevie walked into the kitchen aided by a night-light that was set on a timer. She walked around the room, touching and looking, pride surfacing. Everything was just like she'd left it—shiny and clean.

She was so lucky. She hadn't realized how lucky until she had landed in the Minneapolis airport and stood shivering in the cold waiting for a cab for twenty minutes.

She owed her future to Uncle Buz. She wished she could tell him how much it meant to her that he had shared such a precious gift with her.

With every setback, a new door opens.

Yes, the Muddy was her open door. She knew that now. Knew that she belonged here. It hadn't taken twenty-four hours for her to realize that, and ever since she had, she'd been aching to return.

Stevie left the kitchen and slipped behind the bar to look out over the Muddy's dining room. The lit-up jukebox in the corner aided her, and she looked around, knowing nothing had changed, but unable to stop looking just the same. Looking and smiling. The chairs had all been turned over on the tables, the floor swept and scrubbed, ready for tomorrow's breakfast crowd.

She stepped around the bar, spinning the stool where Jinx always sat. He was quite a character. They were all characters—Nate and Dula, Fay and Arley.

She meandered around the room wearing a silly grin and warming with pride. She stopped and closed her eyes and without any effort at all, she could picture the tables full of customers. They were eating and laughing while the jukebox played and the bar was lined with old-timers.

"Thank you, Uncle Buz," she whispered. "Thank you for trusting me with your life and loves."

In that moment, Stevie realized just how much she

had needed to belong somewhere. How much she ached to belong to someone.

She had wronged Justus, and she owed him an apology. She had jumped to the wrong conclusion and falsely accused him just like she had that day in his office.

*It's called conjecture and it's not admissible evidence in court, honey.*

Stevie had stopped at the Henny-Penny on the way back into town. When she'd gone inside to pay for her gas, Sissy Folly was at the checkout. She'd said, "I'm sure glad you're back in town, Stevie. I'm getting tired of being blamed for selling Arley all those balloons. If I had known what he was going to do with them, and that you were going to have a hissy-fit over it, I wouldn't have sold them to him. But I didn't know what he had planned. Honest. You shouldn't be too hard on him, though. He's been pretty low since you left, blaming himself for ruining things between you and Justus."

"Call it, and it's yours."

Stevie spun around to find Justus behind the bar. He must have been upstairs. She hadn't heard him come down, but there he was, wearing a white dress shirt that looked like it belonged under a suit jacket. It was unbuttoned, and the sight of his bare chest brought back a flood of hot memories.

"I'll have a cosmopolitan, heavy on the cranberry juice, please."

"One Bullfrog comin' up…with cranberry juice."

"No cherry."

"Yes, ma'am."

Stevie slowly walked back to the bar and slipped onto a bar stool. "Did I wake you? It's after one."

"No. I just got back from Nawlins about an hour ago. Had business there."

"Who kept the Muddy running while you were gone?"

He set the vodka and cranberry juice on the bar and reached for a glass. "Fayda Mae and Nate."

"Nate?"

"He's decided that bartending is his calling. Besides I told him if he was willin' to come to work for us all his BLTs would be on the house." He mixed her drink, set it in front of her, then gave her his full attention. "I've missed you."

His eyes penetrated hers, searched. Stevie had missed him, too. So much, she hadn't had a decent night's sleep since she'd left.

"What's been going on, honey? Where have you been?"

"I went back to Minneapolis."

"Runnin' off never settles much."

"I never ran off. Connie had an accident that put her in the hospital. She needed me to come."

He frowned. "So that's why you took off. That's what you meant by somethin' awful happened."

"What?"

"That's what you told Arley at the Henny-Penny the day you left. You sayin' it wasn't the balloons that sent you runnin'?"

"I told you I didn't run. Well, I did at first, but I would never have left town if it hadn't been for the phone call."

"You ever think that maybe you should have let me know where you took off to? That I might worry?"

"Did you?"

"*Oui.* Every day."

"I'm not used to having to check in with someone. I guess I didn't think." Stevie suddenly realized she had been very irresponsible. "You're right. I'm part-owner in the Muddy. I should have called and let you know I wasn't going to be able to be here. I should have explained how long I would be gone."

He stared at her, his intense blue eyes unwavering. He hadn't cracked a smile since she'd turned to look at him. She missed his smile. Missed the way it warmed her inside.

"I owe you an apology. Sissy Folly told me tonight that Arley bought the balloons. I made a mistake."

"I did, too. I should have run after you when you took off out the back door."

Stevie watched as Justus reached for the phone behind the counter and punched in a number. He waited a minute, then said, "Say, Leland, you can cancel that investigation we discussed this mornin'. There's no need. Catch you next time I'm in town."

When he hung up, Stevie said, "You hired an investigator to look for me?"

"Leland is an ex-lawyer turned private investigator. You haven't told me much about your life in Minnesota so I didn't have much to go on. I did locate your ex-boss, but he wasn't much help. He said he hadn't seen you since you'd moved. You should have cleared it with me, honey. I've been losin' sleep."

"Cleared it with you? I haven't had to clear anything with another person besides my boss in years."

"Best get used to it."

"I will not get—"

He placed his hands on the bar and in one easy motion, vaulted over the top of it. Before Stevie could get off the stool, he had her spun around, and she was pinned between the bar and his powerful body.

Stevie hiked her chin. "What now? Are you going to manhandle me?"

"That's one way of puttin' it." He reached out and threaded his fingers through her hair, at the same time he tugged her head back. "You all right with me kissin' you?"

He was towering over her, his legs spread wide, cradling her between them. Her back was against the bar.

"Give me an answer, honey."

She nodded.

"That'll do."

The kiss came fast, loaded with possession and hot scorching passion. Stevie moaned, raised her arms and slid them around Justus's waist. She opened her mouth and let him take what he wanted. As he continued to kiss her, he lifted her off the stool and urged her to wrap her legs around his waist. He walked to the jukebox and set her on the lit-up glass top. "I want more," he muttered against her lips. "I want it all."

"Are you saying I turn you on, Justus Walker?"

"You turn me on, over, upside down and inside out honey, and you know it."

Stevie touched his cheek. "Yes, I know. You don' hide it very well." She reached out and ran her hand along Justus's zipper. He moaned, pressed himself against her hand.

"Right here," he said.

"Yes, here," she agreed.

"Let's get rid of these jeans."

Stevie leaned back, closed her eyes, and hung onto the sides of the jukebox as Justus unzipped her jeans, then peeled them off.

"Candy-apple red."

"What?"

"Your panties. I love the taste of apples. Let's get rid of the T-shirt, too."

Stevie sat up. "I don't have a bra on."

"I know."

He pulled her shirt up and encouraged her to raise her arms. As she did, he slipped her purple T-shirt off over her head. The minute her breasts were bare, he lowered his head.

Stevie closed her eyes and threaded her fingers through his hair. She loved the way he touched her, how unhurried and gentle he was. She shoved his shirt off his shoulders, wanting him as bare as she was. "You make me crazy," she whispered. "Have I told you how much I love everything you do to me, Just? Everything inside and out."

Stevie lay naked on Justus's bed content to watch him sleep. They had made love on the jukebox, then on the stairway three steps away from his apartment door.

Now hours later, he had fallen asleep with his arms

wrapped around her waist and his face pillowed between her breasts.

She bent her head and kissed his temple, stroked his hair. Studying him, she decided he was absolutely the most sexually hot, exciting man to ever exist.

She sent her eyes over his naked body, again appreciating him in detail, marveling at all the controlled power that held her—loved everything about him from his sturdy hips, and beautiful butt, to his rock-hard legs and flat abdomen.

"Am I a keeper, or are you goin' to throw me back?"

The question brought a smile to Stevie's lips. "A keeper? Hmm... I'm not sure."

She felt his hands slowly release her, then suddenly he came to his knees and jerked her beneath all that controlled power. Straddling her, he said, "You're not sure? What aren't you sure about? You seemed pretty sure on the jukebox."

He laced their hands together and flattened them to the bed. His smile slid a little and he said, "Stevie, honey, have you come home to stay? I need to know."

The seriousness in his voice sobered her. "I'm here aren't I?"

"But for how long?"

"There are some things we need to discuss, Just."

He rocked back and, still straddling her, rested his hands on his bare thighs. "This would be the time, honey."

"I've changed my mind."

"Changed your mind about what? The Muddy?"

"Yes. I can't make it work...without a joint menu

like we talked about before I left. And I really have found a way to take the grease out of the Buzzard burger, and keep it juicy. Want to hear?''

He looked down at her for a long minute, then slowly his smile returned. ''You're stickin' then?''

She nodded. "Yes."

He leaned forward and kissed her gently, then with more fervor.

Stevie didn't remember when he flattened out and slipped between her legs, when he entered her and took possession of her body. But it didn't really matter when it had happened, only that it had, and that Justus was there, filling her up and taking her on another heavenly ride.

Justus Walker's heaven was this side of nowhere Stevie had ever been before. Each trip, new and exciting. Each touch more potent than the last.

''I love you,'' he whispered. ''Love everything about you, honey. Welcome home.''

As he slid deeper and began to move, Stevie closed her eyes and clung to him. Home... Yes, she was home. Home in every way that mattered. Home in Justus Walker's capable arms.

# Chapter 11

"I hear Stevie's friend is a big city secretary. You think she's got what it takes ta stick like our Stevie?"

Justus glanced over the top of Jinx's head to where Connie and Arley sat at a table near the window. They had eaten lunch together. Actually they had eaten lunch together yesterday, too. And like yesterday, they were both grinning like love-struck kids.

He watched as Connie raised her fork and fed Arley a bite of low-fat strawberry cheesecake. He couldn't help but smile over that.

"Somebody said you offered her a job."

"I did. The police station could use some organization."

"Did she accept?"

"She did. Said she would be happy to take the job. Guess she approves of me dating Stevie."

Arley had told him what Connie had said about him two nights ago—shooting him between the eyes and burying him in the swamp if he didn't measure up.

"This here dating business, Just. Don't you think you're a little too old for that sorta thing? I mean, why not up and marry Stevie and get it over with. You two are doin' it anyways."

Justus angled his head and looked at Jinx. "Doin' it?"

"You know what I'm talkin' about. Long as she's yours, you oughta be claiming her before she gets a wild hair ta run off again. Or Elroy gets another notion. I heard his yard is mowed and the junkyard is around back of his house now."

"Drove by yesterday." Justus shoved Jinx's burger platter a little closer to him, hoping he'd take the hint and put his mouth to better use. "Yard looks pretty sharp."

"That might be," Jinx agreed, "but I was just starting to know where things was at out there. Heard he's still talkin' about indoor plumbin'. I think you should be poppin' the question before he gets that stool ordered and you're plumb flushed out of the picture."

Justus raised a black eyebrow. "You make another bet with Nate?"

Jinx's cheeks turned red. "A small one. Now don't go gettin' riled. It's in your best interest, boy. I'll cut you in for half if'n you get to it first before Saturday."

"First? You sayin' Elroy's in on the bet, too?"

"I ain't for sure, but Nate's got somethin' up his sleeve."

"What about Nate?"

At the sound of Stevie's sweet voice Justus turned his head, his smile spreading. She looked pretty today. She was wearing jean shorts and one of those skinny-strapped tops of hers. This one was red.

Like always all he had to do was think about her eager response to him and it sent his body into motion and his heart pounding.

"Hi, honey."

She acknowledged his greeting with a smile, and then some. "Hi, yourself."

Jinx cleared his throat to pull Stevie's eyes around and get himself noticed.

"Afternoon, Jinx. Something wrong with your burger? You haven't touched it yet."

"Nothin's wrong with it, Stevie. Looks fine. You look real fine, too. Come ta think on it, you always look fine these days. Don't she, Just?"

Justus ignored the way Jinx was giving him the go-ahead nod, and sent his eyes over Stevie again, this time a little slower—he didn't want to miss anything. Taking inventory with pleasure, he said, "*Oui*. She's an eyeful."

In the few days she'd been back, they had settled on a joint menu, and things were progressing nicely at the Muddy. They had hired two waitresses, and a salad girl, and with Nate behind the bar a few hours every day, Justus had been given some breathing room.

"It's good ta have you back in the Muddy's kitchen, Stevie." Jinx finally cut into his Buzzard burger and sighed. "Sure do like the way you make these burgers so juicy. Guess you gave up that fool notion of taking the grease out, ya?"

"Actually, I—"

Justus wrapped his arm around Stevie and pulled her close. "Jinx ain't interested in the lowdown, honey. Only the taste. You get enough sleep last night?"

She smiled up at him, slipped her hand around back of him and gave his butt a pinch, then wiggled out of his arms, and asked, "You were saying something about Nate. What about Nate? He's all right, isn't he?"

"He's fine. Say, Stevie, you gonna help with the big shindig on Saturday?" Jinx asked, around a mouthful of burger and grits. "The Muddy always celebrates Valentine's Day with a shindig. Everybody in town shows up for a burger and a beer."

"A party?"

"It's a big'un," Jinx guaranteed.

"This is the first I've heard of it."

"Last year Buz outdone himself and decorated the Muddy with balloons. Even ordered napkins with hearts on 'em. Burgers was shaped like hearts, too. Arley and some of the boys pulled out the fiddles after a fashion, and we moved the party outside when it got dark. We had ourselves an all-night mudbug boil."

"Arley plays the violin?" Stevie couldn't hide her surprise.

"Here we call it a fiddle, honey," Justus said.

Stevie shrugged. "Whatever, Just."

"Our boy, Justus, plays, too," Jinx added. "He's got a sackful of talents. 'Course I figure you already know that."

Stevie looked at Justus. "You play the fiddle?"

"Jinx is stretchin' it, honey. I don't play near as good as Arley."

Stevie didn't believe him. She was in agreement with Jinx. Justus had a sackful of talent. More than a sackful. He could be a high-powered lawyer anywhere he wanted to. Or do anything else he chose to do. But instead he'd come home to Crawford because he'd made a promise to Mamma Dula.

Nate came through the door of the Muddy and covered a bar stool. When he looked at Stevie, she knew what was coming.

"So, Stevie, you give my heart-smart idea some thought?"

Yes, she had, but as much as she was in agreement with him, she was nervous about popping the question.

"Stevie, honey, what idea was that?" Justus asked.

She smiled pleasantly at one and all, then to Justus, she said, "Maybe we should discuss this in private."

Nate cleared his throat. "Witnesses would be best if'n you're planning a speech. Case there's a dispute later on."

He rubbed his fingers together, and Stevie knew what he was trying to tell her. He was concerned with winning the bet he'd made with Jinx.

She didn't really care who won. The bottom line was she wanted a steady diet of Justus Walker. An everyday diet of him, and she was determined to have it. And if Mamma Dula was right, Justus wasn't going to make the first move. She said that he was concerned with moving too fast for her, and knew she wasn't ready to make a permanent commitment, even though he was.

How dare he say she wasn't ready. She was ready. More than ready.

She glanced across the bar to where Dula sat at her favorite table. As if the woman had been summoned, she raised her eyes and nodded her encouragement. It was the shove Stevie needed, and her mind was made up. She slipped her arms around Justus's neck and encouraged him to wrap his around her waist.

He said, "What's going on, honey?"

"I've got something to ask you." On tiptoes she kissed him, then angled her head back to check his response. "Just...honey," she began.

Jinx groaned. "I've lost. She's your ace in the hole, ain't she, Nate?"

"You bet your boat, she is," Nate laughed.

Stevie kissed Justus twice more, then whispered, "I'm ready."

"Ready for what, honey?"

"Ready to commit." Stevie paused, then said, "I'm asking you to marry me, Just."

Nate let out a catcall, while Jinx lowered his head and put his mouth to better use, digging into his burger like a starved animal.

Even though Justus said nothing, Stevie felt his arms tighten around her, and his lazy smile touched his eyes. She said softly, "I love you, Justus Walker. If you love me, too, say, 'Yes, Stevie, honey, I'll marry you.' Say it, Just. Say yes."

He laughed, squeezed her a little tighter, then said, "Yes, Stevie, honey, I love you. You hear that, boys?

I love her. Sounds like we're tyin' the knot on Saturday, and afterward we'll have the biggest Valentine's Day celebration in Crawford's history. Hosted right here at the Muddy.''

# Epilogue

The wedding was the biggest ever in Crawford. Mamma Dula put the word out, with an open invitation to anyone along the river and beyond who was interested in witnessing the marriage of her boy, Justus, and the prettiest filly this side of anywhere.

Henrettia Penny had called in a rush order on red balloons and another tank of helium, and the men started netting mudbugs.

Come Saturday morning the Muddy's backyard was lined with picnic tables, a mess of well-wishers, and too many red heart balloons to count. Connie walked up the grassy aisle first as Stevie's maid of honor, followed by Stevie on Arley's arm wearing a summer white dress, carrying a single red rose. After the ceremony was over, the fiddles were pulled out, and enough food and mudbugs to feed the entire parish.

*Just Say Ye*

The day was one of the happiest of Stevie's life. She brushed a tear from her eye, and again silently thanked her uncle Buz. He had given her more than the Muddy. So much more.

"Stevie, honey, where did you go?"

"I'm out here." Stevie turned from the railing to see Justus standing in the doorway of the cabin. He was so handsome in the moonlight wearing blue jeans and his white shirt.

"We sure had a wild day, didn't we?"

"You bet we did."

"Speaking of bets. How much did you make?"

Surprised by the question, she asked, "You knew?"

"'Course I knew."

"You knew Nate recruited me? How?"

"I heard about the bet a day earlier. Jinx was bettin' on me proposin', and Nate took up the challenge claimin' you'd be the one to pop the question first. When I heard that Mamma had joined Nate's side, I knew the smartest thing to do was to keep my mouth shut. That is until you popped the question."

Stevie was speechless.

"Now, honey, it's all right. It really doesn't matter who asked who, does it?"

"Mamma was in on the bet?"

"*Oui.*"

"I was set up."

"I'd say from day one." His hands slid over Stevie's backside and he drew her against him. "I'll let you in on a little secret. I've heard Jinx and Nate have made another wager."

"On us?"

"*Oui*. It involves both of us."

"What is it this time?"

Justus nuzzled her neck, then whispered in her ear. "How soon we can make a baby."

Stevie jerked her head back. "They're making bets on our children now?"

"Jinx says the first one will be a boy. Nate says it'll be a girl."

"And what do you say?" Stevie asked, slipping her hands around the back of him to squeeze his sexy butt.

"I say...whatever."

Stevie angled her head back an grinned. "Whatever?"

"Boy, girl... One of each. Four of each. How's your wind? You up for a marathon tonight, honey?"

She slid her hand over his hip and touched him there, along his zipper. "Feels like you're up for a marathon, and then some." She kissed him. Sucked on his bottom lip. "I finished the book. Chapter five is titled the 'Main Course.' There's a checklist involved."

He let out a heavy sigh, then lifted her off her feet and into his arms. They were on their way back into the cabin when they heard giggling out in the middle of the bayou. Stevie reached for the flashlight on the side of the cabin and while Justus held her, she scanned the bay. Seconds later she located Arley, Connie and Ruby Duke.

"Hi, Stevie. Hi, Just. Nice night, ain't it," Arley hollered.

"What are you two doing?" Stevie called back.

"Connie's going froggin' with me. Don't that sound like fun?"

Stevie glanced at Justus. "Connie has no clue," she whispered.

"If she did, she wouldn't be grinnin' ear-to-ear," Justus offered.

"What should we do?"

"Wave."

"Wave?"

"Come on, honey. Maybe if we're lucky they'll get lost and it'll give us a couple extra hours to work on that checklist before they find their way back."

Justus raised his hand, and Stevie followed suit. "You two have fun," she called out cheerfully.

"Now douse the light."

\* \* \* \* \*

## Forrester Square

### LEGACIES . LIES . LOVE .

He made her a once-in-a-lifetime offer....

# TOO GOOD TO REFUSE

by

# Mindy Neff

Millie Gallagher's ordinary life is about to take
a fairy-tale turn. Hired as a nanny for Sheikh
Jeffri al-Kareem's young son, she soon finds
herself at odds with her headstrong boss.
To Jeff, Millie is endlessly exasperating—
and equally intoxicating....

*Forrester Square...Legacies. Lies. Love.*

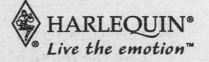

**HARLEQUIN**®
*Live the emotion*™

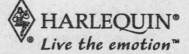

**Coming in March 2004
to Silhouette Books**

Widower Harrison Parker needed a nanny for
his three young children so he could work on a
top-secret government project. But he hadn't
counted on finding such a beautiful and intriguing
woman, who just might capture his heart....

**Five extraordinary siblings.
One dangerous past.
Unlimited potential.**